The Knights of Black Chapter

Ken Bourne - Turner

London, UK

Cover design Jim Bailey

© 2008 by Ken Bourne - Turner
All rights reserved.

ISBN: 978-0-9559936-0-2
LCCN

Printed by Lulu.

Ken Bourne-Turner has written and constructed working modules for career development, business and personal performance psychology. He has spent the last five years researching the intriguing world of freemasonry and developed the full story line for *The Knights of Black Chapter*.

He is a practising Freemason and Knights Templar of the St Amand Preceptory. Under oath his full allegiance is to: The United Religious and Military Orders of the Temple, and of St John of Jerusalem, Palestine, Rhodes and Malta in England and Wales and the Dominions and Dependencies of the British Crown.

A sequel to *The Knights of Black Chapter* is planned.

Acknowledgements

I would like to thank my wonderful wife Gill for her patience and understanding, whilst I spent many months intermittently locked away in my study pulling all the research into the storyline. I am also indebted to her for agreeing to spend time with me researching on the islands of Crete and Capri!

My thanks also go to Adrian Eakins for the faith he showed in me and his continual support and ability to bring the novel into fruition. And to Denise Ward whose tireless skills as a proof reader and editor assembled the novel correctly and put the punctuations in the right places. And lastly to Jim Bailey, the freemason and excellent artist who designed and produced the front cover.

I would also like to acknowledge my wonderful craft lodge, Strongman No45. In February 2008 we celebrated its 275th anniversary. The companionship we all share at Strongman is a terrific legacy of true freemasonry, especially in the sense of brotherhood, companionship and commitment to charitable offerings we all share. And my final acknowledgement must go to the Preceptory of St Amand where I attend as a Knights Templar a place at which I never fail to be overwhelmed in the unfolding spectacular events of history.

The Knights of Black Chapter

1

The special red phone snugly concealed in the President's desk was white hot. It was the middle of the night, but the man himself had been in the Oval Office with the receiver pinned to his ear for the best part of an hour.

The nicety of a pending state visit to London was not the issue being discussed by the two leaders at such an ungodly hour. A crisis was happening of major proportions. Some four and a half thousand men, women and children had been slaughtered, thousands more were injured, many seriously. There had been one incident in New York, another in London and a mid-air explosion had blown a 747 out of the air - all in the space of twenty-four hours.

The USA and Britain stood alone over the Gulf War, now they were paying a horrific price. The terrible statistics were an epitaph to the blunders and security failings of both countries. For almost three decades Britain had experienced her mainland being violated by the bomb attacks of the IRA. However, following the 'Good Friday' treaty and economy drives imposed by the Treasury, security had been down-graded. The country was left exposed, especially the capital, and now London had been targeted once again. It was no better in the USA: the bombings in Atlanta and Oklahoma were a long time ago, people soon forget and besides we're talking about America for God's sake... bombings only happen on movie sets and in someone else's back yard!

A cluster of bombs strategically placed had ripped through the United Nations building in New York. Flight *Alfa Bravo* 971 had left Johannesburg bound for Chicago, crammed full with Americans returning home for the July 4th celebrations. There was also a smattering of British businessmen and some South Africans hoping to beat a trail across the Promised Land. Devices strapped to the bodies of two suicide bombers, one at the front and one at the rear of the aircraft, were detonated simultaneously some four hundred and fifty miles off the North African coast. A Royal Naval Frigate cruising in the vicinity was

The Knights of Black Chapter

scrambled but had found nothing except mutilated bodies and wreckage.

In London, the majestic splendour of the Duncannon Building that had once towered high above its Victorian neighbours, now lay a smouldering wreck. The force of five explosions had twisted its steel framework into a tangled mess. Glass from its windows had been reduced to fragments and blown with velocity across a radius of almost a mile. The incident had left London's banking district in total chaos. As with New York, these bombs were designed to kill as many people as possible without prior warning. A BBC news flash had described the incident as the worst attack on London since the Second World War!

Despite the air conditioning cooling the Oval Office, the pyjama-clad President was covered with a blanket of sweat. He had been scheduled to take a private trip to Kentucky to look over a horse which, like him, had Irish blood running through its veins. President William P. McCain had a passion for fast horses and even faster women. The Kentucky trip was to look over a filly by the name of *Sunnydown Lady* and watch her being put through her paces, not to mention a secret liaison with another filly - the former junior press secretary who had begrudgingly left Washington, her promising career in tatters because of her rumoured relationship with the President. She was young and exceptionally beautiful, exactly how WPM liked his women. In one brief, stupid encounter she had spread her legs in wild frenzy, her torn clothes exposing her half-naked body as she rolled across the Oval Office floor locked in the clutches of her lover. Her future in Washington had been destroyed in seconds... a future she had worked so hard to develop.

The encounter had cost the President a cool half a million dollars to set her up in business, back in her home state. As for the cleaner who'd walked in on them... the authorities had miraculously discovered that there were doubts over the validity of her visa. She was quietly deported back to Peru the very next day. The lady's tragic death was reported to her family just twenty-four hours after her arrival on native soil – she had been killed by a hit and run driver on a mountain road near Macchu Piccu!

This had been WPM's first opportunity to arrange such a trip without the usual fanfare heralding his arrival. His intention was to get back a little of his investment and leave the young lady with a memory she'd never forget. But events during the last few hours had totally screwed up his plans; scorn and criticism was being hurled at his name from almost every country throughout the world.

The two leaders finally agreed that a high-level meeting should be arranged between the Joint Chief of Staff and the Foreign office, hopefully to instigate a damage limitation exercise.

The world's press was set to explode with headlines clearly connecting these devastating explosions with the air strikes on Iraq. Saddam Hussein had used the Anglo American attacks to rally support across the Arab nations and clearly his strategy had worked.

* * * * *

"Say honey you don't really expect anyone to eat that stuff do you?" bellowed John Joseph Curtis as he watched the buxom black girl struggling to push her long-handled spoon into a huge stainless steel bowl of pasta.

She beamed back at him from behind the glass serving counter. "Hell man, it's two am in the mornin', this stuff's been under lamps since last night, what do you expect?" She let out a belly laugh at John's expression that made her entire body rumble like an earth tremor. Her laughter was contagious, even at that time in the morning.

"Well at least drown that stuff in chilli sauce."

"I sure will, Sir," replied the canteen girl, who according to the plastic badge pinned on her tabard was called Lulu.

John Joseph Curtis had eaten the majority of his meals in the White House canteen for the past two months and it was clearly showing, especially around the belt line. His latest wife, the fourth in a line of catastrophes, had uprooted and left. Clare was most definitely going to be the last. Shadowing a series of Presidents wherever they went was not the way to kindle married bliss. Unfortunately the US government provided no compensation package for a broken marriage, even though it was in the line of duty. And whenever a President partied, his men were supposed to party also... and when he fornicated... well it was all in the line of dutiful obedience and after all presidents of the USA were the most powerful men in the world!

But it was his close involvement with Freemasonry that mostly freaked out his ladies. John Joseph Curtis, known to his friends as JoJo, was on the edge of fifty-five. With his shoulders right back he could just claim to be six foot two inches tall. Six-two gave JoJo that feel good factor and made him just a little bit special. He had a thick mop of wild, red hair that grew like bracken and despite his years not one grey hair had forced its way to the surface. The hair made JoJo look just that little bit younger which was good, especially as this latest president preferred his staff younger than himself. Younger made WPM happy.

Like his predecessors, WPM inherited JoJo along with all the other fixtures and fittings. At their first informal meeting JoJo had declared that he was only forty-seven years old. And for months afterwards he tried every stunt in the book to get hold of his personnel file from Human Resources where his true age was recorded. He was convinced that if the President ever found out his actual date of birth he'd be immediately wheeled into the retirement parking lot.

The balance between presidents he'd served and women he'd married was running at evens. JoJo only wished Carolina Clare, as he affectionately called his latest folly, had hung on in there. He really loved those cute expressions and that tiny turned up nose. And after all she knew exactly what his job was all about; he had even discussed his position in the thirty-three degrees of Masonry. She also knew he couldn't talk about things that much, but she said she understood and that it would be okay. Goddam it, he even explained why his other three marriages had failed and despite everything she had still wanted to marry him.

JoJo had served his country well for the past thirty-six years, first in the Airborne Infantry then moving to Intelligence and Security Command at Arlington, Virginia. Most men of his age could afford to retire and perhaps take a nice home in the Washington suburbs or buy a condominium on the coast. Maybe even have a long lens Canon draped around the neck like a typical American tourist. Even grand-kids to share Thanksgiving with, but JoJo's world had not panned out that way.

Life had really given JoJo Curtis the bum deal. What with a monster mortgage on his apartment, just ten blocks from the White House, and a bank account that fluctuated faster than the national debt - not to mention three hungry ex-wives to feed, plus a fourth pending? Things really were tough.

During the past month or so, since Carolina Clare had left, his apartment was a place he visited infrequently except maybe to collect clean laundry or crash down following a 'let's drink away the blues' binge at Mickey's bar around the corner.

Nancy Weaver did his accounts and the cleaning; in fact she'd actually cleaned through all his wives. Nancy was the only lady to stick by JoJo and charged him heavy money for the privilege, making sure her account was the first to be paid, in full.

JoJo crossed the empty canteen with his tray of pasta and a mug of steaming black coffee. His position as Senior Security Officer entitled him to eat in the executive dining room. He concluded however that the food was basically the same and paying a premium to be served by bored waitresses at white linen-covered tables did not justify the additional expense.

He unbuttoned his jacket before sitting down and adjusted the holster housing his long-nosed Smith & Wesson; the side arm had been cutting into his shoulder all day. Wearing a holster was part of JoJo's permanent dress, like socks! For him, a gun hanging under his arm had the familiarity of a wart.

"Take JoJo," suggested the President. "And make sure this meeting is held *in camera*. We need to do whatever it takes to knock over the bastards behind these atrocities. Use the Brits; they love crawling about on their bellies in the name of glory. But for Christ's sake make sure this country's not implicated. I don't want to be caught with my knickers down any further. Have you got that Bud? Am I coming over loud and clear?"

Bud O'Dowd held a dead receiver in his hand, which he slapped down so hard the body of the blue phone cracked upon impact. "Just like that, we've got a major catastrophe on our hands and Willy boy wants me to hold Kodak talks with the limeys.... Great!"

O'Dowd stared hard at the Amadeo Gennarelli bronze of Chief Sitting Bull lethargically astride his Mustang. The sculpture took pride of place at the right side of Bud O'Dowd's enormous, Chippendale, partner's desk. The sculpture provided a symbol of solidarity almost as if the battle-weary Indian provided some form of unanimity. Sitting Bull had been the sounding board for the Chief of Staff on innumerable occasions.

Bud O'Dowd picked up another receiver, this time from a black phone close to his right elbow. This one had been the seventh telephone installed in less than six months, he'd smashed the rest.

The Knights of Black Chapter

"Amy, get me CIA and the FBI Top priority, my office and tell those guys to make it fast." Down crashed the receiver.

Amy had been Bud O'Dowd's secretary for the best part of four years and if it weren't for her religious beliefs, yoga and the Anthony Robbins seminars, her valium intake would have put her in the funny farm.

O'Dowd's Irish temper never really cooled, it just simmered close to boiling. He was fat, bald and fifty. And according to his doctor a heart attack had been long overdue, especially with his blood pressure so high on the Richter scale. O'Dowd carried an amazing bundle of responsibilities which had driven his predecessor to chronic alcoholism.

Amy put out calls to the respective directors' PAs, inducing the network to hum in search of the two men.

James Parker had been Director of the Central Intelligence Agency for the past six months. Hand picked by the President himself, the forty-two-year-old fitness freak was lean and mean with a carefully prepared image that manifested itself into his position. His haircut resembled designer stubble, far removed were the baby curls that grew naturally if permitted. Parker's suits were cut in Manhattan by Mani Cowen who had the knack of enhancing his already broad shoulders and developed chest. James Parker was a man of ultimately correct proportions who kept his private life as secret as the service he directed.

Parker was the first to arrive in the lobby of Amy's office and took a chair to await the arrival of Frank Decapio.

Born to an Italian fruit seller on New York's east side, Decapio had literally clawed his way up from those humble beginnings to become one of America's most influential sons. Decapio had received the call just as the black helicopter landed on the White House helipad. His trip had not been a pleasant one, assessing the devastation that formed a gaping wound in central Manhattan. New Yorkers had been violated and were scurrying around, fearful that more explosions would follow.

Decapio knocked and entered the lobby. He shook James Parker by the hand and offered Amy a friendly Italian smile. His dark piercing eyes were both evil and sexy. Amy was unsure whether she'd have an orgasm or pass out with fright if he ever made a pass at her.

"Mr Decapio and Mr Parker are here Sir," reported Amy. She replaced the receiver. "You can go straight in, Gentlemen."

The lady from Williamsburg felt nervous whenever either of these two men was around, knowing the awesome power they had behind those friendly smiles and polite mannerisms. Amy, like most of the department staff, had her suspicions about the death of the Peruvian cleaner and therefore seeing these men together frightened the hell out of her.

"Come in guys," said O'Dowd, greeting the two men with firm handshakes. Even Bud O'Dowd treated these two with weary respect.

"So Frank, what's the position in New York?"

"Pandemonium, Chief, total," replied Decapio, taking a seat in front of Chief Sitting Bull. "The Mayor's in a flat spin, every hospital within a hundred mile radius is bulging at the seams, they've called rescue workers in from everywhere. And still people are being pulled from the rubble." Decapio crossed his legs and leaned on the desk towards the Indian as if to whisper in his ear. "Chief, the President must come forward and make a statement, even if it is a pile of bullshit."

O'Dowd leaned back in his red leather button-backed chair and looked across the desk at Decapio. "Knowing Willy, it will be; right now he's sitting in the Oval Office nursing an aborted erection, feeling really lonely and unloved."

"Chief, New Yorkers have been rocked to their socks by this... Hey, what am I saying? The whole country has taken a hit. We need to calm things down big time," said Decapio.

James Parker agreed. "Chief if ever guys out there needed a leader, now's the time!" Parker's words echoed around the office concurring with O'Dowd's feelings and Sitting Bull's predicament, albeit decades before.

Bud O'Dowd gently stroked a chubby hand over his bald head as if searching for hair that had long since disappeared. "I hear what you say guys, the country wants the words and the script's not been written yet. The President has agreed with British Prime Minister Blain to hold a high-level meeting. Both of them feel Saddam Hussein is kicking the crap out of their popularity ratings. I've been asked to arrange this meeting with our cousins, and gentlemen, I'd like you both to be there!"

Decapio shook his head. "I'm straight back to New York, Chief; the Bureau's stretched, like big time. I've got Senators across America demanding agents in place at every public building."

James Parker glanced across at Frank Decapio and smiled. "No problem Chief, where's this meeting going to take place?"

he asked standing to take a cup of coffee from the tray Amy had appeared with.

O'Dowd shrugged his shoulders. "Search me James, you arrange it with MI6 in London. Although apart from discussing who's going to win Wimbledon, Christ in Heaven knows what we're going to talk about." O'Dowd took a sip of coffee.

"We're going to talk about knocking out Mohammed Abu Atif and the Al Val Sinda. Chief. This guy's got more followers than Gandhi and by comparison he makes Osama Bin Laden and Al Quaida look like Snow White and the Seven Dwarfs," said James Parker. "Trouble is he's harder to pin down than a Jack Rabbit in a burrow. We know it, the Brits know it, and the whole goddam world knows it!"

O'Dowd took another sip of coffee which burnt his mouth. "Fuck that was hot... Frank, the President needs some breathing time. We need a stooge, a fall guy. What do yeah say?"

Decapio stood and walked over to the window and peered out over the plaza. "Georgia's full of Muslim fundamentalists itching to help the cause," he said turning towards O'Dowd whose face had brightened a little.

"Then make a name for yourself, pull someone, anyone, but make it fast. Give CNN the exclusive, let them carry the pictures. We need to show the world Americans don't hang around when it comes to catching violators."

Both Parker and Decapio frowned at O'Dowd's remarks but by now he was in full creative mode. "Let's show some bum covered in a blanket, a nameless immigrant say, in orange overalls, chained up, leaving the court house under heavy guard. You know the scene. Make sure you're in the picture Frank. I want to see the faces of top brass in on this one."

O'Dowd felt uneasy vibes emanating from both men. "Look we must ease people's nerves and help the President, give him a basis for his address-to-the-nation speech - not to mention a kick in the balls for those guys in Congress who think this country should welcome any crap onto our shores in the name of freedom." O'Dowd looked squarely at Frank Decapio. "I need to offer Willy. P. McCann something good, let's give the guy a break. How long do you need Frank?"

Decapio placed his cup and saucer carefully down on the desk and smiled. "Leave it to me Chief. I guess we can have a limp soul hanging from a chain within forty-eight hours."

O'Dowd rose from his chair, a broad smile spread across his scarlet face. He shook Decapio's hand. "Great, I'll tell the

President we've got a suspect and that an arrest is imminent. He'll be delighted, so will the media."

The Knights of Black Chapter

London had been basking in a heatwave. England were playing surprisingly well at Lord's against a restrained Australian side who might just relinquish the Ashes. Wimbledon had its courts packed with the usual enthusiastic crowds revelling in the heat that was providing the famous fortnight with the rare treat of not one rainy day. Strawberries and cream, with chilled Moet, were consumed with profuse regularity.

The long-range forecast predicted that this dry, hot spell was set to continue. The lush, green lawns of Henley had enjoyed a massive throng of visitors eager to shout on their teams during Regatta week. The Leander Club had been packed with cotton frocks and straw boaters, 'Pims' flowing as energetically as the Thames.

The entire country harked to the sound of leather striking willow on village greens; barbecues glowed from patios across the land. The sun was out, England was at play.

Now 'HEATWAVE' had hurriedly been pulled from the front pages of every national newspaper in the country and replaced with 'HORROR'. The entire City of London had been brought to a halt. An area from Whitechapel to the Tottenham Court Road had been cordoned off, making ground movement in central London impossible.

New Scotland Yard's Special Squad had sifted through the debris in the hope of discovering some clues. The IRA had used the special call sign to declare their innocence of the atrocity. Summer sunshine continued but it didn't seem to matter any more.

Television screens on every channel gave a detailed description of the appalling devastation. Bomb experts were interviewed along with the emergency services. Broadsheets and tabloids alike packed their pages with coloured pictures graphically depicting the mangled remains of the Duncannon building.

Politicians were using every phrase in the thesaurus in an attempt to side step blame, especially when being asked leading questions on their policy for the reduction in security. The country demanded information about catching these perpetrators.

'*Baghdad must pay. Bomb the crap out the Middle East*' was the message from grassroots Britain over the airwaves of a Channel 4 call-in programme.

Jeremy Paxton-Smyth always walked from the mews cottage he was renting in Chelsea to his office in Whitehall, where he'd spent most of his time of late. This walk had become a ritual since his appointment barely three months earlier. The old Etonian and Oxford Blue adored the ambience of London's splendid facades. The stroll across St James's Park after brown toast and sparkling water, taken at a tiny cafe in Shepard's Market, provided him with a good start to any day before jumping into his hectic life style.

After Sandhurst, Paxton-Smyth had commenced his career in the Coldsteam Guards. There had been a Paxton-Smyth in the Coldstreams almost since General Monk formed the Regiment back in 1659. Following an albeit short but glittering career in the Brigade, Paxton-Smyth passed a selection course for the Special Air Service where he had spent six intensive years before accepting a position in Military Intelligence. And in true Paxton-Smyth tradition, promotion was swift and continual.

The sombre, pale face of Kathy Parnell greeted Paxton-Smyth on his arrival at the office. She carefully placed the morning's post and his first cup of fruit tea down on his desk.

"I've got Washington on hold for you, Sir, someone called James Parker."

Jeremy glanced up from his desk, "Are you okay Kathy? I told you to take a couple of days' leave. I know what its like to loose a friend in a bombing."

It was as if the mere mention of bombings had taken Kathy's emotions over the edge as tears began to flood down her attractive middle-aged face. "It's better to be at work rather than stuck at home alone," she said, mopping up her eyes with a handkerchief kindly provided from Paxton-Smyth's top pocket.

"Well if you feel that way fine, but I'll leave it up to you. Put the Director through Kathy." He took a sip of the raspberry tea as the telephone began ringing. A security scramble continued for a few seconds before the line opened. "Good morning Mr Parker, sorry to have kept you. My name's Paxton-Smyth."

"Paxton, how the devil are yeah? Congratulations on your appointment, Head of MI6 must be one heck of a job?"

Always ask a Brit how they are then tell them how much you love London, say it's your favourite city in the whole world and hey presto, you've got a friend for life was the sound advice offered to James Parker by a CNN reporter friend prior to his first trip to England.

"My name's Jeremy Paxton-Smyth, Paxton is part of my surname, it's double-barrelled, my given name as you Americans call it!"

"Well okay Jerry, only where I come from the only thing double-barrelled is my old papa's huntin' gun." James Parker laughed, amused by his own joke. "Okay Jerry I'll come to the point, as you know our big guys have summoned a meeting and my Chief has asked me to liaise with you. Who's the fella you're bringing to this party?"

There was a brief pause on the scrambled transatlantic line whilst Paxton-Smyth checked his file. "It would appear the Minister of Foreign Affairs; a little pimple-nosed squirt called Martins," Parker laughed.

"Hey Jerry, you and me, we'll get along just fine. My guy's the Chief of Staff, got an ego the size of the Empire State along with an Irish temper."

Paxton-Smyth was forced to smile at the way they were acting, like a couple of schoolboys comparing tittle-tattle notes about their respective teachers. "Mine looks like a garden gnome," went on Paxton-Smyth.

"Say Jerry what the hell's happened with you guys since Maggie quit?"

"Not a lot," replied the Head of MI6.

"Well I guess we're in for a real bunch of fun, your garden gnome and my fat fella discussing the greatest violation in my country's history, or at least since you guys tried to stuff the crap out of us over some tea party in Boston!" Parker laughed then continued, "I suggest we hold these talks on a yacht in the Caribbean. I have a friendly Senator who owes me a bunch of favours, his yacht's moored in Antigua."

"Sounds good to me," replied Paxton-Smyth, placing his mug down on a green mat with the Harrods crest.

"How about the day-after-tomorrow or do you guys need more time to wind up the rubber band?"

"No Mr Parker, I think the RAF can supply an aircraft with engines capable of getting us that far! I'll ask the minister to pack his bucket and spade!"

The Knights of Black Chapter

Bud O'Dowd relaxed like a tourist, sprawled out on Senator Summerville's yacht anchored off a tiny bay near the St James Club. The bow of the splendid, pristine 1950s motor-yacht tugged very gently on its anchor chain. Not a ripple dared break the lush, blue water.

From the luxury of his cushion filled steamer, strategically placed for him on the yacht's after-deck, O'Dowd could look across at the tiny whitewashed cottages of the St James Club village, shaded from the sun by huge palm trees. A fragile looking wooden jetty partly submerged by soft golden sand reached out across the aquamarine blue sea like a finger pointing towards him.

O'Dowd shifted his heavy frame slightly to one side and took a sip of Pinnocolata; he then raised a freshly lit Romeo and Juliet cigar to his chubby lips. This was the closest he'd come to a vacation in almost two years and he intended milking it for all it was worth.

It felt good slipping out of his typical dark blue suit, albeit briefly. He crossed one heavy leg over another causing the towelling robe to fall open to reveal a giant pair of Bermuda shorts emblazoned with 'Hallo Sailor' motifs.

"Yeah know, I should move my office out here," said O'Dowd letting out a mouthful of smoke as James Parker appeared at the rail holding a pair of binoculars.

"Looks like the Brits have finally arrived," said Parker as he watched the blue water give way to white foam as the bow of a motor launch powered its way towards them. O'Dowd sunk the remaining dregs of his cocktail and wedged the cigar firmly in the corner of his mouth before raising himself up with some difficulty from the cushions of his steamer. He gripped the yacht's deckrail and yanked himself up to a standing position.

"Yes that's them okay, I can see JoJo at the helm. He's got a clean-cut guy next to him and someone at the back covered in a straw hat, who I guess must be the gnome?"

"Give me a look see," insisted O'Dowd taking the glasses with a chuckle. "Ye gods and you reckon this guy ranks right up there with the Prime Minister? This could be a bunch of laughs."

JoJo soon had the launch skilfully brought alongside the bathing platform at the stern of the yacht. Paxton-Smyth skipped nimbly off the launch clutching a bowline, which he secured to a ring on the platform, he then held the side of the boat for the Minister to alight. Just as he did so the wide-brimmed hat slipped from the Minister's head and dropped into the water. Martins made a frantic bid to retrieve the monster, almost falling overboard in the attempt.

Using a boat hook JoJo skilfully scooped the dripping thatch from the surface, placing it where the Minister could catch hold. Martins shook it vigorously then installed it back onto his bald head. Both James Parker and O'Dowd looked down from the esplanade deck in stitches.

"Gee I think I've just bust a rib, but it's been worth it," said O'Dowd trying to contain himself.

JoJo Curtis led the way up the steps onto the after-deck. He glanced across at his countryman and smiled, sharing their amusement.

The tiny Minister, wearing a creased fawn suite and dripping wet hat, greeted Bud O'Dowd with a bony outstretched hand. "Good morning, I'm Philip Martins, Foreign Secretary to her Majesty's Government... and you are?" he asked with visible aloofness.

"Bud O'Dowd," replied O'Dowd wiping the remnants of Martin's clammy handshake down the side of his robe.

Everyone else exchanged greetings as O'Dowd escorted them to a prepared table. Martins pulled a large polkadot handkerchief from his breast pocket and proceeded to mop perspiration from his brow. Unfortunately the action lifted his hat sufficiently for it to roll onto the back of his head and uncontrollably bounce off the deck rail before floating majestically down to the surface of the water like a giant autumn leaf about to land on a pond.

"For some reason Minister you and that hat seem destined to part," exclaimed Paxton-Smyth. The whole group watched as the hat headed back to shore.

"The natives will have used it as a new roof on a hut by nightfall," said James Parker, with a chuckle. O'Dowd began a rumble that developed into a king-sized belly laugh, almost bringing on a convulsion.

"Yeah know I haven't had as many laughs as this since I saw Bob Hope on Broadway," exclaimed O'Dowd in between coughing bouts.

Martins looked very red and hot, his knuckles turning white from gripping the rail with frustrated anger. "Mr Paxton-Smyth I insist you go and retrieve my hat immediately," he commanded. "I shall fry in this ridiculous heat."

"Well guys let me ask you a question. Are you going off hat fishin' or do you intend helping us to put the goddam world to rights? Me I'm easy," said O'Dowd pouring himself a glass of chilled orange juice.

"Perhaps I can pick up my hat later!" replied Martins reflecting upon O'Dowd's comment.

Eventually they all took seats around the large oval glass table, everyone began watching Martins as he proceeded to tie a knot in each corner of his polka dot handkerchief and then position it carefully over his head.

The spectacle again reduced Bud O'Dowd to howls of uncontrollable laughter, which infected the others, much to Paxton-Smyth's embarrassment.

"Now I've seen it all. You Brits sure are on your own," said James Parker.

"I suggest we get this meeting underway," said Martins, not exactly appreciating such frivolity, especially at his expense.

Bud O'Dowd stuffed the butt of his cigar into an empty glass.

"Before we commence gentlemen I'd be most grateful if we moved into the shade, I'm not comfortable in this heat, it doesn't suit me. I can't think for the life of me why such a place was chosen," said Martins removing his handkerchief and wiping sweat from his face.

"Dracula had exactly the same problem," whispered Parker in O'Dowd's general direction.

"Mr Martins, I spend most of my life stuffed up in an office, however just for you... please follow me." There was a tone in O'Dowd's voice reminiscent of his normal attitude. He pushed back his chair and raised his heavy frame from the table before leading the way into the saloon. He escorted them to a lounge area consisting of two very large semicircular, cream leather settees surrounding a huge, low, glass table. Stewards were called to move the refreshments to the new location. Martins again removed his handkerchief and wiped his freckled face before sitting down.

"Whatever happened to *'mad dogs and Englishmen go out in the midday sun'*?" asked James Parker.

"The Minister's a Scot," replied Paxton-Smyth.

"Open the goddam windows it's like a Turkey oven in here, that's if our distinguished guest has no problem with fresh air?" said O'Dowd, clearly agitated at having to sit inside. He positioned himself right along side Martins as if to purposely dwarf the little man, intimidating him sufficiently just to make a point.

"Right let's cut the crap and get down to business, this yacht's on rent and it's my budget taking the hit," said O'Dowd.

"Gentlemen," said Martins almost startling the others in a loud matter-of-fact voice as if he was about to address the House of Commons! "The British Government has assisted the United States in practically all its endeavours in the Middle East and, may I say, to the outrage of our European partners. We agreed to the bombings of Scud Missile sites and Iranian strongholds. In fact we provided active support by sending in fighter aircraft as back-up. However, clearly the violations experienced by both of our countries are a direct result of these actions."

The entire saloon fell into stony silence. O'Dowd wiped a handful of thick fingers across his forehead as Martins continued. "My government has been extremely embarrassed by this devastating attack on our capital. We stand alone, isolated from Europe and ridiculed by the Commonwealth initially for actions taken against Baghdad and now the death, destruction and devastation experienced in London."

O'Dowd looked carefully at the little man with the sandy tufts of hair ruffled by the experiences he'd endured. "Mr Martins you choose your words carefully and I detect the makings of a danger limitation exercise being put together here."

Philip Martins looked up the nostrils of the big man and then across the table towards Paxton-Smyth as if seeking support; however no body-language to that effect was forthcoming.

"Tell me Mr Martins, if we could put the clock back and the US were just commencing these actions, are you suggesting the British Government with hindsight would abstain or even opt out from supporting us?" asked James Parker with a serious expression on his lean, tanned face.

Martins looked clearly agitated. "No, not at all," he said finally. "I'm simply stating our position as I see it."

Paxton-Smyth thought intervention for the sake of British diplomacy might be prudent at this time. "Saddam Hussein is the ultimate reason for these bombings, the blood of innocent people is on his hands and the blame should be squarely placed on his shoulders," he said boldly.

Martins looked a little bemused as if he had a different agenda for this meeting.

"We are here," continued Paxton-Smyth, "for the sole purpose of jointly investigating ways to take the focus away from our respective countries, especially Prime Minister Blain and your President who clearly need this Middle Eastern issue to calm down significantly before the G7 summit."

"Okay Jerry, you're in the chair," said O'Dowd.

Martins threw O'Dowd a disapproving stare but said nothing.

Paxton-Smyth took a sip of orange before continuing, "Gentlemen I suggest we are all aware who is directly responsible for these bombings and I recommend a *modus operandi* to eradicate this desert scum once and for all."

Martins shook his head slowly and permitted a smirk to form across his insignificant face. "Mr Paxton-Smyth's comments are laudable, however my Government will not condone cavalry charges across the Middle East."

"Well my friend, I think it has merit," said O'Dowd.

"I will not agree to gung-ho tactics Mr O'Dowd," said Philip Martins as he leaned forward to pour orange juice into a glass. He then pushed his index finger down the collar of his shirt to allow a little air to ease his humid discomfort.

"Mr Martins, why don't you loosen that neck-tie and take off your jacket along with your attitude an' lighten up a bit, for Christ's sake? We're all on the same goddam side," said O'Dowd, frustrated by the spectacle at his side.

Martins ignored the suggestion and continued, "We have seen the result of your attempts to stop Al VL Sinda before and each time it's ended in failure and retaliation. We all know these latest atrocities are an eye for an eye. The Pan American aircraft bombed over Lockerbie, killing two hundred and seventy people in 1988, for example. And remember the deaths of two hundred and ninety civilians in the unwarranted shooting down of that Iranian passenger aircraft by guns deployed from an American warship, The USS Vincennes, I believe?"

O'Dowd moved with some discomfort in his seat at the remarks. Martins had the big Joint Chief of Staff on a hook and he was going to show him why Prime Minister Anthony Blain had made the right choice in appointing him Foreign Secretary.

"And correct me if I'm wrong Mr O'Dowd but I have it on good authority that it was your navy who shot down an airbus on a scheduled flight from Bonder Abbes to Dubai, mistaking it for military aircraft. I'm also reliably informed that the US is paying sixty million dollars in compensation to the families that were killed!"

Paxton-Smyth was waiting for the Irishman to explode at anytime and therefore jumped in again to defuse the potential 'situation' taking place.

"I suggest we deploy a very small task force to go in undercover and flush out Mohammed Abu Atif. If we can remove him it would disorientate AL VL Sinda and their so called disciples of war. Muslim fundamentalists across the globe treat him as if he's a god!"

James Parker concurred. "Jerry could be right; a small task force might work. We got real close to this guy once but the bastard slipped through our fingers like the proverbial sand. Even our naval bombardment right at the heart of his command post failed to flush him out. This Abu Atif has infiltrated our administration, ransacked the place, taking blank passports and other documents. According to our people on the ground in Albania he stole thousands of passports from there as well. He's hit you Brits also if I'm not mistaken, Jerry?"

Paxton-Smyth nodded in agreement. Philip Martins made no comment, he simply dabbed his red face with the handkerchief.

James Parker replenished his glass from a freshly delivered jug of orange and continued, "Small is beautiful, maybe just a couple of guys, say one of yours and one of ours, plus an observer. This guy Abu Atif's a cunning bastard, he can pull an army of terrorists together for whoever's got enough money to pay him and plenty have, take Saddam for example."

Everyone looked across at Martins for a sign or comment. He looked thoughtful for a moment before responding, "If we carried out such an exercise these men should not directly represent or hold allegiance to the British government or, I suggest, you people in Washington. If the world were to learn that we are directly responsible for such an attempt we'd slip even deeper into the abyss."

"Mr Martins you're right," agreed Bud O'Dowd, "My President's already off the world's Christmas card list as it is. If such a task force failed and he was directly responsible, he'd be wearing his balls for a neck tie, goddamit!"

A smirk re-appeared across Martins' flushed face - yet another Yank he'd won over!

"Mr Martins, outside it's a beautiful sunny day, in here it's hotter than hell's kitchen but I'm afraid I'm going to keep you guys here for quite some time. Let's get one thing clear: this is not simply another hit by religious fanatics. We are talking about a movement so deep-rooted it goes back to the Crusades. If we intend to clear the world of these Terror groups we need a fundamental understanding of how they tick and who's behind them. Smash the foundations and the building falls down!"

Bud O'Dowd leaned forward resting his forearms upon each knee; the action prompted his ample stomach to forcibly sag between his broad thighs. He first glanced across at Paxton-Smyth then focused his attention again on Philip Martins.

"What do you guys know about *Incanda*?"

Martins' face remained expressionless; however Paxton-Smyth looked interested.

"Well, *Incanda* was a breakaway group from Rex Deus," continued O'Dowd, "who perhaps you also have not heard of Jerry?"

O'Dowd looked for a flicker of knowledge or even a mere sign of understanding from Philip Martins, but none came.

"Were Rex Deus not the instigators of the original Knights Templar movement?" remarked Paxton-Smyth.

"Correct and you'd know that Jerry because you are a Knight Templar, are you not?" replied O'Dowd as he opened a humidor to select a cigar.

Philip Martins gave Paxton-Smyth a disapproving stare as if he'd just been accused of something indecent.

"Well yes," replied Paxton-Smyth adjusting his posture on the settee. "In fact I've been a Freemason for the past fifteen years. I was exulted to the Order of the Knights Templar about two years ago. As I understand, and believe me I'm no scholar of Rex Deus, in translation it means 'Kings of God'. I'm not sure of its origin but I know the Order we associate with Knights Templar originated with a number of Jewish priests who escaped from Jerusalem following its destruction. Apparently they fled to Europe. I know that the higher rituals of Freemasonry can trace this lineage back to the building of King Solomon's temple some two thousand years before Christ and indeed back again to the time of Moses."

The Knights of Black Chapter

Bud O'Dowd looked impressed. He turned to JoJo Curtis who smiled back at him.

"JoJo here is of the Thirty Three Degree Masonic Order as indeed I was until this goddam job got in the way. I hate to leave you out of this Masonry stuff Mr Martins, as I know you're not a practising Mason although I hear your father was! He followed in your grandfather's footsteps but apparently you had no interest in joining the Masonic movement!"

Philip Martins looked a little aggrieved to discover that this fat, brash Irish-American had delved into his family history. "I'm intrigued to learn what else you might know about me, Mr O'Dowd. Is it common practice to investigate every Senior Minister of Her Majesty's government before meeting them?" asked Philip Martins with an almost cutting edge to his voice, his face appearing even redder than before.

"You bet Minister," replied James Parker, "We know what you had for breakfast two years, ten months, three weeks and two days ago. When anyone engages in a meeting at this level we turn 'em inside out and upside down. Don't be aggrieved, you passed - but only just!" James Parker smiled, so did Paxton-Smyth.

"Gentlemen we have expert knowledge of *Rex Deus* and how it works today. We believe that if its function were unlocked we would find a way of removing these violators once and for all," said O'Dowd, cutting the end off his chosen cigar. He waved his hand to gesture at a fairly inconspicuous character standing motionless near a pair of open glass doors. "Ask Professor Weigner to join us now please."

The security guard initially ignored the Chief of Staff and looked across to James Parker for instructions. A nod from Parker prompted him into action; he crossed the floor and descended down a narrow staircase.

"I guess you could say Bernard Weigner is one of the world's leading authorities on Rex Deus. As a practicing Roman Catholic, Mr Martins, you may find some of the things you are about to hear concerning, maybe even a bit frightening. It could go against the religious instruction you had during your time at St Mary's Junior School where you were probably brainwashed by the teachings of Catholicism before you became a server of the host during communion at mass in St Catharine's Church in Aberdeen." Bud O'Dowd smiled smugly from behind his chubby hand and fat cigar.

The left eye of Philip Martins began to twitch uncontrollably, a nervous affliction he thought had been eradicated after some very private and expensive coaching sessions in preparation for his first exposure to a cabinet post. "Mr O'Dowd, this is all very interesting and I congratulate you on such a detailed investigation, especially as this meeting was only arranged a couple of days ago, but I really cannot see how historical religious beliefs - and indeed Freemasonry - can affect the situation we have here," said Philip Martins.

Bud O'Dowd raised his hand as if to symbolise a halt in the procedures. "Mr Foreign Secretary, please be assured, all will be revealed quite soon. You know like most things, religion has been a primary cause of trouble throughout the world ever since time began. The situation we find ourselves in right now is in no way unique. How about the troubles in Northern Ireland, Catholic against Protestant? And as you know, most countries around the globe have had their fair share of problems through differing religious beliefs!"

Just as O'Dowd began to raise a glass of orange to his lips the guard reappeared escorting an elderly man towards the table. The old gentleman looked desperately thin and frail; the hump on his back caused him to stoop over a stout walking stick that he relied upon for support. All three Americans scrambled from their seats on the settee, clearly reacting to the sudden presence of a person they obviously held in high esteem.

"Professor Weigner, please accept my apologies for keeping you so long, I hope you were looked after down there?" said Bud O'Dowd who was now gently shaking the Professor's hand as if it were bone china. He continued holding it until a chair had been brought to the table and the professor could be assisted into it. "Gentlemen I'm very proud to present Professor Bernard Weigner!"

JoJo Curtis bowed respectfully, accepting the Professor's hand. Everyone was unsure whether he was about to kiss it, as if the Professor was the Pope, or give it a gentle shake. James Parker offered the Professor a broad smile and left it at that. However Paxton-Smyth felt obligated to formally introduce himself whilst Philip Martins simply smiled and remained seated throughout O'Dowd's formal introduction.

"Professor Weigner kindly accepted my invitation to come here to help us guys understand exactly who we are up against. I've had the privilege of attending a number of the Professor's seminars and found them fascinating."

The Knights of Black Chapter

Bernard Weigner sat through O'Dowd's introduction without showing a modicum of change in his expression, accepting O'Dowd's accolade as if it was an everyday occurrence.

"Professor, over to you," said Bud O'Dowd as he flopped back down onto the settee.

"Gentlemen! Some of you will be shocked by what I'm about to reveal. You may feel some things are far-fetched, mythical even. Names of famous people throughout history will be described in ways unfamiliar to you, but you must be enlightened to the fact that the world is not all that it might seem and many parts of our history have been massaged and manipulated for the benefit of unparalleled greed, power and the conquering of mankind at any cost!"

Paxton Smyth was a little surprised to hear a very English accent emanating from this old gentleman.

"Professor, do I detect an Oxford accent?" he asked at an appropriate opportunity.

The flicker of a smile scurried briefly across the old man's face. "Yes I am English although I have spent the major part of my life in America. Perhaps I should commence by offering you a brief glimpse into my background. I was born in Worcester and educated at King's. I read Ancient History at Oxford and eventually became a Don. It was whilst I was a student at Oxford that I became a Freemason. I was eventually invited to become Head of Historical Studies at Harvard. I have spent the past forty years working at both of these wonderful institutions."

James Parker poured a glass of orange and handed it to the Professor. He accepted it gratefully and took a sip before continuing. "If power is corrupt and men who are powerful are corrupted by it, then potentially this could apply to all men: those who run countries, companies, departments and religions of all kinds. In fact the whole philosophy of corruption has been ingrained into our daily lives. For thousands of years it has become accepted as the norm."

The old man's tired, pale-blue eyes briefly scanned the faces of his audience for any sign of disapproval.

"Gentlemen, permit me to take you back centuries before Christ, in fact to the building of King Solomon's Temple. The Phoenician King Tyre, called Hiram, was reputed to have supplied the designs and in fact many of the materials to build this Temple. The actual name of this king was 'Ahi-ram'. We know this because the letters and communications between him and Solomon were lodged in the Tyrian archives."

"A second Hiram built a foundry in the valley of Jordon between Zeredatha and Succoth; it was here that Hiram the worker of metals, cast the great pillars of Boaz and Jachin; they were cast to form the supports for the entrance of the Temple. These two pillars will be referred to several times; they are symbolically used in every Freemasons lodge throughout the world."

"We are of the belief that this worker of metals is the man known amongst Masons as Hiram Abif, appointed by Hiram, King of Tyre. Hiram Abif was a senior brother of *Rex Deus* and it is our belief that his line still exists to this day under the Order known as Knights of Black Chapter. Hiram Abif met an untimely death, plotted by fifteen stonemasons who were eager to extract the secrets of Rex Deus from this man they referred to as their master."

"Hiram Abif became the principle architect of the Temple. Just before the temple was completed he was set upon. He had taken time at 'high twelve' to give praise to a God who was described as the 'most high'. Let us ponder on the description 'most high' because it will play a significant part in the fundamental understanding of religious unity, at a level at which most people have little knowledge. Most would be horrified to learn of its existence because it turns religion completely on its head!"

"The sun being at its zenith in the sky, this Canaanite artisan known as Hiram Abif would have been worshiping the Sun God - hence the description 'most high'. Fifteen plotted Hiram's demise but only three masons actually carried out the deed. He was struck a violent blow upon his forehead by a mason who approached him from the south gate of the temple. He attempted to make his escape by running to the west gate where a second mason was lying in wait. There he received a second devastating blow to the head. Now groggy and bleeding badly, in great terror he instinctively ran to the east gate where the third perpetrator was lying in wait. As he approached the third mason emerged from the shadows and lashed out, delivering the coup de grace."

"Today these actions are practised symbolically as part of the ritual when raising a Mason to the third degree. Following these symbolic attacks, the candidate, known as the 'Cadaver', blindfolded and therefore in total darkness, is laid in a makeshift grave."

"Following this ordeal the masons of the lodge parade around the circumference of the grave. Three attempts are made to snatch the candidate from the clutches of death. The first two fail because they are mimicked from the previous two degrees. However the third, used specifically for the third degree, is successful. With the help of the deacon of the lodge the candidate is resurrected - a special grip is used by the Worshipful Master to accomplish this. The candidate has now been raised to a standing position. A difficult manoeuvre then ensues between him and the Worshipful master. They embrace and touch each other at five distinctive points; these points are called the five points of friendship. This action accomplished the candidate is then shown the tomb directly behind him from which he has been raised. A real skull and crossed thighbones form the head of the grave, these represent the candidates own remains."

"The candidate is directed to the east to view a five-pointed star that shines out from the darkness between two pillars. These pillars represent Boaz and Jachin. The star signifies the bright star of the morning. We presume this represents the planet Venus that rises just before the sun at dawn! From this moment on the candidate will have been elevated to that of a Master Mason and will remain that way for the rest of his life. This ritual replicates the slaying of Hiram Abif. Do you also see the similarity Gentlemen between this act and the rising of Christ?"

Professor Bernard Weigner glanced around the table as if analysing the expressions upon the faces of these very powerful men.

Only one showed any signs of scepticism. Clearly Philip Martins was moved by the similarity the old man had pointed out, but refrained from comment.

With his audience now captured, the Professor continued: "Almost since time began groups of people have existed as families, united by various common causes and aims! *Rex Deus* was such a group. Traditionally a specific offspring, normally the firstborn or chosen one, would be called to one side and informed of the secrets and working knowledge of the Order. No other member of the family would have any knowledge or even be aware of this involvement. Not even a wife would know that her husband was connected. This tradition gentlemen, is still practiced by both the Knights of Black Chapter and *Incanda* to this very day!"

"Long before the birth of Christ, Priests of the Temple in Jerusalem arranged and ran schools for boys and girls. These Priests all took their names from angels and out of respect were always referred to as such. When a girl student was past the age of puberty she might well be selected for copulation by one of these Priests, purported to be directly from the holy bloodline, his seed was induced into the young woman in a bid to maintain the 'pure' lines of Levi and David. Upon confirmation of her pregnancy the young girl would be married off to a respectable man in the community. The girl, described as the Virgin Mary was so seduced by a Priest known as Gabriel."

Philip Martins suddenly drew in a gasp of air and visibly moved on the settee, as if suddenly being subjected to a stabbing pain. The professor glanced briefly across at him. This was a common occurrence in his experience and one he had learned to ignore.

"Mary was married to the man called Joseph who was, naturally, much older than her. Despite her difficulty coming to terms with the marriage they eventually settled down and in fact had seven children - three girls and four boys. Traditionally the first born from the virginity, upon reaching the age of seven was destined to return to the Temple to commence formal education and so the cycle would continue. As Jesus grew into manhood he was not particularly popular in the Temple or in fact in Jerusalem itself. James, his half brother, was by far the more popular of the two, especially after his untimely death at the hands of the Romans. Zadok was James's Jewish name. After his death the brothers of Rex Deus were referred to as the 'Sons of Zadok'!"

"The entire population of Jerusalem rose up in revolt following the demise of James, which started a very bloody war between the Jews and the Romans. The power of the Romans was immense, they literally razed Jerusalem to the ground and many Jews were slaughtered whilst others were sold into slavery. Just before the Temple in Jerusalem was destroyed a group of Nasorean Priests escaped to Greece and over time they eventually dispersed in different directions across Europe - a number of these Priests were Rex Deus. I should mention that Greece plays a very significant part in this area of history involving *Rex Deus*. There is little evidence, but it is believed that the Knights of Black Chapter were conceived on Crete!"

"Napoleon Bonaparte invaded Egypt in 1796 and as you know from history his attempt was a complete disaster, and he was defeated by Nelson at the battle of the Nile in 1803. Napoleon Bonaparte was almost certainly a brother of *Incanda* but we are uncertain at what level. We do know the *Incanda* down line eventually passed to Napoleon III who'd spent much of his life living in the shadow of his famous uncle. Napoleon III seized an opportunity when an Islamic sect known as the Druze slaughtered over 30,000 Christians in Syria. He sent an army to destroy the Druze and unlike his uncle he succeeded in his quest. It's thanks to him that we have an understanding of Cannaan. Bonaparte sent an army of scholars to study the ancient history and cultures of Egypt; consequentially Egyptology became an academic subject."

"Not to be left outdone, his nephew, forever wishing to prove himself as a worthy leader in service of *Incanda*, in 1860 sent a force of French troops to assist the sultan of Constantinople who was attempting to quell the many killings going on, inspired by religious beliefs."

"An excommunicated priest from the Catholic faith called Father Renan, a well-read man in semitic languages, was instructed by Napoleon III to investigate the history of Phoenicia. His journeys took him to the Phoenician town of Byblos. The Greeks used the name *Byblos* to describe writing materials and papyrus. The name *Byblos* became the word *Biblion* that eventually became *Bible*."

"The Nazarene Priests I mentioned had been prominent in this area under Rex Deus. A hand full of them returned to the ruined city of Jerusalem in an attempt to discover the remains they referred to as the Savoir. They were successful in their quest, these remains were sent to Greece for safe keeping and in fact remained there until AD600 after which they were returned to Jerusalem and carefully placed back under the ruins of the Temple."

" The Jerusalem Temple possessed a honeycomb of archives and a labyrinth of tunnels and passageways, most of these passageways had inscriptions upon their walls with the names of the young girls sired by the temple priests. The names went back to the times of David and Aaron."

"The group who returned the Savoir to the Temple were of the *Rex Deus* brotherhood. During that time Jews were not permitted to enter the city of Jerusalem and in fact they were barred entry for some five hundred years. Members of *Rex Deus* were able to avoid this persecution because they adopted other religious faiths and practices. This was accepted so long as they followed a single God. Gentlemen, Incanda eventually evolved from these former Priests. Perhaps you can now appreciate how this *high degree* has divested itself of any one single religion or belief, be it Muslim or Christian and that is why it has been very dangerous for so many centuries."

"So you are leading us to believe that this *Incanda* movement is ultimately behind the Middle Eastern problems?" asked Philip Martins, almost smirking… almost, because there was a clear sign of fear hidden behind the smugness.

The professor held an index finger in the air. "All will become clear, have patience Mr Martins. King Solomon developed a 'grade' known as the 'Master Elect of Nine'. This grade was awarded to nine of his closest companions, all of whom were of *Rex Deus*! It is from these nine that the original Knights Templar was eventually formed. For many centuries the nine each handed down their mantle through their direct bloodline. Jesus Christ and indeed his brother James were of this bloodline through their mother Mary, being of *Rex Deus*! Yes, Gentlemen, women figure in *Rex Deus* and, as Greek history demonstrates, women were regarded as the principals of the human species for many centuries.

"It is believed that Mary's *Rex Deus* connection came from a Norwegian line via the so-called God Thor and a beauty called Freyia. Freyia was said to represent the Planet Venus, her power was immense, even over life and death. She was said to posses all the gold of the then known world. She also cultivated certain species of flowers and in particular the rose was initially associated with her - the very same rose that was later depicted upon the ceiling of the Rosslyn chapel in Scotland long before this flower was even known about anywhere in western civilisation, let alone specifically grown in Scotland. It is a fact that the direct line of Freyia, through Mary still exists to this very day!"

"So what you're saying is that there's a direct descendant of Jesus and his brother David still living today and he or she is aware of this fact!" Phillip Martins almost stood to deliver this divine revelation.

"Let Mr Weigner continue," barked Bud O'Dowd from behind a cloud of cigar smoke.

"Thank you," responded Bernard Weigner. "For precisely nine years, nine Crusaders lived in Poverty. The new King of Jerusalem by the name of Baldwin provided their only support.

The Knights of Black Chapter

Many answers to the puzzle surrounding these nine were found by the discovery of a copper scroll at Qumran on the banks of the Dead Sea in 1947. This metal scroll that is now know commonly known as the Dead Sea Scroll had been written just a few years after Christ's death. The scroll in fact contained information suggesting the whereabouts of over 60 locations where items of immense value had been buried at the commencement of the Jewish war against the Romans.

"The Dead Sea Scroll was intended to act as a reference and map for the benefit of those Jews who had survived the war. It was meant to guide them to where these sacred and precious items had been buried, especially as treasures might well be needed to continue the long and expensive battle for Jerusalem. The Dead Sea Scroll goes on to say that a second copy can be found! It also contains a very descriptive list of the vast amount of precious items of treasure, together with details of twenty-four other scrolls hidden beneath the Temple."

"In 1860 the British Army were deployed to excavate below the Temple. They dug down more than 80 feet but discovered nothing save a few belongings of the Knights Templar. Back to our lineage of nine! The task of Rex Deus was to carry out research in an attempt to obtain certain relics and manuscripts that contained the secrets and traditions of Judaism and of ancient Egypt going back to the days of Moses."

"Perhaps that's the reason why Napoleon was so keen to conquer Egypt, to try and discover these manuscripts and learn of their secrets, he could then gain the ultimate power he craved." suggested JoJo.

The professor nodded in agreement. "Yes in fact the quest of Incanda has always been to possess these secrets to secure ultimate world power and domination," said the Professor looking directly at JoJo. "After the Romans defeated the Jews, Emperor Hadrian in AD135 eventually rebuilt the city of Jerusalem. He renamed it Aelia Capitolina and called the province of Syria, Palestina. All Jews were banned from entering this new city and as I've mentioned before, for over five hundred years no Jewish community resided there! In Rome the Christians merged the myths of their Gods into one cult conceived by Pope Paul who wanted to create a religion that would appeal to the masses. On the 20th May AD325 the Emperor Constantine who was not a Christian, convened a council known as the council of Nicaca for the purpose of taking a vote. Was Jesus a deity or not? Following this vote it was proclaimed that Jesus was indeed a God! The outcome of this vote began the Romanised Christian era. This also brought about the period in history we call the Dark Ages. A period when time stood still, blanked out from the western world for some twelve hundred and seventy years. These dark ages actually remained until the power of the Roman church was undermined by the reformation.

"The library in Alexandria, which contained recordings of the world's great wealth of knowledge, was completely destroyed by fire at the hands of Bishop Theophilius. St John Chypostom declared that this great achievement was to rid the world of 'old' ideas. All traces of the old philosophies and literature of the ancient world had vanished from the face of the earth."

"Progress and the natural evolution of western civilisation had been brought to an abrupt halt. Life in many parts diminished into a state of barbarism. The church banned education in an attempt to halt the spread of knowledge. All freedom of thought was outlawed for fear that free thinking would destroy the foundations of the church."

Philip Martins sat with a transfixed expression upon his face. He'd asked many questions of the faith from in which he was raised, as any intelligent person naturally would, especially at junior school where most people of his age enquired as to the why's and wherefores of the Catholic teachings. The answers in response had often been inadequate or had made little sense to an intelligent young mind. Philip Martins therefore sat like the rest of the group intently listening to the words uttered by this frail old man that began to make perfect but scary sense.

"Science eventually succumbed to superstition," continued the Professor, "engineering was lost. All things one could describe as proper and good were despised. Human achievements were repeatedly ignored in the name of Jesus Christ. The subjects of art, science, philosophy, literature, astrology, mathematics, medicine and indeed sex all became taboo. Sex was for procreation only; if women actually enjoyed the act but did not conceive they were considered to be copulating with Satan and often burned as Witches."

"Gentlemen, at the hands of Catholicism a very important piece of history was destroyed in that there were actually two Messiahs!" The professor immediately looked across at Philip Martins who, surprisingly, showed no outward signs of emotion or disbelief and as for the others, they simply sat motionless. "Exactly 35 years after the crucifixion of Jesus Christ," continued Bernard Weigner, "disease and death ravaged the lands of his birth. People were dying terrible deaths, literally in their thousands. Centuries later history repeated itself, but this time with even greater devastation, exactly 35 years after the death of the second Messiah who, incidentally, was to be subjected to a similar fate to that of Jesus and in almost identical circumstances.

"Mr O'Dowd and Mr Curtis here are both practicing masons of the thirty-three degrees. Each degree represents an important key to history. If we consider these thirty-three degrees as a storyboard, they begin with a very early civilisation. A terrible flood swept the lands and the history of the temple builders was almost lost. This prompted a man called Enoch to preserve knowledge and history for whom so ever would survive. This knowledge would provide future generations with the ability to build cities and great mansions and to develop new cultures."

"Enoch cleverly built two massive pillars and carved the great secrets of life onto them. About 3,200 years BC saw the founding of the Egyptian civilisation. It is said that one of these two pillars was discovered at that time and that by its teachings the first king of Egypt, called Osiris which incidentally in translation means Prince, had risen from the dead to develop civilisation. Parts of the second pillar were found by the Jews close to the spot where King Solomon's temple was eventually constructed, over three thousand years later. This would explain how the Jews obtained their teachings, which pre-date history itself."

"Following this supposed happening to Osiris, resurrection became a fashionable cult of the Egyptians, hence the practice of mummification which they undertook and which is known to common history. The Jewish culture that evolved was very similar to that of the Egyptians. Actually the name Moses is of the Egyptian tongue!

"During the 'dark ages' eleven Knights from the families of Christian princes took vows of secrecy. These were the second wave of Knight Templars; their Order was established in 1118. These eleven removed parts of what was left of the one great pillar of Enoch from below the Temple in Jerusalem and transported it along with scrolls and artefacts to Scotland, to a place called Kilwinning in Ayrshire. It was here at Kilwinning that the first Masonic lodge was formed."

"During these times the high priesthood of Yahweh was re-introduced in Jerusalem by the Knights Templar. Grand masters were appointed. Jacques de Molay and Hughes de

Payen both held these supreme positions. Jacques de Malay was often depicted directly at the side of Jesus on a cross. This is symbolic of the fact that he was viewed as an equal, the second messiah. Freemasonry was, and indeed still is, all about truth - this occurrence was described as the royal secret."

"Both Jesus and his brother James taught the ancient secrets from the originals transcribed from the great pillars of Enoch. These teachings were inherited by the Knight Templars and eventually bequeathed to Freemasonry. Therefore hidden deep in the bowels of Freemasonry is the knowledge that there was actually this second messiah! This was another reason why the Church of Rome was determined to continue wiping out a whole swathe of history."

"The need to coerce people into subservience at all costs, was significant. In the late 13th century the theologian Thomas Aquinas even decreed that the consecrated Eucharistic bread and wine is automatically transformed into the actual body and blood of Jesus Christ upon its consumption - a cannibalistic concept."

Again Professor Bernard Weigner glanced sharply at Philip Martins as if half expecting a ton of abuse to be hurled towards him. None came.

"A second messiah you say?" remarked Paxton-Smyth, who was almost transfixed by the knowledge this man could provide: knowledge that he, like most people, had often sought but never found.

"Yes. A man by the name of Joachim of Fiore, who was a Calabrian Abbot, had an apocalyptic vision of the future, developed from complicated numeral systems derived from the analysis of the Bible. As the tarot pack of cards, through Major and Minor, had numeral connections with both the outer and inner worlds, so the Abbot used this analysis to calculate events between the Old Testament and the New Testaments of the Bible."

"He estimated that the time of the Son was closing and that the time of the Spirit would be dawning. He also estimated that there were exactly forty-two generations between Adam and Jesus. He was therefore convinced that forty-two generations following Jesus, a new age would dawn and that its arrival would be in approximately 1260. He predicted that there would not be a smooth transition. His estimates were to be proved absolutely correct!"

The Knights of Black Chapter

"Following Joachim of Fiore's death, ideas based on his thinking were gaining pace, along with others of similar belief; to the extent that one group called themselves the Apostolic Brethren. This group commenced an armed resistance against the Church of Rome. It was their belief that God had withdrawn authority from the Pope; they proclaimed that both he and his clergy would be annihilated in a battle, a battle that would lead to the 'Age of the Spirit'. The Apostolic Brethren hid out in the Alpine valley in wait for the end of the world; which for them, as for the Templars, commenced in 1307. For these people, their world ended by the sword at the hands of the Church at Monte Rebello."

"At the millennium birth of the fourteenth century, the people of Europe were deeply concerned. The Church they followed was falling apart and the predicted messiah had not arrived. Joachim's apocalyptic vision was soon to become true, as the Black Death would spread like an evil blanket across the Christian world."

"During this period Jacques de Molay was of the belief that he had won his battle with the almost bankrupt King Philip IV of France and Pope Clement V, to stop the amalgamation of the Templars with the Hospitallers. Jacques de Molay had brought a fortune with him to France and made sure the king was aware that this incredible wealth had been deposited in the Temple in Paris. It is reasonable to believe that as Grand Master Jacques de Molay intended to remain in Paris to reconstruct the Templar movement and eventually take control of the situation which was leading to this unwanted merger."

"Regrettably, de Molay did not anticipate the ruthless retribution he was to receive at the hands of the Pope and the huge price he personally was about to pay!"

"De Moray was subjected to an Inquisition, developed as a court of justice; the founder was the Roman Catholic Church. It had been formed to eradicate anything that opposed the official beliefs of the Vatican heritage. Anyone who was brought before this court was either maimed or killed. This decree originated in AD 382, in that anyone charged with heresy would be put to death."

"The Inquisition was permitted to not only kill those accused of so-called crimes against the church, but to cause excruciating pain and a slow, vile death for any suspect. In 1252 this practice had the formal blessing of the Pope who was, ironically, called *Innocent the IV*."

"It was a Friday, Friday the 13th in the month of October 1307. Now you know where *Friday the 13th* came from! Early in the morning the army of Seneschals of France attacked the highly respected Order of the Knights Templar, and some fifteen thousand of them were accused as heretics."

"From his balcony King Philip IV looked on as his men took over the Paris Temple. They removed its entire contents and the fortune stored there by Jacques de Molay, who was arrested along with the other preceptor of Aquitaine, the Prior of Normandy."

"Information about the impending attack had in fact been leaked, prompting a number of Knights to flee, disappearing to safety before the event. A significant number of these Knights ended up in Scotland under the protective banner of Robert the Bruce; whilst others set forth in search of a land they called la Mercia, now known as America."

"A man known as William of Paris was the Chief Inquisitor of France. The King charged him to extract a confession from Jacques de Molay along with other Templars, and granted him free licence to use what ever means he wished!"

"The 'persuasion' of this Inquisition elicited the information that ceremonies were held in private, exclusively by the Knights Templar, in the chapel of the Paris Temple, described as a secret place. The 'secret place' had a black and white chequered floor; non-christian symbols hung from its walls and on the ceiling stars were depicted. Hanging from the centre of the ceiling was an object signifying the letter G. Inside a wooden chest a skull and two thighbones were found together with a white burial shroud."

"Gentlemen, those of you who are Masons will agree that the items I have just described are found in the temples of a Freemason's lodge to this very day! Then, like now, Templars used the shroud to wrap the candidate in following his resurrection into the new life of the Order."

"In total, ten charges were brought against the Knights Templar but the one the Inquisition designated the vilest was that the Knights would subject every novice of their Order to spit and stamp their feet on a cross, suggesting that this cross was a replica of the one used for Jesus Christ's crucifixion. The Paris priests were outraged by this charge. The Pope demanded that William of Paris use torture of the worst possible kind on all the 'heretics'. The King, under Papal directives, ordered that Jacques de Molay be brought to confess by any means at the

Inquisition's disposal. In the hands of skilled practitioners of torture, most souls confess simply to end their pain with death by execution."

"Initially the Grand Master, Jacques de Molay was simply questioned. Because the Paris Temple was used merely as a financial centre, its basements did not contain any equipment of torture. William of Paris, however, had a vivid imagination and therefore pre-arranged a number of things that would have a devastating effect upon the accused. These included whips, large nails and ropes of differing thicknesses."

"De Molay was going to suffer to the extreme for allowing and participating in these ceremonies of resurrection, and for abusing the name of Christ! As was the custom, he was stripped of his clothes. A makeshift crown made from sharp thorns was forced onto his head, cutting deep into the flesh of his scalp and forehead. Ropes were attached to his wrists, he was then beaten repeatedly, using a whip with many tails. Sharpened bones were lashed to the ends of each tail to induce even more indescribable pain... the Inquisition recorded descriptions of many of the means of torture commonly used."

"De Molay was then forced towards a stout wooden door. He was made to stand on a stool with his back propped up against the door. His right arm was then held above his head and a large nail was driven into his wrist, skilfully avoiding the veins between the ulna and radius bones. This action immediately dislocated the thumb, which turned uncontrollably, burying its nail deep into the palm of de Molay's hand."

"His left arm was then brought up to his side at an angle of 45 degress, crucifixion fashion. It too was then pinned to the door by an equally long nail through the wrist. At this point the footstool was then kicked away from under de Molay, the sudden strain caused by his weight dislocating both shoulders."

"His right foot was then laid over the left so that one large nail could be driven into both feet between the second and third metatarsals. This, combined with the nails in his wrists, would support his body for as long as his tormentors wished. Ironically, the blood loss was minimal and although his pain was excruciating he remained conscious throughout the ordeal."

"The Inquisition employed priests who were specialists in cruelty and expert at inflicting pain. For example the door on which de Molay had been nailed would be opened and then suddenly banged shut, the pain this sudden vibration induced must have been quite terrible! All this served upon a man well into his sixties - a highly respected man who enjoyed the high office of Master."

"De Molay was close to death, but not quite. Death was not his tormentors' objective. The treatment made his breathing laboured due to carbon dioxide excess induced by long spasms without breathing because of terrible pain. His body temperature rocketed and his blood pressure sank dramatically, forcing his heart to beat rapidly in an attempt to keep the body functioning."

"William of Paris was both cruel and very clever, just at the point when de Molay thought he was about to die, he was removed from the door and laid onto a shroud, which had been spread out across a mattress. Pillows were placed under his head, and waists, his arms were then painfully laid at his sides."

"The Pope ordered William of Paris not to kill the Grand Master of the Templars. The shroud had been wrapped around de Molay and soon blood and sweat began to impregnate the material. Gentlemen, the shroud that formed the sheet Jacques de Molay was wrapped in, is without a shadow of doubt the garment commonly described as the Shroud of Turin!"

"Again the Professor took a long, hard look at his engrossed audience, especially Phillip Martins who seemed to be staring out over the deck rail towards the St James Club, almost as if in a trance. However, his mind was somewhere else and what he was seeing was not the sun disappearing behind the palm trees, but the priest who'd clipped him around the ear for being late to serve at mass."

"Jacques de Molay," continued Bernard Weigner, "had no family who could look after him, therefore it was the family of Geoffrey de Charney, Temple Preceptor and de Molay's second in command who was also under interrogation, who took him in."

"The shroud was carefully removed so that de Molay could have his horrific wounds tended. Over many weeks Geoffrey's family nursed Molay back towards reasonable health. As for the shroud, it was simply washed and put away with other linens. Eventually in a state of semi-fitness, Jacques de Molay wrote a letter making a full confession; this letter was copied and sent to other Knights Templar begging them to do likewise."

"Jacques de Molay knew that the recordings handed down were accurate and he described them as such to the English

Templar, John de Stoke, saying that Jesus was a messiah of the Jews but was not a god and that there was only one god, the god who created heaven and earth. He admitted in his confession that he did not believe in the cross as a symbol and that he denied Jesus Christ as a god. He also denied the charges of being homosexual."

"On the first of October 1311, Pope Clement summoned a meeting of his bishops. Over one hundred attended from most parts of Europe but only a handful were from France. The purpose of the meeting was to discuss the fate of the Templars, but bishops from countries outside France refused to condemn the Templars as guilty."

"A long time elapsed then eventually King Philip visited Pope Clement. Following this meeting in March 1313, the Order of Knights Templar was dissolved. The Pope allowed King Philip to charge for all the enquiries and costs relating to the abolition of the Knights Templar, these costs took the entire assets from the Order in France."

"King Philip 'the good' therefore obtained the substantial wealth of the Templars without fair trial. Five hundred and thirty six Knights agreed to come forward following the promise made by Philip that no harm would come to them. The King was not true to his word as each Knight was arrested and prosecuted. They were subjected to torture and burned at the stake. The King ordered them to be burned in lots of fifty at a time, one such burning was under the direct control of Philip Marigni the archbishop of Sens. Despite their inhuman treatment not one Knight admitted any guilt of the charges made."

"Jacques de Molay languished in prison along with Hugh de Peyraud, Geoffrey de Charney and Guy de Auvergne at the command of Pope Clement who set up a papal commission under his chosen cardinals, that their guilt should be taken for granted when the sentences were to be given."

"King Philip wanted as much publicity as possible to demonstrate how senior Templars were dealt with as an example to the public at large, and on the 18th March 1314, in front of a huge crowd of people, three papal commissioners along with the Archbishop of Sens sat on a specially erected platform built in the square."

"Each senior Templar in turn was led out of their cell onto the platform and the crowd stood in silence as the alleged confessions were read out by the Archbishop. He went on to pass sentence of life in prison when Jacques de Molay shouted out, informing the Archbishop that he wished to confess his sins himself right there in front of the crowd. He was granted his wish. Gentlemen, I have here the exact words Jacques de Molay used to address the crowd on that fateful day."

The professor reached into the inside pocket of his linen jacket and removed a folded piece of paper. He carefully opened it and commenced reading:

> *It is just in so terrible a day, and in the last moments of my life. I should discover all the iniquity of falsehood, and make the truth triumph.*
>
> *I declare in the face of heaven and earth and acknowledge, though to my eternal shame, that I have committed the greatest of crimes but...*
>
> *It has been in the acknowledging of those who have been so foully charged on the Order. I attest and truth obliges me to attest that it is innocent!*
>
> *I made the contrary declaration only to suspend the excessive pains of torture, and to mollify those who made me endure them.*
>
> *I know the punishments which have been inflicted upon all the Knights who had the courage to revoke a similar confession; but the dreadful spectacle which is presented to me is not able to make me confirm one lie by another. The life offered me on such infamous terms I abandon without regret.*

"De Molay did not decree that the Order of Knights Templar were innocent of the charges although he knew they were! Nor did he express his love for Jesus Christ as saviour. The Grand Master of Rex Deus referred to God on many occasions, but not Christ as God!"

"Following de Molay's speech the commissioners brought an end to the proceedings so that they could report the content to King Philip. The King flew into a rage and without seeking papal approval commanded that Jacques de Molay and Geoffrey de Charney be burned the very next day."

"The deed was carried out on a tiny island called Ile des Javiaux on the Seine. The two Knights were subjected to being slowly burned upon a hot smokeless fire. The heat of the fire was gradually increased; first the feet were subjected to burning followed by the lower legs, then gradually up the thighs and finally to the genitals. This barbaric cruelty exacerbated their suffering to the extreme."

"de Molay cursed the Pope and the King and demanded they be called up in front of 'God' in less than a year to answer for their sins. After many painful hours de Molay finaly died. The many spectators openly wept at the bravery these two Knights had shown. Later that night de Molay's and Charney's ashes were secretly removed for preservation.The chronicle in Paris recorded that de Molay's final words were: *'Let evil swiftly befall those who have wrongly condemned us. God will avenge our deaths.'*

"Geoffrey de Charney was reported as saying. *'I shall follow the way of my master, as a martyr you have killed him. This you have done and know not. God willing, on this day, I shall die in the Order like him.'*

"Within three months King Philip IV and Pope Clement were both dead. The King fell from his horse whilst out hunting and was killed instantly. The Pope died of a fever brought about by a poison planted in the communion wine by one of his priests. His death was recorded as from the bowel cancer, which had first struck him some two years earlier."

"Superstition was rife during the fourteenth century. People marvelled at the accuracy of Jacques de Molay's proclamation. Whilst the Pope lay in state a terrible thunderstorm evolved, a bolt of lightening struck the building, turning it into a flaming inferno. The body of Clement was completely reduced to ashes. France was convinced that God had given his verdict over the guilty."

"The death of the Grand Master's persecutors convinced the people of France that the spirit of de Molay lived and that it had the power to bring the wrath of God down upon them! This fear lasted for centuries even to the times of the French Revolution."

"At the beheading of Louis XV a witness came forward and pushed his hand into the dead King's blood then shook it down onto the crowd. He is reported to have shouted, 'Jacques de Molay, thou art avenged!'

"With Jacques de Molay, died the most prolific Order of crusaders. Dead men of fame become heroes, stories of great deeds were written: Knights involved in great battles, saving damsels from distress; romantic tales of chivalry such as those of King Arthur and his round table. Many were true, by the way, but subject to additions and the imagination of an author's pen! In Fact King Arthur was a Crusading Knights

Templar. His true lifestory was simply romanticised by storytellers!"

"As far as Jacques de Molay was concerned, for forty or so years after his death, the legend was embellished to portray him as the figurehead of a seriously threatening cult. Talk, and even expectation, of a second coming was everywhere. It was the people's belief that this second coming would be heralded by disaster and sickness; talk of the plague was of the commencement of the apocalypse before the Messiah."

"The curse that brought Jacques de Molay's two accusers to their death, proclaimed him a great man. His remains, secretly gathered up following his death, became almost holy artefacts."

"Then it commenced. Europe became gripped by a number of disasters. Exactly 35 years following de Molay's death, Rome was subjected to a massive flood. This was followed by a revolution and just two years later an earthquake damaged the great basilicas, but that was a mere sample of what was to come. A form of bubonic plague called the Black Death, caused by a bacterium passed on to humans by infected rats, flees and flies, was transmitted from one person to another through coughing and sneezing. This dreadful epidemic began in the Gobi desert around 1320. It then soon spread to the Far East. China was struck, with the Black Death killing almost a third of the entire population. About forty million people were wiped out. It then travelled to the Middle East, India and into Europe. By around 1340 the Black Death had destroyed a major proportion of the entire Muslim world."

"A group of fighting nomads called the Kipchaks who were laying siege to a Genoese trading station in Crimea, catapulted corpses infected with the Black Death into the station. This took the disease to Sicily via a ship that contained infected rats."

"The Black Death swept through Sicily, across Italy, Spain, North Africa and France. Around 1350 it consumed Germany, Holland, Belgium, Austria, Switzerland, Sweden, Norway, Denmark and Great Britain. It literally killed the major part of every population. Norsemen took the disease to Greenland and Iceland. Even America did not escape. European traders, long before Christopher Columbus, carried the disease which killed the entire population of what are now the Southern States. The race who were originally evolved from the Apache nations, better known as the Aztecs, were completely destroyed."

The Knights of Black Chapter

"Almost thirty million people in Europe alone had died during the first epidemic. It returned again and again, in fact from 1361 until 1400 it returned five times. The Black Death accounted for a total loss of life on a scale never experienced before or indeed since. Life had been completely transformed by this disease. Christianity was looked upon in a completely different way as it was blamed directly for the Black Death."

"Strange forms of religious practices began to evolve from this apocalyptic event. People became subservient to the anger of God. They entered into strange rituals including beating and whipping themselves. The Jews were blamed and many thousands of them were killed, both in Brussels and Strasbourg. Vast numbers of monks and priests were also put to death in the people's retaliation against the church."

"Jacques de Molay was seen as the second messiah especially by those who knew he had been crucified. They saw this as a very close similarity to Jesus Christ's crucifixion and the aftermath in the decimation experienced across the Holy Lands, where people were completely annihilated."

"600 years after the destruction of the Temple in Jerusalem," continued the professor, now looking quite tired, "the story of a new prophet evolved and was establishing itself across the entire Middle East. Jerusalem then became titled as the Holy City. Mohammed had risen to heaven over the rock that Abraham used in preparation to sacrifice his son, Isaac. The stone was described as the Holy of Holys and formed the innermost sanctum of the Temple of Jerusalem. In 691AD the Muslims created a building called the Dome of the Rock. This building was erected exactly where the Jewish Temple previously stood."

"In 1071 the Turks took Jerusalem. About thirty years later it was declared that these Turks were evil and worshiped the Devil."

"A Christian army of Crusaders was assembled; they marched on Jerusalem, capturing it from the Turks. The Crusaders massacred every man, women and child of the Jewish and Muslim populations, all in the name of God. Pope Urban II instigated this crusade. The clergy were called to arms on the 27th November 1095. A proclamation decreed that Christian knights must form an army to secure the Holy Land as a Christian kingdom."

"Great Lords were offered substantial riches in exchange for their participation. The amassing together of Christians was prolific as word spread. Then the vast journey began from different directions across the length and breadth of Europe all bound for one principle collecting point that would ultimately bring together a mighty Christian army."

"The Byzantine capital called Constantinople was the chosen venue. It took a year to assemble a significant fighting force; the taking of Jerusalem was their ultimate objective. By May 1099 they had reached the northern boundaries of Palestine and by the 7th of June they were camping outside the walls of the holy city of Jerusalem. Baldwin eventually became the first Christian King to rule Jerusalem."

"Nine knights were appointed and took vows of obedience and chastity - these were again referred to as Knights Templar. Records show that these nine were Andre de Montbard, Geoffroy Bisol, Achambaud de St-Amand, Hugues de Payen, Gondemare, Godefroy, Geoffrey de St Omer, Payen de Montdidier and Rosal."

"There is no evidence to show if any of these nine were actually among the originators of either Incanda or The Knights of Black Chapter from Rex Deus, but the co-incidence is uncanny. The leader of the Templars was Hugues de Payen from Champagne. He had a very close association with his brother in law Baron Henri St Clair of Roslin in Scotland."

"Strangely, the moment Jerusalem was taken, two key figures met their untimely end: Pope Urban II and a warrior chief called Godfrey de Bouillon. Both had served their purpose and then were murdered. This was the first sign that Incanda was in existence and very active."

Philip Martins picked up his glass of orange before speaking. "Professor, are you saying that this Incanda is some kind of breakaway group from the earlier organisation you describe as Rex Deus, and that they are the baddies and the Knights of Black Chapter are the goodies?" A smirk blossomed across Philip Martins' face.

Bernard Weigner smiled and shook his head slightly. "Power and riches can do strange things. Some become extravert and flamboyant, almost wallowing in their position, whilst others become introvert and reclusive. One group found a vast fortune the other found the secrets of Enoch. Both groups who exist to this day are equally as powerful now as they were then. So when did Incanda and The Black Chapter actually evolve from the brotherhood of Rex Deus? No one actually knows. However we do know that following the death of Jacques de Molay both movements became far more intense.

The Knights of Black Chapter

"The actual nine families of both Incanda and the Knights of Black Chapter are not known to each other - Incanda has been a thorn in the Black Chapter's side for centuries and *vice versa*. I suppose between them they form the pinnacle of the centreground that balances the world, but to answer your question by name-dropping, we know that both Oliver Cromwell and Adolph Hitler were disciples of Incanda, probably at the rank of Cardinals, but who knows if they were actually a direct part of the blood line?"

"Adolph Hitler was aware that the Jews were still a race of people and not just a religion. Judaism only became a religion when they sought to re-invent themselves. Incanda has always feared they would rise again as a nation and amass power, possibly under the leadership of the Knights of Black Chapter. You must ask yourself why the USA supports Israel so stubbornly."

"Incanda are comfortable with religious uprisings, one movement against another. In fact it actively encourages such goings on. Incanda is the ultimate power over all religions. It also infiltrates movements such as the Mafia, the IRA, the Red Brigade and Al Val Sinda."

"Mohammed Abu Atif, although an important figure and a thorn in the side of the western world, could be but a fringe player in the big picture that is Incanda. I suppose Incanda induce these irritating problems so that a balance can be created; these various figures are merely pawns in the big game! Hitler, for example, attempted to make history repeat itself, as at the commencement of the Church of Rome and the dark ages that followed. Did good triumph over evil? Who knows?"

"Gentlemen, you are principal players in a major event in which today's history is to be written... its ultimate outcome will be in your hands. These lands they call the Middle East still remain the nucleus and balancing point over all life, as we know it, make no mistake. The festering wounds of history will continue to weep until the human race has ultimately been destroyed."

The professor turned his tired eyes towards O'Dowd who took the glance as his cue to intervene. "Thank you professor, we have all learned a lot today, of that I'm sure!" O'Dowd's voice was unusually soft as he spoke; he was clearly moved by the words he'd heard. He glanced around the table as the Professor stood with the aid of his stick and the strong-arm of the CIA officer for assistance."

Parker sat in silent reflection. JoJo seemed distant with a strange half-smile across his face. Jeremy Paxton-Smyth tapped his lower lip with the index finger of his right hand. He felt so many questions of history had been logically answered that afternoon. As for Philip Martins he simply remained silent, staring at his empty glass on the table in front of him.

"Gentlemen to reach into the heart of Incanda will be exceptionally difficult. You must also attempt to get into the inner sanctum of The Black Chapter. You might well discover its Knights are both very powerful and very famous. But be warned, if you are successful in these endeavours you will be exposing knowledge of quite frightening proportions, the results of which I would not like to even contemplate."

Now standing, Professor Bernard Weigner looked across at O'Dowd after finishing his epilogue. Bud O'Dowd struggled to stand. He moved forward and took the Professor's hand. "Thank you," were the only words he thought relevant to use as the Professor took his leave.

"Well people, what the fuck did you make of all that?" said O'Dowd returning to his natural brashness as he looked out over the deck rail at the now darkening sky. The sun had sunk below the St James club leaving behind in its wake a multitude of bright red strands, almost like painted brush strokes across the twilight sky. "Red sky at night, shepherd's delight," he said.

"Red sky in the morning, shepherd's warning," replied Philip Martins.

O'Dowd directed his attention towards the Minister. "Then we'd best make haste. There's much to do and little time to do it in!"

The Knights of Black Chapter

At the end of a Freemason's life the family invariably call upon the Lodge to dispose of their loved one's regalia. This task is normally the responsibility of the Almoner of the Lodge; the Almoner also offers support to the Mason's spouse. Worshipful Brother Albert George Openshaw, Past Provincial Grand Sword Bearer, had spent over fifty years in Masonry and until his recent death had regularly attended his mother Lodge, the place of his initiation.

Brother Harry Blakemore, affectionately now known to his fellow brothers as 'H', received the phone call early on the Saturday morning following Albert's funeral. It had been one of those lousy weeks when nothing seemed to go right and he had travelled miles simply to stand for hours through four very boring auctions and without a sniff of a bargain to show for his efforts. Then, to crown it all, the private house full of good furniture and *bric-a-brac* that he'd been nurturing for weeks suddenly went to a competitor in Conwy.

Hunting for stock to replenish the antiques shop he shared with his partner Clarissa Llewellyn-Jones was a constant frustration and getting more difficult all the time. He blamed television and *The Antiques Road Show* in particular; he blamed all the thousands of little old ladies who sit behind stalls at fairs, fancying themselves as antique dealers, flogging off the family heirlooms.

At one time they would have just picked up the phone and got onto a 'real' dealer, getting a fair price and saving themselves lots of time and trouble instead of spending hours in draughty village halls drinking tea from stainless steel flasks and moaning to their next-door neighbours.

"Thank god it's Saturday," said Harry to himself. A cloudless, early morning sky promised a fine day. The fields across the lane from Harry's cottage were bathed in sparkling, bright sunshine and the heavy dew glistened like millions of tiny diamonds. Everything looked perfect for that round of golf he had promised himself for the past month.

It was hard getting Clarissa to agree, he mused, especially as it was the height of summer - the very time tourists from far flung continents, not to mention Birmingham caravanners and folk from the north, troop through Machynlleth High Street in every type of vehicle known to man.

"Hello H, Mrs Openshaw wants Albert's gear out of the house pronto. I said you'd pop around this morning on your way to the shop," said the Worshipful Master presumptuously.

"I'm not going to the shop this morning," responded Harry indignantly.

"Well, you agreed to be Almoner and as such it's down to you. I've got a tee-off time booked so I must dash. See you at Lodge on Thursday." The continual burr at the other end of Harry's phone indicated that the Worshipful Master had gone.

Despite Aberdovey not being a particularly large place, Harry had no idea where exactly Appletree cottage was located. However, after asking at the post office, he eventually found it tucked away off the coast road. Were it not for the rows of clotheslines draped like telephone wires along the full length of each front garden, the neat oasis of terraced cottages might just be described as picturesque. Harry found the narrow lane difficult to negotiate in his large van with the *Llewellyn-Jones & Blakemore, Dealers in fine Art and Antiques* sprawled across both sides.

The lane opposite the cottages seemed to disappear over a low stonewall, beyond which lay a sheer drop into the sea. The mere presence of an Antique dealer's van attempting a nine point turn provoked a flurry of curtain movement throughout Seaview Terrace. Albert's cottage noticeably differed from the rest with the addition of an enclosed glass porch with a prominent, varnished sign over the doorway bearing the name Appletree Cottage, elegantly scribed in italics. Just to emphasise the name, apples had been artistically painted around it.

Harry felt the presence of a number of eyes watching him as he opened the little gate. The neat garden either side of the pathway demonstrated the results of some careful spring sowing: flowers of many varieties were in abundance on the left side of the path, to the right were row upon row of vegetables. Beanpoles had been meticulously tied together with raffia to form a wigwam effect. Green shoots with small, scarlet flowers attached had already begun to weave themselves upwards promising a bumper crop of runner beans - beans poor Albert would now never enjoy.

Harry reflected deeply on returning life to the soil and, in turn, life springing eternal as he dodged the sudden flurry of a man's shirt pegged by its tails to a bright green, plastic line.

He pressed the doorbell, provoking a peel like the chimes of Westminster. A pale-faced man of about Harry's age opened the inner front door; he peered out through the rain-smeared glass, focusing with difficulty because of the bright morning's glare.

"Good morning! I'm from the Freemason's Lodge. I've been asked to collect Albert's regalia."

"You've wasted no time boyo, bloody stuff's still warm," replied the man with a strong Welsh accent that sounded hollow through the glass.

"Sorry mate, if it's not convenient, I'll call back one evening in the week," replied Harry, keen to make a quick dash to kickstart his well-earned day off.

"Hang on," came the reply, followed by several frantic attempts to yank open the porch door. Eventually it yielded to a mixture of anger and determination. "Bloody wood's swollen again," he said.

"One of your lot built this for me da', charged him a bloody fortune too, bloody Freemasons, supposed to be a charity... charity my arse."

"You never wanted to be a Lewis then?" replied Harry, with a slight defensive tone in his voice.

"Lewis? What's one of them?" asked the man whom Harry could now see more clearly.

"A Lewis is the name given to the son of a Mason who becomes a Mason himself!" advised Harry.

The man smiled and shook his head. "One nutcase in the family is enough, what with me da' spendin' all those years goin' off for weeks at a time without sayin' where. How he kept his job at the Council beats me! Never had a penny docked from his wages neither. And he still kept all his holiday entitlement. Two weeks at Llandudno with me mom, every year without fail."

"Albert who are you talking to?" shouted a female voice from within the cottage.

"Bloke here from da's lodge, he's come for the stuff."

"There's two boxes full under the stairs," came the reply.

"Hang on a mo'," said the man who Harry could now see had the pointed features of his father.

The Knights of Black Chapter

Young Albert disappeared back into the cottage, returning moments later with a large cardboard box, a long sword and scabbard protruding out of the top. "Here's the first one," he said, pushing it in Harry's direction.

Harry found the box surprisingly heavy as he walked back towards the van.

By the time he'd opened the back doors young Albert was right alongside him holding a second box of equal proportions. "Antique dealer then boyo? That'll give these nosy old buggers a few things to talk about."

Harry made no comment as he took the second box from young Albert and placed it in the van alongside the other.

"We have a letter from your father pledging his regalia to the Lodge's museum after his death. I can show you the letter if you like?" said Harry, diving into the back pocket of his trousers.

"Couldn't give a toss me self, it's all junk as far as I'm concerned," replied Albert junior.

Harry closed the van doors before turning to Albert. "Look, as I'm the Almoner of the Lodge, it's my job to see that a departed Mason's wife is looked after, so if I can be of any help at all, perhaps you'd let me know?"

Young Albert looked offended. "She don't need any bloody Masons coming round here, had enough of them buggers when the old man was alive."

Harry thought it best to simply nod in recognition of the message delivered and received loud and clear.

Harry Blakemore was a man with no history, or at least none that anyone in Wales knew about. Harry made it perfectly clear the past was the past and he intended it to remain that way. Respecting this, Clarissa never asked any questions - her own past was filled with incidents she preferred to forget, in particular the sexual assaults she had experienced as a child and the eventual rape by a so-called uncle.

Harry himself had watched personally as his real name and identity were sucked through a shredding machine and then incinerated at the Ministry of Defence. It had been a very weird experience being shuttled into the Westminster building in a bulletproof car with blacked-out windows, knowing that the life of 43939610 Sergeant Bob Richardson of 9 Squadron, 22nd Special Air Service was about to be terminated.

Sergeant Bob Richardson had survived working behind the scenes in Argentina during the Falklands conflict. And, after breaking into the spacious palace of Idi Amin, it had been him who actually stood at the tyrant's bedside, holding a knife at the evil man's throat and delivering the message that sent the violator of human life scurrying out of the public eye forever. It was also him who strategically placed a device that removed a terraced house from its foundations in a Dublin suburb, together with four top IRA occupants. And he was the first out of the Schnook helicopter during the Iranian Embassy siege. The man that his men call 'Rich' was about to disappear from the face of the earth after his identity had been splashed all over a terrorist hit list. In truth, it had not been a total surprise, especially as he'd been discovered laying explosives to remove the property containing Osama Bin Laden, two Iraqi Government officials and a number of Taliban representatives, near to a tiny village on the edge of the Khyber Pass near Kabul.

A neat line of items including a passport, birth certificate and driver's licence, all with the name Harry James Blakemore, lay on a table in a small, sparsely furnished room.

"Am I going to have plastic surgery?" asked the soldier.

"You must be joking Sergeant," replied a small, middle-aged woman endowed with a ridiculously large pair of breasts, prevented from erupting by a tightly buttoned jacket. An identification badge with her photograph and the name McDonald hung from a thin silver chain around her neck. "We're not going to all this trouble and expense to protect you, my friend, this is to protect us... so don't get carried away with any flash ideas that we're going to turn you into a Sean Connery look-alike."

"Well these photos look nothing like me," he said, glancing at the driver's licence.

"Have you ever know a passport photograph to look like its owner?" replied the woman, with a detectable Glaswegian accent. "You are now Harry James Blakemore and you were born at Crayford in Kent." She picked up a brown folder, opened it and then continued, "You are the only child of Harry and Rose Blakemore, both dead."

"How convenient. Why can't I choose my own name and place of birth? I rather like the name Clint."

The woman looked hard at the soldier. "Clint," she repeated with a smirk, and then continued, "You work for Ashford Ridley and Blakemore Estate agents, Surveyors and Auctioneers based in Torquay, Devon."

"Estate Agents, what do I know about estate agents?"

The Knights of Black Chapter

McDonald looked at him disapprovingly, she hated being interrupted. "Please let me finish. You work in the antiques section of the business. According to your file, antiques are a hobby of yours, you specialise in collecting Staffordshire figures. You also have a knowledge of country furniture."

"Very good, so I'm to become an antique dealer, I like the idea of that."

"We try to please."

"Am I married?"

"No, not any more although you have been, twice, I think." McDonald turned over a few pages in the file and continued, "Yes to someone called Avril and a lassie by the name of Donna. Avril now lives in Australia with her new husband whilst Donna broke her neck in a skiing accident. You had no children by either of these ladies. In fact you'll not be too surprised to learn you have no living family at all."

A 'don't care' smile had flashed briefly across the Scotswoman's face. "We need to keep you under wraps for quite a while until you grow into the new identity. You'll need to build a foundation, people that'll just know you as Harry Blakemore – it's called establishing identity. Once you have achieved this you can move if you want. You'll be monitored continually for at least three years. You are not permitted to leave the country and if you travel further than a fifty miles radius you'll need clearance.

"Right Mr Blakemore," she said, handing him a slip of paper from the file. "This is a number that puts you in direct touch with your 'contact'. Remember it and then destroy the paper. You will call the number every day at 7.00 pm for the first month, thereafter weekly until you are downgraded to level two. This file describes in detail the life of Harry Blakemore. Read it, digest it, then burn it."

The new Harry Blakemore took the manila file. "Was Harry Blakemore a real person or a figment of Whitehall's imagination?" he asked, opening the file containing his new life on a few flimsy pieces of paper.

"Read the file. Harry Blakemore was born on the 8th of June 1965. He died of complications caused by his premature birth just three days later," said McDonald as she escorted the new Harry Blakemore to a small office that contained little more than a steel desk and typist's chair. "You can use this office to study the file. If you want tea or coffee there's a machine around the corner, it accepts fifty pence coins. Although I don't recommend the tea, the coffee is passable. I'll be back to test you in an hour."

It appeared the name Blakemore had been added to the estate agent's name for barely a week. The staff had been notified of the new junior partner who would be working strictly on the antiques side of the business. A small apartment had been sourced for him in Ashburton. A bank account was opened in the name of Harry J Blakemore and five thousand pounds had been deposited. Even a bax transfer had been put into place to pay him a monthly salary. Direct debits for the rental of his flat and utilities had also been organised. A bright yellow MG Midget was assigned to him with the relative papers all produced in the name of Harry Blakemore.

"Well you blokes certainly go for detail, I'm impressed," said the new Harry Blakemore upon McDonald's return. "When do I leave for Devon?"

"As soon as you've got your new identity off pat," she said then proceeded to ask him questions from a sheet of paper. Most of the answers came back in quick response. "Good, then you'll be leaving this evening."

"What about my kit, things like clothes and personal effects for example?"

"All gone Mr Blakemore, along with the old you. Bob Richardson is officially dead."

"Just as a matter interest how did I die?"

"Does it matter?" asked Macdonald with a smirk. "Off with the old on with the new, you'll soon get used to it! Right, sign here." She placed an official looking form on the desk beside him. "See... the last page of the file has a rough outline of your new signature. Practice it. You can make a start by signing this form."

"Not till you tell me how I died."

The Scotswoman gave him a piercing stare. "You died when your parachute failed to open. You roman-candled into a ploughed field near Abingdon."

"Abingdon, I haven't been there since I did my first training jumps when I joined the Regiment," he replied.

"Well there you are. Now please sign this form and we can all get on with our lives."

The new Harry Blakemore checked the back of the file and then attempted to copy the signature.

"You can take that page with the signature with you. Make sure you practice signing it until it comes naturally." She finally handed him a thin brief case. "This contains all the paperwork, bank account, statements, lease on the flat etc. A lot of people have burnt the candle at both ends to re-invent you, don't fuck it up."

Harry Blakemore stood and followed McDonald out of the office.

"This way," she said, walking at pace towards a brown, panelled door which opened automatically upon their arrival. Harry found himself in a dimly lit garage amongst a pool of cars.

"This guy will show you to your car," said McDonald pointing to a thin wisp of a man in a pair of brown overalls. His complexion suggested he'd spent most of his adult life working in the semi darkness of this MI6 underground car park.

"What about some clothes?" asked Harry suddenly feeling a chill. "There's a few basic requirements in the back of your car, more will be found in your apartment, all courtesy of Marks and Sparks. This is the last time you'll see me but I'm sure you'll not be too stressed about that?"

"Oh, I don't know, I bet you have some endearing qualities, finding them might be a challenge though."

The Scotswoman gave Harry a half smile then disappeared as the door automatically closed behind her.

"Well you must be 'Q'," said Harry to the ghost of a man. "Has my car got all the latest gismos... oil slick from the rear lights, machine-gun under the bumper, and those swivelling number plates... I've always wanted swivelling number plates?" said Harry, relating to the James Bond character.

The expression on the thin man's face didn't change. "It's got an engine and it goes, that's all I know!" he said as he dropped a set of keys into Harry's hand.

A plain envelope lay on the passenger seat at Harry's side; it contained fifty pounds in cash and a note that simply instructed him to drive to the Exeter services on the M5 and wait in the car park. He checked his new watch; it was just past six o'clock. He estimated that the journey would take him about three hours. He was wrong, there were roadworks on the M4 near Reading and an articulated lorry had spilled its load of empty plastic bottles on the M5 close to Taunton. He therefore pulled into the services just as the clock on the dashboard was approaching ten. After seeking out the toilets and then buying a hamburger and coffee, Harry returned to his car to await instructions.

The Knights of Black Chapter

It had been a long day. He'd travelled from Hereford to London in the back of a plain, unmarked van before being transferred to the official car that took him to Whitehall where he spent half the day in the de-briefing session, and now he'd finally driven to Devon.

Harry had climbed from the car and strolled over towards a waste bin to throw the remains of his plastic-tasting food and polystyrene containers away, and as he did so he scoured the now almost empty car park for anyone who might remotely look like a contact. Returning to his car he switched on the radio, closed his eyes and promptly dropped off into a light slumber. His snooze was abruptly interrupted by the passenger door being opened. The flurry of a cotton dress and the flash of naked thigh startled him. The stale smell of Hamburgers and coffee was soon replaced by the sweet scent of Chanel.

"Hello Harry, sorry for the delay, have you been waiting long?" asked someone whose face was obscured by a huge, floppy-brimmed sun hat, ridiculous for the time of day.

Harry concluded that the legs were the best part as he glanced at the gaping front of her cotton dress which revealed a brown flat chest and ribs he could play a tune on! She turned the brim of her hat back to expose the pretty face of a young woman in her early twenties.

"Sorry," she said again, holding out a long, thin hand, which Harry accepted. "I'm Annie, I've been assigned to look after you."

Harry smiled. "There is a God then!" he said, still holding her hand.

"That's my Mini over there," she said releasing her hand to point at the blue car with the white roof parked a few spaces away. "Would you like to follow me?"

"That's the best offer I've had all day," replied the invigorated ex-sergeant.

Without saying another word Annie bolted from the MG just as quickly as she arrived. She strode purposefully towards her car, wobbling a little on high, cork heels with Roman-style lacing running up her legs. Just then, an unexpected breeze caught her sunhat and flimsy dress both at the same time. Annie giggled and made a grab for the hat as her skirt was lifted high above her waist exposing two long disorientated legs and a pair of white knickers, one side had slipped between the cleveage of her firm, round bottom. After a struggle she opened the car door and climbed in.

The Knights of Black Chapter

"Sorry," she shouted across to Harry with a little-girl giggle and smile.

"No need to apologise on my account," Harry said, enjoying the spectacle especially as he'd not enjoyed even a modicum of involvement with a member of the opposite sex for literally months.

The Mini suddenly burst into life, jolted forward a couple of paces then roared out of the car park at a speed that Harry, fumbling to start his car, had to follow in hot pursuit. Annie had screamed past two roundabouts and was now scorching up the slip road towards the southbound carriageway of the M5 motorway.

"If she screws as fast as she drives, I'm in!" said Harry with a smile, taking the first roundabout almost on two wheels in an attempt to catch up.

It had been close to midnight as the blue and white Mini, driven by the attractive lunatic, screeched to a halt outside the row of terraced houses, just past the High Street in Ashburton. The place Harry Blakemore was about to call home.

Ashford, Ridley and Blakemore had their own car park at the rear of the large, converted double-fronted premises just on the edge of the fashionable seaside resort, close to the Babbacombe road. It took Harry no time at all to settle into this new lifestyle. Calling Annie on regular occasions was never a problem although strangely enough he never actually met her again after that first evening. Their conversations were always brief and strictly formal. And as for Annie, she never failed to find things to say 'Sorry' about.

Harry became quite friendly with the senior partners who had no idea who he really was of course, nor where he'd actually come from. All they knew was that there had been a response to their advertisement in the *Sunday Times Business Supplement* for a working investor. Solicitors had arranged everything, the hundred thousand pounds was deposited and a brief outline of Harry submitted. Their natural apprehension was soon overcome when they got to know Harry, especially with the enthusiasm he soon began to demonstrate and in particular the way he handled stroppy dealers who soon realised they were not going to get away with 'ringing' deals at the monthly auction.

Everything had settled down quite nicely and within just a few months Harry Blakemore had a diary crammed with both business and social events.

The Knights of Black Chapter

Everyone had told Harry Blakemore Gabby was going to be trouble, directly after he'd recruited her as the auction administrator. Harry on the other hand was besotted right from the moment Muriel the office manager had escorted her into his office for an interview. The mere sight of her figure-hugging grey suit, divulging every perfect curve, literally blew Harry's mind… but it was her rich mahogany hair that swept him away into a sea of ecstasy, especially the way its thick, shoulder-length waves framed her beautiful, dark porcelain face, from which two large pools of mystery sparkled at him. The look of disapproval across Muriel's lived-in matronly face went completely un-noticed.

Within two weeks they were dating. In less than ten, confetti was being thrown at Torquay's registry office. No more than six months later, Harry was at the solicitor's office explaining how he'd left the house purchased for the woman he now described as the 'she cat from hell', who'd been caught providing bodily services to three male neighbours in one frantic orgy, all ensconced in Harry's brand new kingsize bed.

She could have the lot as far as he was concerned: the house, its contents, the car, even their joint bank account where most of his money was now deposited. He instructed his solicitor to handle negotiations for sale of his interests in the business. And with a small bag of clothes, his toiletries, the private building society book containing little more than eight thousand pounds and his wallet bulging with fifty-pound notes, Harry was off, just like he'd arrived, 'out of the blue'.

The Knights of Black Chapter

5

Torquay railway station at six o'clock on a cold damp Wednesday evening provided little choice of places to go. Harry decided not to pick, he wanted fate to determine his destination.

"Where's the next train going?" he enquired at the ticket office.

"London," replied a bored looking Asian lady whose crossword he'd interrupted.

"London! I'm not going back there… where's the first stop?" asked Harry, now determining that he couldn't exactly leave everything to fate without a little tinkering.

The lady glanced up at him. "You can get off at Exeter. Do you want a single or return?"

"Give me a single, please." A feeling of immeasurable guilt came over him as he handed the lady a crisp fifty-pound note, which she half-heartedly held to the light.

"It is real, I've just printed it," he said, trying to lighten the way he felt. Two large dark eyes flashed at him disapprovingly. She then glanced briefly at her fingers. "So long as the ink doesn't come off, I really don't care," she said, pushing the ticket and his change under the glass barrier towards him.

Harry ended up in South Wales because he got on the wrong train at Exeter. His intention was to take the Cornishman heading north and get off wherever the mood took him, somewhere between Exeter and the train's Scottish destination. But he allowed fate to take complete charge and after spending a restless night in a three star hotel close to the Millennium Stadium in Cardiff, Harry hired a car and simply drove north through the picturesque spine of the country. His natural liking of coastlines instinctively encouraged him to turn east; Machynlleth was the first town he eventually arrived at, hoping he could get a decent meal and a bed for the night.

The mid Wales town was literally buzzing. It was decked out with bunting tied to any immoveable object. Large banners stretching across every approach road advertised the Machynlleth 'Giant' Antique Fair and - according to the date - the event was due to commence the very next day.

The Knights of Black Chapter

"If you're plannin' to leave first thing in the morning, you'd be best to park on the edge of town, we'll be pedestrianised come daybreak," said the friendly policeman Harry had stopped to ask about a good place to stay. "*White Lion*'s as good as anywhere. Tell Mick I sent yeh'."

"Thanks, I will," replied Harry. The Policeman smiled, nodded and was gone before Harry could ask him his name. He had followed the policeman's recommendation and drove through the town passing the *White Lion* on his left. He eventually found a quiet side road and parked. The conversation he then had on his mobile with Annie was a little difficult to say the least. Her telephone voice sounded nothing like the image Harry remembered from their one and only meeting. She had given him a hard time on more than one occasion but nothing like this encounter; she had a real cutting edge to her voice, and this particular evening Harry was getting the full force of her trained tongue stinging his ear.

"I'm taking a short break," he said, trying to quell her fury.

"Short break! You've separated from your wife, given her the house and furnishings, most of your money and instructed a solicitor to sell your share of the business! ... Not the actions of someone taking a fortnight's holiday, Harry. You know the rules... you need clearance for any big move."

"You're right Annie, as always," said Harry, attempting to bring a little calm to the conversation, "I had an emotional moment."

"Well you must call me twice a week so that I can report your movements back to HQ. Let's call this a holiday and leave it at that for a while. No doubt you'll stop running one day?"

"I'm not running," Harry replied, almost beginning to wish he'd thought matters through and not been so hasty. He had given up such a lot. He'd enjoyed his time in Torbay, and now he was sitting in a hired car in the suburb of a town he'd never been to before. Harry was full of remorse for all of three minutes, whilst Annie was babbling on about security requirements and her job being on the line if he didn't comply. Harry shrugged his shoulders. "I'm moving on Annie, speak to you in two days time."

"You'd better. Where exactly are you now?"

Harry smiled. "Have you ever heard of a place called Machynlleth?"

There was a short pause. "Where?" exclaimed Annie.

"Machynlleth," replied Harry, "How well do you know Wales?"

"Where?" repeated Annie.

"Look, I'll call you in two days."

The landlord at the *White Lion* in the high street served a really fine Welsh 'T' bone steak topped with a mound of fried onions all cooked just the way Harry liked it. The fat, jolly Welshman described the fair as the major event in the town's calendar: antique dealers and collectors would flock in from miles around. Harry sat at the end of the bar feeling comfortable, in fact he felt good and, for the first time since leaving Torbay, at peace. He'd certainly eaten in more salubrious places than the *White Lion* with its strong smell of stale beer and tobacco smoke, but despite these things Harry had a feeling that this part of the country was a friendly place where he could simply drift for a while... and besides, Mick the Landlord kept a fine pint of bitter and, with his room directly over the bar, Harry could sup' to his hearts content.

After his breakfast, which the menu described as the Machynlleth 'belly buster', Harry had decided to continue letting fate take the lead hand. He therefore decided to stay for the fair. He'd learned a lot about antiques over the past two years and was determined to put this newly acquired knowledge to good use. Early oak, pine, clocks and porcelain had become his speciality. In fact he'd often heard dealers from Torbay remark favourably on their Welsh excursions, he could be in for a profitable treat. He also concluded that Wales must be bulging with country antiques and after all he was heading for nowhere in particular. The more he thought about it the more convinced he felt that leaving things to fate might be a really good move after all.

That chubby policeman the night before had been spot on when he'd said the place would become pedestrianized. Every pavement and road had been turned into a bustling market; stalls of different sizes and shapes had sprung up everywhere. Whilst Harry slept a complete makeover had taken place in the centre of town. Then, just as dawn approached, the stall holders invaded, emptying vehicles of their precious cargoes, so that by 9 o'clock the final touches were being made in preparation for what everyone hoped would be a bumper selling event.

Clarissa Llewellyn-Jones's stand was a bit different from most of her contemporaries', not the merest hint of Royal Worcester, Wedgwood or even the odd piece of Clarice Cliff was displayed. Also conspicuous by their absence were the overpriced trinkets normally on show at such events where, in the words of the trade, 'wannabe dealers', elderly middle class ladies, hiked up prices through pure ignorance or sold far too cheaply, much to the annoyance of their 'professional' counterparts.

Clarissa's stand had displayed some seriously strange stuff. Her business cards that were scattered across the green baize tablecloth mentioned 'Artefacts' and 'Objects d'art', but it was the small 'treen' box that had caused Harry to linger at her stand longer than most. He was particularly intrigued by the way craftsmen of the 19th century worked with scraps of different types of wood veneer to produce elaborate things of beauty. This particular example was a cigarette box; the craftsman had intricately depicted a pair of black and white Scottish terriers, crafted with meticulous detail on the lid.

Harry's natural love for a deal had provoked him to make Clarissa an offer after he had examined the piece for any signs of damage. He then finally looked at the price on the ticket.

"Will you take a hundred pounds?" he asked, calmly rubbing his index finger over the surface of the lid in search of any signs of loose veneer.

Clarissa took the box and looked at the price she had written on the ticket. "I've marked it at one hundred and forty, it's a fine example of 19th century treen, the best trade I can do is one thirty," she said, handing the piece back to Harry.

"Make it one, two five and you've got a deal," he replied.

Clarissa smiled. "Tell you what, see that cafe over there? Fetch me a coffee and a bacon sandwich and it's yours for one, two five."

Harry looked in the direction she had pointed to and smiled. "You've got a deal," he said, smiling he shook her hand.

"Strong, white, no sugar, thanks," Clarissa replied, having completed her first deal of the day.

Most of Clarissa's friends thought she was completely mad but selling the treen box had started a successful partnership that was now in its fourth year. Clarissa's specific interests in specialist antiquities and Harry's preference for a more generalist approach proved a successful combination. Besides, the double-fronted shop in the High Street was far too big for Clarissa to keep well stocked alone. It therefore made perfect sense, especially when trying to entice dealers to make a special journey by providing a much wider selection of things to buy during their regular pilgrimages to Wales. Machynlleth soon became a place worth visiting on scouting expeditions.

Except for the odd joke in the bar over a pint, long after closing time, the subject of more intimate relationships and sex in particular was never mentioned. The thought of a relationship beyond the platonic had never been attractive to Clarissa. The childhood experiences she had repeatedly encountered had left her closed to physical contact with either male or female, beyond a peck on the cheek at birthdays, weddings and christenings. It was the girl in the school dormitory that had consolidated Clarissa's celibate lifestyle. She had been tucked up in her school dormitory one night when a girl she barely knew slid under her bedclothes with the red-blooded intention of entering into a full sexual liaison. The experience of being groped between the legs by another girl still sent shivers of shame down Clarissa's spine and would do so till her dying day.

Now in her late forties, Clarissa seemed to have developed a body-change, with her portly figure and her Harris tweed and brogues, more befitting a country gentleman than a lady antique dealer. There was however, a certain charm in the way her naturally thick, wavy, red hair grew around her face out of which, if ever a beautician had been allowed to work on the blank canvas with a little blusher and eyeliner, an attractive female might just have emerged. However the mere sight of Clarissa never induced anyone to think of her as a sexual object, which suited her just fine.

After winning a place at Oxford where she had read Ancient History, Clarissa journeyed across the western Mediterranean, through Egypt and into the Middle East, eventually returning to Crete where she worked as an English speaking guide at the Archaeological Museum of Heraklion. This provided her with the opportunity to study the fascinating Minoan civilisation and, with Knossos on the doorstep, she felt that in some strange way she was following in the footsteps of the Welshman Sir Arthur Evans who had dedicated most of his life to the excavation and reconstruction of this 6,000 BC city.

A fellow antique dealer, Bill Williams from Bala, proposed Harry into Freemasonry and he was eventually invited to become an Entered Apprentice of the Machynlleth Lodge. Harry was the only one initiated that year and therefore soon progressed to the degree of Fellow Craft and finally became a Master Mason within eighteen months.

The Knights of Black Chapter

He had taken the Almoner's job as he felt the position might present him with a few opportunities of commercial benefit, especially as Masons in the area were generally farmers and very old farmers at that! The possibilities of rich pickings could be endless, on their demise - and indeed their widows might well find themselves a little tight for cash. A bundle of notes in exchange for a few dusty heirlooms would do everyone a favour!

Despite his involvement with running the now successful antiques business, Harry was still able to meet Bill for the odd round of golf, albeit that he mostly restricted himself by playing the back nine only. Bill Williams was given the nickname 'Rollie' by the brethren of the Lodge on account of the way the sixty-six- year-old rolled taper thin cigarettes with liquorice paper. His antique shop had been in the main street of Bala for over three generations. It was where he lived in an on-off relationship with 'Mags', his exceedingly longtime partner whom he preferred to describe simply as a bedmate, for fear that the word *partner* might tarnish his reputation as a Welsh oak and pine dealer and brand him with the same image as Mags - whose preference leaned towards ladies' Victorian clothing and costume jewellery. Mags, short for Margaret Smyth-Greenway, was a former Rodean girl and possessed a very large plum in her mouth to prove it!

No one ever really got to the bottom of how they met or exactly when, but according to Bill their fiery relationship was now well past its silver jubilee! She could therefore claim half of everything Bill possessed and as her brother Giles was a London lawyer of some note, Bill was not going to provoke a challenge.

Their relationship however had almost come to an abrupt end a couple of years before Harry came on the scene, after a huge bust up over a house clearance. Mags had packed a light bag and walked out, but cleverly left most of her clothes and her precious stock in place to indicate a positive return at some stage, convincing Bill there was nothing permanent about the disappearance.

He had however taken the opportunity to do some emergency alterations and had called Di Jones into help. Di Jones was a fellow Freemason who owned the largest building firm in Bala. Less than four days later, Mags had stepped from her taxi to discover a breezeblock wall, with the mortar barely dry, had been constructed right through the centre of the double fronted shop, cutting the whole place completely in half. It continued on up the stairs and through their flat, stopping just short of the bathroom where a sign on the door now proclaimed, 'Joint & Several'. As there was only the one bathroom it would remain neutral ground.

The wall stayed for precisely six months. The bathroom gradually became a no-man's land en route to their respective bedrooms, and especially Mags' boudoir where cunning rather than desire permitted Bill entry. The 'Bala Wall', as it soon became known throughout central Wales, was the talk the trade, provoking dealers and tourists to journey for miles to see the spectacle for themselves, long after the wall had been removed.

The Knights of Black Chapter

"I'm leaving these boxes behind the counter," said Harry after removing Albert Openshaw's regalia from the Van.

"Can I have a look?" asked Clarissa, dropping down upon one knee in front of the large glass counter.

"Suit yourself," replied Harry, "I'm off to knock seven bails of shit out of a little white ball."

The day, like the rest of the week, was prone to failure. The now late morning began to cloud over and by the time Harry and Bill were on the tenth, a long par five with the green miles away from the clubhouse, the heavens opened and soaked them both to the skin. It was therefore a very unhappy soul who appeared in the bar of the White Lion to meet Clarissa for their Saturday night steak and onions. The steak supper had become a ritual that normally proceeded a long session into the early hours of Sunday morning. Unlike Harry, Clarissa was in a particularly good mood.

"You're looking pleased with yourself, have we had a good day? I hope so, I could do with being cheered up."

"No crap, this weather's kept everyone at home! I've had a bit of a find though!" said Clarissa in between sips of her whiskey and soda, "You know that stuff you left behind the counter?"

"Stuff? You mean Masonic regalia," responded Harry defensively.

"Yes, well I found this at the bottom of one of the boxes." She took a round looking stick of about fourteen inches in length and just a little thicker than a broomstick from her large canvas bag. Harry took one end whilst Clarissa held onto the other as if they were about to pull a cracker. Eventually Clarissa let go so that Harry could examine the strange artefact more closely.

"Looks like it's made of bamboo. I'd say it was really old, could be something tribal? On the other hand it could be ceremonial, like an army officer's swagger stick but much older. These symbols look interesting," continued Harry, pointing to a number of faint markings. "They look as if they represent symbols of the craft, although I'm not sure from which order."

Harry rubbed the cane through the palm of his hand; the effort highlighted two distinctive bindings towards both ends of the cane. "Hm. Interesting, could these be hemp bindings that have been painted over with some sort of red dye?"

Clarissa smiled. "Well you're right to say really old, in fact I'd say literally hundreds of years old."

"You're joking," said Harry.

"I'm not," replied Clarissa, "Sounds exciting, this is quite a find. We must take it to my old Professor for his opinion."

Harry looked a little doubtful. "Oh I don't know about that, it's destined for the provincial grand Museum."

"Fine, but wouldn't they rather know exactly what it was so that it can be catalogued properly?"

"Well I suppose so," replied Harry.

"I've got a good feeling about this, in fact I think we've got a very important piece of history here," said Clarissa. Taking the cane from Harry she shook it vigorously.

"What are you doing?" he asked.

"I think it's hollow, these hemp bindings could be holding two parts together, see this?" She pointed to a very faint line no thicker than a hair along its entire length.

"I reckon this cane was made in two halves to contain something. These hemp bindings were then used to lash the two parts together, it would then have been painted with some form of red dye. The symbols may have been put there as some kind of coded message."

"You mean something might be inside?"

Clarissa smiled. "I'd put money on it!"

Professor Franklin Thomas lived in a rambling old vicarage, accessible only from a long winding track amidst large open meadows where flocks of sheep grazed. The nearest town was Aberystwyth about ten miles away. Except for his housekeeper, Professor Thomas lived a typical bachelor's lifestyle, married to his reference library and the research he perpetually undertook, often with his students who were both under and post graduates.

The unruly hawthorn hedges that inter-twined with wild blackberries and bracken scratched noisily against the van as Harry and Clarissa drove up to the house. The gothic-looking property had been built as a rectory during the flamboyant Victorian era. Its stone gravel drive and forecourt appeared unkempt and in a serious need of weeding. The wisteria, that almost completely covered the front of the house, desperately required the expertise of a good gardener with a sharp pair of secateurs to bring its massive growth under control.

Clarissa opened the front door. With Harry in hot pursuit she walked into a large hallway with a mosaic floor and a broad, pitched pine staircase rising towards a huge picture window that drew in the afternoon's sunlight, the intricate stained glass evoking a multitude of coloured shafts of light to beam down into the hall. The musty smell and many antique relics indicated a man who had dedicated his life to the past and to Egyptology in particular.

"Come on he'll probably be in the garden room," said Clarissa, "I know this house well. I used to come here frequently as a student to use the Professor's vast collection of reference books. I actually helped him compose his articles for the National Geographic here. I really love this house, it's like a time warp of historical references," she said, stopping for a moment beside a large steel engraving. "This is mine," she said, pointing to the large, detailed study in the gilt frame. "I simply said to the Professor how much I loved its beauty and detail, and bless the lovely man he's bequeathed it to me in his will."

"I can see the quality, but who are the people pictured in it, it looks as if it's telling a story!" said Harry studying the remarkable subject in detail.

Clarissa smiled. "Oh but it is. This engraving was taken from a fresco by Botticelli painted in 1481. He painted it on the left wall of the Sistine chapel in the Monastery of Saint Catharine on Mount Sinai. It shows the meeting of Jethro's daughters. Jethro was the priest of Mid'ian, he had seven daughters." She pointed to the centre of the picture. "Here you can see them coming to draw water from the well, filling those troughs for their father's flock... *Exodus* 2: 16 by the way. Botticelli produced the work in this iconographic arrangement in order to tell the entire story. It shows one of the many wells that provided water to serve St Catharine's."

Clarissa then pointed to the figure at the top of the engraving, a man who was removing a stone from his shoe. "That's Moses stopping briefly on his journey down from the mount. The eldest of the seven daughters, Zipporah, seen here helping her father, eventually became the wife of Moses. I suppose you know as you are a Mason that Moses had an important connection with Freemasonry?"

Harry looked at Clarissa and smiled. "I bet you know far more about Masonry than I do!" he said.

The Knights of Black Chapter

"She knows more than the average Mason and that's for sure," replied a rather deep, educated voice with the merest hint of a Welsh accent.

The silhouette of a tall, portly figure filled the doorway from a dark passage that led towards the light of the garden room. Clarissa kissed the red-cheeked man in a daughterly fashion. Harry estimated the Professor to be in his mid to late seventies, he wore a shabby dark blue cashmere jumper that had clearly shrunk and barely covered his ample proportions. The stains that it displayed down the front almost represented an impressionist's painting, its arms were short in length and sported two holes at each elbow. A blue and white bowtie protruded above the jumper's crew neck, but it was the striking gold ring on the little finger of the Professor's right hand that caught Harry's eye.

The Professor smiled. "You are looking at my signet ring, which you think bears little relation to me and the rest of my attire!"

Harry looked embarrassed. It was as if the Professor had read his mind.

"Don't be embarrassed, Mr Blakemore," he said holding out his large hand with its long fingernails so that Harry could examine the ring more closely. "You're not the first to observe this ring. It sticks out like a sore thumb I must admit." The ring was indeed stocky and looked as if it was made from 'rose gold'. The face of the ring bore an unusual motif. "I bet you are wondering about the engraving, as a Mason you've probably seen its like before."

"It looks like one of the columns, either Boaz or Jachin that formed the entrance to the temple of King Solomon," replied Harry.

The Professor escorted Clarissa and Harry into the garden room where Mrs Jones had laid out a table with tea and welsh cakes, an odd combination amongst the collection of giant exotic plants the professor had collected from his travels across many continents of the world. Three worse-for-wear green Lloyd Loom chairs were arranged around the table piled high with old newspapers and magazines.

"Please take a seat. Clarissa be a good girl and pour the tea," said the Professor as he stared again at his ring. "This ring is my most valuable possession, although many, including Clarissa, would disagree. I must confess however that I wear it as a pretender. I have no actual rights to even own it really. You see I found it in a shop selling artefacts in a village called

Makryteichos, on the outskirts of Heraklion just a few miles from Knossos in Crete. I was visiting this charming young lady at the time." He glanced at Clarissa affectionately. "The ring is of Rex Deus. Tell me Harry what do you know about Rex Deus? Does the name mean anything to you?"

Harry looked a little puzzled, having never actually heard of the name before. "Well I've got to be honest, I'm ignorant of so many things connected with Masonry as I've not been a Mason for long and it's not that easy to find stuff out. I find that Masons who have progressed beyond me are reluctant to tell me about the goings on in the craft," replied Harry, as if almost apologising for his ignorance as he accepted a china cup and saucer with a chipped rim.

"Well then let me explain. Rex Deus was a group of people who reputedly go back to the beginning of time although their first known existence evolved during the building of King Solomon's Temple. Archaeological evidence is very limited about King Solomon's Temple. It was supposedly built in Jerusalem almost three thousand years ago. Reputedly it was the first stone temple to be built in recognition of the storm god Yahweh, who later became the only true God. You are familiar with the use of the capital 'G' that hangs in the centre of your lodge. This symbol of God is widely recognised by millions of people throughout the world. Both the Masonic Testament and indeed the Old Testament describe Solomon as the King of Israel living in the tenth century before Christ. Solomon was the second born of his father David from his mother Bathsheba."

"In both Muslim and Jewish literature Solomon is described as the wisest of all ages, gifted with a power to control the spirits of the invisible world. He was also a great author and had many works attributed to him. In the Bible we learn that Solomon succeeded his father David despite the protests of his elder brother Adonijah. Solomon divided Israel into twelve provinces for expending taxes; this territory extended from the land of Philistines that bordered Egypt to the river Euphrates. He formed an alliance with Hiram King of Tyre who actually designed and built the Temple for Solomon. He also enslaved the Canaanites because they remained on his lands, refusing to leave. These associations caused significant discontent and led to a number of foreign religious cults forming in Jerusalem. Solomon was forced to levy taxes upon the people in order to pay Hiram's significant charges to cover the King's ambitious building plans, which included a huge palace and a harem together with a much smaller temple. Josephus recorded that Hiram paid over three tons of gold from his own resources in advance. The Masonic Testament reveals quite a lot more about Solomon and the Temple than in fact does the Bible."

"Hiram King of Tyre appointed Hiram Abif as chief architect of the Temple. You are no doubt aware that the rituals through the first three degrees in Masonry depict the assassination of Hiram Abif, the master who died to protect the secrets that, some say have been lost forever but clearly linked in some form of magical incantation. In their place these secrets were substituted, a watered down version was created which did not have the significant occult outcome of the originals."

"In the Masonic rituals it says that Solomon initially selected a place near Jerusalem to build the Temple but when the ground was cleared they found the ruins of an old temple, Solomon therefore assumed this must have been the remains of some unwanted God. As he had no intention of using a desecrated spot the location was changed to Mount Moriah. Solomon eventually realised that the site he'd rejected was in fact Enoch's Temple."

"Hiram King of Tyre, Solomon King of Israel and Hiram Abif were the three Grand masters. Personally I'm convinced they were of Rex Deus Lines. They concurred that if Israel diverted from the Laws of Moses and the Prophets, their enemies would rise up and ransack their cities and especially the sacred treasures that would be contained in the Sanctum Sanctorum or, to use its English translation, the Holy of Holies, could be stolen. To prevent this happening a secret underground passage was built directly from the private chambers of Solomon to a vault below the Sanctum Sanctorum. This secret vault was divided by nine different archways in front of nine crypts, the ninth crypt was used to hold all the sacred treasures and Holy vessels that would later be placed in the Sanctum Sanctorum. The chamber was also used by the three Grand Masters to hold secret meetings and where the ritual of the Degree of a Master Mason originated."

"What were these treasures?" asked Harry who by now was becoming really interested.

"Why, my dear friend, precious scrolls containing the secrets of the world's history and the Ark of the Covenant," said the Professor with a boyish smile. "As you know from your three degrees in Masonry, Hiram Abif was murdered from a severe blow to his head. Following the architect's death the two

Kings stopped meeting in the secret vault. Solomon appointed nine Knights to watch over the nine crypts and especially the precious Sanctum Sanctorum. It is believed these Knights were actually selected from other Rex Deus lines. They were the original Knights Templar who actually existed many hundreds of years before their more famous counterparts. They were considered as the guardians of King Solomon's Temple. Its Jerusalem headquarters were located on the summit of Mount Moriah. Decades later the Jerusalem Temple was built upon the same site."

"Make no mistake Rex Deus are by far the most powerful people the world has known. This ring is a ring of Rex Deus. There were but nine men of the Rex Deus direct line, this number did not change until after the death of Christ, who was of the Rex Deus line through his mother Mary. There was no public outcry when Jesus was killed, but the situation was different concerning his brother James who was by far the more popular with the masses, therefore when James was also killed the whole city of Jerusalem rose in revolt and took up arms which led to the commencement of a long and bitter war between the Jews and the Romans. It was at this point we believe that Rex Deus split into two parts."

"James had become a far more important figure than his half brother Jesus in the Jerusalem Church. After James' death and just before the complete destruction of the Jerusalem Temple, a few Nazarene Priests fled, initially to Greece, they began to spread out across Europe. Eventually a few of them returned briefly to the destroyed city to collect the remains of a person they referred to as their Saviour, these remains were taken back to Greece."

"In AD 600 the remains were again returned to Jerusalem and placed back under the ruins of the Temple, which they believed were the safest place to hide them. Under the Temple it is said were many chambers and upon their walls genealogies were scribed, recording the children of priests from the Temple, all tracing their lineage back to the two Messiahs David and Aaron who would one day arrive to establish the Kingdom of God on earth."

"In part, this is the story that a member of Rex Deus would pass onto a chosen offspring, to continue the lineage. I actually found the former owner of this ring who sold it to the shop where I bought it. His name was Paul Chaumont, an elderly

Frenchman who painted for a living - that is, between bouts of chronic depression and alcoholism."

"He told me that he was actually a member of Rex Deus but as he never had any offspring to follow after him, he was unable to continue his line. Paul Chaumont said he was contacted by the 'upper house' and was advised that he'd be summoned to appear but apparently that was years earlier and no one had ever made contact with him. He then told me that he'd moved to Crete after spending four years in a French prison, jailed for faking some painting or other that was to be used for a stage play. Apparently someone had attempted to sell it as an original after the play ended and unfortunately the Frenchman's name and address was plastered across the back of the canvas."

"After our meeting in his tiny, two-roomed studio I periodically called upon him until his death. It was strange, I remember calling one evening, he was always more talkative in the evening. His personal possessions had been cleared from his rooms; no one seemed to know what had happened to him or indeed his body, which had simply disappeared. I was intrigued by these strange happenings and began to do some investigating."

"I discovered to my surprise that Paul had a cousin who lived in Dorset. I have an aunt living down there so I decided to call upon her and make it my business to do some detective work at the same time. I was forever intrigued by the motif on this ring, apart from it being Masonic. I felt there must be something far deeper in its meaning, and possibly historically sinister. I was sure the answer could be found somewhere."

"This cousin was as different to Paul as chalk is to cheese. His name was Humphrey Morgan Sinclair; before he retired he'd been the senior partner in a firm of accountants in Blandford Forum. He was a man in his late seventies when I met him and a credit to his age."

"Was he wearing the same type of ring?" asked Harry.

"No, but although initially he was not very forthcoming, the moment he saw my ring he began to open up. I'm not sure whether he thought I was a member of Rex Deus but he certainly knew the symbol. He said he was born in a substantial house, now pulled down, in Blandford very close to the derelict St Leonard's Chapel. At the time it was being used as a hospice run by a religious order. The Chapel, built in the early part of the 13th century had a direct association with Fontevault Abbey in France. Apparently this Abbey was popular

with the Counts of Anjou, who were related to the early English Kings. It's where Richard I, Coeur de Lion, is entombed.
Interestingly St Leonard's Chapel has connections with the Knights Templar of Templecombe in Somerset, just a few miles away over the Dorset borders. This ring continued to fascinate me, so, as is my nature, I made it my business to learn more and began delving. Interestingly, I discovered that Rex Deus had in fact split into effectively two groups. One group had a genealogy back through the Royal Line of David; this family represented the Mishpat pillar, known amongst Masons as Boaz. This group became known as the Knights of Black Chapter, whilst the other went back along a Priestly line, the families of this group were represented by the Tsedeq or pillar of Jachin. The group known as The Knights of Incanda."

"So the motif on your ring represents the pillar Jachin and therefore is an Incanda ring?" Said Harry.

"Precisely," replied the professor, "This meant that there were two types of ring, each depicting their respective halves of the holy gateway of Yahweh."

"Fascinating," remarked Harry, placing his cup and saucer down on the table.

"Fascinating indeed," exclaimed the Professor. "Now according to Clarissa you have an interesting object, found I believe in the belongings of one of your brethren?"

Harry nodded. He took the baton from a crumpled carrier bag and then handed it over to the Professor who removed the pair of gold-rimmed spectacles precariously lodged across the top of his thick mop of white hair. He fixed them close to the end of his nose. Instantly his expression changed, as if he had suddenly been struck by excruciating pain.

The Professor began to examine the baton closely. Harry looked across at Clarissa who simply smiled. Some time elapsed before the Professor made any comment. He rose from his chair. "Follow me," he commanded as he walked through the open french doors of the garden room.

Obediently, Harry and Clarissa followed. They walked across a yard, stopping briefly behind the Professor as he opened the door of what clearly was at one time the stables. The Professor began to climb up a flight of shabby wooden stairs. On reaching the door at the top he stopped to take a key from his pocket. He unlocked the door and then bid them enter. The large expanse above the stables was brimming with artefacts.

The Knights of Black Chapter

Bookcases lined the walls with leatherbound volumes spilling from their shelves.

Clarissa looked as mesmerised as Harry. "You've kept this place a secret Professor, of all the times I've been here I've never set foot in this place before," she said, sounding a trifle hurt at not being told of its existence.

The Professor smiled. "Normally I never share this place with anyone. Not even my very best students." He gave Clarissa a fatherly smile. "This baton is exceptionally old, I'd guess over a thousand years old in fact."

"Wow, how can you tell that from just looking at it?" asked Harry.

"Experience, I'd say," replied Clarissa with a smile.

"Mr Blakemore, with your permission I'm going to examine it under an x-ray unit."

"Be my guest," said Harry following the Professor and Clarissa towards a long oak table.

After removing umpteen files, papers and books the professor revealed a small black box with a screen at the end. He flicked on a switch, which instantly lit the screen. Attached to the back of the apparatus was a long thick wire. Plugged into a handle at the other end was a tool that resembled a round magnifying glass without a lense. The professor placed the baton on a piece of brown cartridge paper and slowly scanned the hoop along the baton's full length.

The screen began to show a long, dark image as the Professor continued to move the hoop slowly over its surface.

"I was right," shouted Clarissa gleefully, "it does contain something."

"This is a very important find my friends," exclaimed the Professor. He switched the X-ray unit off and picked up the baton.

"Harry I would suggest this baton contains a scroll. To extract the content from the baton will mean we have to break the bindings."

Harry looked sceptical. The Professor glanced at him from over the rim of his spectacles. "What do you think your freemasons lodge will do with it?" he asked.

Harry thought momentarily. "Well ordinarily I'd say they'd put it in the new Museum, but for a piece as important as this... I suppose it would be sent to the Museum at Grand Lodge in London."

The Professor smiled coyly. "Yes and that will be the last the world would ever see or hear of this piece of history ever again,

The Knights of Black Chapter

Mr Blakemore. The United Grand Lodge of all England denies virtually every part of Masonic history prior to the formation of the Grand Lodge in London during the year 1717. There are a number of reasons for this. You see Britain was going through a torrid time around this period, especially between the two Kingdoms of Scotland and England."

"Freemasonry came to England around 1600 with James the Sixth. However, it retained most of its Scottish formalities especially those of the Jacobite nature. Being a Freemason in a Hanoverian ruled country under George I, who had no association with Freemasonry whatsoever, was, to put it mildly, 'tricky'. To the point where several witch-hunts took place. Masons in London where considered as being disloyal to the King. Freemasons therefore left the craft in droves. Those that remained realised that if they wanted to continue Freemasonry it would have to disassociate itself from its Jacobite connections."

"Hanoverians of course had good reason to worry. The Stuart line had bred a boy and although James the Sixth was a weak man his son was the complete opposite. Charles Edward Stuart, known to those who loved him as Bonnie Prince Charlie, was up for the fight to regain the Crown of Scotland and become Charles III. He, like other royal personages, was a practicing Freemason."

"To disassociate itself from Jacobite Freemasonry, England altered the history books to remove many parts of its true origins. The Hanoverian Royal Family were encouraged to join Freemasonry and eventually they did. In fact a duke became the Grand Master. Within half a century quite a number of princes were passed through as its head. This was all at extreme cost in that all traces of the Scottish rituals had been removed. This in turn meant that the original purpose behind Freemasonry would be lost."

"A league of London gentlemen became the ruling body for the craft of Freemasonry. Naturally they were not recognised by many Masons. To establish superiority they announced that the United Grand Lodge of England was officially formed and, as I said before, the year was 1717."

"Scotland decided to produce a Grand Lodge for themselves and in so doing went back to their historical roots and loyalty in that Sir William Sinclair of Roslin would be their hereditary Grand Master. He was a direct descendant of William St Clair, the Crusader and one of the original second coming of nine

Knights Templar, the same man who built Rosslyn Chapel. For some strange reason, on his appointment he sold both Roslin Castle and Rosslyn chapel, perhaps his thinking was that his ancestors' wishes might now be fulfilled?"

"Between the two Jacobite campaigns around 1715 and 1745, during the time when Scotland invaded England, France was using the traditional three degrees. A man from Ayr called Chevalier Ramsey assisted Bonnie Prince Charlie to mount an expedition to re-gain the Scottish throne. Around 1730 Ramsey was granted permission to visit England where he was made a Fellow of the Royal Society by Isaac Newton, its president. Ironically, a Lodge in France, known as the Lodge of St Thomas was formed of which Bonnie Prince Charlie was a member. In 1761 the Grand Lodge of France issued a patent to spread the word across the world. Stephen Morin was given the task of introducing Scottish Freemasonry to America. He was made Grand Inspector in America and was given the right to install inspectors in areas where the 33 degrees of Scottish freemasonry were not practiced. Although these 33 degrees already existed in America on May the 31st 1801 Morin had established The Supreme Council of America in the town of Charleston, South Carolina. After no more than a year this Supreme Council sent a message to every Grand Lodge around the world proclaiming that the start of Freemasonry commenced at the very beginning of the world not in 1717."

"I hope I've not bored you Mr Blakemore with the turmoils of these English and Scottish ancestors, but you see if the United Grand Lodge of England refuse to recognise any form of masonry before 1717 then this baton predates their belief. Incidentally, the English, hypocritically, did in fact select their progression in Masonry from the Scottish 33 degrees."

"Okay Professor I'm convinced, lets do it," said Harry handing back the baton to him.

Clarissa looked like a little girl who had just been promised an extravagant present.

Within seconds a sharp scalpel had cut through the hemp bindings and with the precision of a surgeon the Professor commenced running his blade down the bamboo joints. It took some time before the two halves were eventually parted. The Professor then gradually peeled the two parts away from one another to reveal a perfectly formed, intact parchment scroll. With great care he removed the scroll from the bamboo baton where it had lain for centuries.

"This is a very important moment," said Clarissa as she gripped Harry's forearm, watching the professor carefully place the scroll into a stainless steel dish.

"What happens now," asked Harry, still a little nervous, as he'd not spoken to the Grand Master nor in fact to the Master of Ceremonies himself about the find. The Professor reached up to a high shelf and took down a large brown bottle. "Well first we need to open the scroll, this will take some time as it has been in this rolled state for centuries. To accomplish that we need to make the parchment supple before any attempt can be made to unroll it." He unscrewed the cap from the bottle and began pouring its contents over the scroll. "This is simply a blend of olive oil plus a few other concoctions, I find it works perfectly well."

"You mean you've done this before," said Harry sounding surprised.

"Oh yes," replied the professor.

The Knights of Black Chapter

"Who have we got that's expendable James? I need a guy fast," asked Bud O'Dowd, talking down the receiver of his new telephone.

"It's not been easy Chief, finding someone who fits the bill. We need brilliant but expendable and that was a challenge. However I had dinner last night with Admiral Robert Punter, he's just retired to a Washington desk job from Newport News Virginia. This guy's quite a character, he was commander of the Navy Seals' base in Norfolk for over ten years… so I asked him if he knew of a guy that might serve our purpose."

James Parker paused only briefly but it was longer than O'Dowd's patience could withstand. "And?" he said impatiently.

"And Chief, he sent me some guy's details." James Parker opened the broad, security-sealed envelope and extracted a pile of papers bound in a manila file. "Right, now let's see. His name's Lewis Ford; he left military service about three years ago after spending six months in rehab' following a mission in Albania."

"What happened to him?" asked O'Dowd.

"He got blown up," replied James Parker calmly.

"Blown up! A cripple's no good for this job, James," said O'Dowd, sounding frustrated.

"No, he was not hurt badly, at least not physically anyway. The rehab' was for his mental state."

"So he's a nutcase. I feel I should remind you of the seriousness of this matter. My balls are on the goddam touchline here, and while I'm on the subject yours are next in line."

James Parker was forced to smile at the Chief of Staff's remarks as he began reading out the details. "Lewis Ford served undercover in the Sudan, he infiltrated a guerrilla group in Darfur after the international community failed the people there, the guy was right in the middle of that war-torn region. He also helped to halt an arms deal in Syria involving the Russians, just as our guys were moving out of the Lebanon, remember when we tried to ease the pressure away from Washington? How many times have we done that during the past couple of years? He's been involved in a number of skirmishes in Tehran and has worked behind the scenes in Iraq. He then headed up a snatch squad to rescue a CNN reporter and - according to these notes - he also discovered a French diplomat the Frogs had written off as lost without trace. This guy was quietly given the Purple Heart for protecting Umar Karami in Beirut when the Syrians were withdrawing their forces from Lebanon."

"Okay, so he's got form, the question is, will he play ball?" asked Bud O'Dowd.

James Parker changed the receiver to his other hand, pressing it to his left ear. "Well that's the snag, see - currently he's in prison."

"So spring him, surely that can be arranged quietly?" remarked O'Dowd, still not seeing the problem.

"Well, Chief, the problem is the prison is in Florianopolis."

"Where the fuck's that? Down on the Florida Keys somewhere?"

James Parker shook his head, "No Chief, it's in the state of Isanta Catharina."

"Where in God's name's that, for Christ's sake?" responded O'Dowd.

"Brazil," replied James Parker, trying desperately to search the file for any good news. Sadly, it got worse. "According to the file, he's been charged with murder."

"Oh nothing simple then, like a traffic violation. James, when am I going to get a break? I did mention where my balls are right now!"

"Chief, think positive, this guy's perfect. If we can get him out for a few bucks in the right pocket, he'll be in our hands in no time."

"Would he co-operate?"

James Parker smiled. "I should think so. Murder, in Brazil, means the firing squad."

"Okay James so let's organise it," replied O'Dowd.

"I already have, the wheels are in motion. And by the way this Lewis Ford is a practising 33 degree Mason, and according to these notes he's a fanatic."

"Then get the poor bastard out of there, fast."

"Mr Director, sir, I've spoken to a couple of our people at Cruz Alta in the Rio Grande, they say the only way we're going to get this guy out is to spring him," said Nick Leigh, James Parker's number two.

"That's going to involve too many people and I promised the Irishman I'd keep this in the family."

"Well sir, apparently the jail he's in is the toughest in Brazil, it would take a anti-tank missile to even knock the door down!"

"Then maybe we'll have to use more diplomatic methods. Nick, the fewer people that know about this, the better. You get me on the next flight to Rio de Janeiro."

* * * * *

Nick Leigh had personally managed the travel arrangements for the Director to fly the 850 miles from Rio down to Florianopolis in a small, chartered aircraft. Arrangements had also been made for him to assume the name James Ford in the guise of the condemned man's brother.
A beaten up old taxi, with no air-conditioning and the distinguishable smell of stale body odour was the best the Director of the CIA could find. Its covered plastic seats made the hour-long journey from the small airfield to the isolated jail a most uncomfortable experience. A much-relieved James Parker eventually slid from the rear seat with his trousers and boxer briefs sticking to him. The taxi driver, in a Robin Hood like straw hat and dirty white singlet opened the door for him to climb out

* * * * *

"Hello this is the Chief of Staff's office in Washington. Mr O'Dowd would like to speak directly to the Ambassador as a matter of urgency," Amy said in her official-sounding voice. O'Dowd was put through. "Well, Douglas Hartman! How's it going Mr Ambassador? I hear life in Brazil's one great big carnival."

"I sweat a lot, but I'd rather be here right now than hooked up to a job close to the President."

"I hear yeh my friend," replied O'Dowd, "America's a tough call right now. Dougie, I need a favour. There's a guy locked up in some prison down your way, we need him real fast. I presume you know the right people to get him out?"

"Do you know his name?"

O'Dowd looked at the file on his desk. "Yeah, his name's Lewis Ford. Dougie, this guy's needed for an important job signed off by the President personally. I really need to stress the urgency to you, we need him like yesterday, I've got James Parker flying over on a secret trip as we speak... he'll be personally going to the jail to talk to Ford directly."

"James Parker, director of the CIA, visiting a prison in Brazil to talk with an American inmate? This guy sounds like a real big cookie. Okay I'll see what I can do, only politicians here are a strange bunch and remember I've only been here a year so my network's not that wide yet. You know, I invited the main people to the Embassy for a welcome dinner and only three turned up!"

"Dougie, I feel for yeah, but the White House expects and you know what that means. If you want a plum job in Europe next get this sorted. You hear what I'm sayin' Dougie?"

"Oh loud and clear Bud, loud and clear. Where are they holding him?"

O'Dowd looked again at the file. "Florianopolis, wherever the hell that is," replied O'Dowd. There was a momentary pause. "Hello, are you still there, Dougie?" asked O'Dowd.

"Yes, I'm just looking for it on the map. Got it. Okay leave it with me, I'll get right back to you."

* * * * *

The outer prison door opened with the sound of creaking hinges as if it had not opened for a long time. James Parker showed his pass to the guard, who simply rolled his head to one side as a gesture to bid him to enter.

Parker felt a little claustrophobic as he heard the large iron door close behind him. The guard led him past a row of what could be best described as empty metal cages.

"What are those for?" he asked the guard who responded with a large, beaming smile and a mouthful of gold teeth that shone as a beam of sunlight struck them.

"For the new people, signor. Now we have no new people."

"You mean to tell me you cage people up in those things?"

The guard continued to smile and nodded profusely. "For a few days only," he said, raising both shoulders in a nonchalant gesture.

James Parker was led to an inner part of the main building that was filled with the sound of caged souls: some screaming, others shouting foul abuse. This was combined with hollow, cranking sounds that echoed, presumably from automatic door locks being continually opened and closed. To the uninitiated, this was a desolate world full of humans attempting to exist in squalid conditions; a world James Parker had no desire to remain in any longer than was necessary.

The guard unlocked a door into a small room that contained nothing more than two wooden chairs and a small table. "You wait here," he said.

* * * * *

In no more than half an hour Amy was advising Bud O'Dowd that the Brazilian Ambassador was on the blue phone.

"Dougie, how we doin'?"

"Not good Bud, this Lewis Ford has only killed three people and one of them was a woman."

"Ye gods. In self-defence I trust?"

"Bud this guy's facing a firing squad at the weekend."

Bud O'Dowd wiped the familiar sweat from his forehead and glanced across at the Indian. "What about the trial?" he said finally.

"His trial was an open and shut case... lasted all of a day. He's been in Florianopolis for the past couple of months awaiting execution. Apparently the governor got the nod last week."

"Of all the guys with purple hearts, we have to pick this one. Willie McCain will blow his stack. So what are you saying Dougie? Is there no way we can lever him out... surely money talks in a country like that?"

"I can try talking directly with the President but if I do that and the answer is no, he's going to post an army of guards around Ford, twenty four seven because the Brazilians will know we might get up to something naughty. I have spoken to a trusted guy that says this prison's not exactly Fort Knox. And people have been known to escape before, so getting out is possible but getting away can prove more difficult. The terrain is very open and exposed with nowhere to hide."

"So if there was a way to get him out of the prison, he could be lifted up by air!" said Bud O'Dowd, trying to cling to the possibility of a positive outcome.

* * * * *

It was the best part of an hour before James Parker saw anyone apart from the occasional fleeting glimpse of a uniformed guard passing the partly opened door. Eventually a bedraggled soul chained at both the ankles and wrists stood in the now fully opened doorway; his arms were looped through the arms of two huge guards, standing either side of him. They literally dragged Lewis Ford into the room and sat him on a chair. Much to James Parker's surprise they then left the room and closed the door, locking it behind them.

"I presume you're not wired?" said James Parker as he looked across the table at the man he'd read so much about.

"No," was the only response to come from the man with the bright red beard. He was smaller than James Parker had envisaged, but perfectly in proportion. His shoulder muscles stood out like two rocks under his dirty, pale green overalls.

"I've checked the room. It's solid concrete and clean of bugs," said James Parker.

"So who the fuck are you?" asked Lewis Ford, in an expressionless voice with no distinguishable dialect.

"Unofficially, I'm your brother, naturally here to see you for the last time. Officially I'm the Director of the CIA and I've come to enquire if you'd like to make it out of here... that's if you're prepared to serve your country again?"

Ford raised a laugh that genuinely made his chains jangle.

"You got to be kiddin' me! You're the Director of the CIA and you've come to this hell hole in Brazil, in person, just to ask me if I'm prepared to work for the Government? Is this some kind of wind-up or a new angle on kissograms? Maybe the perverted version." Suddenly Lewis Ford's expression changed. His pale blue eyes flashed with a deadly serious glare. "Whoever sent you, tell 'em thanks but no thanks." He pushed his chair back away from the table in order to stand up.

"Does the name Admiral Robert Punter mean anything to you?" asked James Parker calmly. Ford looked hard into the face of the director as he slowly sank back down onto the chair.

"How is the old guy?"

"He's good," replied Parker.

"He sends you his best and asked me to tell you Pepsi's just fine. Whatever that means."

Lewis Ford's expression relaxed slightly with the merest hint of a smile. "So, Mr director of the CIA, what's the deal?" he asked, casually glancing behind where James Parker was sitting.

"What is it?" asked Parker, turning around just as a large, black rat scurried into a corner. Despite the restriction of his chains, Lewis Ford was off his seat and with one lunge he snatched the struggling rat, and without a moment's hesitation he bit off its head. "Like some?" he asked, gleefully crunching on bone as he returned to his seat. After chewing on the remains, he spat out a particle of brown fur onto the floor.

It took James Parker a great deal of resolve to remain unperturbed by the incident, however he eventually smiled and shook his head. "Me, I've been a vegetarian for years now," he said.

Lewis Ford smiled and as he did so he wiped his sleeve across his mouth. By the time he'd removed his arm the smile was gone, replaced by a deadly serious stare. "This will give you an idea of how good the food is in here." He held up the still twitching carcass to emphasise the point. "You know one fat rat can be traded for two cuts of chewin' tobacco in this dump," he said, throwing the remains of the dead rat back into the general direction of where he caught it.

"I've come here personally because Admiral Robert Punter recommended you. If you take on this assignment it would mean you'd be working in the Middle East to seek out and find a specific person whose name's not important right now. He is however a Muslim fundamentalist and has been causing our country a whole bunch of grief," said James Parker, appropriately moving from one rat to another of the more dangerous kind!

"Yeah, get newspapers, even in this toilet," said Ford. "You mean the bomb attacks on New York, therefore you're talking about a guy by the name of Mohammed Abu Atif. Now let me guess, why me? Could it be that there's a heap of smelly brown stuff on the White House carpet right now and you need an expendable person to take out the elusive Abu Atif. And if this expendable person was to perish in the attempt there'd be no come-back and the President's lilly-white hands would stay clean?"

James Parker smiled. "Got it in one, heh, yeah know what, the Admiral said you were bright, but he didn't say how bright, I'm impressed."

"All good stuff Mr Director, but you're forgetting just one tiny thing, I'm about to face a firing squad on Sunday - that's like six days away," said Ford without showing a morsel of fear or apprehension at the thought.

"I meant to ask you about that," said James Parker. "What happened exactly?"

"Simple, I met a Brazilian lady called Martina in New Mexico, we were getting along just fine. We might have even

settled down together, but she needed to sort out a few urgent things, like getting her five-year-old kid back from his father here in Brazil. So we both came to get him.
We were held up in a hotel down the coast from here at a place called Laguna, close to where the kid was living. Martina went to visit her ex- husband but got a fist in the face for her trouble. I was told that he spent most of his time drinking in a bar across the other side of town. So I thought I'd pay the guy a visit, but he didn't show up all evening so I skipped back to the hotel to find these two guys busy raping Martina as she lay dying with the hilt of a knife sticking out of her neck. Lewis Ford's eyes clouded as tears began to roll down his face."

"I killed both of those bastards with these," he pushed his chained hands, palms down, towards the table in front of James Parker. Thick calluses on both hands from the bottom of his little fingers to his wrists had been honed to an edge almost like the blades of a knife. Each index finger was also callused, the hard skin honed into points. "I pushed my hand into the one guy's stomach and pulled out his intestines," he said demonstrating with the open fingers of his left hand.

"I strangled him with his own guts. Yeah know the other guy just continued fucking Martina's dead body. I tore off his dick and balls and fucked his mouth with them until he choked. Naturally I took the rap for Martina's death as well." The fleeting presence of a smile briefly changed his expression as he looked up towards the ceiling."

"You know they wanted to cut off my hands so that I could never use them as weapons again, but I guess they figured that whilst they were hacking off the one hand, I'd be killing them with the other, and they'd be right of course." Lewis Ford placed both hands down on the rough wooden table."So Mr Director, if I agree to your proposals do we simply walk out of here?"

"Not quite, but moves are taking place as we speak," replied James Parker, ad-libbing the situation.

"And naturally I'd be well compensated for a successful accomplishment and presumably be left alone to live out the rest of my life on some comfortable Caribbean Island. What kind of back-up can I expect?"

James Parker looked at him and smiled. "None. Except you'd have a partner, a Brit'. A top man, he's an ex-pro just like you."

Lewis Ford shook his head. "I work alone, I don't need any partners, especially a Brit'," said Lewis Ford sternly.

"You got no choice, my friend, this is take-it–or-leave-it-ville. And besides the guy's ex- Special Air Service, so he's probably as nuts as you are. In the nicest way, you understand. Now have I come here to get the big, sorry but I'd rather get shot on Sunday routine or have we got a deal?"

"Well nuts I might be, but I'm not that nuts. I presume our wonderful President will have sent a fax to the Brazilian Minister of the Interior saying, "Please can we have our boy back?"

James Parker didn't quite know what to say. The man needed to know how he was going to be released and right at that point the Director didn't have a clue. "Let's just say the political wheel is turning," James Parker said as he stood and walked toward the door, which he knocked hard with his fist. "We'll be in touch," he said.

Lewis Ford nodded.

* * * * *

General Richard Hertmenger was invited to have an early breakfast with the Chief of staff. The fifty-two-year-old head of the Airborne Infantry was everything Bud O'Dowd wasn't. Lean, tanned and in remarkably good shape.

The two men sat at a specially prepared table on one of the many terraces that overlooked the splendid grounds of the White House. The silver service reflected the early morning sunlight as both men sat in the tranquil ambiance.

"Richard, how do we get a guy out of a prison in an isolated part of Brazil?" was O'Dowd's opening question after his bacon and two over-easy eggs had arrived.

The General slowly placed his glass of fruit juice down and smiled. "Simple, blast the place wide open."

O'Dowd broke the surface of one of his fried egg yolks with a toast soldier. "Do you have any other suggestions, a little more quiet and a little less violent?"

"No," replied the General looking at Chief of Staff full on. "If you need to spring this guy without the diplomacy of a political relationship and he's as important as you say he is, then that's the only way."

O'Dowd looked worried. "But Americans can't just go and violate a foreign country like Brazil, it's an act of war."

The Knights of Black Chapter

The General again returned the glass of fruit juice to its coaster. "Why not? We've been doing it for years. Look, apparently this place is one of the most inhuman prisons in South America. It's stuck right in the middle of nowhere land and the sea is no more than five miles away. Perfect."

"You do know that if we did this and something failed your career would be fried like this piece of crispy bacon," said O'Dowd looking a might apprehensive.

"Yours too Bud and make no mistake. Look, right now we've got a Carrier not more than a hundred and fifty miles off the Brazilian coast, she's *en route* to exercises in the Pacific with our British cousins."

"Two red hawk missiles sent from a ground busting, fixed-wing fighter flying low, followed by a snatch and grab helicopter would have the job done in the blink of an eye. The President would have to rubber stamp the operation of course but I'd say we'd be doing humanity a favour.
Of course the place would need a complete re-build after we'd left. It depends how important you think this guy really is?"

O'Dowd sort of let his head nod up and down before responding.
"Well if we do this I hope in the name of god he is. There's no way we can expect Willy McCain to sign off such a deal though."

The General looked at the perspiring Chief compassionately. "No problem, anyone can stray off course and blast the wrong target, especially during international exercises, we're well known for it. A hands up apology and a cheque from congress to re-build the place will resolve the issue."

* * * * *

A Catholic priest was assigned to help Lewis Ford prepare to meet the firing squad. No word, in fact not even a message had been received following James Parker's visit. Lewis Ford therefore became convinced that someone had played a sick joke on him.

Father Pablo Renaldo was a young Brazilian Priest who had graduated from Harvard with a Master's in history before changing direction towards the church. He was ordained in Chicago's Rush Street Cathedral close to where his family had now settled. Unfortunately, two of them constantly lived in fear of imminent deportation. Following his ordination Father Renaldo was instated as the priest of St Catherine's in the

Michigan parish of Des Plains. He soon became a pillar amongst the community, but try as he might there seemed nothing he could do to save his uncle and cousin from deportation, that is until an offer came from the bishop, out of the blue so to speak!

"I have been assigned to stay with you my son, until the great bird plucks you up into the sky," said Father Renaldo as he stood in the open doorway silhouetted by four guards.

"I don't need a priest, especially a Catholic one," responded Lewis Ford.

"Sorry I'm wrong," went on the priest, " I forgot you'd be joining The Great Architect of the Universe, naturally, as a 33 degree Mason."

Lewis Ford looked up at the young priest and smiled as Father Renaldo entered the cell.

"You can leave us now my sons," he said to the guards in Spanish. They politely removed their hats and bowed respectfully towards the priest then closed the door.

"For a Catholic priest you know more than most about Masonry," said Lewis Ford. "Are you the advanced party to get me out of here?"

"Of course my son, do you think I can smuggle you under cassock?" replied Father Renaldo.

"Will you stop calling me your son, I'm years older than you!" said Ford, with a half smile.

Father Renaldo ignored him and continued. "I have a message from the Military. They say you will be taken to the outer quadrangle and put up against a particular wall. You will be standing with the sun's rays shining directly into your eyes. You will be offered a blindfold. Do not accept it. The firing squad will comprise of ten guards. They will be facing you with their backs towards the sun. The governor and any other onlookers will be in the shade close to the main building facing you. The US navy will be despatching a jet fighter, flying low directly towards you. The theory is that you will see the aircraft first. However as the sun's in your eyes it will not be easy to see the aircraft as it approaches from a distance away, so I've been told to stand close to a small building directly to your left. When I give you a signal be prepared to run towards me because according to the person who briefed me, all hell will be unleashed. The Navy have one attempt at this and no practice run. A helicopter will drop a rope ladder and whisk you away."

"How about you, how do you escape? "asked Lewis Ford.

The Knights of Black Chapter

The young priest smiled, "I don't need to, I'll simply leave in the general direction from where I arrived. Now, I'll whistle, I'm a good whistler and can do it quite loudly so when you hear a high pitched whistle, run like crazy."

"What happens if they don't show?" asked Lewis Ford with a doubtful smile. "Is there any back up procedure?"

"Yes, you get shot and my uncle and cousin get deported from the US back here to Brazil."

"Then it better work for both of us."

Father Renaldo spent the entire night with Lewis Ford; they talked about everything from politics to baseball right through until dawn, when the guards arrived. Father Renaldo stood over the now kneeling figure of Lewis Ford to enact the final blessing.

"God be with you my son," said Father Renaldo in Spanish as the two guards gripped Lewis Ford under his armpits and raised him to his feet. He was given a clean pair of bright red overalls and ordered to change into them.

"Great colour, so you don't see the blood," said Ford smiling at one of the guards as he began to strip off. He was allowed to wash and drink a cup of thick black coffee before being taken out of the cell.

It was strange but the entire prison seemed remarkably quiet as Lewis Ford was frogmarched through a series of dark passageways with Father Renaldo bringing up the rear, clutching a Bible. The party stood for a second whilst a guard unlocked a large metal door. As it opened the bright sunlight hit Ford for the first time in over two months, almost blinding him. He squinted and shook his head to try and gain some sort of focus as he was almost carried into the quadrangle. Those prisoners who were not in for violent crimes normally used the area as an exercise yard but not today, it stood empty and quiet.

The infamous wall was quite a few yards away, which gave Ford a few precious seconds to adjust his sight to the glare of the morning sun. Eventually he was turned and as he did so a line of guards marched from a building to his left. Each one bore a rifle on his right shoulder. Lewis Ford looked over towards Father Renaldo who had moved into position out of the line of fire. Right enough there was a small building and the door was ajar.

Ford noticed a small delegation of about six people had assembled close to the door he'd been brought through.

Obviously these were not guards as they were smartly dressed in suits and one was in fact a woman in a white cotton dress.

Despite the time of morning, the temperature was high and the humidity level was gaining momentum, making for yet another unbearably sticky day. Lewis Ford however felt a chill that made him shudder, suddenly realising his time on earth might now be coming to an abrupt end – and in just a few moments. He imagined how gladiators must have felt standing in the hot sun of the arena, but at least they could fight for their lives, whereas he was denied such a privilege. He watched as the squad of guards began loading their rifles, each putting a single round into the open breech. He then heard the sound of the bolts being pushed into the breech and closed down. The guards then put their rifle stocks into their shoulders and pointed the barrels up into the air, holding them there to await the order. A guard somewhat more smartly dressed than the others walked slowly towards Lewis Ford with a black scarf in his hand. He stopped in front of Ford and, standing at a reasonably safe distance, he held out the scarf without saying a word. Ford shook his head. The guard simply nodded and returned to the firing squad. He then raised his hand above his head and as he did so the entire firing squad lowered their rifles in readiness to fire upon his command. Just then the dull hum of a jet engine could be heard, instantly followed by an ear-piercing screech. Lewis Ford just about heard the sound of Father Renaldo's whistle as the entire wall in front of which he was standing seemed to disintegrate in one almighty explosion that was followed by a huge flash.

Instinctively Ford began to run and as he did so he could hear the sound of gun fire followed by a second explosion; within seconds he had reached the flesh-torn remains of Father Renaldo. Within an instant the sound of rotor blades and the sight of a large helicopter appeared through the smoke and flames above the ruins of the wall, and sure enough a rope ladder was trailing from its fuselage just as Father Renaldo had said.

The priest's smashed body provided Ford with a modicum of protection as he viewed the terrain in front of him in readiness to make a dash for the ladder. It was impossible to tell if the guards were still in any form of position as choking black smoke had virtually obliterated that entire end of the quadrangle.

The Knights of Black Chapter

The helicopter skilfully turned at a sharp angle and as it did so the rope ladder swung towards a point close to where Ford was lying. At once he was on his feet and making an almighty leap, grabbing the rope ladder with his right hand whilst the left gained a further grip on a higher rung. By the time he had scrambled up the ladder sufficiently to gain a foothold he was being hoisted into the air, swinging within just as few inches of a part of the wall that remained standing. Then, as the helicopter gracefully turned and commenced gaining height, a winch began winding Ford up into the fuselage.

From the safety of the speeding helicopter Lewis Ford looked down on the scene of devastation. He briefly touched his right eyebrow then threw his hand forward in the gesture of a salute in recognition of the young priest who had been sacrificed to make this all possible.

"Your family will never want for anything, I promise you that, my friend," he pledged, closing the fuselage door.

Harry could hear the telephone ringing from the comfort of his late night bath. He had decided to give himself this rare treat after concluding a nice little 'deal' with a Dutch antique dealer who had paid a handsome price for an early oak Welsh dresser that had been in the shop for barely a week. Deep hot water with plenty of bubbles, a large brandy, a Cuban cigar, a soothing Italian ballad from the Bang and Olson and the Antique Gazette to read, what more could a man ask for?

Suddenly the telephone in the bedroom stopped after no more than a few rings. Harry concluded that it couldn't have been that important, however his relaxation had been broken, especially after failing to hold the fat cigar between his lips whilst turning the page. The result was that the cigar fell from his mouth onto his chest and rolled into the foamy depths.

"Bollocks," shouted Harry as he threw the Gazette onto the bathroom carpet in his rush to stand. He wound a towel around him, finished the last dregs of brandy, pulled the plug and made for the door.

"Hi Harry, if you pick up this message before twelve, please give me a call," was the voice message Clarissa had left.

Harry used a kitchen towel to dry his feet, as he called Clarissa. "Hi it's me, what's the problem? You made me drop my cigar and burn my chest."

"Well that'll teach you not to smoke, especially indoors. I won't ask what you were doing at the time. I thought you might like to know I've spoken to Professor Franklin, he's cock-a-hoop with the content of the scroll."

"You mean he's actually been able to read it?" remarked Harry forgetting all about the smell of singed chest hair and the burning red stripe down his front.

"He wants us to go around to see him."

"When, to-night?" asked Harry.

"No, first thing in the morning. He's planning to travel down to Blandford Forum to visit Humphrey Morgan Sinclair later in the day.

* * * * *

The Knights of Black Chapter

Mrs Jones had prepared toasted homemade bread and coffee in the garden room to await their arrival. The jubilant professor greeted them, still wearing the same shabby cardigan, although the bow tie had different coloured spots.

"Grab your coffee and come with me," he commanded just as Harry was about to tuck into a thick slice of toast with lashings of Welsh butter. He led them into his immense study, purported to be the largest room in the house. A space had been cleared on a heavily carved, oak desk to make way for the important artefact. The scroll was now fully rolled open upon the ink stained red skive, kept in place with the aid of two glass paperweights.

"My friends, this scroll is valuable beyond the bounds of imagination," commenced the professor.

"How much do you think it's worth then," asked Harry getting excited.

"I'm not referring to it in terms of monetary value Mr Blakemore, but in those terms, I'd say it is priceless."

Clarissa gave Harry a disapproving glare.

"What we have here is an account of the splitting up of Rex Deus... remember what I said about one side following the religious route and the other following the Royal line. Well this scroll confirms it. It also establishes the true reasons behind the crusades - something historians have pondered over for generations. I have spent the last few days piecing together some very significant parts of history."

"This scroll tells that following the destruction of the Jerusalem Temple, Rex Deus removed the scrolls and the Sanctum Sanatorium that lay secretly hidden in vaults below the Temple ruins. It seems it was at this point that the split between what was to become Incanda, and the Knights of Black Chapter occurred."

"This scroll has clearly been written by Incanda, probably on the instructions of the one they call the Knight Commander, or High Cardinal. His line would have gone directly back to Ahaz."

"Incanda had and still has a monumentally powerful hierarchy. No doubt you are aware that throughout history religion has been at the very core of wars, confrontation and destruction as indeed it is to this day. Catholic against Protestant, Muslim versus Christian. But so that you will appreciate exactly what this scroll is all about I'm going to take you back thousands of years before Christ."

"The actual origins of Rex Deus still remain unclear however we do know they evolved through a people known strangely as the 'Grooved Ware People.' These were the first stonemasons, a Neolithic people that first appeared in the Northern Islands of Britain over 9,000 years ago. In those days it was possible to actually walk from Norway to Scotland, before the Great Northern plains were flooded. Not long after the glaciers of the ice age melted covering masses of land, the levels of water rose to form the North Sea separating the landmasses. However from these early times it became easy to detect that the Scottish people and the Neolithic Scandinavians share the same ancestry."

"The Grooved Ware People were early stonemasons who inhabited Wales, England, Scotland, Ireland, and France along with the southern parts of Scandinavia and went as far south as Malta and northern Spain. Evidence of this civilisation is prolific across the continent. In England alone there are well over 40,000 sites, which have survived for almost six thousand years."

"Temperatures in those days were far hotter than we experience today; this induced dense forestation, which made overland travel very difficult. These megalithic people were already excellent craftsmen and great boatbuilders. They used the seas as their means of travel and therefore became highly skilled sailors. Soon they colonised the many islands of the northern Hebrides, trading across Scotland."

"These people quarried stone of a particular type found only on the island known as Rum. The stone was used to construct buildings across the mainland. Maritime trading was carried on as far as Scandinavia. Little is actually known about these people, as there was no form of writing to record their history - unlike later groups such as the ancient Egyptians."

"They were therefore simply called the Grooved Ware People on account of the grooved designs that appeared in the clay pots they used during this period. They did however record things in the form of symbols, which can be identified through astronomical references. Often we take for granted the many stone buildings they erected without really understanding their true meaning: Maes Howe in the Orkneys for example, recorded as one of the most of superb achievements of the Neolithic age. These people built 'standing stones' in a number of formations; their earth and tunnel moulds, and ditches are prolific right across Europe including Egypt, Israel and North Africa."

"The structures were built to allow the sun to shine on specific parts of the interior on special days of the year. Many of these sites, including Stonehenge, had alignments that formed a calendar based on the solstices and the equinox."

"An important megalithic settlement had been discovered following a storm in Orkney: when the sand was blown away the well-preserved stone dwellings were revealed. The area known as Skare Brae had been occupied for over six hundred years from around 3000 years BC. These dwellings were used as accommodation for trainee astronomer priests. The dwelling themselves and the furniture contained inside were all built of stone. This included beds, tables and fireplaces - all had been perfectly preserved. They were occupied by an elite class of priests who were rulers and wise men supported by taxes taken from the rural population."

"Others would provide them with food, meat brought in by boats in a pre-butchered state. Firewood was also imported. Their dwellings would have been built for them so that they could devote their entire lives to scientific, religious and intellectual pursuits. This transformed the Neolithic peasants into a more advanced society with intelligent and skilled leaders and wise men. This may well have begun a religious revolution that established a professional priesthood in early Neolithic times."

"Archaeologists have been convinced that Skare Brae was a Neolithic University for religious instruction. This scroll has confirmed the theory."

"For centuries it was thought that the people who inhabited Britain and parts of Europe were backward compared to other parts of the world whereas quite the opposite was true. These people were mathematicians and commonly used standard units of length; their knowledge was widespread across the continents of Europe. It's difficult to believe, but they could produce accurate and precise measurements of vast distances. This was realised following the discovery of the Dead Sea Scrolls and in particular a Jewish text reputed to be over two thousand years old."

"So, in a nutshell, Rex Deus evolved from the Ice Age onwards; it spread through the Grooved Ware People who were the first known people to use technology to build, using stone. These people also were able to record the movement of the sun. They celebrated the summer and winter solstices and the equinoxes. They also studied the science of astronomy. Interestingly, they also believed in the resurrection of the dead through Venus. Those who lived close to the Irish sea almost 6000 years ago, developed a way of recording the dawn rising that occurred within the chamber of their buildings, once every eight years. Venus was identified as the symbol of sex, love and reproduction."

"Clearly the Grooved Ware People influenced the early Jews. Megalithic monuments scattered throughout Israel especially in the Golan Heights and around Jordan, confirm this fact. The Arabs knew these as Kubur Brni Israil, which translated means Graves of the Children of Israel. The features of these buildings are exactly the same in character as those found in both Scotland and England. We know that the strange rituals of Freemasonry originate from pre-history, confirmed through signs at megalithic sites around the British Isles. Their definite links were transmitted through the people of Israel."

"You see, the Grooved Ware People had the principles of knowledge; Rex Deus sat clearly as overlords and their influence spread across the world and especially through the Egyptians and Canaanites. Jerusalem was founded by the Jebusites who were influenced by these teachings. A culture and learning centring on Venus evolved through the Grooved Ware People, spread across the Eastern Mediterranean, was accepted by the Jews some time later and re-energised by the Knights Templar."

"So, my friends, the impact of Rex Deus came by way of the Grooved Ware People. From these King Solomon selected what he called the Master Elect of Nine: the original Knights Templar. The Copper Scroll, part of the Dead Sea Scrolls, with its stamped characters written no more than thirty years after the death of Jesus Christ, lists over sixty locations where items were buried at the commencement of the Jewish war against the Romans. At first I thought the baton scroll we have here was from one of those locations but after further reference I discovered this not to be the case. In fact I believe this scroll originated in Scotland, possibly at Skare Brae. It is therefore highly likely that the dividing of Rex Deus and the forming of Incanda and the Knights of Black Chapter evolved in Scotland, though it maintained deep roots in Norway."

"Clearly the Nasorean Priests, many of whom were Rex Deus disciples, removed the precious scrolls and artefacts from below the ruins of the Jerusalem Temple. Some had one sole mission, to bring them to their rightful resting place, the land where the majesty of knowledge originally evolved - Scotland.

The Knights of Black Chapter

These were to form the group know known as Incanda. The others fled to Greece."

"Make no mistake, Incanda have a direct power so immense that it sits above all religions including Islam, Christianity and Judaism. This power commenced with the astronomical science of the Grooved Ware People, and was passed down over time to the Canaanites through priests who lived in Qumran and the group headed up by Jesus, John and James."

"Incanda has, through its direct line, people in powerful positions throughout every religious group and to some extent through political circles. Was Adolph Hitler of Incanda? Was Oliver Cromwell influenced by them? Was Princess Diana murdered indirectly through them? Or might the deed have been done by the Knights of Black Chapter, because a Christian Princess was bearing a Muslim man's child... who knows?"

"You mean Incanda are as powerful today as they were way back in history?" asked Harry.

"I do indeed, and they are in fact still seeking ultimate power. This has been prohibited by just nine people: the priests who fled to Greece and evolved as the Knights of Black Chapter. But these two extraordinary powers are not just black and white. Their forebears within Rex Deus and the Grooved Ware People also influenced these Knights of Black Chapter to instigate and build great wealth and power from the treasures taken from under the temple. I suppose Hiram King of Tyre was the royalist instigator, so described as the true son of Venus. His father made sure his mother was impregnated during the sexual rituals of the vernal equinox. You see, Venus rose just before the sun at the winter solstice in 1002 BC. Hiram's birth therefore fulfilled the same criteria as that of the Qumran priests who were to decide if a messiah were to be born."

"The birth of a Jewish messiah was heralded by a number of Venus/Mercury connections, which occurred every 500 years. These were referred to as Shekinah. A long time to wait, you'll agree. The Phoenicians therefore accepted that so long as a new king was born before the light of Venus he would be a suitable person to rule over them. The decree that kings are born only when a bright star is visible before dawn was accepted by the Jews. These were viewed as super-kings with God's full approval. They were therefore able to provide for their country and for its people with success and vast fortunes. But they had to be born when this fantastically bright star appeared at the precise moment of birth. This knowledge was acquired roughly at the time of the dedication of King Solomon's Temple in 967BC."

"Clearly the forebears of the Knights of Black Chapter were active in some form or degree even before the birth of Jesus. They could have also been astronomer priests from Solomon's times. The Grooved Ware People, Egyptians and the Sumerians all worshiped Venus, who was considered as a female deity. This bright star represented, birth, death, love and resurrection."

"The rituals of Freemasonry align with astronomy and the royal lineages of Jerusalem... oh and by the way, in translation Jerusalem means city of Venus. This scroll clearly refers to the Ark of the Covenant, which Incanda describes as theirs by divine right, but which they clearly did not have. Therefore one would presume the Knights of Black Chapter have the Ark of the Covenant and Incanda have been attempting to secure it from them for centuries. But who specifically are the Knights of Black Chapter, this group of nine who, like Incanda, slipped into obscurity?"

"Incanda had to draw them out into the open and therefore began a war, a war that has never ended: a clash of civilisations, using the agitation of one religion against another, from the simplicity of the early crusades to the constant struggle of modern times. The continual bomb attacks in Beirut and the occupation by crusaders in the Holy lands only differ by modernisation. In brief, foreigners occupying Arab lands have constantly invaded the entire Middle East."

"In the Middle Ages western Christians believed that the Crusades to the East were sanctioned as divine wars against the enemies of Christ. This scroll however confirms that the crusades were contrived by Incanda to disrupt the Knights of Black Chapter and cause mayhem throughout the world. Gaining the upper hand of authority was crucial for Incanda and I believe still is."

"Religious wars are not an atribute of the distant past. Look at what's been happening in recent history. When the President of America spoke of this 'new war' on terrorism as a 'crusade' he was roundly criticised, his comments were interpreted as suggesting a war between Christianity and Islam. For some in the Middle East, the remark confirmed their assessment of the West as being American and European crusaders. For centuries historians have studied the fundamentals of the crusades, but one burning question has always remained... what was truly behind the reasons that apparently drove thousands to war? Of course, to re-capture the Holy Land was important for western Christians, but were the crusades merely staged to significantly disrupt the world for some other, sinister reason?"

"This scroll reveals it was a move by Incanda to attempt to expose the Knights of Black Chapter and hopefully capture the Ark of the Covenant. Clearly they did not succeed and so this war has gone on with Incanda, niggling away far off in the background. As I've said, during the Middle Ages the Western Christians believed the crusades in the East were divinely sanctioned as the war against the enemies of Christ. So then, with the expansion of the Islamic Ottoman Empire, Europeans were forced to abandon any hope of reclaiming Jerusalem and instead they were forced to commence defending Europe. In the sixteenth century Europe was in danger of a Muslim conquest. At this time the crusades, as a means of defence began to collapse. As one secular authority in Europe expanded so religious unity crumbled."

"The Protestant Reformation did significant harm to the crusades because doctrines had been rejected that were at the very heart of crusading. The view was taken that crusades were the tools of corrupt popes, especially agitated by Martin Luther. Luther was aware that the power of Islamic Turks posed a threat to Christian Europe, therefore the old ideas that Christian unity against the Muslim has never died. Now was Luther a pawn in the game for Incanda? Who knows? Pope Gelasius wrote a letter to emperor Anastasius to consolidate the view of supremacy of the church over all other authorities, stating that although the emperor is lord over mankind, in dignity he should bow his head to those who take charge of divine affairs and seek from them the means of salvation."

"He went on to suggest that the emperor should submit to religion rather than rule. The Pope said that no one should raise themselves up by purely human means. Whereas in 795 Charlemagne, so called Charles the Great, King of the Franks, expressed a different view to Pope Leo III - saying that it was his royal duty to defend the church against attacks by pagans and infidels and to enforce within the church acceptance of the catholic faith. He went on to say that it was the pope's duty to assist him in the good fight by raising his hands to God so that the Christian people would always and everywhere be victorious."

"So, if I'm reading this right, you're saying that this Charles the Great was from the Knights of Black Chapter and Pope Gelasius was on the side of Incanda?" suggested Harry.

The professor looked up at his two companions and pulled a face.

"Maybe, maybe not... it's not simply a matter of choosing sides and then following your choice to the bitter end, like deciding which football team to support. These two groups are far more cunning than that. They needed to win over the minds of man subconsciously, so that the seeds of feeling would grow through generations to the point where vast populations became impregnated with particular views. Incanda could then instigate an action that would unite millions of people and force the Knights of Black Chapter into a confrontation that might expose them to the point where one of the nine Knights would either defect or be overcome and therefore release the Ark of the Covenant - so that Incanda would gain supreme power. The knights of Black Chapter have a more passive tendency until provoked, but so far they have held their lines."

"So far... Professor, that's a scary thought," remarked Clarissa who looked very concerned.

"Incanda have been pitching one religion against another for centuries and are still doing so. Right now we are experiencing a huge build up of problems. In the main, men no longer wear the uniforms of their chosen side with battle standards flying over them: war has become far less visible. Under the name of terrorism, the enemy might well be your next-door neighbour, a workmate, friend or even relation. Incanda sit as high lords creating aggression, death and destruction through the mind games they continue to play."

"It seems to me that the Knights of Black Chapter have a constant battle on their hands to keep the world from total annihilation," said Clarissa.

"And all this has come from that scroll?" said Harry, staring down at the dried up piece of parchment with its faint symbols and weird lines.

"This scroll merely confirms the theories that have plagued historians for generations. Interestingly, part of these writings are in an Irish script called Ogham, a gesture alphabet used certainly up to the 6th century, and then for secret communications between the Druids for magical and cryptic purposes."

The Knights of Black Chapter

The professor opened a large leather-bound book and took a piece of folded paper from between its pages. On the paper were a number of symbols, written by hand in black ink, each with a vertical line and a number of horizontal lines at varying angles running through them. Alongside each symbol was a letter of the alphabet. The professor pointed to a number of tiny symbols on the scroll similar to those on the paper. "These, as you can see, are Ogham symbols. This suggests the scroll was actually written in Britain. Ogham is not uncommon, in fact these symbols can be found upon a number of Celtic stones of this later period. The most famous example is the memorial to King Arthur, they were actually cut into the edge of the stone."

Harry smiled. "You mean to tell me King Arthur was not just a fairy- tale King?"

The professor looked at Harry and smiled back. "Not at all. Of course - as indeed with all things - the tales of King Arthur have been dramatically expanded and romanticised, but Arthur was real and of Celtic birth. The memorial stone I mentioned is called the slaughterhouse stone and can be found to this very day at Camlann. Slaughterbridge is situated on the river Camel, near Camelford on the west coast of Cornwall. In fact this site was the final battleground, where Arthur met his death against Mordred, which ended the Fellowship of the round table in 537AD. However, that's another story. This scroll also mentions the Norwegian connection with Incanda. I would suggest Incanda would really like to retrieve this important artifact, especially as it exposes them to a degree. You see, although the scroll is centuries old, family lines can easily be traced."

"You say you're off to Blandford Forum, is that anything to do with the Scroll?" asked Harry.

"Yes I need to pick Sinclair's brains, I think he can unlock a number of key issues about Incanda, especially with the additions contained within this scroll. Would you like to come with me?"

Harry looked first at the professor and then at Clarissa. "If you intend to take the scroll with you I really think I should."

"Well I'm going down this afternoon. I shall make a point of visiting my aunt first, she's almost a hundred and not exactly *compos mentis* these days. She's in a nursing home just outside Blandford Forum. I normally stay at *The Fox*; it's a small, old coaching inn on the edge of town. I've spoken with Humphrey Morgan Sinclair; he's now living with his son at

Blandford St Mary. I have arranged to see him at two o'clock tomorrow."

"Then I'll leave first thing in the morning. Do you have a mobile phone?"

The professor pulled a face. "I do, but I hate them," he replied.

"It's just that I need to let you know when I've arrived," said Harry.

"Oh very well, I'll make sure I take it with me," said the Professor, handing Harry a slightly crumpled business card with his mobile number on it. "I'll put the scroll away safe and see you tomorrow."

The Knights of Black Chapter

Lewis Ford arrived in the USA under a tight security blanket, escorted by two CIA agents, after being lifted from the SS California. His arrival in Washington was by way of a private jet from Miami. Ford then spent the next four days recuperating, undergoing medical checks and being subjected to a gentle grilling by Nick Leigh in the security wing at the CIA building.

"Well now, you look more like a human being than the last time we met," said James Parker with a wary smile. "I hope you're finding the Washington rats a little more to your taste."

"That was quite a dramatic exit you guys put on, it cost a good guy his life," replied Ford sternly.

James Parker took a sip of coffee from the mug he was holding. "Yeah, and not just the priest's. That FA18 pilot took no prisoners - everyone in the yard was blown away, including the governor and some lady official from a government department. So we've got the mother of a diplomatic incident on our hands. See the lengths we go to when it comes to getting our heroes back."

Lewis Ford looked hard at the shirt-sleeved director. "What a pile of bull shit. If I wasn't needed for this job, I'd be in a five foot pit with a heap of dirt for a blanket by now."

"Okay my friend so let's get down to matters at hand," said James Parker, pulling up a chair to sit at the table close to where Ford was relaxing, now dressed in a dark blue track suit with a gold-threaded insignia of the Intelligence and Security Command, Arlington Virginia, emblazoned on the left breast.

Parker placed a file on the table and opened it. "The FBI desk here in Washington have a young Iraqi woman in custody, apparently she's been living in New York for the past two years. The rumour is that she was a girlfriend of Mohammed Abu Atif, your target."

"How long have they been holding her?" asked Ford, lighting up a cigarette from a pack of Camels.

"Ever since the bombings, but she's in isolation, currently detained incognito."

"Then let her go, if you think she's going to co-operate from a detention cell, you're very much mistaken."

James Parker waved away a cloud of smoke that drifted in front of him. "Okay so what are you suggesting?"

"Secretly drop her back in New York, then keep her under protective surveillance, and I mean protective. There's no way she'll tell her community she's been detained by the FBI and then simply released; because those bastards will think she'd changed sides and rather than run any risks they'd kill her. Let things settle down and I'll take it from there."

James Parker's smile masked his anxious expression. "That could be difficult," he said.

"Oh I get it," said Ford. "You think if you release me onto the New York streets, I'll take a hike and all this will be for nothing. Let me tell you pal, if this lady's been that close to Abu Atif, her knowledge could be instrumental towards a successful outcome, but the only way of getting her on our side is by winning her trust. She knows how vulnerable she'll be back out on the streets, that's where the deal will be done, that's if there's a deal to do of course."

James Parker stood up and in one violent move he kicked the chair he'd been sitting on, right across the room. Lewis Ford remained motionless and unimpressed. "I've got the entire political machine on my back right now. Time's not on our side, the President wants things to happen, especially after our wonderful gung-ho navy destroyed half the fucking east coast of Brazil" shouted Parker, waving his arms in the air.

Lewis Ford smiled calmly. "And I haven't even discussed terms yet," he said, stubbing out his cigarette.

The file described Parseena as a highly intelligent young lady, the daughter of a Sunni saffron grower. She had graduated at Cambridge University, where she read politics and economics.

"How the hell could a saffron grower afford to send his daughter to a top western university?" remarked Ford, glancing briefly at James Parker.

"Search me; perhaps he had a bumper crop that year."

Lewis Ford shook his head. "Since early childhood she would have followed the Shari'ah, the code of Islamic law. The Shari'ah prescribes a complete set of laws for the guidance of mankind so that Good (Ma'ruf) may triumph and Evil (Munkar) disappears from society. Her beliefs would have been like those of the majority of the Muslim people. Shari'ah or Allah's Law is complete and perfect and covers all aspects of human life. Shari'ah is permanent for all people all the time; it never changes either by time or conditions. Drinking alcohol and gambling for example is not allowed under Islamic law. This can never be changed or tampered with, unlike a manmade law that changes to suit circumstances and time. This girl Parseena would have been brought up to believe that Allah was the creator of all laws and that Allah's laws are for all nations, all countries and for all time, Universal. Shari'ah has two other sources: Ijma' - consensus - and Qiyas - analogy, or reasoning on the basis of similar circumstances. Mankind, however, bastardised parts of the teachings of the Qur'an to replace universal peace with hatred. Being caught up in such a situation, a young person, I guess like this gal, could soon bring on a spirit of hatred and be put forward towards a bright future by fundamentalists. But this would start from a very young age, encouraged by the political side of the Muslim faith. Let's look at a few real facts. There are a billion people professing the Islamic faith; over fifty countries have populations that are predominantly Muslim. Islam is the world's fastest growing religion; especially in the post communist world of materialism and decadence, Islam makes sense not only to the poor and oppressed but also to Muslims who seek justice and morality. Then we have the Islamic fundamentalist who the West sees as fanatical and who believes in terrorism. To the Muslim, it's seen simply as a return to the purities of Islam."

"Now, Mr Director, you and I both know fundamentalism is not restricted to Islam. Fundamentalist movements have been gathering strength throughout various religions right across the world. Remember the bombings in Oklahoma City in 1995? The US put out a response that Muslim terrorists were involved, when in fact it was American white terrorists who carried out the atrocity. Let's face the facts, the West is crapping its pants about the power of Islam. Our fathers were wrong to predict that the clash of mankind would be between capitalism and communism. The real clash is between Islam and the West, and buddy you've seen nothin' yet."

"The thing is, the Muslim world is fragmented, thank God. It has many shades of politics and opinions and, let's be frank, why the hell should we really fear a creed that puts such a heavy emphasis on the values of family life and upright behaviour? The US, with all its morals, should welcome an alliance with Islam; after all they have such a lot in common."

"But the Western hatred goes back to the crusades. You sound as if you have regard for these people," remarked James Parker.

"I have, that's because I've lived with them and studied their ways, rather than being blindly ignorant of their teachings. True Islam is a very tolerant tradition, a thing that the zealots forget. Trouble is people have always taken the bits they want from religion and ignored the parts they don't like."

"Let this gal go, Mr Director. I'll get her to co-operate. Now, are we going to talk Turkey about reward? I rather fancy a small, secluded island with a hammock strung up between a couple of palm trees and a bunch of olive-skinned ladies mixing Manhattans all day long."

James Parker smiled. "Your share of six million bucks will buy you enough Manhattans to sink a battleship."

Later that day James Parker was on the receiving end of twittering remarks from Bud O'Dowd, after explaining why he was recommending Lewis Ford and Parseena be set free. O'Dowd sprang to his feet, having listened intently to the Director's explanation. He gripped the phone and pressed it hard against his chubby face then paced across his office until the phone wire became so taut it dragged the body of the phone off the desk.

"Are you kidding me? We're actually going to let this maniac go free to wander around the streets of Manhattan? We need this guy's arse in the Middle East. Now. I don't care what happens then, he can take out Abu Atif and half the goddam Middle East with him for all I care, just get him out of the US fast, those Brazilians will soon figure out Ford's body's not amongst the wreckage."

James Parker, on the other end of the phone, looked up at the ceiling then down at his office carpet, trying to control his frustration. "Look Chief, if the President wants this job doing, plans need to be put into place. We need to give Ford his head, but only to a degree of course. How's our cousins doing, have they got their man on board yet?"

O'Dowd hesitated briefly before responding. "They got a guy in the frame, that's all I know. I presume you're going to shadow this Lewis Ford?"

"Absolutely, he'll be watched twenty four seven, trust me," vowed James Parker.

The Knights of Black Chapter

Parseena was driven to the outskirts of New York from Washington, in a closed car. "Why are you letting me go?" asked the attractive girl with the wide, chocolate-coloured eyes.

The agent whose job it was to sit alongside her during the journey smiled. "Because we're the good guys, once we know who we have in the can and have done some checking, we let people go so they can get on with their lives."

"Yes and hell's just frozen over. Have you any idea the level of danger I'm going to be in?"

The young FBI officer glanced at her attentively. "Why do you think we're going to all this trouble? We could have given you a Greyhound ticket and sent you on your way."

The girl looked a little more at ease with this recognition of her predicament.

"Do you intend staying in the US?" he asked.

Parseena shrugged her slender shoulders. "I'm not sure. Why would I want to leave, I have a good job teaching English at High school... that's if they'll take me back?"

Getting Parseena back onto the street was done via a rehearsed storyline and a number of disguisable routes that ended at La-Guardia airport. Her purported return had been from a flight that had just arrived from Atlanta where she had been visiting an American couple she had met at University. Everything had been made to fit, including her name appearing on the passenger list. Now on her own she was free to return to the apartment on New York's Lower East Side, that she shared with another teacher. The experienced FBI agent appointed to keep a close watch on her followed every step she took, at a safe distance, and in turn Lewis Ford tracked his movements at an equal distance.

Parseena's home was on the fourth floor of the apartment building, on a street of identical properties with their fronts fenced off with heavy wrought-iron railings, approached by a dozen steps leading up to heavy front doors. The hot night enticed a number of residents out onto the steps, some were engaged in idle conversation, whilst others played Gin Rummy or threw dice against the dirty stone façade.

Lewis Ford watched from the distance of the street corner, as the black, African-American agent, dressed in a flower-patterned shirt and broad trousers, merged in with the locals. In fact within minutes he was tossing a ball into the gloved hand of a young baseball hopeful.

The Knights of Black Chapter

Lewis Ford booked into Matilda's Boarding House right across the street from the apartment building.

"Have yeah got a room at the front?" he asked of the buck toothed black lady he presumed must be Matilda.

"No, sorry, clean out of front rooms. I can give yeah a real nice room on the second round back, the trains won't bother yeah none from there," she said with a smile.

"It ain't the trains, honey; I just can't stand the backs of buildings. How much have I got to pay to get a front room?"

Matilda gave Lewis Ford the evil eye. "I told you, man, I got nothin' up front."

"Tell yeah what, whatever yeah charge for a front room, I'll pay double. Now you look like a real good businesswoman to me, what do yeah say?"

Matilda pointed a long black finger at Lewis Ford and smiled. "I'd say there's a bigger reason than just not wantin' a front view."

Ford laughed. "You are one hell of an astute lady, do yeah' know that? As well as bein' a real businesswoman, you know you're absolutely right. See my wife has been having this affair with a guy who lives across the street, I'd dearly like to catch her going into his building."

She looked at Lewis Ford square on. "You know what; I hate infidelity, I'm going to help you, my man, I'll move the guest from 242, you can take that room. It'll cost yeah three times the normal rent, and a week on account."

"What?" shouted Lewis Ford.

"That's the deal, 'cause I don't hate infidelity that much... and you want it an' I've got it."

The room was dark and dingy with a bed, side-table, chair and a kitchenette, but the bonus was more than Ford had hoped. The view was spectacular, right into Parseena's apartment.

Lewis Ford had been given a mobile phone and a direct report line to an agent by the name of Chester Ferguson. Later that evening Ford made a call. "Hi Chester, tell the big man I'm lodged across the street," he said glancing from his window both up and down the street. Earlier he'd seen an FBI agent slip into a blue Chevrolet parked to the left about half a block away. The car was still there an hour later. "Tell Mr Parker he can call off the cavalry, I'll handle it from here."

Chester took a few moments to reply. "The problem is," he replied eventually, "that the FBI are under a different controller, the Director of the CIA has no authority to call these people off."

Lewis Ford became impatient with the bureaucracy. "I don't care what formalities are needed, I want that Chevrolet off the street otherwise I'm not going to play ball, that is unless the car's full of Muslim fundamentalists."

"What are you talking about?" responded Chester.

"Look if Parker wants a swift outcome, he can stage a fake assassination attempt on Parseena."

"I'll call the Director right away," replied the agent.

Lewis Ford's phone went dead. He snapped it shut and put it in the breast pocket of his shirt. Not more than five minutes had elapsed before the phone began vibrating against Ford's chest.

"Mr Ford, I understand you've come up with an interesting proposition?"

"Well Mr Director, I don't plan to stay in this shit place any longer than necessary. If you guys can stage a situation, say a mock up of an Al Val Sinda visit... put the frighteners on her, nothing physical mind... I'll go across the street and blow them away. They'll play dead and I'll have the gal with nowhere to go, except with me."

"Okay, I can do that, give me twenty four hours. I'll call you."

"I'll need a gun filled with blanks of course."

"Okay, like I said, twenty four hours," replied James Parker.

Ford kept a regular watch on Parseena's apartment through a powerful pair of binoculars, but, apart from her watching television, everything remained quiet.

Ford's phone rang just before two in the morning,

It was Chester. "I have the specimen you require," he said.

"Okay, where are you now?" replied Ford.

"Two blocks down from you in a dark blue Honda Civic."

"Okay, stay put, I'll be down."

"The FBI are still staking the street, so be careful."

Ford peered as far as the restriction of his window would permit. "How long does it take for some simple co-operation?" he said.

"God knows. The FBI are free-radicals on this one," replied Chester.

Lewis Ford was at street level within a couple of minutes. The Chevrolet could be seen easily, down the street to the left, a short distance away. Ford turned right, quickly skipping past two drunken men struggling to hold themselves up as they staggered to make a modicum of headway in the same direction as Ford was heading. He hoped the confusion of darkness and the two drunken men would mask him from detection.

He eventually saw the dark blue Honda at the kerbside. The window began opening on the driver's door as he approached. He could make out a bald headed man at the wheel.

"Chester?"

"Got it in one," replied the man in the car. Ford went around to the passenger door and got in. The pungent smell of vanilla from an air freshener stung Ford's nostrils.

"Here, one Browning automatic, complete with a clip full of blanks," said Chester handing Lewis Ford a small paper parcel.

"Good what time's the hit?"

"Not sure yet, the Director's handling this personally, he'll call you in plenty of time. Realistically, we're talking tomorrow night, late."

"The FBI are still hanging around, they could screw up the whole deal," said Ford eyeing up Chester, who was a larger-than-life character around his mid-forties and by the look of his waistline he'd spent far too long behind the wheel of a car. As he turned towards Ford the smell of garlic on his breath was intoxicating.

"As I said we have no control over the FBI, however the message will get across eventually."

"Yeah, whatever," replied Ford opening the door to seek fresh air.

"Just make sure you keep your phone on and wait for the call," said Chester as he drove slowly away.

After taking an early ham and egg breakfast at the café around the corner, Ford spent much of the following day keeping a watchful eye on Parseena's apartment. At four o'clock his mobile rang. It was James Parker to say everything was arranged and that the deed would be carried out at eleven precisely.

"How about the FBI, Mr Director, they're still on the case."

"I know, but they have been briefed. They'll not make a move unless anything goes wrong. Three men will arrive in a black Lincoln. Two of them will go into the apartment building, they will bring the girl out, and that's when you can make your move."

"Okay I need a car parked right across the street," replied Ford.

"That's no problem I'll have one parked up by seven."

The Knights of Black Chapter

"Can you please make sure its fast," said Ford.

"Naturally, and we'll have the key left under the drivers foot mat." replied the Director.

Exactly at seven that evening, a green Grand Cherokee drew up between a parked car and a truck. The driver was Chester Ferguson. He tapped the top of the vehicle's roof, to indicate that that was the one and slowly walked across the street and eventually out of sight.

By nine o'clock the street was fairly quiet especially as it was raining. The Grand Cherokee was now the only vehicle for some distance in either direction. Lewis Ford left the confines of his room and cautiously walked down onto the street. He noticed the Chevrolet, still parked up in the same place. Ford shook his head and smiled as he climbed into the Grand Cherokee's seat and after throwing out the air-freshener he started the engine and drove up the street, taking the first turning on the right. After making a three-point turn he parked right up on the corner, which allowed him a clear view down the street towards Parseena's apartment building and the Chevrolet some distance beyond.

At five minutes to eleven the black Lincoln slowly drove down the street, parking right in front of the apartment block. Ford watched as two men left the back of the car, they glanced briefly up at the building; one was carrying a baseball bat in his hand.

Ford started the Grand Cherokee's engine and then slowly drove up the street and parked directly outside the boarding house, opposite the Lincoln. The occupant behind the Lincoln's wheel nodded at Ford as he passed. The apartment building was fairly quiet except for the muffled sound of raised voices coming from an apartment on the first floor.

Lewis Ford stood for a moment outside the door of Parseena's apartment, at first there was little noise then came a woman's scream. With that Ford hit the door with his shoulder and burst in. Parseena was sitting on a chair, one of the men was standing behind her, holding the baseball bat across her throat, whilst the other was brandishing a knife in his hand. The corner of Parseena's mouth was bleeding and her left eye looked bruised and swollen.

Ford pointed the Browning at the man with the baseball bat and fired, he fell back spectacularly with a spray of blood splashing up the wall. The other lunged forward with the blade of his knife pointing directly at Lewis Ford who let off two rounds at point blank range before the man could reach him; he instinctively fell to his knees clutching his chest before dramatically keeling over in a heap on the floor.

"Quick," said Ford, grabbing Parseena by the hand. "Don't ask any questions, just run."

Within seconds they were at the front door. The entire apartment block was alive with activity; some occupants were rushing down the staircase towards the street. Ford and Parseena used this as an opportunity to be swept away in the rush. The driver of the Lincoln threw the car into gear and screamed off up the street at a roaring pace.

Ford pushed Parseena into the Grand Cherokee's passenger seat then ran around to the driver's side and as he did so he could see the Chevrolet leaving the kerb and heading straight towards them.

"Who the hell are you?" shouted Parseena as she looked back toward the fast approaching car.

"I'm your fairy godfather, the name's Lewis Ford and right now we have the FBI on our tail, so fasten your seat belt, this could be a wild ride."

Ford was doing seventy by the time they passed the spot where he'd met Chester. And after crossing the Brooklyn Bridge he began reaching speeds of ninety miles an hour. He turned left onto the Queens Expressway and by the time he crossed back onto Lower Manhattan by way of the Manhattan Bridge, heading towards China Town, the Chevrolet had gained on them and was now close behind.

Lewis Ford reached alarming speeds as he drove through the relatively narrow streets, crossing one street after another. He swerved to avoid a passing truck, smashing the left wing of the Jeep into a stationary car. He then spun the Grand Cherokee around to face the oncoming Chevrolet, and hit the accelerator. The Cherokee lurched forward with smoke streaming from its screaming tyres. The FBI in the Chevrolet had nowhere to go but backwards or take a direct head-on hit from the madman in the Cherokee. The driver took evasive action and threw the car into reverse gear then accelerated at top speed, the car flew backwards at an alarming pace heading straight towards the Lafayette cross roads. Ford thumped both the front and rear near side wheels up onto the sidewalk and accelerated hard, just as the back end of the Chevrolet reached out into the busy Lafayette traffic.

Ford steered directly at the offside front of the car, smashing into it. He then progressed to push the vehicle at speed into the oncoming traffic. A huge Big Mack truck scooped up the Chevrolet like a paper bag and carried it sideways for at least fifty yards up the street, the car spun round onto its roof and then was bowled right over again. It continued to roll with sparks flying from its screeching body and from the airbrakes of the truck that was desperately attempting to stop.

Then, as if a gust of wind had picked up a leaf from the ground, the Chevrolet flew into the air and descended into the pathway of the northbound traffic and then just lay there on its roof waiting to be hit. The impact took no more than a couple of seconds to happen as a yellow cab had no choice but to strike the car at an angle, and was sufficient to spin the car around several times like a propeller.

Lewis Ford smiled as Parseena eventually emerged from the Cherokee's footwell; she then scrambled back onto the passenger seat.

"Well that'll keep 'em busy for a while," said Ford turning the battered Grand Cherokee onto the Southbound Lafayette, towards East River Drive.

The text message Lewis Ford received on his mobile was from Nick Leigh to say that a room had been booked at the Claremont Hotel on Lexington; they were to leave the Grand Cherokee as soon as possible and take a cab.

Lewis Ford pulled up in a tow-away no-parking zone, close to the Williamsburg Bridge. He climbed out of the car and went around to the crumpled passenger door, and with some effort he eventually forced it open.

"Come on," he said to Parseena, who simply sat there bewildered.

"Where are we going?" she said, her eyes streaming with tears.

"Somewhere safe, by the time your friends learn that their guys have been blown away, your life won't be worth a plug nickel."

The Indian cab driver looked at the two with a curious expression.

"I know its tough but try and look happy," insisted Lewis Ford. "We're going to play the part of lovers about to spend the night together, so act as if you're eagerly anticipating a wonderful time, even though it's bull shit."

Parseena forced herself to half-smile as she climbed into the yellow cab. Lewis Ford put his left arm around her shoulders and then pulled her towards him.

"I'm acting so don't resist," said Ford as he looked through the heavy plastic screen between them and the driver, whose bloodshot eyes were watching their every move.

"Well don't attempt to get an Oscar on my account," Parseena said, reluctantly leaning into Ford's embrace.

The twenty-dollar journey to the Claremont was uneventful with neither Lewis Ford nor Parseena saying a word to one another.

The receptionist had been expecting them and after Ford gave her his name a plastic room key in a cardboard wallet was handed over without the usual formalities of registering and the scanning of a credit card.

Ford zapped the key through the locking mechanism and opened the door onto the blackness of the room. He took the Browning from the wasteband of his trousers.

"Wait here," he said as he carefully entered the room, a quick scan showed no one was lurking inside. After checking the bathroom he finally inserted the card into the switch on the wall close to the bathroom door, which activated the lights.

"I need food," said Ford glancing at his watch.

"Its four thirty in the morning," exclaimed Parseena. "And I want to know who the hell you are?"

"I told you, I'm your fairy godfather, a Knight in shining armour. "

"You must be an agent with the FBI, I thought it strange, being let go just like that."

Lewis Ford smiled as he picked up the phone and called reception. "Can I have two breakfasts? how do you like your eggs?"

Parseena looked at him square in the face."Shove your eggs," she said.

"That's two eggs sunny side up, heaps of crispy bacon, orange juice and lots of black coffee, thanks."

Having placed the order with reception Ford sat down on one of the twin beds and turned towards Parseena. "Lady, do you really think I'm with the FBI when they've been chasing us right across New York for half the night?"

Parseena collapsed down on the other twin bed with a frustrated expression on her face. "Oh! I don't know, so if you're not with the FBI then who the hell are you with, and if you mention fairy godfathers once more I'll scream."

"My name's Lewis Ford, I'm a bounty hunter looking to make the big kill."

"Kill! Kill who?" shouted Parseena at the top of her voice.

"Mohammed Abu Atif, replied Ford calmly. The look that ran across Parseena's attractive face was one of utter fear.

"And sweetheart, you're going to help me take him - alive or dead, I don't give a shit."

"I don't know what you think I can do," she replied.

"Look, it's common knowledge you were one of his women for quite a long time."

"Oh no I was not!" said Parseena defensively.

"Look honey, let's cut the crap and get down to some serious chitty chat here. I've wasted two guys that were clearly sent to cause you untold heaps of pain and if you think the mean machine will give up, you're out of your mind. So you need me just as much as I need you. I can get us both out of the States in no time; all you have to do is to agree."

"What happens to me if you succeed, which you won't?"

Ford smiled. "You'll be well looked after, a change of identity, money, whatever you need."

Parseena looked sceptical. "That's a lot of promises coming from a just bounty hunter."

"Yes, well maybe not everything's as it seems."

"So you're working for the Government, and that's why I've been treated so well."

"Look I am a bounty hunter, at least I am now; whoever pays me and ultimately pays you is immaterial. You play ball and you'll live, if you don't I'll throw you back where I found you, and you know what that'll mean, you'll be dead by this time tomorrow. Such a waste."

Lewis Ford stood up from the bed after hearing a gentle knock on the door. "That'll be breakfast."

They sat in silence whilst Lewis Ford tucked into a plate full of bacon, eggs and a pile of neatly cut triangular pieces of toast. Parseena simply picked without eating much of anything.

"Eat! Because God in heaven knows when we'll get to eat again." Ford said through a mouthful of food. "So you came here to the States on a visa as a teacher, teaching Muslim kids English, but that's not all you've been teaching them is it? You teach them how to pick pockets and steal people's handbags and stuff, like regular little Fagins. All the loot then gets sucked into the big machine and swallowed up to fund terrorist activities." Ford looked hard into her face and then shook his head several times.

"No, no I don't think you'd have been involved in converting young guys into walking bombs, but that'll be just one department away. Tell me; are you still under the influence of Mohammed Abu Atif?"

"Once you get caught up in the web, you get consumed forever," Parseena said softly.

"How did you get sucked into the Al-Val Sinda?"

Parseena took a sip of orange before answering. "My father had great hopes for me, I was seen as a bright student so he spoke to my uncle who was some sort of government official. I was sent to college in Baghdad and from there I graduated. I had no idea my education was being financed directly through the Al Val Sinda. I was then sent to England to study at Cambridge and spent three years there in total innocence until just before I graduated. That's when two gentlemen paid me a visit; the one of them introduced himself as my benefactor. That night, the night of the Graduation Ball, I had been booked into a hotel off the campus, that's where the bastard raped me, the first time." Tears began flowing down her slender face, like a waterfall. "It happened after the Ball; I had such a pretty pink dress with a tiny bow in front. He was the perfect gentleman until it was time to say goodnight outside my room. Then he just bundled me inside and tore my dress to shreds. He'd paid for it so I suppose he thought he could do what he liked. "

"You say the first time, how many times were there?" asked Ford, sounding like the concerned father.

Parseena looked at him, rubbing tears away with the heels of both hands, but more replaced them. "Four... four times altogether," she sobbed."

"The bastard, he needs fixing," said Lewis Ford gripping the e.p.n.s fork until it bent in his hand.

"Well he's not very far from here. If you make sure he comes to an unhappy end I'll help you find Mohammed Abu Atif." A faint smile appeared for the first time on her tear stained face.

"You're asking a tall order," replied Ford

"Well those are my terms," Parseena said in a determined voice.

Lewis Ford carefully wiped his mouth with a napkin. "What's this guy's name?"

"Muhammad Sunan Tirmidhi. I know his address if you want it."

"What's he doing here?" asked Ford, ignoring Parseena's direct question.

"He's a banker, very successful, in fact he's a director of the Kuwaiti bank on Fifth Avenue. He's also behind the syndicate directing the recruitment of young fundamentalists."

"I need to make a call, right now," said Ford standing up from the small table. He walked across the room towards the door.

"Sunan Tirmidhi is a powerful man, he has friends in influential places," said Parseena.

"Does he now? Okay eat some food, I'll just be in the hall," said Ford opening the door.

"Put me through to the Director," said Lewis Ford, surprised that someone else had answered James Parker's direct line. The phone went dead for a couple of minutes.

"Good morning Mr Ford. Right now I'm taking this call in the shower, just in case you can hear running water. What can I do for you today?"

"I've got a problem, have you ever heard of a guy by the name of Muhammad Sunan Tirmidhi?"

"No, never heard of him, why, should I have done?"

"I need him eliminating."

"Fine and apart from this triviality, is there anything else I can help you with this side of breakfast? I've got to say Mr Ford you don't hang around with your requests, you've been on the streets for no longer then forty eight hours and already, you've scared the good people of an apartment block shitless, Christ knows how much damage you've caused with your stockcar racing routine. Oh and did I happen to mention the three FBI agents you almost killed? They'll probably be on sick leave for at least a couple of goddam months. New York's too small and peaceful for a guy like you."

Lewis Ford dismissed the sarcasm and continued. "Look, this guy Tirmidhi seems to be behind a terrorist cell right here in New York. They're training young fundamentalists in the art of self-destruction. Plus he's raped Parseena on several occasions. The only way she'll co-operate is if he's sent to the happy hunting ground."

"Look Lewis I appreciate your predicament, but I can't just go around eliminating people, on the say-so of a young girl just because she's been raped a few times."

"Mr Director this is no ordinary girl, she can lead me directly to the target, or not if she won't co-operate... and besides for all we know this fundamentalist group might well be behind the bombings."

"Okay I take your point, how about if we meet you halfway. Say we bring this guy in and put him in isolation until you're safely on your way, you could tell Parseena the jobs been done."

"Yeah know I thought of that, but she wants proof of the deed," said Ford lying through his back teeth.

"I'll check him out and get back to you. By the way, you'll be flying out to Cyprus via Paris, leaving Kennedy at seven o'clock tomorrow evening. An agent will bring you a package of goodies, first thing tomorrow," Parker said before closing down the call.

Ford returned to the bedroom. Parseena had fallen asleep on one of the single beds. He covered her over with the quilt from the other bed and drew the curtains, shutting out the now quite strong sunlight. It was close to two o'clock in the afternoon when Lewis Ford's mobile began ringing.

"Well," commenced the CIA director, "we've tracked this guy Muhammad Sunan Tirmidhi down. You're right, he's quite a fella in banking circles. He lives a good lifestyle in an expensive Upper East Side apartment close to Central Park, he's got one son currently at high school, aged sixteen, and it seems just the one wife.

"The FBI have had a monitor on him ever since the bombings, as indeed they have upon all middle-eastern immigrants."

"Has he got a bunch of thugs protecting him?" asked Lewis Ford.

"Don't think so. According to the FBI he leads a normal social life, goes to the gym, runs in the park, that kind of stuff."

"I don't suppose you're going to tell me where he lives?"

"No Mr Ford I'm not, the best I can do is to have him picked up and held under alien interrogation law. If he has been encouraging fundamentalists he'll go away forever... least ways we'll hold him until you guys have left the country."

"Okay Mr Director, it's a deal."

Ford gently shook Parseena who nervously leapt off the bed, still half asleep and for a moment unaware of her surroundings.

"Hey, take it easy, you *are* jumpy. You say you've got the address of this guy Sunan Tirmidhi?"

Parseena nodded her head. Lewis Ford took a pencil and note pad from the bedside table. "Okay I want you to describe this guy in as much detail as you can."

"Unfortunately I know him intimately," said Parseena, walking over towards the bathroom. "I need some clothes, I've got nothing to wear."

"Later, we'll get some for you," replied Ford. "Have you ever been to his apartment?"

"No, but I've met his wife and his spoilt brat of a son."

The door of the bathroom closed and Ford heard the lock draw across, then the sound of the shower flowing. He went and stood by the bathroom door, then leaned on the wall close enough to make himself heard. "Do you know which gym he's a member of?"

"Not really, but I know he jogs a lot, especially first thing in the morning, with his friend."

"Friend, who's his friend?"

"He's Tirmidhi's bodyguard, and his gay lover. I don't know his name."

Parseena eventually appeared, wrapped in a large bath towel, a smaller towel was wrapped around her head like a turban, holding back her long black hair.

"Get dressed we're going shopping," said Ford, "then I want you to show me where this guy lives."

The shopping trip onto 5th Avenue was briefer than Parseena had hoped, however. Having Lewis Ford almost fixed to her side like a Siamese twin was embarrassing especially in the Sears lingerie department and particularly when he insisted on sitting outside the fitting rooms.

As for Ford, he bought himself two pairs of jeans, three shirts and four changes of underwear, all in the space of twenty minutes.

"Okay, toiletries department and then we're off," he said collecting up the shopping bags in one fell swoop.

Back on the street, Ford stopped at a florist's and bought a dozen red roses: the florist gift-packed them in a cellophane bag with a large pink bow. The card simply said 'To Mrs Tirmidhi, thank you'.

"What are you going to do with those?" asked Parseena.

"You'll see," replied Ford as he hailed a yellow cab that drove them to the fashionable Upper East Side, just off Madison Avenue.

"That's his apartment block there, number 1222," said Parseena.

"Okay wait in the cab," said Lewis Ford as he picked up the flowers from the seat. He leaned towards the driver's open window. "I'm just dropping these off to a friend, I won't be long. Stay here," said Ford pointing to Parseena.

The commissioner in livery and top hat smiled politely.

"Just dropping these off to Mrs Tirmidhi."

"Go right ahead, sir, third floor."

Ford took the elevator to the third floor and alighted into a hallway that smelt of hugely expensive new carpet. He found apartment 1222 just a few paces down the hallway. Ford knocked on the door. A short, thin-featured girl who looked no more than thirteen eventually opened the door.

"Hello, I have a delivery for Mrs Tirmidhi."

"Thank you," said the girl, holding out her hands to take the flowers.

"Sorry my instructions are to give them to Mrs Tirmidhi in person."

"Who's that? My wife's not in," said a voice from within. The man who appeared at the door matched Parseena's description exactly. Ford therefore knew the man in front of him was Muhammad Sunan Tirmidhi.

"What do you want," he said in a gruff matter-of-fact voice, the remains of a mouth full of food spilling from his lips as he spoke. He muttered something in his native tongue to the young girl who Lewis Ford presumed must have been a servant; she bowed her head as if being scolded and then scurried away.

"I've been asked by the florist's to deliver these flowers to Mrs Tirmidhi."

"Thank you, I'll make sure she gets them," he said then abruptly closed the door in Ford's face.

At precisely 4.00am the following morning the hired car was parked across the street in full view of the apartment block. At six o'clock two people emerged through the revolving doors, they stood briefly under the canopy for a while talking and then began setting off at a steady pace. Tirmidhi was quite portly and therefore his jogging looked more like a painful robust walk.

The other man with him was much leaner, a little taller, and far more agile. Before they disappeared into the park, Lewis Ford left the car and began to jog after them. Ford's pace soon took him within fifty yards of the pair who began drifting slightly apart, the younger man quickening his pace as they approached a fork in the path. Tirmidhi took the left path whilst the other man took the right. Lewis Ford beamed with approval and started to run across the grass moving well to the left of Tirmidhi.

   Within a few minutes Ford was parallel with Sunan Tirmidhi who by now had reduced his pace to nothing more than a purposeful walk. Keeping him clearly in sight Ford sprinted in front but remained on the grass at least fifty feet to the left of the path. He continued at this pace until the path began to bend towards him, but he was now some distance in front of Tirmidhi. Two joggers and a man with a large scruffy dog were approaching. Ford could also see that the path turned sharply to the right which meant it would eventually rejoin the other pathway and presumably Tirmidhi's companion, who obviously preferred to run the longer distance, would then appear. Ford gave the two middle-aged joggers a friendly smile as they passed in front of him, heading towards the now tiring Tirmidhi. Ford then caught site of the man and his dog as they left the path and began heading towards a clump of trees.
   Ford began trotting slowly, keeping a distance behind the two joggers. Within less than a minute they were passing Tirmidhi, and as they did so, they acknowledged him with a friendly wave. Ford stopped, and spread his feet about a metre apart; he then bent over and placed both hands on the ground and began taking deep breaths as if the exertion had been too much for him. With his head now fully down Ford was able to peer between his legs to see if anyone was coming up the path behind. Then as Tirmidhi approached to within inches, Lewis Ford struck. He caught Tirmidhi with a perfectly targeted roundhouse karate kick, striking him on an exact spot on the temple; his victim fell in an instant.
   Ford quickly looked around before winding his left arm around the unconscious man's neck. He then dragged Tirmidhi's deadweight across the path. He was able to pull him into the cover of some bushes just as he began to regain consciousness and as his faculties began to return. Instinctively, Tirmidhi began to struggle and scream.
   A sharp upward blow with the heel of Ford's left hand, at the bottom of Tirmidhi's nostrils, sent the bone in his nose shooting upwards like an arrow straight into his brain. Tirmidhi's body fell limp, his head dropped to one side and his

eyes bulged from the shock of the bone's direct penetration. His mouth then fell open, expelling foul air. Conveniently, a scar of about two-inches in length was clearly visible upon Tirmidhi's left cheek. Lewis Ford took out his knife, opened the blade and cut a chunk of flesh that included the scar from Tirmidhi's stark face. The body began to violently convulse as if the remainder of life was beginning to reluctantly ebb away. After extracting the deep chunk of facial tissue, Ford slipped the flesh into a plastic bag and then made his move.

He was soon back on the path and jogging towards where he presumed he would eventually see Tirmidhi's companion. The man was sitting on a park bench not more than a few hundred yards away; clearly waiting for Tirmidhi to arrive. Ford simply smiled and jogged nonchalantly past. He then gradually increased his pace to that of a full sprint until he had left the park and was back on the street. He then casually climbed into the hired car and drove slowly away. Just as he did so, two men arrived at the park bench where Tirmidhi's companion remained seated.

"FBI! You're under arrest for murder," they said, as one showed the surprised man his badge and the other the open end of a 38 magnum.

"What, you can't just arrest me, you American scum, my partner will be here in a minute, and he's got influence."

"I don't think so chum," replied one of the FBI agents, "You've just killed him!"

10

By the time Harry had given Clarissa a few last-minute instructions about what to say to a prospective Dutch buyer who had shown interest in a heavily carved court cupboard, it was almost ten o'clock.

"Annie, just to let you know I'm going to Dorset, I'll be away overnight and I plan to be back in Wales by tomorrow evening."

"Hello Harry, sorry I was busy texting."

"No worries, I was just leaving you a message. I'm off to Blandford Forum, I'll be back tomorrow."

"Oh I thought you said you were going to Dorset?"

"Annie, how come you were able to entirely skip geography when you were at school? Blandford Forum is in the county of Dorset."

Harry heard a giggle at the other end of the phone. "I knew that really. Have a good trip."

Harry decided it best if he picked up the M5 at junction seven; that would mean he could take the A44 through Crossgates, Pembridge and Leominster where he knew a number of antique dealers and where he felt a spot of business might be had. He followed the M5 south until it forked off at the M4 intersection. The further east he drove the busier the M4 became. He was therefore somewhat relieved to see the signs for junction 17 that would take him off the motorway and down the A350 towards the town of Blandford. Curiosity compelled him to stop off at Shaftsbury, where he bought two treen items from a large antique centre. It was therefore gone six o'clock when he finally pulled the van into the Fox Inn car park.

The Fox's interior was a mass of low black beams, some of which bore polished post-horns and horse brasses. Harry followed the signs that led him to the tiny reception area. He rang the hand bell on the counter top and within a couple of minutes a young woman appeared through a beaded curtain.

"Hello," she said, offering Harry a broad smile. "How can I help you?"

"I have a reservation, my name's Harry Blakemore."

The Knights of Black Chapter

"Ah yes, Mr Blakemore, you rang to say you would be late, no problem. You're in room 14." She gave Harry a registration card to fill in. "How will you be paying Mr Blakemore?"

"By credit card. Can I get anything to eat?" he asked, suddenly noticing the long case clock was just about to strike nine o'clock.

"I'm sorry, the kitchens are closed. I could get you a sandwich or perhaps you could pop into town, there's a very good Indian that stays open late."

Harry pulled a face. "Okay, thanks. Can you tell me if Professor Thomas is in?"

The young woman frowned. "I'm not sure, hang on a mo'." She went down the guest list. "Do you know when he was supposed to book in? I've just come back off holiday."

"Last night, as I understand," replied Harry.

"Well Mr Blakemore, I don't see his name on the guest register. Hang on." She picked up the phone and dialled three numbers. "Oh hi, sorry to trouble you. Do you know if we have a guest booked in by the name of Professor Thomas?" The response must have been brief because within a few seconds she had replaced the receiver. "I'm sorry Mr Blakemore, the Professor apparently had a reservation but someone called and cancelled it yesterday."

Harry Blakemore looked surprised and just a little concerned. "Thank you," he said, taking a key from the young woman who pointed him in the direction of the stairs that bore a sign saying 'Residents Only'.

Harry threw his bag down on the bed then took the mobile phone from his pocket. He placed the crumpled card the professor had given him on the bedside table and dialled the mobile number. There was no response. He re-dialled and again, but nothing.

"The stupid old bugger's probably got a pay-as-you-go and it's run out of cash," he said to himself, before phoning Clarissa. "Hi have you heard from the professor?" he asked as soon as the phone was answered.

"No, why?" replied Clarissa.

"Because, I've arrived at The Fox only to discover that his booking was cancelled yesterday."

"Perhaps he stayed with his aunt instead?"

"I doubt it," replied Harry, "She's in a nursing home." There was a brief pause before Clarissa replied, "Well sometimes these nursing homes have a family room for relations to stay in when they have a long distance to travel."

"Do you know the name of the nursing home?" asked Harry.

"No I don't, can't you raise him on the mobile?"

Harry shook his head in frustration. "Negative, he must have let it run out of credit."

"Okay let me call Mrs Jones, his housekeeper; he'll have spoken to her I'm sure. I'll give her a call and phone you right back."

Harry went back down to reception and rang the bell. The young woman re-appeared through the curtain.

"Your offer of a sandwich, is it still on?"

"Of course, would you like it brought up to your room?"

"Thank you that would be nice and perhaps a pint of beer?"

"No problem, give me a few minutes," she replied, disappearing back through the curtain.

By the time Harry had returned to his room, his mobile had begun ringing. "Hi this is Harry."

"Well, I've spoken to Mrs Jones and she's not heard from him," said Clarissa, sounding worried.

"You don't think he's flogged the scroll and done a bunk do you?" said Harry.

"Don't be so bloody daft, I'm sure there's a logical explanation," replied Clarissa, sounding cross at such an unreasonable suggestion.

No sooner had Harry switched off his phone from Clarissa, when there came a knock on the door. He opened the door to find the young woman holding a tray; a dinner plate was filled with assorted beef and cheese sandwiches and a large-handled glass was frothing at the rim with beer."

"Thank you," said Harry. "Tell me, do you know of a nursing home close to here?"

The young woman thought for a moment. "The only one I know of is Claredon House. Its about ten minutes walk away from here," she replied.

"I'm still looking for the Professor and it was suggested he may have stayed there last night."

The young lady smiled,"Well you could ask the owner, if he hasn't already left, he was in the bar not more than ten minutes ago."

"Fantastic", replied Harry. "What's his name?"

"Mr Walcott, Mr Roger Walcott."

The Knights of Black Chapter

Harry took the tray and carefully put it down on a small table. "Can you point him out to me? By the way what's your name?"

The young woman smiled shyly. "Margaret, but everyone calls me Maggie."

"Right Maggie, please lead the way." Harry followed her downstairs and into the bar. She walked over to where two men were sitting.

"Mr Walcott, this gentleman would like a word." She turned and smiled at Harry.

"Thanks Maggie. Hello I'm sorry to bother you only Maggie tells me you keep Claredon Nursing home."

"That's right I do, why?"

"Well I believe a friend of mine has an old aunt living there, he was coming down to see her and I was supposed to meet him here this evening but he hasn't turned up."

"What's his name?" asked the man a little abruptly.

"Thomas, Professor Thomas," replied Harry.

"That's Nora Bethridge's nephew."

"Yes that's right, have you seen him, is he staying at your place?" replied Harry.

The man shook his head. "No, but he popped in yesterday, late."

"What time would that have been?" said Harry.

"Around seven, he stayed for about an hour and told his aunt he'd drop by today."

"And did he?" asked Harry.

"Not as far as I know. I was in Shaftsbury this morning, got back about twelve. His Land Rover wasn't in the car park so he'd either been and gone while I was away or he hadn't turned up."

"Have you ever heard of a man by the name of Humphrey Morgan Sinclair?"

Roger Walcott shook his head.

"I have," said a man sitting next to Roger Walcott. "He was our family's accountant years ago."

"Do you know where he lives?" asked Harry.

"Yes, up the road from here at Blandford St Mary. He lives with his son and daughter-in-law at the old vicarage."

"How do I get there from here?" asked Harry.

"Simple. Turn left out of the car park, go up the lane for about half a mile then take the first turning on the left, you'll see the village after no more than half a mile. The vicarage is the first turning you come too on the right...there are large white gates opened right back, you can't miss it."

Harry looked at the clock above the bar. It was almost ten o'clock. He thanked both men and left The Fox. He then opened his van and climbed inside. "Clarissa I'm concerned, something sounds spooky," said Harry after explaining about the Professor's strange disappearance. "I'm going to see if I can talk with this Humphrey Morgan Sinclair bloke."

"Yes, well leave it until the morning, its almost half past ten," said Clarissa.

"Okay your probably right, I'll go first thing in the morning."

They bid each other good night and Harry switched off his phone. He sat in the driver's seat of his van for a while, cogitating. "I think I'll just do a bit of a reckie," Harry said to himself as he started the engine. Within ten minutes he was outside the white gates, which were wide open just as the man in the pub had described. The house must have been some distance up the drive as it was not visible in the darkness. Harry parked the van and walked up the driveway until he could see the outline of a large house. The entire place appeared to be in total darkness. He continued up the drive, passing neatly trimmed lawns that disappeared on both sides into black obscurity. Harry noticed the curtains were drawn in two of the upstairs rooms. To the left of the house was a large building that would have possibly been the coach house and stables in the house's hay day.

Harry took a small torch from his pocket and pointed it through a gap in the coach house door. As his eyes became accustomed to the light he caught sight of what looked like the professor's Land Rover. He tiptoed back down the lane. "So that explains why the Professor cancelled his room at The Fox; Humphrey Morgan Sinclair must have invited him to stay at the Vicarage. They'd probably got so engrossed in talking about the scroll that they lost all sense of time," said Harry, muttering to himself as he drove back to The Fox. He returned to his room, drank his now quite flat beer, ate a few sandwiches and then went to bed.

By eight thirty the following morning he was back at the old vicarage, this time he drove the van right up to the door. As he got out of the van he glanced up at the bedroom windows which had had their curtains drawn the night before. The old bell-pull to the left of the door failed to draw anyone's attention so Harry used the large brass ring on the Lion's mask to give the door a hearty knock.

Eventually a thin man in his mid-forties came to the door. He was clearly partly dressed for a city job, with striped trousers, a white shirt, university tie and braces. The napkin in his hand suggested that his breakfast had been interrupted.

"Good morning, I'm sorry to trouble you, is Professor Thomas here?"

The man looked puzzled. "I'm sorry, Mr?"

"So sorry, " replied Harry, "my name's Harry Blakemore. I'm a friend of Professor Thomas, I understand he might have stayed here last night."

"I'm sorry Mr Blakemore, I have no idea who you are talking about. I've never heard of any Professor Thomas."

Harry looked puzzled and more than a little frustrated, he wanted to say that he had seen the Professor's Land Rover parked in the old coach house, but thought it best if he refrained from doing so. "Is this where Mr Humphrey Morgan Sinclair lives?" he asked.

The man's face instantly straightened into a serious expression. "I am Humphrey Morgan-Sinclair."

"No, the one I'm talking about is an older bloke," said Harry looking him square in the eye.

"Then that would be my father, who on earth are you?"

"I told you, I'm a friend of the Professor's. He came to Dorset to see your dad and it seems he's now vanished into thin air!"

"Sorry, I can't help you," replied the man who began to close the door.

Harry placed his hand firmly on the door to prevent it from shutting. "Hang on a minute, can I have a word with your dad, perhaps he knows where the Professor's gone."

"I'm sorry, Mr Blakemore, my father's unwell, he's rarely able to leave the house these days and has not communicated with anyone outside our immediate family for a long time, now if you'll excuse me, I've a train to catch and I'll be late. Please remove your hand from my door."

As Harry removed his hand, the door was closed, leaving him alone on the step. He climbed into the van and drove off down the drive, but instead of turning left, he turned right and parked about fifty yards up the road towards the village and phoned Clarissa. He told her about the Professor's Land Rover and the cool reception he got from Humphrey Morgan Sinclair's son. "Hang on," said Harry as he saw a silver coloured

Mercedes estate car leave the drive, turning left at top speed. "Got to go, talk to you later," he said, closing his mobile.

Harry left the van and walked towards the old Vicarage. He first looked through the gap in the coach house door, as far as he could see the interior was empty. The Land Rover had gone. Glancing around he made his way stealthily to the rear of the coach house. The cobbled yard led towards the back of the house where a number of hanging baskets were hung. They made an impressive show with a variety of summer flowers bursting out over their edges in a blaze of colours. Harry peered through a tiny window into almost pitch-blackness; a larger window near the back door must have brought light into what presumably used to be the boot room.

An inner door was open sufficiently for Harry to see a woman in what was obviously the kitchen, who he presumed must be young Sinclair's wife. He was just about to move to a third window when he spied an old man. He was smartly dressed in a sports jacket and a gold coloured waistcoat, with a watch chain stretched across both pockets. A silk handkerchief flopped casually from his breast pocket, and a bow tie was neatly tied around his neck. Harry could clearly see he was busy in conversation with the woman. Their mutual reactions suggested he was articulate and, when she laughed, funny as well. Not exactly like his son had described!

Back at Harry's room in The Fox a note had been pushed under his door. It was from Maggie to say that a visitor had called whilst he'd been out. Harry skipped down the stairs and rang the reception bell. A middle-aged man appeared through the bead door.

"Good morning," he said.

"Good morning is Maggie around?" replied Harry.

The man smiled and shook his head. "No I'm afraid not, she's off duty now until this evening. Can I help?"

"I'm not sure," replied Harry. "I had this message slipped under my door." He showed the man the message.

"Oh... then you must be Mr Blakemore. Maggie's my daughter. Yes, a priest came into reception, not more than a few minutes after you left this morning. He said that he'd call again later today."

Harry looked puzzled. "Did he say when?"

The owner of the Fox shook his head. "No, he just said to tell you that he would be in touch with you later today. "

"Did you see this priest?" asked Harry.

"Yes it was me who took the message."

"What did he look like?"

"Well I don't know... quite a thin chap, pointed features, about forty, dog collar, you know the usual thing. Bit of a scruff, I'd say. His hair was thin and looked greasy, I hate greasy hair."

"He didn't leave you with an address or any way of contacting him I suppose."

The man shook his head.

"Well thanks, have I missed breakfast? "

"No, go into the dinning room, I'll have a waitress come and serve you."

After breakfast Harry called Clarissa. "Have you heard anything?"

Clarissa replied that she hadn't and that neither had the Professor's housekeeper, Mrs Jones.

"Well I'm just going to wait here until this priest turns up. He must know something."

At nine thirty that evening Harry's phone began to ring. He left the room and took the call in the car park. "Blakemore," said Harry in a matter-of-fact tone.

"Mr Blakemore, I'm Father Macaroni, I need to see you urgently, please come to St Leonard's Church, it's just on the outskirts of Blandford Forum."

Before Harry could ask any questions the phone was dead. He did not feel like leaving the bar to drive to a church. He'd enjoyed a large steak and kidney pie with Cornish potatoes and plenty of fresh vegetables, all washed down with a couple of pints of real ale. He'd also been engaged in a spot of stimulating conversation with a farmer who might well be coaxed into selling a Welsh dresser he'd described as in crap condition and painted, lying in one of his barns. Just the way Harry liked them, cheap but easy to restore and worth a mint. Another pint would have sealed the deal, of that Harry was convinced. Now he was driving to a church and he had no idea where it was or why he was going. He first drove into Blandford Forum and stopped the van at a bus stop where three people were standing. He wound his window down.

"Anybody know where St Leonard's Church is?" he asked any of the three who might oblige.

"Go through town, take the second turn on the right and first on the left," said an elderly gentleman holding a tiny Yorkshire terrier under his arm.

Harry thanked him and followed his directions. In less than ten minutes he drew the van up alongside a graveyard, presuming that the church must be close by. He got out of the van and walked over to a very old lynch gate. Ivy had almost completely covered the entire roof and main supports, the gate itself was missing and the hedges were noticeably unkept. After some effort Harry scrambled through the entrance and stood on the pathway.

"Mr Blakemore," said a voice. Harry turned around to see a very thin man, just as the publican had described, standing on the path behind him.

"What's this all about and who are you?" said Harry, sounding quite annoyed.

"Please follow me," said the priest as he walked past Harry towards what were the ruined remains of the church. Despite it being well past ten o'clock there was incredible light on the ruins thanks to a new moon.

The priest suddenly stopped and faced Harry. "Mr Blakemore, what you are about to see might shock you, although I know you have seen much death and destruction in your life. Or should I call you Sergeant Bob Richardson?"

"Who the devil are you?" shouted Harry. He'd not heard his true name used for such a long time that it scared him.

"Never mind who I am, who's he?" The priest pointed to the strange figure of a man lying on a large tomb. The figure had been draped in a white shroud. As Harry looked closer he had a terrible feeling he knew who he was going to find wrapped in the linen. He carefully opened the blood stained shroud to expose the face.

"Holy Christ!" he shouted, stepping back from the body of Professor Thomas. Part of the professor's cranium was completely missing. All Harry could see was a large hole where congealed blood had turned almost black.

Just beyond where the body lay, close to what would have, at one time been the Eastern doorway of the church, a thick mass of blood and flesh smeared up the remains of the door. Two ornately carved wooden columns had been carefully placed either side of the Professor's head. Harry recognised them from the Masonic ceremonies he attended at the Masonic lodge, as being replicas of Boaz and Jachin, the columns that had formed the archway and entrance to King Solomon's Temple.

"This killing is a replica of the Third Degree, the murder of Hyrum Abif," shouted Harry.

The Knights of Black Chapter

The priest looked on as Harry rushed around finding more of the Professor's cranium at both the Southern and Western parts of the ruin. It was an exact depiction of the enactment. A five-pointed star representing Venus was suspended above the Professor's head.

"How... when did you find the professor?" Harry asked the priest.

"I come here to pray, it is a very holy place. The body was not here then."

"What time was that?"

"Around six o'clock," he replied.

On a flat gravestone embedded in the ground were a number of tarot cards carefully positioned into a figure of eight. The upper circle, nearest to the Professor's feet, commenced with the zero card depicting 'The Fool'. Next, in clockwise direction, was the number one card 'The Magician', then number two 'The Papess', then three 'The Empress', four 'The Emperor', five 'The Pope', six 'The Lovers', seven 'The Chariot', eight 'Justice', nine 'The Hermit', and finally, at six o'clock, the number ten card representing the Wheel of Fortune. At this point a second card had been carefully placed to partly cover the ten to form the lower circle. It was the number twenty one representing 'The World'. Then the lower circle continued... card twenty 'Judgement', nineteen 'The Sun', eighteen 'The Moon', seventeen 'The Star', sixteen 'The House of God', fifteen 'The Devil', fourteen 'Temperance', thirteen 'Death', twelve 'The Hanged Man' and finally eleven 'Strength'.

"What does all this mean?" exclaimed Harry, dropping down on both knees to examine the strange arrangement of tarot cards in front of him. Then, for some reason, he suddenly thought of the ring. He clambered to his feet and opened the shroud surrounding the Professor's body. The legs had been purposely crossed, the right over the left. The arms were bent at the elbow and resting across his chest. The wrists were lashed together so that the palms of his hands would remain clasped, as if in prayer. The little finger of the right hand had been unceremoniously hacked off. The ring was missing.

Harry felt a hand grab his right shoulder.

"Stop right there. Back away and do it slowly." Instinctively Harry did exactly as he was told. "Put your hands behind your back," commanded the voice. As Harry did so he felt cold metal encircle each wrist and tighten as handcuffs were locked into place. When he looked up he could see that the ruins of the church were now crawling with police officers.

A very smart looking female, with long blond hair almost touching her shoulders stood in front of him. "Is your name Harry Blakemore?" she asked in a cold, stern voice that seemed out of character with her childlike face.

"Yes! Who the devil are you?"

"I'm Inspector Caroline George and I'm arresting you for murder. Take him away."

"Hang on," cried Harry. "It wasn't me! I didn't kill the Professor. Ask the priest, he'll back me up."

"Priest? What priest?" replied the Inspector. Harry scanned the entire area only to find the priest had gone, vanished into thin air.

The Knights of Black Chapter

Three people arrived at John F. Kennedy airport in three separate taxis. Parseena was the first to alight at the departure terminal. She was now clothed in a burka, the garment commonly known as a shadier - a long tent-like veil that covers an Afghan woman from head to foot. Traditionally, such a dress was worn to cover jewellery whilst walking amongst poorer, village people - jewellery that was collected and worn as a symbol of wealth but only displayed privately amongst equals to reflect success in the family. But for Parseena the garment was specifically to discourage prying eyes.

Lewis Ford was next. Following the agreement between Pakistani officials and the FBI on the ground in Pakistan, Ford was provided with papers that permitted him to join one of the Afghan Technical Consultancy teams. Recognised ATC teams sponsored by non-government organisations were deployed to help rid Afghanistan of its reported several million land mines, left there from the Russian invasion. The Taliban government allowed ATC members into Afghanistan beyond the perimeters of Kabul, recognising the important work undertaken. This cover would provide Lewis Ford with access into the country's interior.

The third person to arrive was JoJo Curtis. The President himself had recommended that JoJo should attend as the official observer and report back through a special communication channel, networked directly to the White House.

"JoJo, I know you've been hoodwinking me about your age ever since I took office. I also know you're in a pile of financial crap up to your neck, therefore I'm going to do you a big favour. I'm going to recommend you go to the Middle East as a close observer and report back on these two guys we've assigned to remove Mohammed Abu Atif from the planet.

"JoJo, this man must be turned into history, I personally want you to play a role in that. Upon your return you will receive honours befitting a man with such a distinguished service career, a significant lump sum in cash and a suitable pension that will see you right for the rest of your life."

The Knights of Black Chapter

Jo Jo Curtis was cock-a-hoop; this was his big chance to sort himself out. And in acknowledgement of this opportunity he arrived at Kennedy with a head-bursting hangover, having spent a celebratory night throwing double Bourbons down his neck in Mickey's bar.

Both the British and Americans had been targeting a number of places in Afghanistan where it was believed Mohammed Abu Atif had planted military installations and training camps. Sea and air Cruise Missiles were launched to show the world they would not just sit and wait for the United Nations. Someone had to pay for the atrocities in New York and London, and for the destroyed aircraft.

The designated target, Mohammed Abu Atif, was immensely wealthy from private means. Born in Kuwait, he was the youngest son of an oil rich family. He had left the country of his birth in 1980 to fight the Soviet invasion of Afghanistan under the American sponsored Afghan jihad and the Mujahideen. Ironically and embarrassingly, none other than the CIA had trained Mohammed Abu Atif in security procedures. Having proved an exemplary student, he had been a thorn in the side of America ever since.

While Mohammed Abu Atif was in Afghanistan he had founded the Al Val Sinda as a resistance group, with the full approval of the Taliban government. Following the Soviet withdrawal he used his millions to turn the wrath of Al Val Sinda towards the west and transformed the movement into one of the most powerful terrorist groups in the world. Lebanese, Egyptians, Turks, Iraqis and Iranians were soon recruited in their thousands, and thousands more were joining Atif's Afghan Muslim Brotherhood in their struggle against an ideology that spurned religion.

As soon as the Soviet Union withdrew from Afghanistan, Al Val Sinda had turned its attention towards the United States and its allies in the Middle East. The intention was that Mohammed Abu Atif and his Al Val Sinda would be part of an International Islamic Front who would bring together Egyptian, Saudi and other groups in a rallying cry for the liberation of Islam's three holiest places: Jerusalem, Mecca and Medina. What with this and his suspected high rank within Incanda, Mohammed Abu Atif might soon become the world's most dangerous man, especially with his associates spreading at such an alarming pace over forty countries in North America, Europe, Asia and the Middle East.

According to Parseena, Mohammed Abu Atif was approximately forty-nine years of age and had five wives. Lewis Ford's objective was clear; to make sure Mohammed Abu Atif would never reach the half-century!

Flights were being taken from New York to Karachi in Pakistan via Paris, after which Parseena was to take a flight to Kandahar in the hope of applying for a position in the teacher-training centre, a place built to prepare teachers for work in secular education. Lewis Ford was to journey to Kabul, in the guise of a landmine removal consultant, to obtain the necessary papers from the Taliban.

Lewis Ford and Parseena met as arranged at the foul-smelling men's lavatory in Karachi airport. He bundled her into a cubical for some last minute instructions. "I'm staying in Peshawar town, I've booked into the Pearl Continental Hotel until I get clearance to move across the borders into Afghanistan, I want you to call me the minute you arrive in Kandahar. Do you know where you can stay?"

Parseena nodded. "I have a cousin who lives there, I'll stay with her."

"Good, I want you to find out as much as you can about that Al Val Sinda training camp you taught at."

"Such as?" replied Parseena sarcastically.

Lewis Ford grabbed her by both her arms and pulled her towards him in one frustrated gesture. "Look, I need to know anything that might provide me with a clue to Atif's whereabouts. Keep your ears open and your mouth shut. You have my security call signal, use it regularly and remember you are going to be watched, the US have men planted everywhere. All eyes will be on you, if you make a wrong move or try a stitch up, you'll be dead."

He increased his grip on her arms to intensify the point.

"And keep your mobile phone hidden at all times. Only use it to call me or take calls from me and keep it on vibration only mode. Now, I'll check that the coast is clear and signal when it's clear for you to leave. Then go straight to the flight desk and book your ticket - and keep veiled."

Peshawar Town was a filthy place with lots of beggars on the streets with smashed up or amputated legs and arms; some the result of de-bombing escapades across the border in

The Knights of Black Chapter

Afghanistan. Most of the streets were covered in donkey dung. They were full of frontier police, Pakistani Army personnel, local tribesmen and Afghan Mujahideen aid workers.

JoJo Curtis found the five star Khyber International Hotel next to the plush green of the neighbouring golf course far more to his taste and booked in under the assumed identity of an international journalist. The hotel was remarkably comfortable, and as JoJo was not a practising Muslim and possessed the necessary permit with his passport, he could purchase alcohol whenever he felt like it.

Lewis Ford booked into his somewhat less comfortable hotel and immediately called Doctor Abdullah Guru, his prearranged contact, who was to lead the team of ATC consultants who were soon to embark on a trip to Kabul to resume their highly dangerous job of de-bombing.

Doctor Abdullah Guru was a thin wisp of a man in his mid-fifties who smelt strongly of garlic. He smiled when Ford introduced himself and bowed politely. His handshake was weak and feeble but for some strange reason Lewis Ford took an instant liking to him. They sat together in the hotel's over-chilled, air-conditioned lobby.

"I am very pleased to welcome you to our group, it is good to know Western people care for these war-ravaged lands."

"I'm pleased to be of help Doctor," replied Ford as he called a waiter to order drinks.

"Oh please call me Abdullah," said the extremely polite man who accepted a glass of hot, sweet tea.

"Will it be difficult to obtain a permit to work with you guys?" enquired Ford after the drinks had arrived.

Abdullah shook his head. "No, not as you are joining our team, we are formally recognised and indeed sponsored by the French Red Cross, therefore how can they deny a westerner a permit - after all you will be doing the country a service at the risk of your life. Although I think the risks you will be taking may have much more serious consequences," said Abdullah nodding his head slightly. He then smiled and sipped his tea.

Lewis Ford returned the smile; words between them were not necessary at that moment. "Please stop and have dinner with me," insisted Ford, picking up a menu from a table close at hand. Abdullah thanked him and accepted a mutton curry, whilst Ford ordered the beef curry and rice. Abdullah excused himself and went to pray before the meal. Ford took the opportunity to call Parseena, but her phone was dead. In frustration he returned the mobile phone to his pocket just as it began ringing.

There was a loud bleeping sound followed by a series of high and then low pitched notes as if someone was attempting to play a piano with just two fingers and no ear for music. Ford dialled in the security code, connecting him with Parseena.

"Where are you?" he asked.

"I'm in the compound close to the school in Kandahar, I'm staying with my cousin's husband's family. "

"How were you greeted, have you been questioned?"

"I've been accepted by the family with no problem, and no, I've not been questioned. I have a meeting tomorrow with the Malik; he's the headman of the town."

"Then you know what to say. Have you had a sniff about any Al Val Sinda members?"

There was a pause before Parseena replied. "Sorry about that, there were a number of people passing me. This place is crawling with Al Val Sinda, in fact my cousin's husband's brother is an Al Val Sinda officer. As a matter of fact I'm meeting him tomorrow, there's to be a big family dinner. I'm sure my cousin's husband thinks it's about time I was married off, perhaps he's lining me up for someone. He's got no chance!"

"Then find out as much as you can, we'll speak tomorrow." Lewis Ford switched off his phone just as Abdullah was returning from his prayers.

The next morning Ford was up early, he swam several lengths of the pool, then completed a hundred press-ups on his knuckles. He then did a further hundred, this time with his entire weight on just three fingers of each hand.

Back in his room, Ford wound the hemp rope that he carried everywhere around the upright foot post of the colonial bed, so that it could be used as a Milwalki to repeatedly punch and thereby keep the broken gristle of his knuckles in good trim - knuckles that had been crushed into tiny fragments and that had subsequently re-grown into one solid mass that now resembled the head of a lump hammer.

Lewis Ford gripped the fingers of his left hand tightly so that the tips were almost embedded into the top of his palm; he then turned the hand into a fist and closed his thumb over the fingers, locking his hand into a piston-like ram. He then struck one violent blow after another directly onto the rough rope of the Milwalki, firing his hand palm uppermost from his hip at speed then twisting his fist just before each devastating impact. The turning action and straight arm intensified the strike power ten fold. After a hundred hits that became faster each time, he reverted to the other hand and repeated the exercise.

At precisely 7 am Ford was in the restaurant digging into half a dozen lightly scrambled eggs, bread and tea with honey and lemon. It would possibly be the last meal that resembled anything western for some time.

The ATC group consisted of fifteen consultants who assembled on the Kabul road close to Ford's hotel. The convoy comprised of four long- wheelbased Land Rovers, heavily laden with equipment. Ford sat in the lead Land Rover after accepting the offer from Abdullah.

"We must stop off first to have our clearance certificates stamped," he said.

Peshawar was one of the few ancient cities in the subcontinent to have retained its original complexion. The centuries old grandeur and the blind alleyways were enclosed by dilapidated ramparts. The convoy passed through one of the principle Darwazas (gates) on its way to the official building where it eventually came to a halt at a place called Fackeyrabad on the outskirts of town, where the headquarters of the Hazb-I-islami Mujahideen was situated. A number of old Buick taxis were parked outside in the rarely fulfilled hope that an official or two might require a ride to the airport. The interiors of the weary looking vehicles were full of bright pictures, mostly of the drivers' families, and the windscreens were framed with strings of beads.

It took the best part of an hour for the papers to be officially stamped. The convoy then returned to Peshawar where it stopped at the Shah Faisal Mosque on the Karahoram road for prayers. Ford left the heat of the vehicle and stood on the roadside to smoke a cigarette. It was almost noon before the convoy got properly underway on its substantial journey along the Khyber road to Kabul.

The papers and passport Ford had been supplied with that bore the name Richard Carson, passed him through the border guard post successfully and without a hitch. The Khyber road was not exactly of western highway standards and had collapsed in a number of places. Large potholes and lumps of tarmac had been torn up by tracer fire from gun ship attacks on the many convoys of trucks that had attempted to keep the arteries of the country open during the war against the Soviet

Union. The wreckage and remains of burnt of vehicles still littered the roadside as a reminder of that wasteful war.

"I understand you have weapons?" asked Lewis Ford following one of the many stops they made en route.

Abdullah nodded. "We do, but it's unsafe to break them out until we have crossed the border. If you don't mind we'll wait until we arrive in Kabul."

The years of the Afghan war with the Soviet Union had cut a wound so deep into the very fibre of the country, that some said the festering scars would never heal, especially as the Taliban government was now in control of over ninety percent of the country.

Eventually the convoy drove across the dilapidated bridge over the almost dried out Kabul river and into the walled city of Kabul, that seemed to climb right up the side of the mountains.

That evening the Land Rover convoy parked up in the compound of the Serena Hotel and four safety guards were placed to watch over the vehicles. Lewis Ford booked into a room and almost immediately took a long bath to wash away the dirt and dust of the journey. He then wrapped a hotel robe around him, lit a cigarette, poured himself a generous level of whisky and then strolled onto the balcony.

He afforded himself a rare smile as he watched JoJo Curtis unfold his aching limbs from the back of a taxi. JoJo placed both hands firmly on each hip and arched his numb back, looking up he saw a solitary figure standing on a balcony peering down at him. Ford raised his glass in acknowledgement. JoJo's reaction was to quickly instruct the taxi driver to gather up his luggage and follow him into the reception area.

As a large proportion of the hotel was being refurbished Ford would have put money on the fact that JoJo would be put in a room on the same floor. He therefore opened his bedroom door just sufficiently to see him being ushered into the room next door but one.

Ford poured himself another whiskey and returned to the balcony. The gap between his balcony and JoJo Curtis's was no more than four feet. Ford relaxed in a comfortable, teak armchair filled with soft cushions. Eventually JoJo appeared on his balcony.

"Good evening, you must have been sent as my observer?" remarked Ford as he stood and walked over towards JoJo.

"Have I blown my cover already?" JoJo remarked.

The Knights of Black Chapter

"You blew that back at Kennedy," replied Ford with a chuckle.

"Well I'm not the fucking secret service type anyway, I'm here just to watch the action," said JoJo.

"Then you'd better be more agile than you appeared getting out of that taxi... from here on in, it's uphill all the way."

"Don't you worry about me, my friend, I'll be just fine."

"Good, then perhaps you'll have dinner with me this evening?" said Lewis Ford calmly.

"Well I don't think that's such a good idea do you - us both being seen in the same dinning room could send out the wrong message."

"Who said anything about dinning in the restaurant? I thought a cosy meal out here on the balcony would be more appropriate.

"Tell me, what's a guy your age doing on a job like this, you should be tucked up in some Florida retirement condo'," said Ford after their meal had arrived.

"Well let's just say I love travelling on shit roads and eating crap curries," replied JoJo. "Where to next, or do I have to find that out the hard way?"

Lewis Ford looked JoJo fully in the face. "We're leaving about noon to head right up into the Hindu Kush Mountains, I hope you've brought your thermal knickers, its pretty cold up there, or perhaps the CIA have put a helicopter at your disposal."

"You must be kidding, this is cheapville and besides I take my orders directly from the President himself, not the CIA."

JoJo eventually spat out a piece of mutton onto his fork after continually chewing on the grisly meat without even marking the surface.

"Are you sure you're here just as an observer, or is it something much more sinister?" asked Ford after taking a sip of beer direct from the neck of the bottle.

"What do you mean?" replied JoJo, frowning.

"Well... yeh know, although this is a low key affair on the surface, the big guy back in Washington is personally keen for a successful conclusion."

"And you think I'm here in a more productive capacity, which I'm not. In fact I can tell you straight, my orders are specifically to monitor movements only."

Lewis Ford smiled over the top of his curry-loaded chapati. "Oh, okay," he said. "But if I were guessing I'd say you're here as a decoy, a sacrificial decoy. I'd even go so far as to lay money on you travelling under a very similar name to me, I've been given the name Carson, what's yours?"

JoJo Curtis looked visibly shocked. "Carson! But they wouldn't do that to me, it must be coincidence, I'm retiring after this, the President is personally arranging my package direct."

"Yes but you could get body-bagged out here, that's also a kind of retirement, the cheap kind. The hero, lost without trace if things go wrong. So, good buddy, watch your back. I'll help you survive but I need transparency from you, lets both come out of this and retire into the sunset, stateside. I think Thirty Three Degree Masons should stick together don't you?"

After the dinner Richard Carson, alias Lewis Ford eventually wished a somewhat worried JoJo Curtis, alias Roger Carson, goodnight.

At 5 am the next morning the compound was alive with AT.C men checking out their equipment in preparation for the journey. The lead Land Rover had been emptied of its equipment and the metal floor panels were lifted to reveal an arsenal of weaponry and ammunition. A number of Kalashnikovs were clearly visible and what appeared to be a small quality of Heckler and Koch G3 rifles. Lewis Ford moved the Kalashnikovs to one side in order to get at a Heckler and Koch G3.

"Well if the Limey ever appears he'll be cock-a-hoop with these babies," said Ford under his breath, knowing the G3 was a popular weapon of the SAS.

"Would you like that rifle?" asked Abdullah with a smile.

Lewis Ford stroked the G3's stock as if he were affectionately petting a long lost kitten. "I would indeed. This weapon fires 7.62 x 51 rounds of ammunition, do we have such a resource on board?"

Abdullah smiled. "Of course," he replied.

The Taliban officials treated the paperwork as a mere formality, concluding that the ATC men would probably blow themselves to smithereens or at best leave a substantial number of their body parts spread across the landscape. Official passes had been issued the night before en block so that the convoy was now ready to proceed.

Lewis Ford sat in the front seat of the three abreast Land Rover to await the contingent of ATC men attending prayers before setting off. He'd checked out of the hotel and enquired if his brother Roger was still in residence. The reply confirmed that Mr Carson was indeed still in the hotel after spending most of the previous night drinking in the lobby.

Ford glanced up towards JoJo's room which was in pitch darkness. He therefore presumed the observer was in deep slumber, especially as he thought the convoy would not be moving until mid-day. Lewis Ford smiled to himself just as he felt his mobile phone vibrate. He looked around to see if Abdullah and the rest of the crew were still out of earshot before taking the phone from his pocket. The call sign code was that of Parseena.

"Yes what is it Parseena, it's not a good time to call me at the moment."

"Sorry," she replied. "Only I spent last night at that family get-together I told you about and well, part of the time I spent fending off my cousin's husband's brother until he discovered that I had been involved with Mohammed Abu Atif. I told him that I was back in the country hoping to resume my role in a training camp. He told me that Atif is living at a village called Pashi, it's in the Kabul Province."

"Okay. Good girl. What are the chances of you joining another training camp?"

"Pretty good but very dangerous," she replied. "I've got to go," she said and instantly the line went dead.

It was almost half an hour before the ATC men returned to the Land Rovers. Lewis Ford slipped off the seat to allow Abdullah to slide across to be sandwiched between Ford and the driver.

"Abdullah I need to get to a village called Pashi, have you heard of it?"

Abdullah nodded. "I have, we are beginning our work at Vrdak, you will need to hire some help to take you up to the village, it's right across there." He pointed a bony finger towards the Hindu Kush Mountains. "Very dangerous, so I'm told, the pathways are narrow and the region is full of bandits. Al Val Sinda have a significant presence there also, still that's what you are here for, is it not?"

12

Harry Blakemore was allowed one phone call before being put into a detention cell deep in the bowels of Bournemouth Police station.

"Clarissa, I need to be very brief, don't speak just listen. This will come as a terrible shock to you but the Professor has been murdered and what's more the police think I was responsible. In fact I've been stitched up, but that's another story." Harry was forced to stop his revelations in full stream as Clarissa was heard to sob uncontrollably down the other end of the telephone.

"Clarissa, I know this is a terrible shock darling but can you grieve later, the cops have given me a minute and the clock's ticking. Firstly I want to assure you I had nothing to do with the Professor's death and secondly I'm convinced Incanda murdered him. I think our Mr Humphrey Morgan-Sinclair and his son are involved up to their armpits. They must have suggested the Professor visit them, then killed him after taking the scroll. They probably hid the Land Rover until someone could collect it. I saw it around ten thirty last night and when I went back to their house this morning it had gone."

Harry could hear a semi-controlled sob as Clarissa was attempting to control her sorrow. "I know you wouldn't do such a terrible thing Harry. Mrs Thomas had a visit from four men, late last night. They forced their way into the house and ransacked the place."

"So maybe they didn't get the scroll off the professor, which means they must still be looking for it?"

"Poor Mrs Thomas was bundled into a room and tied to a chair, she said they were in the house for hours. Fortunately the postman found her and sounded the alarm. Harry what can I do?"

"Nothing yet. If we start blaming a bunch of Knights called Incanda for the Professor's murder, the police will think we're away with the fairies. One thing you can do is to make sure the police in Wales know what's happened to the professor and then they can start talking to the cops down here."

The Knights of Black Chapter

"Okay time's up," said a burly looking sergeant. "The inspector would like a little chat with you my friend," he said, leading Harry to an interview room that comprised of a metal table with one end pushed towards the wall where a recording device was positioned. A solitary tin ashtray was strategically placed in the centre of the table.

"Take a seat, that one," said the sergeant, pointing to the chair facing the door. With that in walked Inspector Caroline George, accompanied by two others, one in uniform who stood by the door with his arms folded. The other was dressed in plain clothes; the cheap herringbone suit belonged to a lean man in his mid thirties. His tired expression and heavy eyelids seemed to be begging for a good night's sleep. The Inspector on the other hand was exceptionally vivacious for the surroundings, in a pale lemon suit and a white blouse opened at the neck, just above the provocative level. She sat down and crossed her legs, exposing just a little knee. She placed a file on the table in front of her and then stared hard at Harry.

"So Mr Blakemore, tell me why you went to exceptional lengths to murder this man?"

Harry Blakemore stared back at the Inspector. "Do you know who I am?" he said eventually, after scanning her face for a weak point behind the facade.

"No, do tell. Are you the great, great grandson of Jack the Ripper?"

Harry shook his head and smiled. "Try asking MI6. My real name's Bob Richardson."

The Inspector smiled. "Yes and I'm Wai Wai Wong," she replied, flicking a switch on the recorder. "The time is 2.46 am, I'm Inspector Caroline George and I'm interviewing one Harry Blakemore on suspicion of murder. Harry Blakemore what is your relationship to the murdered victim?"

"I'm not answering any of your questions," said Harry with a half smile, attempting to conceal his frustration.

"Oh do come on Mr Blakemore, we have you banged to rights." The Inspector's body language was sending out a completely different message to the one that was coming from her mouth. Harry could tell she would soon become frustrated if he ruffled her feathers by his non co-operative attitude.

"Mr Blakemore," said the tired looking man in the shabby suit, as he came forward and rested both hands on the table and leaned over towards Harry, "You were caught in the act, now why don't you save us all a lot of time and trouble and tell the Inspector why you committed this crime?"

Harry looked hard into the officer's face. "Look stupid, the victim had the top of his head cut off, have you any idea how much blood that would cause? Whoever did this would be covered. As you can see, I've got no blood on me whatsoever, so do yeah think I'd have killed the Professor, nipped home to for quick wash and brush up, and returned to the crime scene just to hang around until you lot turned up? Don't be lazy, go find the Professor's murderer, but first I should get a good night's kip' 'cause yeah brain needs stimulating."

"Very good, so what you are saying is that you were simply passing by a ruined church, thought you'd just pop in for a quick pray and happened to find the victim, dead!"

"Exactly, you've got it in one. Keep this up and you'll go far," said Harry sarcastically.

The Inspector beckoned the officer away from the table with a flip of her hand. "Mr Blakemore, how did you come to be in St Leonard's churchyard at such a late hour?" she asked.

"Probably for the same reason as you lot, I was asked to meet someone there."

"Who?" replied Inspector Caroline George in a now less than calm voice.

"Some priest or other," replied Harry.

"Ah yes, the priest, a vision who must have miraculously disappeared into thin air."

"Why don't you have a word with the landlord of the Fox Inn, he saw this miraculous vision as well. The priest's name is Father Macaroni by the way."

Caroline George smiled. "Don't worry we will."

Taking the inspector completely off guard Harry suddenly flicked off the recorder. "Listen, I suggest you stop fucking around and contact MI6 like a good little girl, tell them you have Sergeant Bob Richardson in custody, otherwise you'll pounding the beat and that'll get your suit dirty."

The Inspector went pale and angrily pushed back her chair. "Take him back to the cells," she said, scooping the file from the table.

Harry dropped off into a restless sleep on a hard green mattress, with the smell of stale urine in his nostrils. He was awoken some time later by the echoing sound of keys being pushed into metal doors. The drunkards that had been rounded up the night before were now being released. Harry's door on the other hand remained locked. He did however receive a cardboard tray with a plastic cup half filled with

The Knights of Black Chapter

watered down orange juice and a paper plate containing cold scrambled egg on top of a piece of hard toast. The tray was despatched through a narrow slide at the bottom of the door. Harry left the tray untouched on the floor at the side of the bed.

It seemed like hours before his door eventually unlocked and two rather large men in plain clothes stood at the doorway. "Come with us," one said. They both dwarfed Harry who was escorted between them up a flight of concrete stairs, along a passage and down steps that led into a covered yard where police cars, incident vehicles and a number of seemingly private cars were parked. One of the men opened the back of a black Ford Transit van.

"Get in," said the other. As Harry did so, the doors were instantly slammed shut. The rear of the van was empty except for one seat towards the front, which Harry virtually fell into as the van suddenly lurched forward.

Three hours or so later the van pulled up in front of two large metal doors, which automatically opened to admit the van to continue into the bowels of New Scotland Yard. It finally came to rest after reversing up to the rear of an unloading bay. The back doors were almost immediately opened.

"This way," said a police officer dressed in a black close-fitting one-piece suit. A black webbing belt was tightly buckled around the officer's middle, which held a number of accessories including a gun holster. A bulletproof vest casually dangled on one of his shoulders. He wore a black beret smartly pulled down over the right eye.

Harry was put into a detention cell that was even worse than the one he'd experienced in Bournemouth. The bed was built of concrete and the combined stainless steel toilet and washbasin had been subjected to extreme violence and therefore rendered useless, hanging limply from the wall, suspended solely from its bent waste pipe.

After about an hour Harry suddenly heard the sound of a voice he'd not heard for a long time. Eventually the door was opened and in walked Jeremy Paxton-Smyth.

"Good God, Mr Paxton-Smyth, how you doing skipper?"

"Better than you, it would seem. What on earth have you been involved in?"

"I've been framed for murder, but I guess you know all about that, especially as now you're the head of MI6. What am I doing here?"

"It's called the system, we need to jump through a few hoops to bring you over to our side. You can make it easy for yourself or exceptionally difficult, depending on how you're going to respond to my proposition."

Harry looked away. "Skipper," he said, "I could really do with getting out of here, what's the deal?"

"Harry I need a little job doing in the Middle East."

Harry frowned. "What kind of a little job?" he said cautiously.

"We need someone eliminating that's all."

"Who," replied Harry.

"Chap by the name of Mohamed Abu Atif," replied Paxton-Smyth with a smile. Harry began to laugh and the more he thought about what he'd just heard the more he laughed. "Skipper, do you know what you're asking? An army of professionals protect this guy, at a location only God knows about. How do you think one bloke could even get close?"

Paxton-Smyth glanced briefly at his former sergeant then looked away. "There would be two of you."

"Skipper, why have I been put into this compromising position? I'm sure there's no actual personal vendetta between you and Atif, so what the fuck's going on?"

"Okay let me explain. Mohammed Abu Atif was directly responsible for the attacks on London and New York. The Prime Minister and President McCain are both internationally embarrassed over their Middle Eastern failings; these attacks have compounded these feelings across the world. If we deployed a joint operational strike force to rout Abu Atif out, the implications would be catastrophic. The job might be easily leaked and banner headlines would cause the attempt to fail... which would cause an even bigger issue, especially with the French and the Germans."

"A decision has therefore been made to send in two experienced men who are no longer directly associated with the military."

"You mean private cannon fodder," interrupted Harry.

Paxton-Smyth ignored the remark. "Both governments must be protected from any blame, should things go wrong," he said smiling.

"Now there's been a bounty on Atif's head for a long time. You'd be a soldier of fortune after the bounty, we'd just give you lots of help and back-up."

"And if it went tits up?" asked Harry.

The Knights of Black Chapter

Paxton-Smyth looked him straight in the eye. "You'd be dead and the government would be protected from any scandal."

Harry nodded his head slowly. "You never did mince your words, skipper. Look, I've cut out a nice life for myself in deepest Wales, why should I jeopardise all that for a job like this?"

"Because you were always up for a challenge, especially an exciting one, and a win would mean you'd never need to worry about money again. Just think of all the antiques you could buy with your share of six million."

"Tell me, skipper, what choice do I have?"

Paxton Smyth smiled and pushed his hands deep into the pockets of his trousers. He then began to slowly pace the tiny cell. "Possibly a life sentence for murder and let's not forget the probability of being pursued by Incanda, which would almost certainly put Ms Llewellyn –Jones at risk."

"You know about Incanda?" exclaimed Harry, looking surprised.

"Yes I was recently made aware of Incanda by an old gentleman on a boat in the Caribbean, since then I've naturally been doing my best to research that group as well as The Knights of Black Chapter. I find their mere existence bewildering and frightening to say the least. I am, Harry, aware that Incanda executed Professor Thomas, although the exact reason why is unclear. Maybe you can enlighten me?"

Harry looked at Paxton-Smyth, feeling a little uncertain, but said nothing. He simply shrugged his shoulders.

"Okay, Harry, my knowledge of Incanda is naturally very limited. However, I do know that it's most rare for them to show their hand like this, therefore their quest must have been substantial."

"You're not a member of Incanda are you skipper?" asked Harry.

Jeremy Paxton-Smyth laughed. "Good God no. But I do feel we need to find a way into their movement somehow."

"Well if you ask me, I think the Professor did find a way in, and it cost him his life," replied Harry.

"Clearly, but the question is how? What do you know about all this Harry, and what were you both doing in Dorset?"

"I'm a Freemason and the Almoner of my lodge; I received some regalia from the family of a recently dead Mason who held provincial grand rank. Amongst the regalia was a scroll encased in a bamboo and hemp bound baton. Clarissa and I took it to

Professor Thomas; he was able to open the scroll. It apparently contains vital information of a religious nature. There could also be some reference to Incanda."

"So that's why the professor was killed, they wanted the scroll."

"Yes, but I don't think they got it because they ransacked the Professor's house looking for it after they killed him."

"Then presumably the Professor hid the scroll somewhere."

Harry looked thoughtful. "Thing is, the Professor insisted on visiting a bloke by the name of Humphrey Morgan-Sinclair, who he was convinced knew a substantial amount about Incanda. This guy Sinclair was the cousin of some strange French artist who the Professor used to visit on Crete; apparently he was a Rex Deus member. They met through a secondhand signet ring that was formerly owned by the artist. If you check you'll find the Professor had the little finger of his right hand cut off, obviously the Rex Deus ring was taken when they killed the Professor."

"Okay so the Professor went to Blandford Forum to meet this Morgan-Sinclair person?"

"Exactly, and as he was taking the scroll with him, I said I wanted to be there. The Professor left the day before me; when I arrived at the local inn I was told someone had cancelled his booking the night before. I found Morgan-Sinclair's house late that evening. The Professor's old Land Rover was tucked up in an old coach house. Naturally I thought the Professor had decided to stay as a house guest, until the next morning when I found the Land Rover had disappeared, and I was told in no uncertain terms by a stroppy git who apparently was Morgan-Sinclair's son, that he'd never heard of the Professor and that his father was not fit enough to accept visitors.. which was a complete load of bollocks."

" I'll have this Morgan-Sinclair family checked out. So if Incanda don't have the scroll, who does?"

Harry again shrugged his shoulders. "Okay skipper, so you've got me here to talk about putting Mohammed Abu Atif to sleep."

"Yes," replied Paxton-Smyth, "but I think that scroll could provide an important link. I'm told that Incanda are indirectly pulling the strings in the Middle East, therefore if we can find a connection further up the Incanda chain of command, it might lead us to Al Val Sinda, the Taliban and Muhammad Abu Atif himself. Harry we need this man's head on a pole because he's gaining so much power and influence it's frightening soon he'll have vast numbers of what he calls his disciples of war spread right across the western world. He'll be able to co-ordinate attacks on any country he chooses, almost at will. Under Atif's direct control Al Val Sinda are becoming increasingly sophisticated; soon he'll just point to a spot on the map and have it destroyed."

"So why don't the British and US governments use their security to do the deed, they have mercenaries at core centres right across the Middle East. After all, both governments sponsor them, we all know that."

Paxton-Smyth looked defensively at Harry. "Yes we do, but so do France, Germany and a handful of other countries. In my opinion we should have no contact with any official organisation. And as far as this job is concerned we want to maintain a wall of silence. Mohammed Abu Atif must be relieved of life quietly and without fuss. If he suddenly goes missing his reputation of being a god will be put into question by his followers. If a security outfit takes him out, he'll become a martyred hero and another will soon replace him. "

Harry nodded. "I see your point," he exclaimed.

"The Americans have a man that would partner you, his name is Lewis Ford; he's been briefed and is about to fly out with a female who we understand used to be Abu Atif's girlfriend."

"A man like Mohammed Abu Atif would have many girlfriends, he'd just use them and throw them away afterwards," said Harry.

"I agree, but it would appear this one was somewhat more special."

"What's this Lewis Ford all about?" asked Harry.

"I don't know too much about him, he's an ex- Seal, a typical American macho tough guy I suppose… there'll be a report in your assignment notes."

"The last thing we'll need is a gung ho yank charging around the Middle East playing Cowboys and Indians," said Harry with a frown.

Paxton-Smyth smiled. "You said we, does that mean you're in?"

"For fuck's sake, skipper, do I have a decent choice?" replied Harry with a smile.

The men shook hands.

"Right, I need to get you out of here," said Paxton-Smyth as he banged on the steel door.

"Make it sooner rather than later, skipper."

"Leave it to me," replied Paxton-Smyth as the door was opened.

Within the hour Harry was removed from his cell and escorted, somewhat more politely, to an office where a change of clothes awaited him. Another closed car took him to the familiar basement car park below the MI6 building. He looked for the sallow faced attendant but there was a younger man sweeping the floor. Harry was escorted to the ninth floor by way of a back staircase and eventually into Jeremy Paxton-Smyth's office.

"Mr Blakemore, can I offer you tea? Mr Paxton-Smyth will be here soon," said Kathy, courteously.

Harry thanked her and said tea would be fine. In no more than a few minutes Kathy arrived with a tray of afternoon tea and a slice of fruitcake. She placed the tray on a coffee table in front of Harry who had parked himself on a leather button-backed chesterfield.

"Have you a phone I can use?" he asked.

"Well, that might be a little difficult. Let me find out." She smiled and left the office.

"Check with the boss first, that's right," remarked Harry to himself.

Kathy soon returned with a hands-free phone. "Just press nine for an outside line," she said.

Harry dialled Clarissa's mobile, the call was answered within just a couple of rings. "Hi Clarissa, it's me," said Harry.

The sound of his voice reduced Clarissa to tears. "Harry," she sobbed, "What of earth's going on? I've been going mental trying to get any information from the police, they won't even talk to me."

"Look, I know how stressful this is for you but believe me I'm okay. I've no idea who might be listening to this conversation so I'll not say much right now nor ask you much either, but what I can say is that I have been released and currently I'm with Military Intelligence in London. Now have you been approached, threatened or - god forbid - even worse?"

"No," replied Clarissa in a now more controlled voice. "Harry I'm scared but I don't think anyone is following me, certainly I've not been approached."

"Okay, we'll say no more for now, I'll be in touch with you as soon as I can." Harry switched off the phone just as Paxton-Smyth entered the office.

"Ah, Harry. I trust you find these surroundings a little more conducive to comfort?"

"Skipper, if I help track down Abu Atif, I want my partner put under protection twenty four seven."

Jeremy Paxton-Smyth smiled. "Don't worry she already is... Especially as she has the scroll."

"What! How the hell did she get that? And how do you know?" exclaimed Harry who stood up and walked over to the vacant chair in front of Paxton Smyth's desk.

"Come on Harry, this is MI6. Clarissa left a message on your mobile to say the Professor had packaged up the scroll and posted it to her."

"Right, so you've been scanning my phone. I get it."

"Better us than the police," replied Paxton-Smyth. "There must be some exceptionally big names behind Incanda: politicians, captains of industry, bankers, lawyers. Who knows who's at the very heart? We do know they have a chain of command and use religious titles essentially of the Catholic line, going right down to that of Server," remarked the head of MI6.

Harry looked out through the window down towards the bustle of Whitehall. "So the Pope's top man," he said, eventually turning to face Paxton-Smyth.

"As I say who knows, although I doubt that very much, don't forget Incanda sit above all religions. And the very top people all inherit the level of nine. It's been suggested that they are called the supreme council of nine and come from locations right across the world."

"Do they operate under any Degree of Free Masonry?" asked Harry.

"You and I are mere fledglings in Freemasonry... therefore we will never know how deep Freemasonry actually goes or how many Degrees there truly are. But if Incanda is a Degree of Freemasonry of some kind, then you can bet the Knights of Black Chapter will be also."

"I presume it's safe to say that the Knights of Black Chapter, who come from the royal line, have members of our Royal Family associated within their top ranks."

Paxton-Smyth leaned back into his high backed desk chair. "Again, who knows?" he replied.

"You do, skipper," responded Harry. "Head of MI6... who else would be called upon to do the Royal Family's bidding. Getting rid of a certain Princess, for example."

Paxton-Smyth stood up from his chair and walked around his desk to stand closer to Harry. "Not at all. These two bodies don't work like that; their depth is so immense and goes back centuries. Remember, we're talking about two groups that are hundreds of years old with direct descendants in a family tree that pre-dates time. Between them, Incanda and the Knights of Black Chapter run the world, make no mistake, but departments like mine are mere pawns in a game so big it's impossible to even comprehend."

"Do you think there are any members of MI6 in Incanda or Knights of Black Chapter?"

"Without a shadow of a doubt," replied Paxton-Smyth. "But on the other hand there may well be just one person and that person might just be a Server who reports to his next in line, who I'm told has the title of Curate. You may also have both sides working for this organisation. Naturally, just as we are unaware, *they* would not be aware of each other's existence. Harry, one thing is abundantly clear, Incanda are instigating the disruption of the Middle East, something they have been doing for centuries, but now it's huge and at the point of rolling out of control. Getting rid of Abu Atif might be just the strategy needed to throw a big spanner in the works, his followers think he's immortal."

"So he's definitely an important member of Incanda then?"

Paxton-Smyth nodded his head. "Absolutely," he said. "But at what level is open to speculation. That scroll might only help us trace the line of a high ranking family member of Incanda. Naturally we have not taken it away from your partner as yet because we're banking on Incanda making a move towards her."

"You mean you're hanging her out as bait?"

"Harry, I told you, she's under total protection."

"Then how do you know one of these guys you've appointed to protect her is not under Incanda control?"

"Good point Harry," replied Paxton-Smyth. "Naturally we had thought of that, therefore placing four men to watch over her. The odds that all four would be Incanda is extremely remote. As far as Humphrey Morgan-Sinclair is concerned, we're checking him out as we speak, and I'll keep you informed of our findings. There is a possible connection with the Sinclair family of Rosslyn in Scotland, but we'll find out."

"Now Harry, about this assignment. The help you can expect to receive either from us or the Americans will be minimal I'm afraid, if this goes wrong you'll be on your own as we've discussed. You will simply be a privateer following the big reward. You can have five days to prepare. Go back to Wales, but don't talk to Clarissa about the assignment, it could put her life in even more danger. Find out whatever you can about the scroll through Clarissa. As the ex student of Professor Thomas she might well be able to interpret parts of it, who knows? We won't relieve her of the scroll until you have left the country."

With that Paxton-Smyth went back around to the drawer side of his desk and took out a broad envelope, he then began extracting the contents. "Here are a number of photographs I persuaded the police to provide us with."

Paxton-Smyth began handing Harry each photograph in turn. They were taken to show different angles of the Professor's body. The re-enactment of the murder of Hyrum Abif was also shown where the Professor's remains had been daubed at the points of the compass. And finally there were three photographs of the tarot cards.

"Do you have any idea what these tarot cards symbolise?" asked Harry.

"Not yet, we know that Knights Templar used tarot cards as a way of teaching others and communicating their ritual when the Catholic Church criminalized the order and made it illegal to become or remain a Templar. I know you are a Craft Mason Harry, but how far have you gone in Freemasonry?"

"Oh not very far," Harry explained. "I'm currently the inner guard of my Craft Lodge and last year I was invited to join Royal Ark, but that's as far as I've gone. I'm the Almoner in Craft but that's not a progressional rank."

Jeremy Paxton-Smyth nodded. "Well I'm a Knights Templar and a Knight of Malta; my Preceptory is at Grand Lodge. I have already spoken to the Eminent Preceptor who has promised to look into the tarot card issue; although I fear the message they contain will be merely symbolic."

The envelope also contained a credit card, mobile phone and a bound file of papers.

"The phone has a few special numbers programmed into it." Paxton-Smyth handed Harry a paper containing a short list of names. "This list of names will be your way of communicating with us. If you prefix the numbers 7071 followed by the two initials representing the person you wish to call then scroll down to the relevant number you will obtain the contact required, but the line will be scrambled to any possible intruder."

"Which one's the Yank?"

Paxton-Smyth smiled, "Right at the top."

Harry looked on the sheet. "Lewis Ford. Okay, so by prefixing 7071 followed by LF then pressing the top number I'll get a performing seal."

Harry tried the number; it rang a number of times and then was answered. "So you're the Limey appointed to help me! Do me a big favour, stay out of my space and we'll get along just fine," said Lewis Ford.

"This is a test call my friend and you failed, so that's about par for the course?" replied Harry. "I'll call you when I need you, which with any luck might be never," he continued. Without giving Lewis Ford the opportunity to reply, Harry switched off the line.

"That sounded like a love match forged in hell," remarked Paxton-Smyth with a half smile.

The Knights of Black Chapter

13

The road to Vrdak was long, dusty and very rough, like the town itself. The convoy turned off the road into a shallow valley about a mile outside of the town.

"We will make our camp here then in the morning I will meet the town's officials. These are mostly Pushtun people and quite friendly, but there's an element here who would steal anything they could get their hands on. It's best to be here, outside town in the open where we will not be disturbed," said Abdullah.

"Good, then perhaps I can go into town with you to find the help I need," suggested Lewis Ford, thankful to have finally left the Land Rover to stretch his legs.

Tents were pitched in a circle like a Western wagon train, with their opening flaps facing inwards. A three-foot high heavy barbed wire fence was then erected right around perimeter; the Land Rovers were parked in the centre of the encampment where a telescopic pole, extending some thirty feet into the air had been inserted into brackets on the side of one of the vehicles, to provide radio communication.

By nightfall the camp was complete, guards had been mounted to patrol the perimeter fence and a generator provided a modicum of light.

"Very cosy," said Ford as he sat down to eat a naan bread and rice, washed down with sweet tea. Ford spent the rest of the evening cleaning the Heckler & Koch. He then fully charged two magazines with rounds of ammunition before bedding down for the night.

The next morning Abdullah and Ford, escorted by two Pakistani members of the convoy, drove into Vrdak. Abdullah asked a small group sitting outside a long, low and very shabby-looking building where they could find the Malik. An elderly man pointed to a building across the street.

"This place is the best hotel in town," said Abdullah smiling.

Ford glanced back for another look. "Well I'll take your five-star camp every time."

The Malik was a portly man of about fifty. Abdullah jabbered away to him in Pashto, a language Ford had a mere smattering of; he was therefore reluctantly forced to remain a mere bystander.

"I informed the Malik that you wish to hire some assistance to help you reach Pashi. He said he would send four men out to the camp this afternoon. You will need camels and donkey's, he will also arrange these for you. You pay him, half now and the rest you will give to the headman who will be your guide."

Ford looked sceptically at Abdullah who smiled and raised his shoulders. "It is the way," he said.

"Okay, I'll give him one hundred dollars," Ford said, reaching into his back pocket.

"That will be very fine," replied Abdullah.

The Malik's eyes glowed as he watched ten and twenty-dollar bills being counted out into the palm of his outstretched hand. They then sat and drank sweet tea to consolidate the arrangement before returning to the camp.

* * *

JoJo Curtis was mad. He had been awoken at ten thirty as requested, only to find that Lewis Ford and the convoy had departed in the early hours. His direct report was straight into the Defence Intelligence Agency whose offices were deep in the Pentagon. The DIA contact was a female with the code name 'Gabby'.

"Gabby. I am leaving for a place called Vrdak… the subject is aware that he's being shadowed because some goddam fool has given us both the same surname. So I've put a time gap between us. He moved out with the ATC convoy earlier this morning, I'm leaving now."

"Your report has been noted and will be passed on," replied Gabby almost robotically, as if her voice was mechanical. With that the phone line went dead.

"And fuck you," shouted JoJo so loud it made his hangover pound like a kettle drum.

"I need someone who can take me to a place called Vrdak," JoJo said after paying the bill at reception.

"One moment sir, I'll call the manager, he'll know how to help you," replied the hotel clerk politely.

Within less than a minute a smart man in a western suit and a tie that had the thin back tail longer than the front, appeared from a back office. JoJo hated badly tied ties.

"I am told you wish to go to Vrdak sir?" he said.

"Yes buddy, and quickly," replied JoJo.

"Quickly is somewhat difficult, the road to Vrdak is very bad."

"Right, but can you get me a cab that will take me there?"

The manager shook his head. "No sir, you will need a private limo' service."

"Okay and you know of one, right?"

"Right it is, of course sir," said the manager, smiling gleefully.

He then went back into the office, returning a few moments later. "All arranged sir, a limo' will be here at noon tomorrow."

"Tomorrow's no good. I need to leave now," shouted JoJo.

The manager waved his hands in front of him and shook his head, dismissing JoJo's demands. "Oh, no, no, no sir, tomorrow," he said.

The limo, when it did finally arrive twenty-four hours later, was in the shape of a canvas top American army jeep. The driver was a man who appeared to be not much more than twenty years old. He had an older man with him dressed in a shabby gundra. The driver spoke perfect English. He introduced himself, and the older man as his father.

"Okay so this is a family business, that's nice but haven't you got a vehicle that's more comfortable than this thing, preferably with air conditioning?"

The young driver shook his head. "This American car is the best for the rocky roads to Vrdak," he said as he commenced loading JoJo's knapsack into the rear of the Jeep.

"Please sit in the seat at the rear," said the young man.

After taking one look at the older man's beaming smile and the ancient Royal Enfield 303 slung on his bony shoulder, JoJo said, "No chance, the old guy can ride shotgun in the back, I'll sit up front."

The young man nodded and instructed his father to climb into the rear of the Jeep.

"First payment please," said the driver.

"Okay buddy, I presume you take greenbacks?" asked JoJo, struggling to get a foam cushion positioned under him to provide a little more comfort on the seat.

"Greenbacks? I don't understand," replied the young driver.

"Greenbacks... dollars to you my friend."

"Oh, dollars," he said, now beaming from ear to ear and holding out his hand, "Yes dollars, twenty dollars."

"Okay," replied JoJo. "And if you get me there by nightfall, I'll give you another five."

"Good show, my name is Abash, good to do business with you."

JoJo put the money into Abash's hand. "So what's your dad's name?"

"His name is Abash also."

Abash senior smiled in recognition of his name being mentioned, then nodded a few times.

"Does he know how to use that thing?" asked JoJo pointing to the old rifle.

"Oh yes, my father was a Mujahideen fighter during the Soviet occupation."

This prompted the older man to burst forth with a volley of information that JoJo could only acknowledge with a smile.

It was just gone ten o'clock and freezing cold when the Jeep entered Vrdak.

"Is this it?" said JoJo as he looked out at the squalor in the streets, picked up in the jeep's headlights.

"I need a hotel, they do have hotels here I presume?" said JoJo a little nervously.

Abash laughed. "Of course, this is it," he said, pointing to the long house Ford had seen the day before.

JoJo got out of the jeep and walked over to half a dozen men who were squatting down close to the entrance. "Any of you guys speak English?"

They all began to jabber in JoJo's direction but in a language he did not understand.

"Abash, come over here," JoJo commanded. Abash cautiously left his driver's seat whilst his father took a grip of the rifle.

"Abash, I need a goddam hand here, none of these locals can speak a word of English."

"I do," said a voice somewhere behind him.

JoJo turned to see a man walking out of the shadows of the low overhanging roof of the building. JoJo could just make out his appearance in the dull light that came from a single flickering light bulb perched on a pole above the doorway. Abash returned to the driver's seat, waved his hand towards JoJo in farewell and drove away.

JoJo looked hard into the subdued light to get a better look at the man who began walking towards him. "You will need a room because you should not be on the streets after dark, it's dangerous," he said.

"You goddam well bet I need a room. And one that's got a fan in it," said JoJo sternly as he picked up his rucksack.

"Fan?" repeated the man with a smile. "It will have a bed, a table and chair but no fan. You follow me." He took JoJo's rucksack from him and walked into the house.

The room he took JoJo to was primitive to say the least, the single bed was comprised of a mattress that appeared to be stuffed with straw and a pillow that was covered in brown speckles like rust stains. A number of blankets were piled at the foot of the bed in readiness for the exceptionally cold night ahead. The only other furnishings were a rickety wooden table and two chairs. A metal shutter was hinged to close off the open window. JoJo ensured it was secured and that the catch was firmly in place. As there was no lock upon the door, JoJo pulled the table up in front of it. He then put one of his clean shirts from the rucksack over the pillow to lie on. He checked the bullet clip of his Browning automatic for a little reassurance, and tucked the gun under the pillow before settling down for the night.

By 5.30 am the following morning Lewis Ford was dressed in a gandura, in keeping with the local dress. He took a drink of sweet tea whilst the first call came for morning prayers. He then sat perched high in the air on the back of a flea-bitten camel, all set for the journey.

"What's your name again?" Lewis Ford asked the man who had introduced himself as the guide the previous evening.

"My name is Abu Hassan but most western people call me Red." Red broke out into a belly laugh that was contagious.

"Okay that'll do for me, Red. Now what I have here is a hundred dollars, split this whichever way you want between the four of you. You will get another hundred when we are safely out of the region and back here at camp."

Ford reached down from his camel to hand five twenty-dollar bills to Red who looked pleased but not exactly ecstatic. They then set off climbing a rugged, stony pathway that ran in parallel to a feeder stream trickling down the mountain towards them. By mid afternoon they had reached a plateau where Red stopped. Ford jumped down from his camel and walked over to Red who was peering through the lenses of a pair of binoculars.

"What do you see?"

Red handed the binoculars to Lewis Ford then pointed towards the mountain range in front of them. "Smoke," he said.

Ford adjusted the focus of the binoculars and scanned the area. A thin spindle of white smoke formed an almost straight line some miles in front of them.

The Knights of Black Chapter

"Who are they, Red?" asked Ford.

"Bandits without doubt," replied Red.

"How about Al Val Sinda or Al Quaida?" responded Ford.

Red shook his head. "I would suggest they are bandits, this is opium country. We are right on an opium trail. And we'd better leave before it gets dark."

"Okay, I'm all ears, when can we get off the trail? And where can we get to before nightfall?"

Red pointed towards the pathway well above them. "There are many caves up there, we will make camp in a cave."

The pathway became even more narrow as they proceeded up from the plateau, so much so that Ford decided to walk and lead the camel who simply plodded along unperturbed by its surroundings.

* * *

JoJo spent a very restless night, falling in and out of sleep several times, fearing that he might be set upon. He took a walk the following morning, glad to be in the typical bright sunshine that gave the town a completely different appearance. JoJo spied the strange man who could speak English and who had shown him to his room the night before. He was talking with another man over a glass of tea. The other man was far older and looked as if he had been virtually starved to death.

"Excuse me, are you the guy from last night?" asked JoJo, breaking into their conversation.

"I am," he replied, "Did you sleep well?"

"Yeh, thanks, look I need to see the Malik, do you know where I can find him?"

The man pointed to the house across the street. "There, but today is a holy day, you will not be able to speak to him until tomorrow."

"Yeh, but I only need to ask him a couple of questions," replied JoJo sounding frustrated.

"Tomorrow," repeated the man, turning back towards his companion as if there was nothing more to be said.

"Do you know where I can get any food around here?" continued JoJo.

The man stood up, clasped his hands together then bowed towards his companion who returned the salutation. "Follow me," he said.

JoJo nodded at the older man and then followed him along several identical poor and deprived streets, where the occasional woman could be seen brushing dust and rubbish off the high stone pavements in what seemed a never ending task.

The man stopped outside a building with a bead curtain across its doorway. "In here," he said.

JoJo gave the Browning that was pushed into the waistband of his trousers and hidden from view under his long creased shirt a reassuring pat. He removed his sunglasses and when his eyes became acclimatised to the dark interior he could see he was in a thirty-foot square room. The place appeared nothing like an eating establishment, or at least of the type JoJo had seen before. There were half a dozen white plastic patio tables, with four high-backed wooden chairs pushed under each one of them.

The man pointed to a table suggesting JoJo should take a seat. "You want food and hot tea?"

JoJo looked up at him. "Have they got any eggs?" he asked.

The man smiled. "Eggs, no. You wait."

Eventually a plate with two naan breads arrived and a glass of hot tea, delivered by a girl with the most striking pair of large brown eyes JoJo had ever seen. He thanked her and sipped the sweet tea. She returned moments later with a bowl of thin, brown liquid.

"What's this?" asked JoJo, peering down at the slimy surface.

"Mutton curry," she replied in reasonably good English.

"Ah you speak English, what's your name?"

"Nadia," she replied. JoJo estimated her age to be no more than eighteen. How he would have dearly loved her to sit with him and just talk. The isolation he was feeling in this deprived, desolate and hostile land was already getting to him. Nadia skipped away through a curtain-covered doorway that JoJo presumed led into the kitchen.

He glanced sceptically at the uninviting spectacle in front of him, however without the benefit of dinner the night before he was starving. JoJo broke off the corner of one of the naan breads and dipped it into the bowl then shook it a couple of times, examined the surface for any sight of indigestible foreign bodies and eventually began to eat. The strength of the curry made his eyes water but hunger prevailed and another piece of naan was broken off and dipped into the liquid.

JoJo's attention was soon drawn to the noise and clatter going on in the kitchen; he then heard a scream, presumably from Nadia. He left his chair and paced across the floor towards the kitchen doorway. He pulled the curtain back sufficiently to peer through. He saw a man gripping Nadia by the wrist, she had been forced down on her knees, and was shielding her head from the long cane the man as brandishing above her.

"Hey buddy, drop that fucking stick," shouted JoJo.

The man ignored him and brought the cane down across Nadia's back. JoJo strode forwards pulling the Browning automatic from his waistband, and pointing the barrel directly at the man's head.

"I said drop the stick goddam it," shouted JoJo again as he moved closer. He then took Nadia by the hand and pushed her behind him so that he was now standing between Nadia and her assailant.

"Who the fuck is this guy?" he said.

"My uncle, he beats me all the time," she replied with a sob.

"Well not any more. Tell him to put the stick down."

Nadia repeated JoJo's instruction in a tongue the man understood. He dropped the stick to the floor instantly.

"That's better, now tell your uncle that I said you are to come and sit at my table while I eat that pile of crap you call food. "

Nadia repeated the instruction. The man collapsed to his knees and bowed.

"Good that's more like it," said JoJo as he pushed the gun back into his trousers.

Nadia looked very nervous, to the point of being visibly frightened.

"You speak good English, how come?" asked JoJo.

"I was brought up in Kabul and went to the English missionary school there," she replied.

"Then what are you doing serving in a shit tip like this?" replied JoJo.

"I came here to get married, but the man I was chosen to marry was killed. "

"Oh, I'm sorry, had you known him for long?" asked JoJo softly.

"No, I'd never met him. The marriage was arranged by my uncle, the man in there." She pointed back towards the kitchen.

"Why was that bastard about to beat you?"

"Because I keep refusing his advances."

"Do you mean that he's been trying it on with you? You're his niece for Christ's sake."

The girl nodded. "Now mister, please let me go back, I'll be in even bigger trouble if I stay here talking to you."

JoJo reluctantly nodded. Talking to Nadia and looking into those wonderful dark eyes made the pangs of manhood stir. Now as she skipped away he felt frustrated and unfulfilled. The last time he'd felt like that was when he first set eyes on Carolina Clare. Hunger had by now left him; he therefore just drank the remaining dregs of tea and stood up to leave. He moved the curtain to one side to see Nadia and her uncle deep in conversation.

"Can I have the check?" said JoJo.

"The bill? My uncle he say there is no charge."

"Okay, well this is for you." JoJo handed Nadia a fifty-dollar bill. She smiled; it was the first time JoJo had actually seen her smile. The spectacle was well worth the money. "And there's plenty more where that came from," he said, turning to leave.

"Thank you, you are a kind man," said Nadia handing the money over to her uncle who bowed courteously.

JoJo went into the scorching heat of the sun wondering why he'd just made such a statement. He began walking in what he thought was the direction of the hotel but ended up in a bazaar where fresh fruit, nuts herbs and spices were on display. A swarm of young children congregated around him like flies round a jam pot. JoJo had no idea why, but he still had a pocket of nickels and dimes which he grabbed and threw into the air. The spectacle provoked a mad scramble for the money, which diverted the children's attention away from him, albeit briefly, but just long enough for him to buy some oranges and half a watermelon.

JoJo felt like the pied piper as he walked through the bare, uninviting streets with a trail of screaming children following behind him. They stayed behind him until he reached his lodgings. The children then encircled him en masse, their faces ablaze with smiles of anticipation: smiles that JoJo felt inspired by, despite these children's deprived existence in a country that was ravaged by war and death and fighting for its very soul. Their future would be at best bleak, and very uncertain. JoJo fell head over heels for one pretty little girl who could not have been much more than four years of age. Despite her shabby clothes she was a perfectly formed, tiny beauty who, given time and the right opportunities, would set pulses racing wherever she went, especially with the way her hair fell in beautiful, natural ringlets.

JoJo entered the hotel determined to do something for those poor kids upon his return to the USA. Perhaps he could adopt one; perhaps Carolina Clare might just see her way to give him another chance if there was a child involved. He went to his room with a definite plan forming in his mind. He began to feel remarkably more positive, it was as if these scruffy street urchins had brought the possibility of a productive future for the last chapters in his life.

That night there was a knock on the door. It was the man from outside the hotel who spoke English. "Mister, you were talking to Nadia, her uncle asks if you would like her?"

"What.... What the fuck are you talking about?"

"Nadia expressed an interest in being with you, if you give money to her uncle." The man simply stood in the doorway without any form of expression on his face.

"Do you mean Nadia is prepared to spend the night with me, if I throw a buck or two at her uncle?" Clearly the slang JoJo used did not connect, however the words 'spend the night' certainly hit a cord.

"If you wish," he replied.

"If I wish...you better believe I wish," said JoJo feeling his heartbeat increase in anticipation of what was to come.

"You wait," said the man. He then closed JoJo's door.

JoJo quickly poured some water from a jug into the bowl on the table. He then splashed his face with the water, wiped his face with a thin towel and applied a generous amount of aftershave. He smelt under his armpits and was applying a little more aftershave directly under each arm when a knock came on his door. JoJo wiped his left hand across his face in nervous anticipation, then brushed it over his thick bushy hair.

He hesitated momentarily; this was precisely the moment he could refuse the offer and remain alone. "Hey what the fuck... here we go," said JoJo to himself as he walked over and opened the door.

Nadia was standing between her uncle and the hotel man. The smell of body odour hit JoJo directly. He concluded, however, that it must have been emanating from one or both men!

"Okay so what's the deal?"

"My uncle wants a hundred dollars and this man wants paying also."

"Okay Nadia, and how do you feel about all this?" asked JoJo, suddenly feeling the pangs of guilt as a potential benefactor in such a cold and calculated arrangement, and besides he'd never paid money for a woman before.

"I'm fine. You are a nice man," she replied with a smile.

"Okay, one hundred bucks for you and fifty for you," JoJo said handing the cash to both men. The uncle bowed, the other man did nothing, he just turned and walked away. With the door now shut and the two of them alone, JoJo's first reaction was to go over to the window and close the metal shutter against prying eyes and the pitch-blackness.

As he turned, Nadia approached then stood within just a few inches from him. JoJo was taken aback a little; he'd thought maybe a conversation first and then to gradually get down to more intimate business a little later. Nadia however clearly had different thoughts. JoJo placed his hands on her waist and drew her gently towards him. Their lips met in an instant. The first kiss was brief; the second was long and wet. JoJo felt the smoothness of her soft young tongue as it searched his mouth eagerly. He moved his large hands to the fullness of her breasts and heard her take a gulp of air as his thumbs softy moved across her nipples.

Their foreplay was much shorter than JoJo had originally hoped; however greed mixed with passion, and the burning desire of anticipation, gave way to impatience as they collapsed naked onto the bed.

* * *

The climb up to the place Red had alluded to was extremely slow and laborious. One minute they were bathed in blazing sun and then, almost as if someone somehow switched off a light, blackness enveloped them. Red moved his camel towards Lewis Ford and pointed to a place where the pathway widened out.

"There are the caves just up there," he said.

"Well come on, let's get a move on," replied Ford, pulling on the reins to induce the camel to speed up, but the animal simply extended its neck and turned around to look sleepily at Ford, who gave the reins an almighty tug that finally resulted in a reluctant, gradual increase in the beast's stride.

Just as Red had indicated, this part of the mountain was honeycombed with caves. The small group made their way up towards a cave that seemed adequate to contain their entire party. Upon reaching the entrance Red switched on a powerful torch, which provided just sufficient light to enable them to see where they were walking. Red raised his hand to halt the group.

"We can coral the camels and donkeys over there, this will do for our camp," he said, waving the torch around so that Lewis Ford could see the space in front of them.

"Have you been here before, Red?" asked Ford, taking his torch back from the guide and peering as far as the beam of light permitted.

"Yes, once," replied Red.

"Then do you know if there are other ways into here?"

Red shook his head. "No, I don't think so, this is the only way in."

Ford moved forward to look further into the cave. "Okay then let's pitch up here until morning."

After the pack animals had been unloaded and corralled a distance away, they set about assembling a makeshift camp. A hurricane lamp was lit and a fire prepared.

"Red, put a man on guard at the entrance," said Ford as he unrolled his bedding. Red simply responded by raising his hand; he then spoke to one of his men who picked up his rifle and disappeared towards the entrance.

After prayers the party sat down to eat. Lewis Ford was starving and appreciated the first naan to come off the flat piece of stone that had been heated in the fire. Ford was intrigued to watch one of Red's men take the urd flour and mix it with water to form dough and then pat it into shape. Within no time there was a batch of naan breads piled up on a large plate. A quantity of what looked like stagnant water was then poured into a steel pan and placed on the fire. Soon the smell of curry wafted around the encampment as the contents of the pan began to heat up.

The taste of the green curry was more palatable than its appearance, especially to a hungry man in such a desolate place. Hot sweet tea was consistently good and Lewis Ford enjoyed two large cups before eventually turning in for the night.

All of a sudden there was the sound of automatic rifle fire from close by the entrance. Ford leapt from his bed and ran towards the mouth of the cave. Dawn was just rising, providing sufficient light to see across the clearing towards the pathway. The rifle fire had come from Red's man placed on guard, who looked bewildered and was chanting something to himself. When Red arrived he asked the man what he'd been shooting at and was told that he had seen two bandits with guns run behind the large bolder he was pointing at.

Ford was angry and told Red in no uncertain terms that this fire would bring a response and very soon. He took the binoculars and scanned the area. "Sitting fucking ducks," he said as a hail of bullets smashed into the entrance of the cave, a number striking the guard whose body turned and twisted as it took one hit after another.

"Red, get the other men," commanded Ford.

Red instantly ran back into the cave and returned moments later with the three others. "They want more money to help. I'm sorry, but they have wives and families to support," said Red looking worried.

"I understand, that's not a problem, just tell them to hold their fire until they have a clear target to aim at."

After the tense and uncertain moments of silence following the first round of gunfire, there came a much more intense hail of bullets despatched from automatic weapons striking the entrance of the cave. Bullets were ricocheting in all directions. Red ran back into the cave, returning moments later with an RPK light machine gun.

"Where the fuck did you find that?" asked Ford, affording Red a rare smile.

Red just returned the smile and set the gun up on the floor at the entrance. Ford took charge of the gun and sent a spray of bullets across the clearing, striking the base of the large rock. Two bandits broke cover as Ford turned the RPK round towards them and as they attempted to run round the bend in the path, he opened fire, cutting them down unmercifully as they fled.

"Red, what do you know about these bandits?" asked Ford.

Red looked at him and shrugged his shoulders. "Nothing much, they tend to work in small groups."

"What would a small group comprise of?"

Again Red shrugged his shoulders. "Maybe four or six," he replied.

"So let's assume that there's six of them, I've just taken out two that could leave four. We'll wait here until nightfall; I'll then scout around to see what we are up against. How well do know your men and how good can they handle those Kalashnikovs?"

"They have fired them a few times," replied Red.

The Knights of Black Chapter

"Okay well ask them to reserve their ammunition and keep their rifles on single shot, not semi automatic... every round is precious."

The blackness of evening fell swiftly without a shot being fired.

Lewis Ford checked his Heckler & Koch; he had exactly one hundred rounds of ammunition after he had recharged the clip and locked it back in the rifle. "Red, I'm going to scout around and see what the deal is, I'll be back before dawn."

The guide just nodded an acknowledgement as he nervously crouched behind a rock at the mouth of the cave.

Ford crouched low then quickly moved out of the cave under the cover of now almost pitch darkness. Not even the moon was visible as he made for the large rock on the other side of the clearing. Nothing seemed to stir; the entire area seemed as still as death, as night approached. Ford decided to make for higher ground as a new moon partly lit the mountains with an eerie hue. To the left of the cave was a steep rise, but the angle, although acute, seemed climbable. Ford quickly looked around before making a dash for the place he'd chosen to climb.

Within a minute he had scaled a jagged overhang onto a ledge. The loose shale under his feet made the climb difficult. However, after a few near falls he was soon able to reach a flat piece of rock that took him onto a shelf where he was almost able to walk upright. By now he was about five hundred feet above the cave. Checking his watch, he saw that, incredibly, it had been over an hour since he'd set out. By now the moon was glowing brighter in the black sky and providing slightly better visibility. Ford took the binoculars and scanned the area below him.

To his left he noticed a glow that might well be coming from a hurricane lamp. However, as he watched the glow more intently it began to move and flicker as if a flame had suddenly been caught by a gentle breeze. Ford estimated the fire to be about five hundred yards away from the cave. He scanned the area to see how he could possibly get closer without being seen. Ford cursed the desolate terrain for its barren lack of foliage.

He carefully picked his way across towards a ledge. To the left of a ridge was a downwards slope which looked precarious; it was steep and covered in loose shale. Ford removed his jacket and placed it under him to control his slide and restrict his movement over the loose shale, as he slowly descended until he reached a flat shelf. He stopped momentarily and raised his binoculars again to look down towards the fire. As he was now a lot closer he could see figures moving about.

All of a sudden, a vivid green light came from a huge barrage of tracer fire aimed directly at the clearing near the cave, far below and to the right of Ford's position. He looked on helplessly as the tracer fire increased, ripping into his party. Then came a sudden blast that literally lit up the sky as if morning had arrived. It had clearly come from a grenade aimed directly at the mouth of the cave.

Ford quickly looked around him but there was no simple or quick way down. He concluded the only possible route was to go further left and then climb up several feet onto a flat ledge where what appeared to be a goat track might provide a means of winding downwards.

With a mixture of anger and frustration Ford proceeded to climb until he had successfully reached the flat ledge. The tracer fire had by now stopped and no return of fire could be heard, which was worrying. Ford hated the deafening sound of sudden battle silence as it invariably meant annihilation!

It seemed to take him hours to carefully pick his way down the narrow track with its dangerously loose shale. One wrong move, or simply a loose foothold, would send him hurtling to his death.

With his hands cut and bleeding from the razor-sharp shale, Ford eventually climbed back down onto the pathway. He soon realised that his expedition had taken him left of the mouth of the cave by a few hundred metres. Still everything remained silent; no gunfire could be heard from either side. He therefore decided to circle round towards where he'd seen the campfire. He scrambled up a rock to gain sufficient height to see the small encampment. One person was clearly visible. He trained his binoculars towards the camp and then scanned the surrounding area but failed to pick out any other signs of life. Ford presumed that the direction from which the tracer fire and grenade assault had been mounted meant the other bandits must have set themselves up quite a lot closer towards the mouth of the cave and might well be still in position.

Ford crouched low as the sound of impromptu gunfire broke the silence. He estimated that the sporadic volley had come from the bandits; worryingly there was again no return of fire. As soon as the gunshots had stopped, Ford made his move. Within a few minutes he was right on the edge of the camp just a few feet from the sole bandit who could be seen putting sticks on the fire. Ford fanned his hand and brought it down in a devastating karate chop right onto the bandit's neck. His limp body dropped onto the fire, where Ford left the unconscious bandit with his clothes on ablaze.

He quickly pulled the webbing sling of his rifle over his head and released the safety catch, then ran away from the fire towards the darkness. Dropping to the ground he took up position with his rifle, bearing down towards the bandit who by now had regained consciousness and had rolled off the fire in a ball of flame. His screams could be heard echoing right down the mountain. Three men could be seen running into the camp only to be greeted by a volley of bullets as Ford immediately opened fire with the Heckler & Koch in semi-automatic position showering the entire area with a curtain of death. Within seconds the bandits all lay still, including the one whose clothing was still burning.

Ford lay in position for a few minutes before standing. He then cautiously walked over to the dead men. After checking that life had completely left them, he proceeded towards the cave; stopping momentarily to examine the RPG grenade launcher the bandits had left before walking into Ford's trap.

The cave had been devastated, body parts were blown in a number of directions, entrails of raw flesh hung like limpets from the walls but Ford couldn't be certain if any belonged to Red. He moved deeper into the cave. The camels and donkeys had been corralled someway inside therefore the chances were better than average that they had survived. Ford searched as deep into the cave as he could see, but found nothing. He flicked his cigarette lighter; the flame was briefly sufficient to light his immediate surroundings. There was a passageway to the left. Ford kicked the ground in frustration, angry with himself for not carrying out the basic textbook procedure of first checking out any possible exit routes. He had trusted Red and that was against all his training and experience. Red had made his escape through this passage and obviously taken the livestock with him.

Except for the brief intermittent glow from his gas lighter Ford was in complete blackness, every step therefore had to be carefully searched first by leaning on the back foot and toe-poking with the other. By the time Ford had reached an opening to the outside dawn was just breaking.

He trained his binoculars on the pathway but unfortunately the range was restricted to a few hundred metres. Ford assumed Red would be at least a good mile or two in front and

with water and sustenance for a journey. Reluctantly, with no food or water, Ford was forced to start the long journey back to Vrdak on foot. He passed a dead camel on the pathway. The poor animal had lost part of its leg. Blood had gushed from her wound and was splattered across the pathway where she had struggled, stumbling on just three legs for several hundred metres.
Ford touched the underside of her belly… it felt warm. The saddle was still on her back but the side-bags containing the water carriers were empty.

With the sole aid of a small pocket compass and his tattered combat jacket, which served to protect him from the blazing sun during the day and the extreme cold at night, it took Lewis Ford just over two incredibly difficult days to get back to the ATC encampment.

* * *

JoJo was awoken by the door opening and four figures walking into the room. He quickly felt for Nadia alongside him but she was not there.
Thankfully the Browning was still under his pillow. JoJo grabbed the gun just as the men made a rush forward. Instinctively JoJo opened fire at the figure that appeared directly in front of him. Two bullets hit the attacker in the chest at point blank range, sending him spinning across the floor; just then JoJo felt a crashing blow to his head that knocked him out cold.

The remaining three men carried JoJo's naked body out of the hotel via the back door. He was then unceremoniously dumped into the back of a truck with his hands lashed together behind him. The force with which he was thrown onto the steel floor caused him to roll uncontrollably, splitting his head open against the wheel arch.

Naked and in a state of semi-consciousness, JoJo rolled around the back of the truck as it drove over the rocky road heading out of town. It was almost dawn before he began to regain full consciousness, as the truck eventually came to a halt and the tailgate was lowered.

Two heavily armed men climbed up into the truck and manhandled JoJo out into the bright sunshine. His head felt like lead, and the back of his neck ached from where he had been struck. JoJo's body began to shake, reacting to suddenly being subjected to the scorching heat of the morning's sun after so many hours of extreme cold. He shivered uncontrollably, partly from the sudden temperature change and partly from indescribable fear.

He was in the desert in an encampment of large tents, being roughly dragged towards a tent with two men guarding the entrance. Both were armed with Kalashnikov rifles. JoJo was taken inside and immediately tied to a pole in the centre of the tent.

"Hey guys, what's this all about? If I broke some law with Nadia, hear me, I'm sorry," shouted JoJo frantically, attempting to bring some mundanity to the situation, but his words were completely ignored. He suddenly felt in his heart of hearts that this was not just some angry members of Nadia's family... this was a serious group and, by the way they were armed, a serious bandit group.

JoJo was frightened, more frightened then he'd ever been in his life before. With his head and body wracked with pain from bouncing around the back of the truck, coupled with the cold, and fear of what was to become of him, JoJo lost all personal control and began to urinate down his legs and onto the floor.

Eventually a man entered the tent; the lower part of his face was covered with the loose end of his turban. He began to laugh at the spectacle in front of him. He then grabbed JoJo's testicles and squeezed them until the pain was excruciating.

"You are going to die my friend, but first you are going to confess."

"Fuck you," responded JoJo.

The man simply laughed and increased his grip, sending waves of pain surging through JoJo's body. He then simply released his grip and left the tent.

Minutes later four men entered the tent. They released JoJo from the pole and bound his hands behind his back. Then they manhandled him outside. By now the typically hot morning sun was blazing down. JoJo suddenly began to shiver again as his body temperature tried to adjust to the extreme changes. He was taken into another tent, a little smaller than the first. It contained a trestle type table and a number of straps. The low hum of a generator could be heard somewhere close by.

JoJo capitulated without resistance as the four men lay him face down on the table with his arms stretched out above his head. They then secured his wrists with two straps that were bolted to the table; two more secured his hands, palms down onto the rough wooden surface. JoJo turned his head to one side so that he could see his captors.

"You know you've got this all wrong, my name's Roger Carson. I'm a journalist, I'm here to send clear messages back about the de-bombing that's going on. Do you know how many mines have been de-activated in the last year alone? And if this is about Nadia then that's not my fault, her uncle wanted money."

But JoJo's attempt at logical explanation fell upon deaf ears as one of the four strode forward and stooped down to stare close into JoJo's face. It was the man from the hotel, the very same one who had taken money from him during the negotiation for Nadia's favours the night before. He looked JoJo right in the eye.

"You are going to die, you western dog, but first you are going to tell us exactly who you are and why you are here. It's our belief that you are here to spy upon the Al Val Sinda and that your intention is to kill our leader Muhammad Abu Atif. Tell all and you will die quickly, if not you will die a very long, lingering and painful death. It's up to you American, either way you will tell us and you will die. You are from the US, of course we know that, but you are too old to be in the military - so who are you?"

"I told you, I'm a journalist," replied JoJo.

JoJo suddenly felt his left hand being gripped but with his arms outstretched above his head it was impossible to see what was happening.

He then felt something being attached to the end of his finger, and then followed the most extreme pain JoJo had ever experienced as the nail of his little finger was literally torn away. He let out a scream that echoed around the tent, drowning the noise of the generator.

Without a word the electric attachment was then fitted to the next finger, as JoJo lay helpless and frightened on the table. Having the second nail ripped from his finger was even more painful than the first.

Through his saliva and tears JoJo began to mutter.

"I thought you would have asked me again after you fucked up my first finger," he said.

"Very well, tell us exactly why you are here and who else is with you and we'll just shoot a bullet into your head."

"I'm a journalist," shouted JoJo as loud and as aggressively as he could.

The Knights of Black Chapter

The third and fourth fingernail and then eventually his thumbnail were each ripped away in turn by the Russian-made electric contraption, leaving JoJo's fingers pumping blood and torn to shreds. One of the men then took a pair of pincers and began plucking lumps of flesh from the raw, tender skin normally protected by the fingernails. JoJo screamed so intensely his entire body shook as if thirty thousand volts had just gone through it.

His mind became incoherent as it started disappearing into a foggy mist of pain. It then began flashing distorted pictures like a television on the blink; first the pictures were of Mickey's bar, then the Executive Canteen at the White House. This was quickly followed by each of his wives in turn; he then searched through the mist of unbearable pain for Carolina Clare's pretty face which eventually came into view so clearly that it almost seemed as if she was standing in front of him.

"He's smiling," remarked one of the men, but JoJo hardly heard the words in his delirious state. His mind had by now almost blocked out the pain and replaced it with fond memories of things and people that for him were now gone forever.

JoJo felt the straps around his hands and wrists being fumbled with, someone then grabbed hold of both his ankles and suddenly he was being dragged down the table until his feet were touching the floor. His body was now simply bent over the table. JoJo offered no resistance as his legs were pulled apart and straps buckled to each ankle.

"You are going to experience a thrill so painful you will beg to die. But first you have just one chance to explain why you are here and who sent you," said the man from the hotel.

JoJo could hear himself scream the word "No".

"Very well, this is called the Abd al Aswd or, to you western filth, the Black Slave. It was used upon our Muslim brothers at government jails in Beirut, now it will be used upon you."

One of the men took a two foot long, round metal bar with a wire attached to one end. As the noise from the generator increased the free end of the bar began to glow as if it had been pulled from a furnace. Soon it became almost white hot. One of the men then threw a switch on a machine positioned under the table, to which the wire attached to the bar was connected. Almost instantly the glow at the end of the bar began to diminish and cool down.

A delirious JoJo felt the heat from the bar burn into his back passage. He let out a scream so loud it made his lungs ache. The bar was then slowly pushed higher and higher into

JoJo's body. He tried to counter the pain by letting out a continual scream so intense that his entire body went into a convulsion. Through the tears of pain he watched a man smile at him and then flick the switch on the machine. The end of the bar, now inserted up into JoJo's stomach, began to heat up again, burning into his intestines. The bar was suddenly withdrawn and then rammed right back up inside again. The man from the hotel bent over JoJo and spoke softly into his ear.

"Well my friend, are you ready to tell?"

JoJo just intensified his continual screaming.

The excruciating torment went on and on for hour after painful hour as excrement mixed with blood poured from JoJo's back passage. Eventually he collapsed into a state of unconsciousness. Suddenly he felt strangely at peace: the pain had gone and he felt a calmness the like of which he'd never experienced before. He felt as if he was floating and that he was able to look down on a table surrounded by all of his wives. They were holding hands as if at a séance. Carolina Clare looked up with tears rolling down her pretty young face. JoJo wanted to touch her, he felt in his mind that he was reaching out towards her to wipe away her tears, but although he was able to effortlessly caress her cheek, he couldn't stop the tears from rolling down her face.

JoJo's naked and blood and excrement covered body was simply dumped in a ditch within a minefield area, some ten miles outside of Vrdak.

The Knights of Black Chapter

14

Harry arrived back in Machynlleth just as the town clock was striking twelve midnight. Regardless of feeling exceptionally tired, Harry first went to the shop, unlocked the door and switched off the alarm. The few days that he'd been away seemed almost like a lifetime.

Subconsciously, Harry blamed himself for the Professor's death and indeed for putting Clarissa's safety in jeopardy by bringing the baton scroll into their lives... but he was not prepared to beat himself up over it.

He smiled when he noticed that four pieces of furniture had red 'sold' stickers attached to them. "Good girl," he said, allowing himself a smile.

As the flat above the shop was in total darkness, Harry presumed Clarissa was in bed, fast asleep. He went into the small room at the back that was used as an office and took the business daybook from the top drawer of the pine desk. It was the book both Harry and Clarissa used to record the happenings of the business and to leave messages for one another. He switched on the art nouveau desk lamp, which bathed the top of the desk in a soft, orange glow. The last entry had been written in a somewhat shaky hand and simply said, "Harry, check out the real Chip', the lever's sticking."

Harry read the entry again; in fact he read it several times before the penny dropped. They had two Chippendale pieces in stock: one was a Victorian reproduction of a side-table that had been purchased in a job lot; the other was a genuine Chippendale of the period, it was a large, ornately-figured, writing box. Its rosewood veneer was awaiting restoration.

Harry immediately went into the back of the shop where a collection of pre-sale stock was awaiting attention. With the lid open, the box became a sloping writing desk covered with worn, brown, ink-stained skived leather curling up at the edges. Harry carefully pulled on the tiny, thin piece of leather protruding between the desk and the body of the box, and the hinged slope opened to expose a second lid and a number of compartments and drawers covered in a remarkably fine, pale blue, water marked satin. Each drawer had tiny, ivory handles.

The Knights of Black Chapter

Harry removed the loose lid at the back of the box and with his index finger he felt around until he found a lever.

A gentle but firm pull forced a spring-loaded secret drawer to pop open revealing a neatly folded piece of paper inside. Harry took the paper and carefully pushed the drawer back in place. He closed the box and took the paper back to the office. The handwritten note read:

> *"Dear Harry, I don't know what kind of a mess you are in but whatever it is, I believe you are completely innocent of poor Professor Thomas's death. The Professor called me the evening he arrived at Blandford Forum to say that he had not taken the scroll with him. He discovered that it contained information so important that if it got into the wrong hands it could affect the balance of world power, and that Incanda could use it to destroy the Knights of Black Chapter. Apparently the scroll reveals the exact timings through astronomy and the celebrations of the summer and winter solstices, pinpointing the Preceptory meeting times of the Knights of Black Chapter that occur once every hundred years. This is when the nine Most High meet. It's something to do with the sun being between the two pillars of Boaz and Jachin, which mark the extremities of the sun's passage north and south at the solstices, in front of the Temple of Yahweh in Jerusalem or something like that, but it's at such a time when they are at their utmost risk and vulnerable to attack.*
>
> *The Professor asked me to take the scroll to Scotland for safekeeping; I have also spoken at length to Guy Pendleton who is an old and trusted friend. He studied under the Professor with me. Guy works at the museum in New York; he's dropping everything and flying into Manchester. I've got a new phone; it's a pay-as-you-go. I think I'm being watched and my old phone has been tapped because there's a funny background sound every time I answer it.*

The note was finished off with Clarissa's name and her new number. Harry read through the note again and programmed Clarissa's new number into his phone, prefixing the access code arranged by MI6; he then burned the note in one of the antique chamber pots and - just to make doubly certain - he flushed the ashes down the drain.

Harry peered through the window of the shop to see if there was any movement around the sleeping town. He then locked the front door after arming the alarm system.

It was almost nine o'clock the next morning when Harry stirred from his bed. He called Clarissa. The phone rang several times before Clarissa picked up. "Harry we're in Loanhead near Rosslyn in Scotland."

"What are you doing up in Scotland and why did the Professor ask you to take the scroll up there?" asked Harry almost in one breath.

"Because, Harry, the Professor said that the scroll would be safer up here, and he told me exactly where to hide it. Harry you have no idea how important this scroll is, if it got into the hands of Incanda it could literally change the balance of the world."

Harry listened to her words but felt an uneasy scepticism. "I find that hard to believe, Clarissa," he said.

"Then come up to Scotland now and find out. You need to talk to Guy, but not on the telephone."

"Okay, I'll make some enquiries about flights to Edinburgh and call you back."

There was a flight leaving Manchester at two o'clock that afternoon. Harry booked his ticket online and left the cottage for the three-hour journey to the airport. He tried to telephone Jeremy Paxton-Smyth but his line was on answer-phone. He then dutifully called Annie.

"Hi Harry, right now you have been removed from my system."

"I sound like a commodity," replied Harry sounding a little indignant.

"No, only now you are moving overseas, I'm no longer your point of contact."

"Then who the hell is?" he shouted.

"No idea, I'm afraid. Bye for now, Harry."

"No, wait!" bellowed Harry, but it was too late… the line was dead.

He tried to re-dial but got an unobtainable signal.

* * *

Clarissa stood with a very tall, elegant-looking man close by her side, awaiting the arrival of the Manchester flight, which was less than half full. They easily spotted Harry dressed in pale blue jeans and a dark blue linen summer jacket. Clarissa smiled and waved like an excited child on seeing Harry as he appeared at the arrival gate.

"Hi Harry, am I glad to see you!" said Clarissa entwining her arm in his and giving him a welcoming kiss on the cheek.

"Well that's a first," he remarked smiling.

Clarissa ignored the sarcasm. "This is Guy Pendleton and before you exchange pleasantries I think we should get to the car. I've got this creepy feeling I'm being watched all the time."

The journey to the old country hotel took them about half an hour. Harry sat in the back of the car with Guy at the wheel.

"Okay people, what have you found out so far, besides the little matter of the world coming to an end of course?" asked Harry jovially.

"This is not a funny matter, Harry," replied Clarissa.

"Let's wait until we're at the hotel."

"Harry I realise this might sound like a story from a Hollywood Sci Fi but believe me this stuff is for real," said Guy, as he glanced periodically into the rearview mirror to watch for any expression change on Harry's face.

"Harry, Guy and I have booked in under the name of Mr and Mrs Bradburner, we said we're on holiday from London."

"Mr and Mrs?!" exclaimed Harry with a coy smile. "You'll have to tell me your secret sometime, Guy," he said with a chuckle.

"Nothing like that I can assure you," replied the American defensively.

Clarissa ignored Harry's remark and simply shook her head. "You've been booked in as Dave Clifford," she said.

"Dave, who?" replied Harry.

"Dave Clifford, he was an uncle of mine, an ugly bugger if I remember correctly," said Clarissa.

After Harry had booked in under the assumed name they all went into the lounge, which clearly had at one time been quite a grand drawing room. Now, however, the carpets looked the worse for wear and the furnishings appeared shabby and in need of re-upholstering.

A rather tall, thin elderly looking gentleman with a long wispy beard and a kilt brought in a tray of tea, which he placed down in front of them.

"This'll be your tea," he said, rolling his words in typical Highland fashion.

"Thank you Hamish," replied Clarissa. She waited until the elderly Scotsman had disappeared through a door in the panelled wall close to the large fireplace before speaking. "Harry, the Professor knew his life was in danger, that's why he gave me the scroll and told me to bring it up here. "

"Where is it now?" asked Harry, helping himself to a piece of shortcake.

"I've done exactly as the Professor asked and hid it at Roslin, it's vital Incanda don't get their hands on it."

"And did the Professor tell you whereabouts to hide it?" asked Harry.

"Yes of course."

Harry looked sceptical. "There seems more to this Professor Thomas than meets the eye," he exclaimed. "Like how did he know specifically where to tell you to hide the scroll in Rosslyn Chapel?" continued Harry, now munching on a second shortcake biscuit.

"Who said anything about Rosslyn Chapel?" replied Clarissa, sounding defensive. "I said Roslin. Roslin's the village on the road to Penicuik. Penicuik is a government experimental farm producing cloned sheep and just past there, is a turning, which leads up to the ruins of Roslin castle. The Professor left me this drawing."

There was a particular sharpness to her voice as if she felt the need to defend her actions. She handed Harry a folded piece of paper, which he opened and placed on the table in front of them. Clarissa pointed to a cross marking a particular spot. "This is exactly where he said we would find a loose stone in the wall."

"And was there, miraculously?" asked Harry.

"Yes and that's where we placed the scroll," replied Guy, who thought it appropriate to interject.

Harry looked first at Guy and then at Clarissa. "How do I know you two are not servants of Incanda?"

Clarissa looked aghast whilst Guy simply smiled casually. "You don't," he replied eventually. "But I think it safe to say that if we were, we would not have dragged you up here and certainly not mentioned the Professor's instructions."

"Fair point," said Harry.

Clarissa gave him a scolding look through tear-filled eyes. "How could you think such a thing?" she bellowed, sniffing back the tears.

"I'm surprised the Professor knew exactly where you should hide the scroll that's all," Harry replied, attempting to defend his comments.

The Knights of Black Chapter

"The Professor's exact words to me were that if anything should happen to him I was to get in touch with Hugh McDonald, who apparently is a Thirty Three Degree Freemason. So I did. It was him who gave me the name of this hotel and told me to book in here, and to wait here until he gets in touch."

"Harry can you tell me exactly how you found the Professor's body? Was it in a state of ritual in any way?" asked Guy.

"Absolutely," replied Harry. "It seemed to be a re-enactment of the Third Degree of Craft Freemasonry."

Guy looked at Harry full in the face. "Or perhaps the murder of Hyrum Abif in the inner sanctum of the temple?" he replied.

"Well yes," said Harry. "In fact I've got some detailed photographs of the exact scene," said Harry unzipping his overnight bag. He took the photographs from the envelope Paxton-Smyth had given him and handed them to Guy. The first was a close-up shot of the Professor's head and the point where his cranium had been literally sliced open.

"Harry, as a Third Degree Freemason yourself, you will be aware that the Third Degree ritual which advances you is a facsimile to the enactment of the murder of Hyrum Abif, and that a skull and crossed thigh bones are placed at the head of the candidate who lies in his tomb. Did you know that currently there are over fifty thousand skulls being used in Lodges throughout the world?"

Harry nodded and handed Guy the next photograph that showed the full length of the Professor's body.

"See here," said Guy, "The Professor's legs have been crossed, with his left leg over the right. Templars were always laid to rest in such a fashion, this goes back literally centuries, and if you look at the tombs and effigies of nobility across Europe you will find those of the Order are depicted in this way. And see here..." Guy pointed to a word painted on a card placed directly at the side of the Professor's body, it read. 'Baphomet' "...This is a Jewish code that originates in the first century. It's called the Atbash cipher, it was used to conceal the names of individuals to protect them from persecution. This same code appears in the Dead Sea Scrolls, it's also used in modern Freemasonry, and it features in that scroll of yours, which we have now called the Baton Scroll by the way. Baphomet reveals the word 'Sophia', a Greek word for wisdom. Clearly by using this word in connection with the Professor they are placing a sign of respect in some bizarre way between him and his executioners. The same respect a conquering warrior Knight would have with the opponent Knight he had just slain."

"What do you make of these cards?" asked Harry showing Guy the next photograph detailing the tarot cards laid out in two circles.

"Mmm, interesting," said Guy looking closely at the photograph.

"Tarot cards were used by Knights Templar when the Catholic Church destroyed most of their heretical cult. The Templars adopted this Eastern way from the Saracens who used picture cards for story telling, the cards would have different versions and meanings depending upon how they were shuffled and placed. The Templar cards were designed with two separate layers of meaning. They were therefore safe to carry around as a training aid, eliminating the danger of discovery. The tarot pack has fifty-six cards, these are known as the Minor Arcana and the twenty-two picture cards are called the Major Arcana; these later became the basis of playing cards commonly used today. The Templars' cards contained cups or grails that are now referred to as hearts; wands that are now clubs; pentacles that are diamonds and swords that are now spades."

"In the original deck each suit contained fourteen cards; the Page, now known as the Jack, the Knight, the Queen and the King. Four cards were removed to form the deck of fifty-two that we are familiar with today. These were the Knights from each suit. They're removal was instigated by the Church who had a passion for eradicating anything that depicted a Knight and in particular a Knights Templar."

"The twenty-two picture cards that make up the Major Arcana all had numbers; these largely disappeared except for just one, the Fool. The church proclaimed that these cards represented the rungs of a ladder leading to hell. When a large proportion of Knights Templar were arrested, confessions were given proclaiming that the true purpose of the cards was the content of coded messages and secret teachings. Interestingly this Major Arcana was also identified as the suit of Trumps or the Great Secrets. The Fool escaped the censorship; this card is now known today as the Joker. In Templar teaching the Fool represented the novice, who is now referred to in Freemasonry as the entered apprentice, embarking on his journey to enlightenment and the Third Degree. The other twenty-one

The Knights of Black Chapter

cards were removed by the clergy for fear that the messages they contained would damage the Church."

"The name 'Trumps' was adopted from an ancient word in Latin meaning a Triumph. Stories through the ages have a strong connection with the goddess Ishtar and her consort Tammuz who died and was resurrected, centuries before Christ."

"The Church hated the High Priestess card, known as the Papess card, as it represented the female pope. The belief was that the first pope was female, and not St Peter as we are lead to believe. This High Priestess was in fact Mary Magdalene. The gospel of St Philip clearly states that Jesus loved her above all others and that she received her holy spiritual authority as pope directly from Jesus Christ himself. You can see why the Church was up in arms at such revelations, especially as the Roman Catholic Church was constructed around the domination of women by men. Even now the Vatican gets really pissed off with the liberal views of other Churches who accept women taking holy orders."

"A cult was created called the Black Virgin, acknowledging that Mary Magdalene was actually black, that she was the pope and married to Christ. If you look in the Bible you'll see a line in Solomon verse 1:5 that says, 'I am black, I am comely, O ye daughters of Jerusalem'. Mary Magdalene was supported and to a degree protected by the Knights Templar. The Black Chapter was the cult supporting the Black Virgin and it was from here that The Knights of Black Chapter possibly evolved by name after the split with Rex Deus."

"The Papess card was called on occasions 'Joan'; clearly the Templars discovered ancient documentation that identified Mary Magdalene as the first pope. The tarot cards show her seated in between the columns of Boaz and Jachin and having a scroll in her hand. Notice here," Guy said, pointing to a small strange circle close to the tarot cards in the photograph, "That's called a *Mobius strip*, it's made by taking a single length of paper, twisting it into a cord and then joining the two ends together. The surface then has no end like the figure of eight; represented by the tarot cards this demonstrates death, resurrection and infinity. If Incanda did enact this terrible deed they have symbolised in the tarot cards their wish for the Professor to be resurrected. Strange though it may seem, this layout of cards is very strongly opposed to Christianity. Templars and Jews alike believe the Fool or the Novice will achieve salvation without the Church, or indeed Christ. The

Church on the other hand, teaches that the grace of God can only be achieved through faith in Christ alone."

"See this top circle of cards," said Guy, pointing to the upper circle of the figure of eight; this is the solar sphere of daylight with the Fool at zero. So the Professor was murdered of course but his body has been respectfully laid to rest in honour, as would befit a noble Knight. He has been adorned with the two pillars forming the porchway and entrance of the Jerusalem temple that was the home of the original Knights Templar."

"Fascinating, you certainly know your stuff," said Harry.

"Well, as you can imagine, I find the subject of significant interest. I stumbled across the existence of Incanda and The Knights of Black Chapter before the Professor purchased that signet ring in Crete. I first read about the Knights of Black Chapter when they were mentioned very briefly on a piece of parchment I found tucked into an old Bible. From then on I've been attempting to piece together as much as I can about them. Discovering their colossal power was quite a shock I can tell you."

"Are you a Mason in the States?" asked Harry.

Guy shook his head. "No, but my brother is and my father was. But not being a Mason has never limited my interest. When you delve into history you begin to see just how powerful these respective Degrees are. Take, for example, your British constitution. The Queen is really powerless as a parliamentary monarch. She reigns at the discretion and will of the parliament, especially as England has no written constitution. On the surface the Monarch is powerless to champion any individual rights and liberties. Prince Charles, as the present heir to the throne, has attempted to buck the system on a number of occasions but he experienced recriminations from the establishment. Bankers, industrialists and lawyers control the fate of the United Kingdom and within their ranks one would definitely find the apostles of Incanda at differing levels."

"Did you know there is no actual British constitution? The title used here just describes a number of old outdated customs and precedents regarding parliamentary actions. The oldest constitution in existence today is in fact in the good old USA, adopted in 1787, ratified in 1788 and then effected in 1789, the same year as the French revolution abolished the monarchy in France. You can bet Incanda were instigators, getting one over their arch rivals, The Knights of Black Chapter."

The Knights of Black Chapter

"Those responsible for the morally inspired constitution of the USA were Freemasons and members of a group called Rosicrucian's, such as George Washington, Benjamin Franklin, Thomas Jefferson and Charles Thompson - who designed the great Seal of the United States of America and was a member of Franklin's American Philanthropical 297 Society. The Philanthropical 297 Society had, and of course still does have, a link with Britain's 'Invisible College'. When you hear and read of the American and British special relationship, it's not the romanticised hands across the water, bond of friendship bit, there is an intertwined brotherhood instigated at the time of the constitution."

"It's run almost like a Masons' chapter and controls both Britain and the USA. A club the French dearly wanted to join, and maybe they would have, if the revolution had not abolished the monarchy."

"And is this the reason why Britain is able to retain its monarchy?" asked Clarissa.

Guy looked at her and smiled. "Yes of course and despite your left wing activists, it always will. However, it's my theory that there's a serving member of the British monarchy at a high level in the Knights of Black Chapter... Even as high as one of the nine Knights. And my guess is that this could be a person who has Greek blood running through his veins, probably from when part of Rex Deus fled to Greece from Jerusalem."

"You mean Philip! Prince Philip could actually be a Knight of Black Chapter?" said Harry.

"Who knows?" replied Guy. "Another interesting connection which symbolises the power of Freemasonry is the Great Seal of the United States of America. The imagery of the seal directly relates to the alchemical tradition inherited from the allegory of the ancient Egyptian Therapeutate. The Eagle, the Olive Branch, the Arrows and the Pentagram - these are all occult symbols of opposites: Good & Evil, Male and Female, War and Peace, Light and Dark, Incanda and Knights of Black Chapter, to name but a few. On the back of a dollar bill is a truncated pyramid indicating the loss of old wisdom, severed and forced underground by the church. Thankfully above this is the All-seeing Eye that was used during the French Revolution."

"Yeah know the good old Americans could see beyond the idea of a parallel monarchy. Did you know George Washington was actually offered a Kingship, which he turned down because he had no heritage? In November 1782 he went to the House of Stuart with three other Americans; they arrived at the Palazzo

San Clemente in Florence, Italy where Charles III lived in exile. Charles was invited to become the King of America. The offer was declined."

"Tell me something Guy, do you think one of the nine of the actual Knights Black Chapter is an American?" asked Harry.

Guy smiled. "Not sure, but my guess would be that at least one of the Knights of Black Chapter definitely resides in the USA. One of the main reasons Charles III turned down the offer was simply because he had no heir and therefore the throne would fall into Hanoverian hands and if it did, he felt independence would be lost. So the question is, was Charles from Knights of Black Chapter? Clearly Incanda influence was directed towards Hanoverian hands."

All of a sudden their conversation was interrupted by a knock on the sitting room door and Hamish appeared on the threshold. "I have a visitor for yeah," he said, twisting his tongue around to accentuate his highland accent.

"That will be Hugh McDonald," said Clarissa, "Can you please ask him to come in?"

Almost immediately Hugh McDonald walked in from behind Hamish. He was a dapper little man in his late fifties wearing a tweed suit, waistcoat and brogues. He calmly greeted the three with a faint smile and firm handshake.

"Can we offer you a drink," asked Guy who was the last to shake the man's hand.

"You can, you can indeed, laddie, I'll have a dram of highland malt if yeah please. If I remember correctly Hamish keeps a Mortlach."

Hamish nodded and left, only to return moments later with a silver tray on which sat a full bottle of Speyside nectar.

Hugh picked up the bottle and read the label. "This describes the whisky as being bottled after 19 years of cask-aging in sherry wood, showing a touch of spice to a long velvety finish. The words are poetic are they not?" Hugh smiled and carefully placed the bottle back down on the tray along side four cut-crystal glasses and a jug of water that had been placed on the table in front of them. Hamish left without a word.

Guy poured a generous measure into each glass and then offered one to Hugh McDonald.

"Hugh, I have followed your instructions to the letter, the scroll has been put in the place you suggested," said Clarissa.

"I know lassie," he replied, "It has now been removed into safe hands."

The Knights of Black Chapter

Harry looked aghast. "And I trust you are going to tell us where that might be?" he asked.

Hugh McDonald shook his head. "No, but please be assured its now at rest in the possession of the rightful ones."

"Well I'm not assured, in fact I'm very pissed off actually - firstly because it's cost a man his life and secondly it should be in the museum at Freemasons' Hall at least, or ideally in our new provincial museum."

"Mr Blakemore, the very reason it is out of your possession is to protect both you and it. Incanda are now aware of the scroll's whereabouts, you therefore will not be pursued. If on the other hand you were still in possession of the scroll, all of you would be subjected to the same fate as my good friend Professor Thomas. As far as the so-called Grand Lodge and Freemasons Hall is concerned, that's the last place where it should be. Some of the recordings in the scroll date back before the time the St Clairs received the Barony of Roslin from Malcolm III in 1057, they built their castle in the vicinity. Below the castle in sealed vaults lies the Templar treasure brought here from France during the Catholic Inquisition. Therefore Scotland is the rightful resting place for the scroll you stumbled across."

"Then at least tell us who's got it now?" said Clarissa.

"I think we can work that one out," replied Guy.

Hugh nodded. "Of course it's with the Knights of Black Chapter. And like you, I mourn the loss of Professor Thomas, a very nice and good man."

"How did you know the Professor?" asked Clarissa, with a touch of defensive sharpness in her voice.

"My dear, I first met him when we were invited to decipher the codes contained within the Dead Sea Scrolls. In fact I have spent the last ten years of my life working on them."

"Was the baton scroll originally part of the dead sea scrolls?" asked Clarissa, sipping her whisky.

"No," replied Hugh. "The Dead Sea Scrolls date from well before Christ. They were discovered by a shepherd boy simply searching for his lost sheep, at a place called Quram near Jericho. The boy stumbled upon a number of earthenware jars. The find was reported to the authorities, which prompted a number of archaeologists to commence a search right into the wilderness where many more jars were discovered. Over five hundred Hebrew and Aramaic manuscripts were brought to light, including community recordings dating back to 250 years B.C."

ludlowadvertiser.co.uk/leisure

Focus

Grim jail spell gave rise to a novel idea

By David Edwards

news@ludlowadvertiser.co.uk

THE road from successful businessman to author has been a dramatic one for Ken Bourne Turner.

Ken, aged 65, is a director in a personal development business and has also embarked upon a career as a novelist with his first book, *The Knights of Black Chapter*, just published.

The book, a thriller set against the backdrop of the world of Freemasonry, is intriguing but arguably hardly any more intriguing than the story behind its birth.

Ken started to grow the seed of an idea into a real book during a terrifying period when he spent four months in prisons in the United States and France.

"It was back in 2002 and I had arrived in Washington on a business trip. As I went through customers I was taken to one side and told that there was an irregularity with my passport," said Ken.

What he thought at first was an administrative mistake turned more sinister when after two days of questioning Ken was taken to prison.

"I spent three weeks in a prison alongside murderers and drug dealers. It was a terrifying experience."

But this was only a start because he was then deported from the United States to France.

"Initially, I was in one of the toughest prisons in France before being taken to another prison in Nantes, where I was kept most of the time in solitary confinement. The only thing to keep me sane was a pencil and lots of paper.

"This is when I turned the germ of an idea into the basis for a real book."

> "It was a nightmare and a terrible time for my family. My arrest came completely out of the blue."

Eventually after three months, he was released on bail. But it took nearly two years and a hefty legal bill before Ken was told the matter was being dropped and he had cleared his name.

The reason for his arrest is complex but related to a business deal nearly a decade earlier when a firm that Ken was previously involved with had opened a plant in France with the help of state aid and had then been forced to close.

"It was a nightmare and a terrible time for my family. My arrest came completely out of the blue. I had been to the United States unmolested on occasions prior to my arrest, said.

"What I think happened in the aftermath of 9/1 were paying particular att to passports and I have c ered that Interpol had mark against my passport

Ken has now moved on taking forward a busine writing career from his h Burford near Tenbury.

Developing the outline f *Knights of Black Chapte* Ken another outlet to co trate on during the time worrying over clearin name.

He has researched the i ing world of Freemasoni come up with a tale beg with simultaneous attacks on New York, L and a passenger aircraft, leave the popularity of t President and British Minister in global meltdo

A surprise guest at Anglo-American talks Caribbean reveals the sc unimaginable power dee bowels of Freemasonry, t the Ark of the Covena Holy Grail.

Puiblished by Ken B Turner, it is available fron bookshops, and to or download in e-book f from online retailers.

▶ Ken Bourne Turner. 0938

"Why were they hidden in such a way?" asked Clarissa.

"What, in earthenware jars? Earthenware provided good protection. They were hidden because of the Jewish revolt against the Romans, sometime between AD66 and 70. The intention was to retrieve them but they never were retrieved. The Old Testament provided evidence of their existence in the book of Jeremiah verses 32-14 which clearly states:*Thus saith the Lord of hosts. Take these evidences and put them into earthenware vessels that they may continue for many days.* A principal scroll was the Copper Scroll because it contains an inventory and gives the location of treasures from Jerusalem and the Kedrom Valley cemetery. A war scroll was also discovered giving a full account of military strategies and tactics. Another scroll also found was a manual of disciples, it details laws and legal practice along with customary rituals; it also describes the importance of a designated council of twelve who preserve the faith of the land. The excavations at Qumran found relics dating back over three thousand five hundred years B.C."

Just then Harry's mobile phone interrupted Hugh. Everyone turned towards Harry who struggled to take the phone from his trouser pocket. The screen showed that Code 3 was calling.

"Excuse me, I need to take this call, I'll just take this outside," he said leaving the room and closing the door behind him. Harry touched the buttons that opened up the security line as he walked briskly into the garden. "Hi Skipper," he said.

"Harry," replied Jeremy Paxton-Smyth, "we have some sketchy information on Humphrey Morgan-Sinclair and his son. The family are closely related to the St Clair family of Roslin in Scotland. In fact their connection has a definite link with Incanda."

"Skipper, I'm up in Scotland now, my partner followed the Professor's instructions and brought the scroll to Scotland, and through a bloke by the name of Hugh McDonald the scroll is now somehow in the hands of the Knights of Black Chapter."

There was no sound from the other end of the phone, which prompted Harry to shout, "Hello, Skipper can you hear me?"

"Yes I'm still here, I'm just thinking. Look I want you on the job we discussed as soon as possible, but if what I hear is true, these Morgan-Sinclair's have a direct connection with the Middle East, through something to do with banking... so take a couple of days to see what you can discover up in Scotland.

There just may be a connection that could lead us to the target. Right now the Morgan-Sinclairs are under surveillance and I'll make sure they remain that way. If there are any developments I'll let you know, in the meantime report back to me every twelve hours or so. I need a good reason why you have not left on the assignment; the last thing I want is for the Americans to think their man is doing this alone."

"This Hugh McDonald guy seems pretty clued up, I'll see what I can find out. He did say that Incanda would be aware that the scroll was now in the possession of the Knights of Black Chapter. He also said that Incanda would not be coming after us, which is a comforting thought, I hope he's right!"

Harry closed his phone and walked back towards the house, he then rejoined the others. "Tell me Hugh, who are you?" asked Harry, casually breaking into the discussion that had been proceeding during his absence.

Hugh McDonald smiled. "I wondered when you were going to ask me that," he said. "I am a Grand Officer, my mother Lodge is the Kilwinning Lodge Number O, the Mother Lodge of all Scotland. Personally I have a direct line going back to Robert the Bruce who reserved himself the right to be Royal Grand Master. He instituted the Royal Order of Herodem after the Battle of Bannockburn in 1314."

"So you are a Thirty Three Degree Mason?" asked Harry.

"I am indeed, as were my forebears since Robert the Bruce. I am also a Provincial Commander of Knights Templar."

"How about the Knights of Black Chapter?" asked a cherry red-faced Clarissa, sipping her third dram of whisky.

Hugh smiled slightly. "Oh I will never be of that rank, lass," he replied.

"Then what is your connection with them?" interjected Guy.

Hugh took a swig of whisky. "Let me explain," he said, "There are so many levels in Freemasonry as indeed you will be aware. The lower down the Orders you travel, the closer you come to the ultimate that was Rex Deus. When Rex Deus split and Incanda and Black Chapter evolved they both required absolute protection, so Degrees further along the line took up this mantle, and naturally many of these Orders became almost as secret as those they were protecting. I am a member of an Order that is in the chain, but many Degrees away from the Knights of Black Chapter, or indeed Incanda.

"We maintain exactly the same ritual of passing our mantle down to our eldest offspring, irrespective of sex - either boy or girl."

"Hugh, what do you know about the Morgan-Sinclair family? Because I think they played a part in Professor Thomas's murder," said Harry.

Hugh McDonald picked up the depleted bottle and poured a measure into his glass, he then carefully added just a splash of spring water and took a sip, closing his eyes as if to savour the experience. He then raised his head as if to help the whisky to slip down. After carefully putting the glass down on the table he turned to look at Harry.

"I discussed the existence of the Morgan-Sinclairs with my friend Professor Franklin Thomas the day before he went to Blandford. I warned him of the danger he was letting himself in for, the Morgan-Sinclairs are members of a Middle Eastern Chapter, who have allegiance to Incanda. The scroll you discovered would have been a huge prize for Incanda's trophy cabinet."

"Permit me to explain briefly. An Earl Rognvald ruled a place called 'More' which was part of Norway. More was the land around the city of Trondheim. The Rognvald family were given the Orkney and Shetland Isles by King Harold; these islands were ruled by Earl Rognvald's brother Sigurd, as regent."

"The St Clair family evolved when Rognvald's son Hrolf invaded France and took Normandy in the eighth century. A peace treaty was eventually signed with King Charles, the Simple of France; this was later known as the Treaty of St Clair. Hrolf More and his cousins decided to take the name of St Clair in recognition of the treaty; they then established themselves as the Dukes of Normandy. I presume Professor Thomas talked to you about the Grooved Ware People, it was a big subject for him and one he researched intently - anyway, the More Family re-united two strands of the Grooved Ware People's philosophy, that was over 3,000 years old. These strands were brought together through marriage and developing a new bloodline, together with the name St Clair which in translation means 'Holy Shining Light'. This was the name for the ancient Jewish concept of the Shekinah, when it was later combined with the Gaelic word Roslin. The family became recognised as both Norse and Jewish."

"The name Sinclair originates from the St Clair name, almost as a bastardised translation. The actual name Sinclair was originally taken by one of the cousins who was ostracised and went off to do his own thing. Both families were involved

in the break up of Rex Deus. The St Clairs and what turned out to be the Sinclairs, used the Pelican as their symbol, and it is believed that Incanda also use the Pelican within their mantle. The Pelican is a symbol of resurrection. They truly believed that if their ancient ideas were to rise from their long slumber, the fulfilment of an old prophecy was required. To the families within the Chapters close to Incanda, the most important book of the New Testament is Enochian, the book of Revelations, also known as the Apocalypse. It concludes the Bible by talking about the New Jerusalem that will one day be built. It was written for the faithful to be prepared for the final intervention of God in human affairs, for the dawning of the New World, but for exactly one thousand years the terrors and evil doings of the existing world were to increase and significantly intensify.
Lets borrow a Bible from Hamish."

Hugh stood up from the settee and left the room.

For a moment Harry, Clarissa and Guy sat in silence intrigued by the revelations they were hearing. Soon Hugh returned clutching a large black volume with faded gold leaf page edges; a blue silk ribbon with a frayed edge hung from somewhere towards the middle.

"Here we are," he said, after carefully turning the frail pages. "Revelation chapter 20... it says... *I saw an Angel come down from heaven, having the key of the bottomless pit and a great chain in his hand. And he laid hold on the dragon, that old serpent, which is the Devil and Satan, and bound him a thousand years, And cast him into the bottomless pit, and shut him up and set a seal upon him, that he should deceive the nations no more, till the thousand years should be fulfilled; and after that he must be loosen a little season.*

"*And I saw thrones, and they sat upon them, and judgement was given unto them; and I saw the souls of them that were beheaded for the witness of Jesus, and the word of God, and which had not worshipped the beast, neither his image, neither had received his mark upon their foreheads, or in their hands and they lived and reigned with Christ a thousand years. But the rest of the dead lived not again until the thousand years were finished. This is the first resurrection.*

"*Blessed and holy is he that hath part in the first resurrection: on such the second death hath no power, but they shall be priests of God and of Christ, and shall reign with him a thousand years.*

"*And when the thousand years are expired, Satan shall be loosed out of his prison, And shall go out to deceive the nations which are in the four quarters of the earth, Gog and Mogog, to gather them together to battle: the number of whom is the sand of the sea.*

"And they went up on the breadth of the earth, and encompassed the camp of the saints about, and the beloved city: and fire came down from God out of heaven and devoured them."

Hugh closed the Bible, put it carefully on the table and collected his glass. "It was of course the Romans who brought about the first destruction, turning Jerusalem into an unholy place. The prophesy clearly stated that those who died in the destruction around 70 AD would be resurrected a thousand years later when a godless power would take Jerusalem. Exactly a thousand years later the Saljuk Turks took Jerusalem. The first crusade was organised and took place around 1096, a thousand years later.

"Incanda have been active to instigate the prophecy again, The Knights of Black Chapter were inaugurated to stop them and so the never-ending battle continues. But I fear Incanda are gradually winning, especially from the point where it all began, the Middle East, where money, corruption and power fuel and influence the battleground.

"Rosslyn plays a significant part in both Incanda and Knights of Black Chapter. It replicates Jerusalem in so many ways. The timing of its construction coincides with the construction of King Solomon's Temple, exactly 1,440 years after the world's flood, before the coming of Enoch and Noah. Jesus was born exactly 1,440 years after Moses led the Israelites to safety through the Red Sea and Rosslyn was commenced 1,440 after Jesus was born."

"Rosslyn was built with symbols and coded messages carved and sculpted into its stonewalls... you could say that the very place is a work of reference, like the Columns of Enoch and the scrolls that are still entombed deep below Rosslyn's foundations. There are, for example, four lozenges etched into the south wall of the crypt, they represent the four places the St Clair family held dear: Jerusalem, Roslin, Orkney and Trondheim. These have been verified and the lozenge that represents Trondheim is actually pointing to the exact compass bearing of the city and is accurate to one degree. In fact each lozenge represents the chart references of each of the St Clairs' favourite places. The position of one top lozenge matches the Solstice Sunrise at Trondheim. The next one down has an exact angle to the Orkney Solstice, and the next again directly corresponds to the Roslin Solstice and finally the top lozenge points to Jerusalem. Experts have examined the angles; all are virtually pinpoint accurate."

"When Rex Deus split and Incanda and the Knights of Black Chapter were formed, Trondheim became Incanda's centre of activity."

"So does that mean Incanda meet at particular times in Trondheim and The Knights of Black Chapter meet in Jerusalem?" asked Harry.

"That might be viewed as speculative, but certainly I think you'd find that you would be much closer to Incanda in Trondheim and of course don't forget the Norwegian Earls were the Sinclair Earls."

"Do you know anyone in Trondheim I could talk to?" asked Harry.

Hugh had a blank expression for a moment before answering. "Historically, the Sinclairs figured very vividly in Norway of course, but the double barrelled name Morgan-Sinclair was not the coming together of two families. In fact the name Morgan derived from the name More, this could have come from a little interbreeding, who knows, but one thing is certain - the name Morgan was not a separate family. But to answer your question, the only connection I have is with a Lodge in Trondheim and specifically with a provincial Grand Sword Bearer from the Lodge, a man by the name of Thor Olson. He can be contacted through the Lodge, but you are treading on very dangerous ground. There must be quite a number of Incanda followers operating in the region and I have no idea who is protecting them."

"Well Hugh, this meeting has been fascinating. We intend to get to the bottom of Professor Thomas's murder. Thank you for spending time seeing us," said Clarissa, standing to suggest the meeting was now closed.

Hugh also stood and accepted her hand. "It was a pleasure, but as I say, be very careful: you are playing with a fire so powerful the outcome could be devastating. My advice would be to let matters rest where they are, mourn our mutual friend's death and get on with your lives."

Harry and Guy also left their seats. "Well, we'll see what transpires," said Harry, taking his turn to shake Hugh's hand.

Clarissa saw their guest to the door and bid him good night. "Well what did you make of all that?" said Clarissa, returning to her seat and collecting her almost empty glass from the table.

"If you ask me, it's a bunch of smokescreens. I bet this guy McDonald is deeper into the levels of Masonry than he's letting on," said Guy.

"Harry, we have a direct transcript of the baton scroll, the Professor made a copy and I'm going to make it my job to find out who these people are. Guy has volunteered to help me, will you help too?" Clarissa gave Harry a girlie look that was uncharacteristic of her normal personality.

"Clarissa, I need to talk business with you in private, no disrespect Guy."

"None taken," said Guy, who emptied the dregs from his glass and stood up. "I need my bed anyway. I'll see you people in the morning." He gave Clarissa a sisterly peck on her cheek then waved at Harry and closed the door behind him.

Harry moved his place on the settee to sit along side Clarissa. She smiled at him nervously.

"Well life's never dull where you're concerned," she said with a faint smile.

"Listen, gorgeous, I'm just about to put all my faith and trust in you."

Clarissa shook her head. "I'm not sure I want to hear this, are you a serial killer or something?"

Harry smiled. "Not quite, at least, not illegally anyway. For a number of years I was in the Special Air Service, my name was planted on a hit list and for security reasons my name had to be changed."

"You mean you're not Harry Blakemore?" said Clarissa with an expression that showed both shock and concern. "Who the hell am I in partnership with then?"

Harry smiled and tapped the back of her hand affectionately. "I am who I am, love, I've just had a security blanket around me for the past few years that's all." Harry went into detail about his time in Torbay and exactly how he arrived in Wales. "I have been selected to assist the Americans to perform a task in the Middle East... ironically there is a connection between the job I'm engaged to perform and Incanda. The person responsible for the attacks on New York, London - and of course the bomb on the aircraft - is a man called Mohamed Abu Atif."

"And you have been assigned to capture him?" replied Clarissa.

"Well something like that. It means me going out to the Middle East in a couple of days, but I'm going to Trondheim first, I want to find out exactly what these Morgan-Sinclairs are all about. I think they could be routing funds through to Al Val Sinda which is the movement this Abu Atif heads up. Now you say you've got a copy of the baton scroll, does your friend Guy think he can break the code?"

"Oh yes, I think so. I want to find out who actually killed the Professor and if that means breaking the code to do it, than so be it."

Harry smiled and poured two drops of water into their glasses as all the whiskey had gone. He then raised his glass and Clarissa touched it with hers. "So tell me your real name then."

Harry took a little water into his mouth then shook his head.

"Is that to help the water go down or are you shaking your head because you're not going to tell me?"

"Harry Blakemore is my real name. The rest's in the past and I intend it to remain that way. "

"Bud, I'd like you to attend a telephone conference with the Brits. I'm planning it for tomorrow morning at nine."

"Yes, Mr President, have we got an agenda?" replied Bud O'Dowd.

"Sure, top of the list; why the fuck did we destroy half the Brazilian coastline to spring a psychopath who's now killed JoJo Curtis?"

Bud O'Dowd wiped the beads of sweat from his forehead and raised his eyes to the ceiling as if to appeal to the almighty. "Mr President, we're not sure Lewis Ford actually killed JoJo Curtis. And besides you know JoJo was there as a decoy anyway."

"Bud, we have men on the ground, I gotta believe them when they say the goddam psycho killed JoJo. Did James Parker tell you about this guy catching a rat and eating it alive, right there in front of him?"

"Yes Mr President, circus stuff, but eating rats and killing fellow Americans are two different things," replied Bud, whose irritability level was ready to explode. He threw a mean glance at the phone, ready to destroy it.

"Bud, will you quit this Mr President bullshit when we're having a one-to-one conversation. Anyway, I've told Parker I want this guy off the planet and quick, he's putting men onto it right away."

"Don't forget the Brits have got a man going out there any time now," replied O'Dowd, wishing he'd been somewhere else when the President called.

"Yeah know, I don't give a finger lickin' fuck. If this Brit relieves the world of Abu Atif, he can have all the reward. I'll even give him a Purple Heart. Bud, be ready for nine in the morning, okay."

With that the phone went dead. Bud O'Dowd just threw the receiver onto his desk and left for the night.

* * *

The Knights of Black Chapter

"Tony, how are you?" asked the President the following morning.

Prime Minister Blaine took a little time to reply because he'd burned his mouth with hot coffee. "I'm well, Bill, thank you for asking, except I've got my egotistical wife ready to set the world alight with a tour across America - maybe you heard, although what rubbish she'll be talking about, I shudder to think."

"How about this affair you've been having with that guy Henderson, wasn't he the one you gave two separate ministerial jobs, and had to sack him from both, how the fuck did you keep that under wraps? Your press would have killed yeh?"

"It wasn't an affair, just a few schoolboy growing pains," replied Tony Blaine defensively.

"Oh don't worry Tony my friend we all have skeletons in the closet. So this G8 summit, what the fuck are we going to major on?"

"Well Bill, the big thing here is climate change, my advisers think it's a big vote winner."

"Right, and I guess you guys need a vote winner right now, but that means reducing emissions and America runs off cheap gasoline. Tony it's about balance... decades ago you guys went off and conquered other lands, you pillaged and plundered, now it's our turn, only this is the 21st century. Oil is the game, cheaper than we can extract at home, so we need to do a bit of pillaging and plundering ourselves.

"You know my old man went into Iraq, won the war and came out with fuck all except dignity and yeh can't run America on dignity. So guess what, I'm going in again only this time I'll rout the place and Tony I want you to help me. Did you hear that Iraq are building a nuclear device that Saddam intends training on the west?"

"What proof has that been founded upon?" replied the Prime Minister, sounding cautious.

The President laughed. "Founded on Tony, why bullshit of course. Get the PR men working, send investigators out there, you know just to make things look real, maybe they may even discover a few things that can be used as evidence, who knows. Hey, yeh know Hollywood invents fantasy, we're masters of illusion. You control that wonderful institution the BBC, the whole goddam world believes the BBC; if they said the universe was turning pink everyone would believe them!" The President laughed.

The Knights of Black Chapter

"Yes but a scam of this scale, it would mean invading a sovereign state. How could we get away with that?" asked Blaine, sounding really nervous.

"Simple Tony, how many other countries are involved in Iraq to the extent that we are? None, so we drop the hint at the G8, then gradually let the ripple turn into a wave of fear. The whole world knows that Saddam's a complete bastard, we could liberate his people all at the same time, after all he's persecuted them for so long, we'll be showing the planet what real good guys we are. We help them appoint a new government with the 'right' people, all in our pocket of course, which would give us economic control. I got to tell yeh Tony, before you know it we'll be heroes, plus it will deflect the serious home and international issues we've both got right now. The Brits will gather around you as their leader, they'll be like bees round the hive, and why? Because it's a time of emergency, that's why. Ask yeh self, did the Falklands war damage Maggie's popularity? Think about it."

"I am," replied Tony Blaine.

"A consolidatory union with me Tony, would be worth millions to you personally, And when that first lady of yours goes on tour again, flocks of people will hang on her every word, no matter what bullshit she'd be talking about. Just think of it, you and me walking side by side towards two podiums at the Whitehouse, shoulder to shoulder. Our countries' flags behind us, two nations again united in one common cause. Freedom. I got ta tell yeh Tony, the world would be eating right out of our hands, rather than kicking us in the balls like it's doing now. Let's fuck those French bastards into the bargain. I truly believe those shit-stirring garlic-crushers have been supplying Saddam with weapons."

"I share your concerns, Bill but you must understand the British people are far more sceptical than Americans."

"Look Tony, historically what has war done to popularity ratings? Zoom, that's what."

"Okay Bill I'm in but I think this must be a slow process, we need to really allow experts to sift through Iraq and it's a big country. Saddam's not just going to welcome them in with open arms of course. Foreigners trampling across his lands are the last thing he'll agree too."

"I agree, but the good times start when we announce that we believe Saddam has the makings of a nuclear capability, we can then develop from there. Hey Tony, changing the subject, I hear you guys are going to make it difficult for your citizens to smoke in public?"

"Well yes, we are, doing our bit for health."

"Well Tony, I think that's great, as you know most of our states banned smoking years ago. It's going to cost you guys plenty though, the amount of taxes you charge on tobacco."

"Oh we've got that covered, through the emissions - we're going to hit big cars with heavy fuel costs, and road licences. The treasury have calculated we'll actually come out better off."

"Wow and your people will just bite the bullet? Your gasoline tax must be the highest in the world now."

"It is, but you see we have exploited the sell-off of public transport. Our predecessors privatised it which meant they gave away control to greedy shareholders, therefore by and large public transport is very poor. People are obliged to use their cars, and the privileged who live in the country have no choice if they want to move around."

"You really hate those guys from the country don't you."

"England is a small country, too much of the land is in the ownership of too few people and most of them vote conservative. Those that don't, vote Liberal Democrat and that's a complete pile of horse manure." The Prime Minister was heard to giggle.

"You know Tony, I don't go a whole bunch on this global warming bullshit."

"No but it's a very good scam to bring fear to the people, and revenues into the treasury. Did I mention a vote winner also, because it will be!" replied Tony Blaine.

"Right gentlemen welcome to this conference call. I've already got Prime Minister Blaine on the line, so let's each have a shout, just to see if we're all here. Can you please call out in turn to say who you are, for the benefit of those who don't know you. Your name will do just fine."

"Hi Mr President, this is Frank Decapio, head of the FBI."

"Morning Frank, good to have you in on this conference."

"Good morning, gentlemen, I'm Jeremy Paxton-Smyth, head of MI6."

"Hi Mr President and you all, this is James Parker, Director of the CIA."

"Hello, I'm Philip Martins, I represent her Majesty's Foreign Office."

"Hi, Bud O'Dowd, Chief of staff."

"Well gentlemen, by the power of technology I welcome you all to this telephone conference. For the sake of formality, I'm

The Knights of Black Chapter

William P. McCain and it is my privilege to be the President of the USA. The reason I have called this meeting is to discuss our united front against terrorism and the ongoing problems in the Middle East. I refer in particular of course to Iraq. Our intelligence on the ground there has discovered what appears to be the makings of a nuclear capability of some kind. So far the information we have is very sketchy, however the merest possibility of Saddam having such a capability puts the safety of the West seriously at risk."

"Sir, that's quite a statement to make. We have people in Iraq, they have not reported such a potential problem."

"Who's speaking," replied the President sharply.

"Oh I'm sorry, Philip Martins, Mr President."

"Thanks, Phil, only if we don't say who we are then it's impossible to detect the guys who are with us and ones that are not, if you see my point!"

"Mr President, I'm not saying I'm not with you, I'm simply saying our people have not reported such a possibility."

"Well I presume that's Phil again. Phil, Iraq is one mother of a size, lots of it is covered in sand, so maybe your guys have not heard of this yet, our guys have. We trust their reports. So if we say there could be a problem, please listen."

Bud O'Dowd smiled to himself. "One nil to us I think," he said to Chief Sitting Bull.

"Did you say something Bud?" asked the President.

"Hi, this is Bud O'Dowd, not a thing Mr President."

"Good morning, Tony Blaine here, the President and I have discussed the possible danger such a capability might represent to the West as a whole, we therefore must act to discover where such a capability is being developed and put a stop to any process immediately. Phillip, perhaps you and I can have a conversation about our people in Iraq after this conference."

"That's him fucked for promotion," whispered Bud O'Dowd to the Indian.

"I can tell you gentlemen, that as Prime Minister I will put my complete weight behind an investigation to clearly discover exactly what's going on in Iraq. They are a conquered country we therefore have rights under international law to investigate any activities that might be seen as contrary to terms of defeat. Saddam signed the peace treaty which precludes any activities that may contravene or put the treaty in jeopardy, especially if it may become a threat to peace."

The Knights of Black Chapter

"Hi, this is Frank Decapio. My people tell me this guy Mohammed Abu Atif and his Al Val Sinda are gaining more and more popularity in the Middle East, have we got guys on the ground yet who can sort this guy out?"

"This is the President. We have a man who was selected to carry out our part of the bargain. This particular person has presented us with a bunch of embarrassing problems. James Parker has his finger on the pulse. James I'll leave it to you to explain, over to you Mr Director."

"Hi, I'm James Parker, CIA. I have a number of agents in Afghanistan, they are there to infiltrate the Taliban and report back any movements that take place. They have also been monitoring the assignee we appointed to seek out Mohammed Abu Atif. The difficulty we had was in engaging an independent person with the necessary experience required for such a job - naturally someone who would be prepared to take significant risks, especially if things went wrong, a suitable guy who could also take the blame away from our respective countries. Unfortunately the person we selected is a free radical and it looks like he's killed one of our trusted people, who we appointed as an observer."

"Hi James this is Jeremy Paxton-Smyth, our man is about to leave, are you saying your appointee has been brought in?"

There was an uncomfortable silence before James Parker replied.

"Jerry, good to hear from you! Let's talk in detail after this conference, but briefly this news is hot off the press and currently my department is responsible for closing him down."

"Phillip Martins here. Are you saying that there's someone in Afghanistan, appointed by the CIA who's so dangerous he has actually killed one of your people and is currently on the loose? Good god the media will have a field day, I did warn you of the dangers of such a risky idea."

Bud O'Dowd felt the need to come into the conversation to quell Phillip Martin's egotistical attitude before he began lording it over the conference. "This is Bud O'Dowd. Firstly we have no categorical proof Lewis Ford was responsible for JoJo Curtis's death and until we do let's be professional and not jump to conclusions with the old 'I told you so routine'. Jerry, what's happened to your guy?"

"Well Mr O'Dowd, we had a problem, in that our man was arrested for suspected murder."

"For fuck's sake, gentlemen, Tony Blaine and I had a very simple idea to quietly appoint a couple of free-lance mercenaries, not psychopaths who kill to get a fix. Surely, gentlemen, with our combined resources we can find a couple of suitable guys who can go in, do the job and leave for instant retirement. Like Phil says, if the goddam media get a hold of this, we'll be well and truly in the brown stuff."

"Jeremy Paxton-Smyth again, Mr President. Our man was not responsible for the death of Professor Thomas, the police have been duty bound to release him without charge. This man has worked for me in Special Forces, he's good and my judgement of his abilities are accurate... that's why he was selected."

"Good, well I hope he gets the job done. Let's give him all the co-operation we can without being seen too, you understand," replied Bud O'Dowd.

" This is the President again, I'm sure I speak for Mr Blaine when I say we'll leave you and James Parker to sort out the details, but we need results, fast, and if we can link the end of Abu Atif with Saddam and the probability of finding hidden capabilities in Iraq, I'd be a really happy President."

The conference call continued with the agenda changing to other business for the G6 summit. When it was eventually over Jeremy Paxton-Smyth felt the need for a good wash in cold water, especially to bathe the ear that had had the phone pressed to it for almost two hours. On returning to his desk he called Harry Blakemore.

"Harry, how's Scotland?"

"Very revealing, Skipper," replied Harry as he stood in Edinburgh Airport waiting to board a flight to Trondheim. "I have an important lead that I'm following up so I'm off to Norway."

"Harry, that priest in Blandford, father Macaroni, we have checked him out and strangely he's actually from Nicaros Cathedral in Trondheim. He was born and grew up in Naples where he took his vows. The route that took him to Norway is unclear but historically the Norwegian archdiocese comprised of Iceland, Greenland, the Faeroes, Shetland and the Isle of Man. We have found that he spent some time in the Isle of Man before moving to Trondheim. "

"Well it's my guess he's a down-the-line servant to Incanda," replied Harry.

The Knights of Black Chapter

"Yes you've probably right. Harry, I need you on the ground out there quickly. The Americans have been asking about you. It looks like their man has killed an observer. The President is personally having him removed from the field, it would appear there's quite a few red faces in Washington."

"So who's replacing him?" replied Harry, somewhat bemused by the revelation.

"I would suggest no-one, you're on your own."

"Fantastic, at least I can work faster and pick up the full reward which, I presume I'm now entitled to, Skipper?"

Paxton-Smyth smiled. "Naturally," he said.

Harry's flight to Trondheim was uneventful. He checked in at the Rainbow Thon hotel, a short distance from the Norwegian University of Science and Technology, where Thor Olson was a lecturer. He then spent the afternoon looking around Trondheim.

With all the revelations and snippets of information surrounding Freemasonry, the compulsion to learn more prompted Harry to acquire as many publications as he could on this vast subject - and on Freemasonry and Knights Templar in particular, especially with regard to their obsession for gathering wealth, banking and the law. He also read about the churches they built and in particular round churches that were placed in certain geometrical patterns. Harry learned that Borholm had one church in particular called Osterlars Round Church where a deep hollow had been discovered in the floor containing an abundance of precious jewels and coinage. The find was known as the Treasure of the Knights Templar.

Harry was not due to meet Thor Olson until later that evening, he therefore decided to explore the town. However as he was leaving the hotel his mobile, which he kept on silent mode, began vibrate.

"Hello. Is that Mr Blakemore?" said a female voice.

"Who's that?" responded Harry, a little surprised to receive a call from a woman with a slight accent.

"I'm Thor Olson's assistant. I'm so sorry, Thor has a prior engagement this evening and will not be able to join you. He must attend a Craft Lodge in his official capacity. He conveys his apologies and suggests perhaps you would like attend the Craft Lodge as his guest."

"Great, but I have no regalia," said Harry sounding just slightly obstructive.

"Thor asked me to say that regalia will not be a problem and that you and he will be able to talk freely at the festive board."

"Okay, but where's the Lodge and how do I get there?"

The Knights of Black Chapter

"Thor will have a car pick you up at your hotel around five thirty."

"Fine, thank him for me and tell him I'll look forward to meeting him later."

"Thank you Mr Blakemore, I will." The phone immediately went dead.

As it was only 2.00 pm Harry decided to take himself off to the Museum. The museum had formerly been the Archbishop's palace and according to the tour guide it was the place to go to discover the important parts of Trondheim, and indeed Norway's history. Artefacts and sculptures that were originally in Nidaros Cathedral were displayed at the southern end, whilst the northern wing which dated back to 1160 featured the great hall behind which the archbishop had his private quarters and would receive visitors.

"Can you tell me if the curator is around?" Harry asked a young and particularly attractive attendant. "I'm from the historical research branch of the British Museum."

"Just a moment sir, I'll find out," replied the attendant.

Harry was impressed. "Amazing, having to come all the way to Norway to hear perfect English spoken, unlike London," Harry said to himself.

The attendant returned and smiled. "Mrs Ottoman will be pleased to see you sir, will you please come this way?"

Harry followed the attendant through a pair of very large old doors, which led into what appeared to be a labyrinth of corridors. Eventually they came to a modern door with Mrs Ottoman's name on a brass plaque. The attendant knocked and entered with Harry right behind wondering what to say next.

"Good afternoon, I'm Muriel Ottoman, it is always a pleasure to meet a member of the British Museum. I am sorry but no one notified me of your visit."

"That is indeed my fault, Mrs Ottoman, my visit is purely on the spur of the moment. I work for a very small investigation branch, loosely associated to the British Museum, the department now comes under the EEC."

"Oh dear, what have we done wrong?" responded Mrs Ottoman, her face changing to a shade of pale pink.

Harry laughed. "Nothing, nothing at all Mrs Ottoman, I work almost entirely in population movement, I've been assigned by Brussels to investigate the historical movement of the population of member states. I understand there are quite a large number of Italians living in Norway?"

The expression on Mrs Ottoman's face began to relax and then change into a formal and official look. "I would think that most countries throughout the world have a community of Italian people Mr...?"

"Sorry," apologised Harry, "Jack Greenway. Naturally we realise that. However, if my research is correct Norway and indeed Trondheim have a long association with Italians through Catholicism and indeed banking.

"Mr Greenway, with the greatest respect I think your enquiries should be directed towards the government department of statistics, or indeed the arch-diesis." Mrs Ottoman became nonchalant towards her guest as she picked up a file and began opening it.

Harry was on the back foot, he needed to adopt a more direct approach if he was going to glean any information from this lady. "Mrs Ottoman I know, but these institutions merely have figures on pieces of paper, I'm looking for the human view. For example have any Italians been influential in Trondheim in any way? Have there, for example, ever been any Italian priests or teachers working in schools and of course churches? You see this is a cultural thing not just a statistical view."

Mrs Ottoman's formal expression lightened slightly. Harry's ad-libbing had taken him to the brink of being slung out on his ear but now his words were getting a more serious, thought-provoking response.

"We had a young priest from Naples here, up until a year or so ago. He was a little strange if I remember but very popular in the Cathedral. I believe, like most priests he moved around quite a bit. My bank manager as a matter of fact is from an Italian family who settled here some time way back in history."

"That's exactly the type of information we need. You see we can link people with family members who might still be in their country of origin.
Do you remember the young priest's name?"

Mrs Ottoman frowned. "I have no idea Mr Greenway. You should ask at the Cathedral. As for my bank manager, his name is Mr Ricardo Francini."

Harry thanked the curator and left without bothering to view the museum, instead he headed straight for the Cathedral. The impressive interior was buzzing with tourists and at least three guided tours were underway. Harry spied a wizened old man in a black cassock coming through a small oak door marked 'private'.

"Excuse me," said Harry raising his voice to gain the old man's attention, as he was several feet away. "I'm sorry to bother you only I'm trying to find a Father Macaroni. Do you know if he's still here at the Cathedral?"

Instantly the nonchalant expression of the old man's lived-in face changed. He looked stony eyed at Harry. "Father Macaroni is no longer here," he replied and began to scurry off in the general direction of the Mary Altar. Harry took a few quick paces and began to walk alongside the old man.

"Father, I'm a private investigator working for Father Macaroni's family, they have not heard from him in a long time, his mother is seriously ill and they are desperately trying to make contact."

Harry felt that he should go on a guilt trip, lying in the house of God, but that was for later. This old man's body language was saying interesting things and Harry needed to find out whatever he could. The priest turned to Harry; his white, wrinkled face looked cold and unfriendly. "The Priest of which you speak has not been here for a long time, I suggest you look elsewhere."

Having made the statement he began to walk away. Harry took him by the arm and drew the old man closer. "Can you tell me where he might have gone to from here?"

"Leave me alone," screamed the old man who began to struggle. Harry immediately released his arm and apologised.

Within a split second four very large priests dressed in purple cassocks had gathered closely around Harry. "Let us escort you out of the Cathedral sir," one said in a firm but polite voice.

"I'm only looking for Father Macaroni, do any of you blokes know where I can find him?"

The four priests responded by simply ushering Harry towards a fire exit. "Leave, Mr Blakemore and don't come back," said one of the priests. A gentle push put Harry between the four in a huddle like a clutch of rugby players; he was then gradually manoeuvred out into a courtyard. The door was instantly closed behind him. Harry was alarmed that they had referred to him by name; he therefore decided it best to leave without making a fuss.

Harry's senses seemed to detect a presence, as if he was being followed. He stopped and sat outside a small street café where he purchased a cup of coffee. From his table he could see both up and down the busy street. He opened the literature he'd taken from the church and began nonchalantly reading it, periodically glancing up over the brochure just to see if anyone was observing him, but nothing seemed untoward.

After purchasing a white shirt and a black tie in preparation for attending the Lodge, Harry returned to his hotel and immediately called Jeremy Paxton-Smyth to update him on the events. Paxton-Smyth agreed to look into the background of Ricardo Francini.

Harry took a long shower, dressed and was about to go down to the lobby to await his lift to the Lodge when he heard a gentle knock on his door. Then he saw an envelope being slipped underneath. Harry opened the door but found the corridor was empty. He picked up the envelope and closed the door. Inside was a typed note, which simply read: *'For your sake do not pursue your enquiries any further. Both you and Clarissa Llewellyn-Jones are in extreme danger. Leave Norway immediately.'*

Harry sat in the car that collected him, in reflective mode. He had tried to speak to Clarissa but her mobile had gone directly to answer- phone. He therefore left a message telling her about the note. The driver was a Mason whose English was not particularly conversational; however the drive from the hotel to the Lodge took less than ten minutes.

Harry was going to witness an installation of a new Worshipful Master and in turn the new Master would be appointing his officers, therefore the
event would be substantially longer than usual. As Harry had not reached the rank of Worshipful Master, he was asked to leave the Lodge during the installation ceremony. The outer guard asked one of the cooks preparing the Festive Board to provide Harry with refreshments whilst he was out of the temple.

Following the installation Harry was allowed back into the temple to witness the remainder of the ceremony. Glancing across the Lodge, now in a different seat, Harry saw a face which seemed strangely familiar. According to the apron and collar the person was a past Provisional Director of Ceremonies. The penny dropped when Harry suddenly realised that he was one of the four priests from the Cathedral.

Harry had been given a summons that showed the Lodge's name and number on the front cover, together with the name of the outgoing Master and his junior and senior wardens. The inside provided a list of the serving officers and the names and addresses of the current Worshipful Master, secretary, almoner, charity steward and treasurer. On the reverse side was the entire list of the Lodge's brethren.

Harry read through every name on the list. He first came to the name Ricardo Francini, who apparently had joined the lodge in 1981, which meant he was a joining member and therefore had a mother Lodge somewhere else. To join another Craft Lodge a Mason needed to go through the Three Degrees of his mother Lodge first.

Harry needed this list of names checking out. Then a name sent his pulse racing; it was that of Father Macaroni. Interestingly he was also a joining member, Harry worked out that his joining date was about five years earlier. Now, hopefully, Paxton-Smyth could have him traced more easily. Unfortunately the priest across the temple from Harry would be more difficult to identify without knowing his name.

The priest periodically glanced at Harry and then smiled when he caught Harry's direct eye contact. He certainly was a big man with broad shoulders that made the provincial collar around his neck seem quite tiny.

As the guest of Thor Olson, Harry was privileged to sit at the top table next to him. It was the first time they had actually spoken. Harry for some reason expected his host to be quite a large Norseman of around fifty, with a mop of wild hair and a fair complexion. He was therefore somewhat shocked to find the complete opposite, as Thor was short, thin, dark and almost completely bald.

They shook hands formally upon being seated. Thor apologised for the disruption to their arrangements, to which Harry replied that he was grateful to be given the opportunity of seeing how a Lodge in Norway worked. Unfortunately, as there were quite a number of speeches, the opportunities to speak to Thor Olson were very limited.

From his seat at the top table Harry could see most of the dining Masons but, search as he may, he could not see the big priest, who, it appeared, had not stayed for dinner. During the break to ease springs, Harry took the opportunity to tackle his host.

"Thor, the brother sitting opposite me in the temple, a really big bloke wearing the regalia of a Past Provisional Grand Director of Ceremonies, do you know him?"

Thor thought for a moment then finally shook his head. "This is not my Lodge, Harry, I'm only here to officiate. Why do you ask?"

Harry thought for a moment before responding. "It's just that I thought I recognised him from my trip to Nidaros Cathedral earlier today."

Thor looked across at Harry, who could detect that he seemed uncomfortable at the question. "In Britain, is it not common for members of the clergy to be practising Freemason's?"

Harry thought for a while before answering. "You know, I have no idea. In my Lodge there are no members of the cloth. Does the name Father Macaroni, mean anything to you?"

Thor shook his head just as those brethren who had the compulsive urge to visit the bathroom began to return to their seats.

After the festive board a large number of masons picked up their cases from the robing room and left; those who stayed went into the bar, leaving Harry and Thor with the opportunity of remaining at the table.

"You are a friend of Hugh McDonald?" said Thor Olson when they were alone.

"Not really," replied Harry, "What has Hugh told you about me?"

Thor shook his head. "Nothing really except that you are keen to learn more about Masonry and the connections that have existed between Norway and Scotland."

"Did he mention a baton?"

Thor presented a blank expression to the question, leading Harry to conclude that Hugh had in fact told him very little. "Thor, I'm very interested in the Knights Templar who after all started Masonry. I understand the connection between Norway and Scotland is through the Templar movement."

Thor smiled for the first time. "The connection is substantially deeper than through the Knights Templar. Let me explain a few facts to you. Firstly did you know that a pentagram that's over a thousand years old covers the southern part of Norway and that this pentagram was initially constructed by using the cities and monasteries of Norway as markers? These cities and monasteries were strategically placed in relation to one another using an ancient formula called the Golden Section.

"The Golden Section is the key to the geometric construction of the holy pentagram symbol. The key line of the Norwegian pentagram was marked at the ends of all round churches; their ruins lay specifically in the cities of Tonsberg and Nidaros-Trondheim. These ruins are on a longitude path exactly 290 miles apart from one another."

Harry interrupted Thor and apologised for doing so, but he needed to cut to the chase. "Thor I am really interested in the untold power behind the visible side: the power that has the entire world in its grip. Naturally I'm talking about Incanda and the Knights of Black Chapter."

Thor remained expressionless as he picked up his firing glass to drain the dregs from the bottom. "I know nothing of these orders you refer to," replied Thor, trying to remain calm and collected. However his body language had tensed up dramatically.

"Hugh McDonald was of the opinion that you do, in fact he mentioned that I should talk to you specifically about them."

Thor glanced briefly at Harry and then at the glass in his hand. "Mr Blakemore you are taking a very dangerous path, one that only foolish people follow and often to their bitter end."

"I realise that Thor, but I'm completely fascinated by the subject. Tell me - if, historically, the Knights Templar were both warriors and bankers, has the latter been harnessed by Incanda?"

"The Incanda movement is everywhere, the degree of their power is unimaginable - over law, banking, religion and even with significant footholds in governments. The following of Incanda down through the generations is so immense no one has any idea how big it really is. There are many tiers in terms of rank, emanating down from the original families. Some areas are slowly progressional. Incanda is like a shadow; you can see a part of it one minute and progress so far, then it simply disappears out of existence."

"Have you ever come face to face with Incanda?" asked Harry.

"What, and lived to tell the tale? No Mr Blakemore, in fact just talking as we are now creates a significant danger."

"I'm told that Trondheim is the home of Incanda?"

Thor shook his head. "Who knows, Mr Blakemore, who knows? Historically, Scandinavia, France and Jerusalem have been closely linked. In fact there is a small Island called Bornholm in the Baltic Sea where fifteen mediaeval churches and hundreds of standing stones mark the island as a sacred site. These ancient markers and churches demonstrate the fantastic skills for geometry, mathematics and land-surveying that people had during these early times. They naturally learned much from the culture known as the Grooved Ware people," said Thor, attempting to skilfully manoeuvre Harry onto a completely different course.

"And does Incanda figure prominently in this Island's history?"

"Incanda, like, for that matter, the Knights of Black Chapter, are in all things. Templars were great seamen you know. At their height they sent ships out right across the Mediterranean and into the Atlantic. They sailed across the Black Sea and the Baltic. Significant traces of them have been found in America as well, so certainly they crossed the Atlantic, in fact their great wealth probably evolved from silver mining in Central America long before the Spaniards. Vikings established settlements on American soil, initially landing in Canada. The first known site was on the Newfoundland peninsula in l'Anse aux Meadows, around 1070.

"Henry Sinclair of Rosslyn was part Scot and part Viking. He went to America in 1390 shortly after the Vatican outlawed Knights Templar. Proof of his visit was recorded in Rosslyn Chapel. Maize heads and Aloe cactus were carved into the construction of Rosslyn, both these species were only found in America. In Rosslyn there is a ship depicted with one single mast and two sails. History suggests that there was more than one journey made to America. Sinclair appointed an Italian, Antonio Zeno, an experienced explorer, to manage the voyage. The journey was planned and involved at least ten ships. They sailed down the eastern seaboard to Westford Massachusetts. A tombstone was found there belonging to Sir James Gunn who apparently died on the journey. A shield carved on the tombstone portrays a single masted ship, identical to that in Rosslyn. The Gunns were a Scots clan closely associated with the Sinclairs. A tower was built in Rhode Island called the Newport tower. It was built around the time of Sinclair. The Templar seal illustrates the dome of the Rock of Jerusalem and comprises of a number of arches, identical to the tower in Rhode Island. Again a replica can be found in Orkney called the Orphir Chapel, replicating the Holy Sepulchre in Jerusalem."

"The Sinclairs got themselves about quite a bit then. Was it them who established business and banking in America?"

asked Harry. "I thought Christopher Columbus was the man who found America?"

Thor smiled at Harry's question. "Christopher Columbus was probably a captain of one the ships in the convoy, he actually only got as far as Cuba. He was himself a member of the Order of Knights of Christ. It was John Cabot, or, to use his Italian name, Giovanni Caboto, as he was born in Italy. John Cabot was the first to wade onto the Newfoundland shores of America, on the 24th June, St John the Baptist's day in 1497. John Cabot was known to sail from the port of Bristol, in fact a tower was built in Bristol and named after him, the Cabot Tower."

"So what with Antonio Zeno and Giovanni Caboto, it sounds like the Italians were quite close to the Sinclairs?" remarked Harry. "How about the names Macaroni and Francini, do they ring any bells in history?"

Thor stared hard at Harry then dropped his gaze to the tablecloth.

"Mr Blakemore, there are so many connections, too dangerous to even think about discussing in idle chatter," replied Thor Olson.

"So there could possibly be a connection between them and Incanda?"

Thor ignored Harry's remark. "The Templar movement was very secret about their maritime voyages," said Thor, again attempting to steer Harry away from a discussion he did not want to participate in.

"Knights Templar were by far the best business people of their particular period in history. They would have guarded their empires with significant care. Not difficult, as the Templars' belief was based upon confidentiality of the principal hierarchy. The more trustworthy a person was proved to be, the higher that person would climb in the ranks of big business."

"So this philosophy is still used by Incanda and the Knights of Black Chapter to this day?" said Harry, relating one to the other.

"It is the way of all Freemasons is it not?" replied Thor. "The Templars acquired their skills from their historical roots as far back as the Bronze Age - the Minoans, the Mycenaeans - and of course the Phoenicians who were all great sailors. Templars who were derived from Norman and French ancestry, were basically Vikings who went to France in the Middle Ages. The name 'Norman' comes from the Norsemen, meaning Men from the North."

"Fascinating, so the cycle has turned back in part, insofar as Incanda, being part of Rex Deus and in turn Knights Templar, eventually returned to their roots in Norway - here at Trondheim?"

"Maybe they never really left in the first place," replied Thor.

"Templars had a very strong hold over large businesses and probably still do," he said with a half smile.

Harry glanced at his host, knowing full well that Thor was very uncomfortable with anything to do with Incanda, but he kept pressing him nevertheless.

"Thor, tell me, do you think with the Italian connection that the Mafia have an involvement with Incanda?"

"Incanda, and for that matter, the Knights of Black Chapter are a life force: two dynasties intermingled in all things; their massive power is beyond the comprehension of us all. They are like two giants underpinning and controlling the world. They clash periodically but if or even when Incanda wins over the Knights of Black Chapter the populated world as we know it today, will end. Now, if you'll excuse my rudeness, I must leave as I have an important lecture to co-ordinate for the morning and I need to run through my notes."

Harry sat in total silence for a short while; it had now finally dawned on him that this planet was a massive battleground that constantly threatened the population of the world. So much was contrived, but the human race was ignorant as to how and why. "I now know the meaning behind the words, 'the struggle of mankind'," he said, leaving the table to follow Thor.

"I'm taking one of the Brethren home in my car. Do you mind if we drop him off first?" said Thor.

"You know, Thor, I think I'm going to take a walk back to the hotel, if you don't mind," said Harry.

"Oh very well, Mr Blakemore... it has been a pleasure meeting you, I'm sorry if I have failed to be as explicit as you had wished, but I'm sure you understand. Now my car is parked in the car park at the rear of the building so I will leave by the back door. If you leave by the front door and turn left, and walk for no more than twenty minutes, your hotel will be on your right-hand side, quite simple to find."

The two men shook hands and left in their separate directions. The street outside the Lodge was completely deserted, no lights shone from any of the buildings.

The Knights of Black Chapter

Harry turned left and proceeded to walk up the road. Suddenly a huge explosion broke the quietness. Harry instinctively dropped to the pavement. It looked as if the rear of the temple had been completely blown away. Harry dashed back towards the front door and entered the Lodge; his mind racing. He could clearly smell burning oil, which stopped him in his tracks. To his left was the gents' toilet. Harry pushed open the door and went in. He could see a red glow through the small frosted glass window, which he was able to open after a struggle. It was as Harry had feared: Thor's car was a blazing inferno. Clearly a bomb had been planted with the intention of killing both him and Thor.

Harry did not return to his hotel, instead he went straight to the airport. It would take some time for the police to identify the bodies in the car, hopefully there would enough time for him to leave Norway.

17

Lewis Ford had expected the ATC camp to be in total darkness as it was gone twelve o'clock when he finally struggled into its midst.

He was tired beyond belief having walked almost non-stop for two days over unbelievably rough terrain. He found Abdullah sitting at the bedside of one of his ATC men, holding a cold compress to his forehead.

Parts of the ATC man's body simply hung like raw meat stripped into shreds, exposing both bone and organs. There was almost nothing left of his right leg which had been virtually blown away. Abdullah was holding what appeared to be a ball of red slime, which in fact was all that remained of the injured man's right hand. As Lewis Ford looked down at them he saw the man who – incredibly - was still conscious, move his lips in an attempt to speak. He looked young, no more than in his late teens or early twenties. He had by now gone well past the pain barrier, his body was wrecked and his spirit was ready to abandon the remains. Ford had seen this mutilated death scene many times before and had witnessed the brief void just prior to the spirit separating itself from the body so that it could drift into restful peace.

Eventually Abdullah rose from the bed to face Lewis Ford. Stricken with grief he nodded several times then wiped his bloody hands with a cloth. "I've lost many men doing this work, but when it is your son, it's much harder." Abdullah turned to hide his grief and Ford placed a hand gently on his shoulder. "I must go now and pray to help my son's spirit arrive safely with Allah. I will be gone for some time."

Lewis Ford stood and watched as Abdullah covered his son's body with a blanket, he then left to allow a father to grieve in peace.

* * *

"Where have you been, I've been trying to call you for days?" said Parseena the following morning. "I've been appointed to work at one of Atif's universities of Jihad. Like before I'm going to be teaching English there. It looks like they're planning something major. I'll know more when I get there."

"Where's 'there'?" asked Ford.

"Pashi Village in Kabul Province. It looks like Mohammed Abu Atif is definitely held up there and has been since the triple bombings."

"I tried to get to Pashi but we were ambushed by opium bandits and I lost my men in the attempt," said Ford with a certain degree of embarrassment. Have you spoken to Atif yet?" he asked.

"No of course not, he's too important to speak to me," replied Parseena, laughing.

"When do you leave? I need to get out there somehow as soon as I can."

"I'm travelling later today, that's why I've been desperately trying to call you. I can't take this phone with me, if they find it, I'm dead."

"You must Parseena, otherwise we won't be able to communicate," said Ford in a tone of authority. Hide it on you. Leave it switched off if you don't want to keep it on vibration mode, but phone me as often as you can. Do you know where you'll be staying?"

"I'm not sure, I do know that the position of women in that area is particularly bad, which I'm not relishing. I met a man at that party I told you about... my brother-in-law introduced me to him. I think it was he who organised my teaching job in Pashi. According to my brother-in-law, this man's family has been involved in a blood feud for generations. The civil war going on here is killing hundreds of thousands of people, perfect for Abu Atif who can keep a low profile and move in and out of any regime. Okay, I'll take the phone, but please don't call me, ever."

"Okay, look Parseena, phone me when you know where you're staying and be careful, you hear me?"

Ford closed his mobile and went in search of Abdullah, who had just returned to camp from the desert where he'd spent the night in solemn prayer. He was now preparing for his son's final journey. Ford related the trouble he had encountered and how he'd lost the guides in the caves. "The head guide, a guy who they call Red, I think he escaped, the rest are dead," said Ford in a cold, matter of fact way.

"The Malik must be paid especially if you have lost his men," replied Abdullah.

"Fair enough, they had no chance, swatted like flies," said Ford,

"I need to see if this guy Red is back in the village. I've got to get to Pashi and fast."

The Malik was somewhat surprised to see Lewis Ford accompanied by Abdullah but a broad smile appeared, across his blotchy face, albeit quite false. Speaking in Pashto, he greeted them and bid them sit.

"He says that he heard you had some trouble," translated Abdullah.

"You could say that. Tell him I've come to pay him the rest of the money and to pray for the souls of the brave men that were caught up with the opium traffickers."

It was as if the Malik understood every word... he placed his hands together as if to pray, then touched his lips with the tips of his fingers and bowed his head ever so slightly. "Allah is the All Seeing Eye, he will have received them into the divine kingdom. And the westerner also," he said in very broken English.

"Westerner, what westerner is he talking about?" said Ford with a frown.

"The dead man found outside of town," replied Abdullah as the Malik peered longingly at the bank notes Ford had in his hand.

Very slowly Lewis Ford began counting out twenty-dollar bills, one after the other, onto the table - then he stopped. "Do you know who this man was? When was he found?" asked Ford.

The Malik shrugged his shoulders nonchalantly. His body language was, however, saying 'get on with the counting'. Ford was using the money as a means to lever information from him. Abdullah spoke to the Malik in his native tongue, which received an instant response.

"The Malik says two men from the village found the remains of a naked westerner. The body was collected by four men and driven away."

"JoJo Curtis!" replied Ford, looking concerned, "Abdullah, ask the Malik if he knows where Red is, I need to get out of here and head to Pashi, fast."

The message was repeated to the Malik who remained looking at the small pile of notes, hoping it would be increased very soon.

"Ask him if he knows where I can find Red."

Again Abdullah repeated Ford's question. The Malik's reply was brief.

"He is back in the village and will be sent to our camp before nightfall," said Abdullah.

"Good," replied Ford, who much to the Malik's delight recommenced slowly counting out money onto the pile. He finally stopped and bundled the heap of bills up into a neat handful then gave them to the eager village Head. "Tell him I'll give him more when Red comes to the camp."

Before leaving the town, Ford confided in Abdullah as far as to tell him that Americans from the CIA might well visit the camp and question him about his whereabouts.

"I shall say nothing except that you went off several days ago."

"Good, cos' they just might think I had something to do with JoJo's death. Can we trust the Malik?"

"Not unless you keep bribing him. They, of course, may well give him money for information... if however he thinks he's going to get more from you, he'll take their money and then lie about you."

"Okay then let him think it. Here take this two hundred dollars and tell him I'll give him another two hundred upon my return."

"Would you like to take one of the Land Rovers? There is another way to Pashi, although the road is rough and long."

Ford smiled. "That's the best offer I've had in a long time," he said as they walked into the camp.

Dr Abdullah Guru looked on as Lewis Ford prepared the Land Rover for the journey. By seven the sky was its usual pitch black but, strangely, no moon or stars could be seen. Red entered the centre of the camp like a man walking hesitatingly towards the gallows. Lewis Ford caught a glimpse of Red advancing out of the corner of his eye, as he was rolling down the tarpaulin side of the Land Rover and securing it to the body with rubber toggles. By now Red was standing at his side like a naughty schoolboy waiting to be scolded. For a few moments Ford ignored him. He then suddenly turned and grabbed a fistful of Red's clothing and with one violent turn he pinned him to the Land Rover.

"So Red, you thought you'd just take off and leave your men alone to die."

"No master, it was nothing like that," exclaimed Red, "I was there with them until the end. Because many bullets were bouncing off the walls of the cave I moved further inside, that's when I noticed an opening leading somewhere. I took the camels and donkeys and eventually found a way out. I used one of the camels to guide me. Camels have a great sense of direction and she led me out. Unfortunately one of the bandits was watching the entrance and opened fire. I was able to use the camel to shield me until I could clear the cave and get the bandit in my sights. I then killed him, master. I collected the donkeys and returned back here. Master I thought you were dead, otherwise I would have come looking for you."

Ford released his grip ever so slightly but kept Red pinned against the Land Rover. "I'm leaving for Pashi and you're coming as my guide."

"Of course, master, I'd be honoured," replied Red, pleased to think Ford was not going to throttle him.

"Right, we leave tonight," said Ford releasing Red from his grip.

"Tonight, master? Tonight is very dangerous."

"Did you see the men who came to the town to collect the dead American?" asked Ford, looking hard into Red's face for any sign of a mistruth.

"Of course... they came down by helicopter, collected the body and left."

"Right, well they'll be back and I don't want to be here when they come, so go to your prayers and meet me here in one hour."

The journey was difficult, over roads that had been blown up by missile attacks on Afghan convoys during the Russian occupation. They passed a number of burned out tanks and armoured personnel carriers which littered the roadside, left there like tombs reflecting the death and misery bequeathed upon a country where peace seemed impossible and even unimaginable.

Ford purposely moved slowly, especially as they were crossing Pashtun tribal territory. They travelled only at night, using scrim nets to hide the vehicle during the day. It therefore took several days to reach the outskirts of Pashi.

"This is as close as we go. From here on we're walking," said Lewis Ford.

The Knights of Black Chapter

"We will act as typical nomads and guess what, I'm your lady!"

Prior to leaving the camouflaged Land Rover, Red dressed in a pair of baggy cotton trousers and a long shirt that hung down below the knee, tied at the waist by a broad sash. He also wore a skullcap and over that a turban. Lewis Ford on the other hand had dressed in the tent-like burka that completely covered his face and all other extremities. He had repeatedly washed his face and hands in permanganate of potash, which had given his skin a brownish-yellow tinge.

It was common to see nomads passing through villages from their summer highland grazing grounds on route to the lowlands where encampments were built in preparation for winter. Traditionally villagers allowed the nomads to graze their flocks which in turn re-fertilised the harvested fields. Nomads would buy supplies such as kerosene, wheat and tea, and in exchange the villagers would buy milk products and wool. This trading relationship had gone on for centuries, therefore the sight of Lewis Ford and Red slowly walking along the goat track towards the village did not provoke any suspicious attention. It was early afternoon when Lewis Ford and Red reached the outskirts of Pashi.

"Look," shouted Ford, pointing towards what looked like the ruins of a building. "Let's check it out," he said.

Within minutes they were inside the remains of what at one time would have been a house, approximately a quarter of a mile from the village. Pashi nestled in a quite fertile oasis; trees and shrubs broke up the normally desolate terrain. The ruin was perfectly camouflaged in bushes and afforded them a certain amount of freedom of movement without any danger of attracting too much attention.

"Perfect," remarked Lewis Ford as he entered the ruin. "Why would this place be left to fall down?" he asked Red whilst removing his Burka to reveal an arsenal of ammunition belts across both shoulders, like that of a bandolier.

"The Russians were very active around here, master, maybe they killed the family that lived here. This village is mostly populated by farmers, they are peaceful people. The house would be a sacred place and left to fall down as a mark of respect."

Ford needed to speak to Parseena, despite his promise to wait for her to call him. The phone rang several times before it was answered.

"Give me five minutes, I'll call you back."

Ford closed his phone. "Let's prepare to hold up here," he said as he hoisted the sling of the Heckler & Koch rifle over his head. Red took off the heavy goatskin pack that contained rations, ammunition and water. Within a couple of minutes Ford felt a familiar vibration in his pocket. A quick glance at the screen of his phone showed that Parseena was on the line.

"Hi, where are you?"

"I asked you not to call me, I'm right in the middle of an Al Val Sinda camp about five miles north of Pashi."

Ford ignored the understandable anger in Parseena's voice. "Okay, we're holed up on the south side of the village, so I guess I'm about six miles from you. Have you heard anything about Abu Atif?"

"No, nothing, but there are westerners here."

"So what's going on?" replied Ford.

"This is a new camp, it's only been set up recently. There must be at least forty young Muslims from Europe here and these three white Irishmen."

"What happens there?"

"I'm not exactly sure, but young Muslims are being trained in bomb making along with these Irishmen. My job will be to teach other young Muslims to speak English, I presume they'll then be scattered across Europe and the US as disciples to spread the word of the Jihad and where necessary to be sacrificed."

"Are you able to leave the camp? What restrictions have been placed on you?"

"None," replied Parseena, "right now I'm staying in the village, they're treating me like royalty, presumably because of the relationship I had with Abu Atif. At night I'm taken down to the village where I stay in a room next to the Mosque, but I'm really not sure how long that will last, especially when Mohamed Abu Atif returns."

"Shit," replied Lewis Ford, "So he's not there at the camp then!"

"No, apparently he was here but left about two weeks ago. There are a number of these camps dotted around Afghanistan so when he'll actually come back here is anyone's guess."

"Listen, I need you to find out who's in charge of the camp and see if whoever it is has a direct line to Abu Atif, " said Ford, angry that this job was going to take longer then he had hoped.

"I can't do that because, okay right now I'm treated with a certain amount of respect but that would be stretching it."

"Right, but why not say that you are desperate to see Abu Atif soon... You know, make up some love and hearts story."

"I'll see what I can do, but I'm not promising."

"About what time do they normally take you back to the village in the evening?"

"Around seven, when they go to the Mosque to pray."

"Okay, how do I find the place?"

"What!" shouted Parseena, you can't come into the village!"

"You want to bet? Just tell me what to look for."

"Well, if you face the Mosque, you'll see a small building on the left, that's the boarding house. I'm in a room at the back on the ground floor."

"Which room?" asked Ford, sounding a tad frustrated.

"There are only two, I'm in the one on the left. Look Lewis, I'm frightened and I don't want to hang around here once these Al Val Sinda and Al Quaida men find out Mohammed Abu Atif has no interest in me... I'll be treated worse than a dog."

"You won't be. Look, if you can find out what I need to know, I'll pull you out of there right away. Expect to see me tonight, late."

It was gone one o'clock in the morning when Lewis Ford crept from the ruined house. He moved quickly and silently using the trees and shrubs that bordered the road as camouflage. Fortunately the entire village was in darkness. Pashi was not important enough to warrant a domed Mosque, however Lewis Ford had seen enough Mosques in his time to recognise the first building on the left side of the road as being a place of prayer, and there was the small building to the left exactly as Parseena had described.

Ford took the 9mm Browning handgun from his belt and, crouching low to the ground like a stalking cat, he moved cautiously but swiftly towards the back of the building. The facing gable wall had two crudely made boxwood shutters covering windows on the ground floor and two directly over them on the floor above.

With somewhat of a struggle Ford was just able to push his fingers between the gaps either side the wooden shutter that covered the left hand window. It was quite loose but obviously fastened from the inside.

He put the Browning back into his belt then rubbed the fist of his left hand several times into the palm of his right hand. He then stood side on to the window with his feet spread several inches apart. He casually looked around for any signs of life and then quickly turned on the balls of his feet smashing his fist right into the centre of the shutter. The impact produced a loud cracking sound that instinctively made Ford run around the corner of the building into the protection of pitch darkness.

As the noise had not provoked any sign of life Ford emerged to discover his fist had split the shutter right down the middle along the grain - it now lay in two halves displaying an opening into the blackness of the room.

"Parseena, are you there?" Ford said in a loud whisper. There was no response. Again he repeated his call only this time his head was halfway through the window. Again there was no response, Ford collected the Browning from his belt and hitched himself up sufficiently to straddle the window-sill. As he was unable to see anything in the darkness, he climbed into the room.

A flick of his lighter gave sufficient light to produce a sight that made even Lewis Ford's stomach turn over. The lighter's flame suddenly dimmed and went out, eliminating the visible horror in front of him. Ford, almost in desperation, attempted to restore some form of light into the room in the vain hope that his mind might have been playing tricks on him, and that it was not Parseena lying there. The lighter failed to yield to his erratic attempts to re-ignite the flame. Then he noticed a torch on a small, rough, pine table at the bedside. He switched it on. Nothing. He gave it a few violent shakes and suddenly a beam of light glowed up onto the ceiling and bounced down towards the bed in front of him.

At first it was difficult to see exactly the detail of the horror in front of him. Her eyes were open and staring up to the ceiling but the bottom of her face seemed to be bloated by mounds of blood covered flesh. Ford pointed the beam of the torch directly into Parseena's face.

"Fuck," he said, instantly turning away. Both of her breasts had been hacked from her chest and forced into her open mouth. Eventually Ford allowed the beam of light to scroll down the full length of Parseena's naked body until it came to rest at the dark hair of her vagina. Her thin young legs lay wide apart - she seemed to be straddled across what looked like the hilt of a bayonet. Its long blade had been pushed to its full extent into her womb and by the look of the numerous open cuts across her stomach, had been rammed into her several times, puncturing her abdomen as the point had repeatedly broken through the soft flesh of her belly.

The Knights of Black Chapter

With tears of anger and sorrow mixed, Lewis Ford removed the bayonet and closed Parseena's legs, to provide her with a modicum of dignity. He rolled her broken body into a sheet and tied a knot at the top and bottom. He then sat cross-legged upon the floor and just stared at the bundle in silent reflection, blaming himself for the terrible waste of her life.

His senses returned to him in an instant as he heard the movement of the door handle turning. He scurried to the end of the bed and then crawled around to the other side between the bed and the wall. Two men entered the room; one had a kerosene lamp in his hand. When they saw Parseena covered in the sheet, the one with the lamp shouted something to the other who then ran from the room. In a flash Ford leapt from his hiding place and threw himself across the bed, taking the man completely off guard. Ford twisted his fingers into a clenched, tight bunch and pushed them into the man's face: the honed calluses at the ends of his fingers piercing his eye sockets. His incredibly strong hand pushed his fingers deeper just as if he was clenching a ten-pin bowling ball. The screams of pain were brought to an abrupt end by Ford's right hand that came crashing down, chopping the man's carotid artery. He instantly collapsed into a lifeless heap on the floor.

A rain of bullets then began smashing into the plaster of the wall opposite the open door. Without hesitation Ford jumped through the window, and with the safety catch off his Browning he quickly surveyed the landscape, which was by now changing in the gloomy light of pre-dawn. In front of him was the comparative safety of some undergrowth but that meant a fifty-metre dash across open ground without the protection of cover.

There was no choice. Ford lifted his Browning and deposited a flurry of high-powered bullets through the window into the room, in the hope that they would give him just enough time to make a dash for it. He began to run for all he was worth, as he heard the frightening sound of gunshots followed by the whistle of high velocity bullets skimming past him, too close for comfort. He had just reached the beginning of the undergrowth when a bullet caught him on the right thigh; the instant slash of pain was like a hot needle suddenly penetrating his leg and the shock made him briefly drop down onto one knee. He had experienced the sting of a bullet wound before; he therefore quickly looked down at his leg and felt around in an attempt to discover the extent of the damage, and although the pain was intense, thankfully the bone had not been affected, it was nothing more than a deep flesh wound. Relieved by the results of his examination, Ford moved as quickly as he could further into the wooded area. He needed to make a left turn in order to get back to the ruined building where Red and the weapons were located - weapons he was now clearly going to need in an attempt to survive.

Whilst Ford had been away, Red had attempted to re-instate an old planked door, which further restricted the view of their movements inside. Ford suddenly crashed into the house and instantly began to count the number of rounds contained in the Heckler and Koch rifle. Fortunately, the back of the ruin faced open terrain while the other side provided a clear view towards Pashi village.

"Red, we'll soon be getting a visit," said Lewis Ford. "Where did you get that from?" he asked, pointing to the RPG-7 Soviet-made rocket propelled grenade launcher. The broad grin on Ford's face was rare to behold, it also gave Red a glimmer of satisfaction that he'd done okay.

"While you were in the village I ran back to the Land Rover and collected it."

"Great and do we have any grenades to fire from it?"

"Of course master," replied Red with an air of offended dignity.

With Red looking on mesmerised, Ford broke out the first aid kit and began attending to his leg; first he washed the deep slash in the thigh muscle and then carefully dabbed the surface before sprinkling antiseptic powder over it. He then took a needle and thread, not exactly a normal item found in any regular first aid kit but one most special forces personnel carry as an optional extra. He ran the flame from his lighter over the needle to sterilise the steel as best he could. In all, the entire wound took five very untidy stitches that closed the gap to Ford's satisfaction. After applying another peppering of antiseptic powder he wound a wide field bandage around his thigh, he then raised his trousers and buckled his belt. "Okay, so let's get ready for a fight," he said finally.

It was well over an hour before either of them saw any sign of movement. Three men, who Ford thought must be Al Val Sinda eventually came briefly into view: they could be seen approaching the ruin about twenty feet apart from each other, with weapons held in front of them, ready for use at any time.

One of the men must have suddenly noticed the ruined house in front of him. First he dropped down into a crouching position on one knee. He then began flapping his arm up and down, suggesting the other two should do likewise.

"Well one thing is clear, these guys are not local," said Ford to Red, "cos' they didn't know this ruin was here."

"I have one in my sights, master," said Red with a sense of nervous anticipation.

"Leave him for now, I don't want to draw the entire camp down here yet."

After the three had knelt for a while without anything happening they rose to their feet and cautiously moved closer to the point where Lewis Ford had no choice but to dispense three deadly rounds, one into each of them, instantly dropping all three to the ground with a tiny hole in each of their foreheads. Due to the type of ammunition in use, the back of their heads were completely blown away.

Ford smiled, pleased that his marksmanship in rapid target fire was still as good as ever.

"Look master, in those trees over there!" Red pointed to a small copse of trees that seemed crawling with movement. Al Val Sinda fighters were massing like ants, the sound of Ford's gunshots now saw them scurrying for cover.

"Okay, Red let's give 'em a grenade up their arse." Ford loaded the RPG-7 grenade launcher, then hesitated briefly as he'd not checked the weapon out first - a really basic exercise taught to rookies at boot camp.

"Oh what the hell," he said, activating the launcher. A loud whistle sounded as the grenade left the breach. Its screech then suddenly died, to be instantly replaced by a huge explosion, reducing the copse of trees into tiny splinters joined by body parts and chunks of flesh all blasted into the air. A beam of satisfaction lit Ford's face but it was instantly wiped away as sniper fire arrived with gusto right into the centre of the ruin.

"Where the fuck did that come from?" shouted Ford.

"Up there master, in that tree," replied Red.

Ford raised the Heckler & Koch, locked it over into rapid-fire mode and blasted the foliage until two limp bodies dropped out. A long pause followed. After at least an hour, Ford glanced at his watch, it was half past ten in the morning.

"Break out some of the rations," Ford said eventually. "Either this training camp's devoid of fighting men or they're planning something. Either way let's eat first."

Except for the odd sporadic burst of gunfire that fell well short of the ruin, nothing happened until later that afternoon. Ford put Red on watch whilst he took a nap, shading himself behind the far wall from the now intense heat of the sun. He'd not been asleep for more than a few minutes when Red roused him. "Look master, children," he said.

There on the roadway were two young girls, one must have been around ten years of age, the other much younger. Ford estimated the little girl to be no older than five. They walked slowly towards the ruin, hand in hand. Ford scanned the entire area immediately behind the children to see if they were being used as decoys, but no movement could be seen. Suddenly the older child stopped and bent down as if to speak to the younger one, she then pointed to the ruin, turned and walked swiftly back towards the village.

The little girl then slowly began to walk onward, stopping briefly to turn around and watch the older child who was by now some distance away; she then proceeded towards the ruin. Both Lewis Ford and Red could now see the clear features of this young child's pretty face; she had long, thick, wavy hair that bounced around her shoulders as she walked.

"Red, you're looking at a dead girl," said Ford as he pointed his rifle in the child's direction.

"No master," shouted Red rising from his position to face the little girl. Upon seeing Red, the child smiled gleefully and began running forward, raising her arms as if to be picked up. One solitary bullet left the Heckler & Koch finding its target right in the centre of the girl's chest. To Red's horror the impact flung her backwards into a small clump of foliage, and was followed by a massive explosion that took Red clean off his feet, sending him backwards into a heap against the wall. He lay there dazed looking up at the sky until Ford's face blocked his vision.

"Master, I don't want to be here any more," he said, coughing and spluttering on his words as a trickle of blackened blood began running from the corner of his mouth.

"Sorry Red, the kid was loaded, she'd been sent to explode in our faces," said Ford as a tear dropped from his face and fell down onto Red's torn body. The explosion had released a package of metal fragments that had ripped his body apart.

"Am I going to die now?" cried Red as he peered up into Ford's face.

"Yes," replied Ford.

"Good, then please Allah make it swift, this pain in unbearable."

The Knights of Black Chapter

Ford raised the upper part of Red's blood-covered body and dragged it up onto his lap, he then began to nurse him close to his chest until he felt Red's life drain completely away.

After burying Red's body amongst the bricks and debris from the ruin, Ford gathered up the supplies ready to make his move. He set the loaded grenade launcher up facing the pathway and then ran a wire from the trigger mechanism towards the path. He then put a stake in the ground close to where the remains of the little girl lay and secured the wire to it, raising the taut wire on the top of two sticks so that it was stretched just a few inches high across the path.

As darkness fell, Ford dropped onto his knees in silent prayer. He prayed for Parseena and the little girl whose life had been so cheaply extinguished, and lastly he prayed for Red, a man who had turned out to be a good companion and a true friend.

Ford thanked the heavens for not glowing that night; even the moon was miraculously missing. He left the ruin, moving into the open terrain at a steady jog, determined to put as much distance between him and the
village as quickly as possible, and in particular the Al Val Sinda training camp beyond.

He dived under the scrim net that camouflaged the Land Rover. "Okay SAS man where the fuck are you?" Ford said as he plugged his mobile phone into the charger wired directly through the vehicle by way of its cigarette lighter. He turned on the ignition to receive the welcoming glow of both red and green lights; the screen of the phone soon began to boot up. Ford went through the security procedures and then put the phone to his ear.

"Don't say a word, just listen," said Harry Blakemore. "You have been chosen to take the rap for some guy's death. The President's jumping up and down calling for you to be removed, so every CIA agent is looking to make a name for himself. You need to get back into Pakistan, just grunt if you understand."

"Fuck you, I'll give you, grunt."

"That'll do, just get over the border, I'm on my way."

"Well, it's about goddam time; I was beginning to think you were letting me have all the fun."

"We'll speak in twenty four hours, either way," said Harry and with that the phone went dead.

Ford checked his watch, it was just gone eleven. He removed the scrim net and turned on the ignition, the engine started at the second attempt. With the help of the four-wheel-drive and in a slow continual movement, he eventually got the Land Rover back onto the excuse for a road. He took a compass bearing and checked his map before proceeding east. As dawn gradually appeared, streaks of vivid red flashed low across the horizon. Ford resisted the temptation to continue on his way; instead he pulled off the road and scrimmed up after emptying the last-but-one jerry can of diesel.

At dawn on the third day, Ford pulled up off the road for what he hoped would be the last time on his journey. His food had all gone and the water he had left was barely enough to quench the thirst of an ant.

He thought he heard the faint hum of rotor blades and left the vehicle to listen. He was right and the noise was getting louder. Ford quickly checked the scrim net, hoping that it would sufficiently camouflage him. The ear-shattering sound was a helicopter that suddenly appeared over the top of a hill. It hovered no more than twenty feet above the road, then suddenly turned in one sharp movement and flew in the opposite direction, like an Eagle stalking its prey.

The sound of the helicopter's engine suddenly stopped as if it had gone away. Ford could just about hear the rotor slowing and concluded the aircraft had landed. His first reaction was to get the Heckler & Koch out and move into a defensive position, but unfortunately his view was restricted by the incline of land directly in front of the Land Rover - good for cover but bad for visibility.

Then all hell was let loose as four heavily armed men came into view. Ford took a direct hit in the shoulder and one in the side. He screamed in anger as he let the lethal rifle open fire on the four men: two dropped instantly to the ground, the third threw himself down onto his stomach to take up a prone assault position. The fourth disappeared altogether.

Ford, dazed by pain, shook his head several times in an attempt to ward off unconsciousness. His vision suddenly became blurred but he thought he saw the man lying in front of him quickly look to his left and then start to get to his feet in an attempt to scramble away, only to be mown down by what appeared to be a swift volley of bullets. Then Ford felt his heart begin to race as he disappeared into a cavern of darkness.

It was the horrible stench of smelling salts wafting under his nose that eventually brought him, albeit briefly, to his senses.

"Mr Ford, I presume?" said Harry Blakemore, beaming.

The Knights of Black Chapter

18

Lewis Ford fell in and out of consciousness several times, but on hearing the gradual sweep of the rotor blades of a helicopter as it began to pick up speed, he regained his senses. He opened his cold blue eyes as if he'd suddenly been shocked by a thousand volts. He turned his head both left and right, but even this slight movement sent bolts of excruciating pain through his entire body. Try as he may he felt any movement restricted.

"You're tied up with a bunch of half hitches to a stretcher," said Harry peering down at him.

"Then you'd better untie me and fast," replied Ford, squirming to free himself despite the pain.

"Not a fuckin' chance. If I do you'll die," said Harry casually.

"I'll be the goddam judge of that," shouted Lewis Ford struggling beneath the series of triangular bandages securing him to the stretcher.

"You've been hurt pretty bad, my friend," said a voice that came from someone standing behind Harry Blakemore. Ford tried to peer through the veil of pain to see who else was there, but the more he moved his head the more intense became the pain and his vision became distorted.

A dark-skinned man with a pile of black wavy hair came and knelt down close to Ford. He was dressed in full combat kit and an armband that bore a familiar Red Cross upon it.

"Who the fuck are you?" said Ford hanging onto consciousness by a thin thread of pure grit and stubbornness.

"We're a private security group called Purple Rain, I'm a doctor, and this guy saved your fucking life." Harry smiled in acknowledgement of the recognition. "Right now," continued the doctor, "medically speaking... well how can I put this so as you'll understand... you're in deep shit. And, if you keep trying to bust free of those bandages you'll haemorrhage to death, so hold the fuck still. Now this is what we call bye-bye juice."

Ford felt a prick in his arm as a syringe full anaesthetised him into a state of total unconsciousness.

The Knights of Black Chapter

Harry covered Lewis Ford with a blanket before attempting to make contact with Jeremy Paxton-Smyth, but the noise from the helicopter's open fuselage made hearing almost impossible.

"I'll call you when we're on the ground skipper," said Harry.

The helicopter eventually landed close to Khorough in Tajikistan.

Purple Rain had licence to move freely around Tajikistan without interference from the authorities. The US had made it perfectly clear, following careful negotiations with Russia to develop a debt re-structuring agreement that instigated the write-off of $250 million from Tajikistan's $300 million debt, that quite naturally this US investment required close protection.

A proposed investment had been agreed to finish off the construction of the hydropower dams of Rogun and Sangtuda. This would substantially increase electricity production which could then be sold for profit as the country ranked as high as third in the world for water resources... it was estimated that Rogun was to be the world's tallest dam.

The Chinese, in the form of the Shanghai Cooperation Organisation, were also keen to invest especially in road improvements and electricity transmission networks, so that a substantial amount of electricity could be cabled directly into China to feed their rapidly growing economy. To assist in northern trade routes the US were committed to constructing a 36 million dollar bridge, linking Tajikistan to Afghanistan.

Purple Rain was the appointed security firm, chosen by the Americans to protect their interests. Their highly equipped, semi-permanent camp with a purpose-built road leading right into town, was situated on the outskirts of Khorough. Satellite bases had been set up close to other areas that required the special protection that such a highly experienced group could provide.

Tajikistan had for many years been a transit country for illicit narcotics bound for Russia - some of which were constantly being filtered into Western Europe. This landlocked country had celebrated its independence from Russia in 1991, after the break up of the Soviet Union. The Tajik people had been under Russian rule since the mid nineteenth century, but with their independence had come civil war. Hence the requirement for a strong independent presence such as Purple Rain, some say too strong a presence as it was rumoured the organisation was being privately paid to assist in the safe transit of illicit narcotics.

Khorough, situated in the south east of the country sits right on the borders of Afghanistan, amidst the vast Pamir range of mountains. With over eighty percent of the population in Tajikistan living below the poverty line, and life expectancy only sixty-five years, bribery was common and cheap to administer to the extent that Purple Rain had a strong grip and a powerful influence over the people. Officially labelled a security company, it could best be defined as a sophisticated group of international mercenaries, ex-professional, highly trained soldiers. One such was an American by the name of Edward Ray, better known as X-ray. X-ray had been a SEAL who applied for a secondment to the SAS. After passing the selection course he spent almost three years working out of Sterling Lines, the SAS base in Hereford.

Harry had first met X-ray when he picked him up from RAF Lyneham when he had flown in from the SEAL base in Florida. After the traditional banter that naturally ensues between rival Special Forces personnel, X-ray and Harry soon became good friends. For a time X-ray even shared a room at Harry's house in Bromsgove, the market town some forty miles from Hereford. And just for fun they would jog up to the summit of Pen-y-Fan together via the infamous Jacob's ladder, with weighty burdens on their backs.

Pen-y-Fan, being the highest point in the Brecons, boasted spectacular views right across the Black Mountains. X-ray and Harry would sit right on the top and talk whilst eating cheese sandwiches and cold sausage rolls. It's said that the view from Pen-y-Fan is so engraved in a SAS man's mind that it's the very last vision he sees before death!

Harry had lost touch with X-ray for a time after being sent to Llangwern, the Army Training Area just over the welsh border, following his selection to go on the four months NI (Northern Ireland) training course in preparation for his first tour of Belfast.

After his stint with the Regiment, X-ray had returned to the SEAL base in Florida to complete his service. He had joined Purple Rain soon after and eventually became a group leader.

The reception for mobile phones was very poor in the Khorough area with intermittent breaks in the signal that resulted in Harry having to re-dial several times in his attempt to have a conversation with Jeremy Paxton-Smyth.

"Hi skipper, the Yank is clinging onto life by his fingertips right now. He was hit right in the guts," said Harry eventually, following several unsuccessful attempts to make contact.

"Harry, what on earth have you done, the entire CIA are gunning for you?" replied Paxton Smyth.

"Simply protecting myself, skipper, how was I to know those guys were CIA, when you're being pelted with lead you don't ask for credentials before returning fire."

"Okay where are you now?" There was a long pause. "Harry, are you there?" shouted Paxton-Smyth down the phone.

"Yes skipper, but that's like asking an escaped convict where he's hiding."

"Harry, trust me. I'm not convinced that American was responsible for the observer's death... in fact I think the whole thing stinks, but that's my private thoughts."

"Okay, we're just over the Afghan border, held up in a security camp," replied Harry.

"What are the chances of that American pulling through?"

"Who knows? He's basically in a field medical centre at the moment receiving attention, but I'd say his chances are pretty slim, but he's a gutsy bastard so I suppose only time will tell."

"I presume you're with a security firm, and if I'd be guessing I'd say an outfit like Purple Rain."

There was another deafening pause whilst Harry collected his thoughts. Then the line was lost. Almost immediately afterwards Harry's phone began to ring. He peered down at the buttons and pushed the reply digit. "Hi, yes skipper, correct I'm with Purple Rain."

"Okay, we need to get you out of there somehow," said Paxton-Smyth.

"Leave that to me Skipper. This is a crap line, I'll keep in touch, Oh and skipper, take my word for it someone wants us stopped. I've rattled a few cages especially in Norway... this Incanda is for real and it's my belief there's a face in the CIA who'd like us to become history before we can get to the target."

"I understand and concur," replied Jeremy Paxton-Smyth. "Just keep me in the loop."

"No problem skipper," said Harry, closing the phone.

"Well how's the Yank?" said Harry the following morning over coffee with Nan bread and eggs.

X-ray looked at Harry and smiled. "He's a SEAL, tough as rawhide. Apparently he's been effing and blinding since three o'clock this morning."

"You're kidding?" replied Harry with a smile.

"No honestly, this guy's something else. Seven o'clock last night it was touch and go if he was going to make it, they reckon his heart stopped twice on the operating table, but by midnight he was shouting for water, then at two o'clock he wanted to shag the nurse. Have you seen his hands? They're like fists full of butchers' knives."

Harry smiled. "I need to see him," he said.

"Okay no problem. Say, what are you two guys up to?"

Harry looked straight at his old friend. X-ray knew that look from old. "Okay, it's none of my business."

"Let's say we'll pay our debts to you when the job's done," said Harry leaving his chair.

"Fair enough," replied X-ray offering his hand to Harry, who accepted it. The two men went into a masculine embrace and then Harry walked off in search of the American.

Lewis Ford had been put in a tent alone, wired to monitors and drips. The trunk of his body was bound in a swath of bandages that seemed to embalm him like a mummy. He lay motionless with his eyes closed until he heard the flap of the tent opening.

"Come to see if I'm dead?" said Lewis Ford without stirring.

"You dead? Now what a waste of my time that would have been," replied Harry pulling up a chair.

"So what's new in the West?" asked Ford, slowly closing his eyes.

"Well apart from the entire US administration wanting our guts in the sand for killing a few of their own, not a lot really," said Harry with an uneasy smile.

"The guy they called JoJo was an observer, that in itself was fine but he was given virtually the same goddam name as me, so I thought they were hanging him out as a decoy to cover my tracks, but then the CIA moved in with guns blazing which blew that theory."

"You're a Thirty Three Degree Mason, I'm told," said Harry.

"Sure, but what the hell has that got to do with it?"

"Nothing directly, but how deep is your knowledge of the low degrees? For example, have you heard of Incanda?"

Lewis Ford opened his eyes. "Who?" he replied.

Harry explained.

"So you think this Incanda is behind the scenes, trying to stop us reaching the target?"

Harry nodded.

"Then we're fucked, if they're as powerful as you say they are and have their fingers everywhere we've got no chance of hitting this guy."

Harry shook his head. "Not necessarily, who pulled you in for this job?"

"A guy by the name of Parker, James Parker. Matter of fact he's the goddam Director of the CIA, the bastard, if only I could get my hands on him now."

Ford gripped the bedclothes with both hands, either from a sudden bout of excruciating pain or giving a sign of what he'd like to do if James Parker was in his clutches.

"Think about it, they went to extraordinary lengths to pull you out of Brazil."

"Oh you heard about that."

"Of course, so we can assume that this Director is not in the pocket of Incanda. And I know my Skipper's kosher, so that's two guys that should come around to our way of thinking."

Ford looked sceptical. "I need to blow this place and soon, who's the guy they call X-ray?"

Harry explained. "Look, I'm going to call my old Skipper again and see how he can help to get us out of here."

Harry stood up and placed the chair to one side of the bed. Ford had closed his eyes again as if the effort of talking had tired him out. Harry therefore decided to say no more but just creep away.

"Hey limey………. Thanks…. I owe yeah."

Harry smiled and left.

* * *

"Harry, I dare not make any physical attempt to help you. God knows who might be watching my every move right now. I can however tell you this; our chaps on the ground are convinced that the American has caused sufficient trouble to un-nerve Mohammed Abu Atif to the extent that he's restless and not settling in any one place, which means he may not even be that far east. Rumours are rife, he could actually be in Albania."

"Thanks Skipper," said Harry, briefly closing the phone. He then thought for a moment, logged the scrambler numbers into the phone and called an old friend.

"Sergeant Keith Turnbull, can you speak? This is Bob Richardson here?"

"Fuck me stupid, Bob. They said you were dead."

The Knights of Black Chapter

Harry briefly explained. "Keith, what are you on at the moment?" asked Harry.

"Oh well you know, still the same old stuff. Currently I'm on detachment, working in the Fire Brigade at Longbridge."

"What you mean the car factory?" replied Harry sounding a little shocked.

"The very one, this is how things are progressing. Do I call you Harry now?"

"Of course," replied Harry.

"This job detachment means that some of us are being filtered into what they call stand-by jobs, mixing into the community. It's the new initiative, fucking load of bollocks if you ask me. I suppose I'm lucky, the Duke's working in the shoe department at Rackhams and Quiggers is cutting hair."

"And how about Doddie?" interjected Harry.

"He's in the Fire Service with yours truly. I gotta say there's a lot of action around Birmingham at the moment, especially IRA cells, so I suppose it all makes sense, working in conjunction with MI5. Still it gives me the chance to live at home with the wife and kids."

"Better you than me," remarked Harry.

"I joined the Regiment as a military man," he said. "Well, at least it's better than sitting in the ops room at Hereford supping tea all day. Working in counter terrorism is where it's at right now. We can be scrambled within minutes, like just a few days ago; I also do a few shifts with Birmingham fire service. We got a shout in the middle of the night to Moseley to a house with a suspected chimney fire. Only me, the Duke and Quiggers dropped into the house next door. It was suspected of being an ammunition holding point. The cellar was heaving with bomb making materials. So like all good firemen, we cleaned up the mess, climbed into our big red fire engine and fucked off, job done. Now the house can be put under surveillance. We rigged the cellar so that MI5 can monitor the place and if relevant blow it to kingdom come with the IRA cell in it. Picture the headlines; IRA bomb makers accidentally blow themselves up. All good stuff."

"Are you still part of the SP team?" asked Harry.

"Of course and so are most of our original group from G squadron, but its nothing like the Special Projects team you were in, this is purely a counter terrorist detachment now. Some call it MI5 and a half."

"Are you still in blue team?" asked Harry.

"You bet, we all are. So tell me Bob, 'er sorry Harry, what's going on with you?"

Harry, in between continually getting cut off, explained briefly what was happening.

"Keith, I'm going to need some kit," said Harry.

"If it's the kind of kit I think you're meaning, that's going to be tricky. Not impossible, but tricky."

As the days went by Lewis Ford made remarkable progress. Within just three days after having two bullets removed from the depths of his stomach he was up and walking around. But it was when he got dressed ready to leave that the damage was done. Bending to put his boots on gave him so much pain it was as if a mule had kicked him in the stomach.

"The stupid bastard, I bet he's gone and busted the stitches I sewed his intestines up with," said the doctor who was forced to re-open Ford's stomach to examine the extent of the problem. Fortunately the damage was minimal and within forty-eight hours Ford was recovering again, only this time his left wrist and right ankle had been chained to the bed.

"Albania," replied Ford after Harry had related Jeremy Paxton-Smyth's comments, "I know people in Albania, get me out of this fucking bed, I've got someone to speak too."

Harry shook his head. "No chance, where's your mobile phone?"

"It's in my kit over there, but I need to find out the guy's number."

"Okay, let me try, who is he?" replied Harry drawing up the chair to Ford's bedside.

"Guy by the name of Malik Ahmed, he's the deputy head of Shik, the Albanian Intelligence Service."

"Right, I'll get a message to him. You rest, you'll need all your strength to travel."

Harry left the tent to phone Paxton-Smyth. Upon opening his phone he noticed he had a missed call from Clarissa. He wondered how she was getting on, but called Paxton-Smyth as a matter of priority.

The head of MI6 was not exactly pleased to hear Harry had made contact with a serving member of the 22nd SAS, however he saw the benefits once Harry explained and promised to filter anything relevant through Sergeant Keith Turnbull.

"Skipper, can you get me connected to a bloke by the name of Malik Ahmed, he's the..."

. "Yes I know who he is..." Paxton-Smyth butted in.

"Well, Lewis Ford knows him and he reckons he'd help us."

"Okay, but I daren't have you patched through, leave it with me, I'll find out his direct number and call you."

Harry's next call was to a very excited Clarissa.

The Knights of Black Chapter

19

"Harry, thank god, where are you?"

"Never mind that right now... how are you? Is Guy looking after you? Are you still in Scotland?"

"Harry, so many questions! Of course Guy's looking after me, although I'm a big girl and can take care of myself, remember."

Harry smiled and related his experiences in Trondheim and the warning that he had received about their safety, giving good reason for his concern.

"Well so far nobody has bothered us. Mind you we're still using false names, it's all quite exciting really. Listen Harry, we've learned such a lot from the notes the Professor left regarding the content of the Baton Scroll- we're convinced Rosslyn was built for one very specific reason."

"And what was that?" replied Harry nonchalantly, not really wanting to get too much involved in history right at that very moment, especially as Jeremy Paxton-Smyth's call might well come through at any time advising him of Malik Ahmed's number. "Look Clarissa, I may well need to cut you off because I'm waiting for a very important call to come through."

"This is important, I'm important, what we've discovered is bloody important."

"Okay, calm down, of course you're important, it's just that the call I'm waiting for could mean life or death and especially my life or death."

"Oh," replied Clarissa, "then why didn't you say? Okay, if the phone goes dead, I'll know it's your life or death call. Harry, listen this is breaking news. Rosslyn was actually built as a tomb, a tomb to contain Jesus."

"What, you're saying Jesus is actually buried in Rosslyn?" replied Harry sceptically.

"Oh yes, and that's not all... Mary Magdalene was also enshrined there. When the Knights Templar returned to Jerusalem after its destruction they took the scrolls that were secretly hidden beneath the Temple and they also took the remains of Jesus. They then built Rosslyn to provide a safe resting place. You see the ground plan of Rosslyn Chapel is an exact mirror image of Herod's Temple. In the arched roof of the Chapel there's a decorated arrowhead suspended from the centre, it's known as the Sinclair Engrailed Boss. The arrow points directly down to a keystone in the floor. We're convinced that below this keystone lie the remains of Jesus and Mary Magdalene."

"So what draws you to this spectacular conclusion? ... that's pretty powerful stuff," said Harry, beginning to forget his present predicament.

"Okay," went on Clarissa, "Mary Magdalene died around AD63. She actually died at a place called La Sainte Baume, a small place in southern France. In the New Testament Mary was described as the woman out of whom went seven Devils. It's all in the Book of Luke chapter 8 verse 2. She's also said to be a sinner, and portrayed in the Gospels as Christ's loyal companion. Now before she got married Mary was under the ruling of the chief Scribe Judas Sicariote. He was classified as a Devil Priest. In fact Judas was Devil Priest No7. These seven Devil Priests were established to oppose the seven Priests who were called the Lights of Menorah. Hugh McDonald and Guy are convinced that the Incanda has evolved from these Devil Priests and not just directly from the Rex Deus line, although this needs more careful research for clarification."

"Well if that were the case, could it be possible that the Knights of Black Chapter evolved from the seven Priests of the Lights of Menorah?" said Harry, now getting totally absorbed.

"Very possible, in which case the split would have come much earlier than we're led to believe. Anyway back to Mary M. One of the jobs of these seven Demon Priests was to manage the female celibates. When Mary got married she was naturally released and became free to engage in sexual practices although these activities were regulated. Now because Mary spent long periods away from her husband, she was actually classified as a Sister. You know like a nun would be. Now, Mary had an attachment with an eminent Father, a man by the name of Simon Zelotes and also to his sister Martha. Martha means 'Lady' by the way. The difference between Mary and Martha is that Martha was further up the pecking order than Mary and was therefore allowed to own property. In those days Sisters were placed at the same level as Widows or 'sick women', positioned apparently below that of an Almah, which in translation, means virgin. Marriage normally changed this status to that of Mother, which meant you moved up the rankings. But unfortunately, because Mary spent long periods alone, she was demoted to the unmarried level.

"Mary was about nine years younger than Jesus, and approximately thirty years of age when she got married for the second time. In AD33 she gave birth to a daughter called Tamar, the name given to the river that splits Cornwall from Devon, named in her daughter's honour when she visited there, but that's another story. Four years after that, Mary had another child, a son who she called Jesus the Younger and in AD44 she gave birth yet again, this time to another boy she called Joseph. By this time Mary Magdalene was living in Marseilles. In those days the official language there was Greek and remained that way until the 5th Century.

"Now back to Martha. She was born into a Royal Family and was officially described as the hostess to the Lord Jesus Christ.
Her Mother and Father originally came from Syria. Now after Christ's death and when his disciples had all left, Martha, her brother Lazarus and Mary left by ship to Marseilles, their mission was to convert the inhabitants there to the faith of Christ. This really is how the Magdalene cult commenced and many shrines were built including her original burial place at St Maximus. Her tomb and sepulchre were guarded by Cassianite monks from the early part of the 400s. Her remains however were secretly removed."

"Now this is the interesting thing... you know that some teachings describe Mary Magdalene as black and we've discussed this on several occasions, well Mary became the head sister of the Nazarite order and as such she was entitled to wear black. Consequently a cult emerged called the Black Madonna: we believe this is how the Knights of Black Chapter originally got their name. The church in France saw Mary as a threat and that's why her remains were removed for safekeeping."

"So she could have become a member of the Seven Lights of Menorah?" said Harry, attempting to piece all the logical bits together.

"Well, we're convinced Jesus was of Rex Deus, therefore he could have handed his mantle over to Mary before his death. Her direct line to this day is definitely one of the nine Knights of Black Chapter. All we have to do is find out who he or she is."

The Knights of Black Chapter

"Well I wish you the best of luck, but this doesn't explain why Jesus and for that matter Mary came to be buried in Scotland," said Harry.

"I'm building up to that. About six hundred years after Mary Magdalene's death a small sailing boat was discovered bobbing about just off the harbour of Boulogne-sur-mer in the northern part of France. The boat had nothing on board except a three-foot tall statue of a Black Madonna and child. Also found in the boat alongside the statue was a copy of the Gospels of Syriac. It was a complete mystery, however it raised all kinds of speculative thoughts. The statue became known as Our Lady of the Holy Blood. In Boulogne it eventually became the insignia for the Magdalene cathedral of Notre Dame. It became classified was a very important item in Notre Dame until it was destroyed in the French Revolution.

"This statue became known as the Black Madonna of Boulogne, it connected Mary with the sea. It soon became an emblem and the badge of pilgrims. This emblem was actually found in Scotland long before armorial seals were used. Now here's the really interesting stuff. In the 11th century the Port of Leith, Edinburgh's port, designed an emblem that depicted Mary as Mary of the Sea and her Grail Child, all depicted in a boat. But because of shamanism, heraldry ignored the emblem in their compilations."

"Most emblems used by Knights, noblemen and Royalty were feudal and emblems didn't actually commence until the 12th century. This emblem was non feudal and had female associations but the Port of Leith adopted it, why? We are convinced it was used by Leith to commemorate Mary's visit or her resting place. We've been looking into any recordings of Mary we can find and discovered that an Archbishop by the name of Raban Maars actually compiled six volumes dedicated to Mary called the Life of Mary Magdalene. It confirms that Mary, Martha and a number of their followers actually did leave Asia. These recordings describe their journey in great detail, how they travelled across the Mediterranean between Europe and Africa, stopping on the west coast of Italy, then eventually landing at Marseilles in the Gaulish province of Vienne."

"Guy has had colleagues in Paris check other recordings and apparently libraries there hold a number of manuscripts that also endorse Mary's presence in Provence. The remains of Mary were buried at Tarascon in the French province of Vienne. Recordings confirm that a visit to her tomb was made in the late 5th century. Her remains were exhumed for preservation in the Abbey of St Maximus, about twenty odd miles away from Marseilles. In 1279 Mary's remains were again exhumed, this time by Charles II of Sicily; he had her skull and, for some reason, her humerus set in gold and silver cases where they remain on display to this very day."

"The remainder of Mary's ashes were placed in an urn, and eventually uncovered by Sire de Joinville around 1250. Sire de Joinville was a knight who visited the cave they called Mary's solitude. As the St Clair family were formerly appointed as guardians of ancient knowledge, Mary's ashes were handed to them for safekeeping. The notes the Professor wrote from his observations quite clearly state that ancient scrolls and the remains of Christ and Mary were held in France until the Knights Templar were outlawed and Jacques de Molay was burned at the stake. St Clair secretly smuggled these precious artefacts, scrolls and remains out of France over to Scotland. They were kept at Roslin Castle and remained there until Rosslyn Chapel was completed in 1490."

"In the first century BC, Marcus Vitruvious Pollio said that great buildings should be constructed in compliance with nature and therefore nature must always be kept in mind. This decree was interpreted in a number of different ways including using the proportions of the human body for architectural measurement and layout. Hence, Leonardo Da Vinci's Vitruvian man, with the navel as the centre point. By extending the tips of the fingers around the body, a perfect circle is formed. We're convinced that all the wonderful theories that have evolved about the earth's movements and degrees of tilt in line with devastating experiences, and about how these theories were depicted in the great works of art as warning signs, is a complete load of poppycock."

"Leonardo Da Vinci and many other great artists were also architects, commissioned to design buildings. Vitruvian Man evolved as a very good system of measurement from the centre pin of the belly button. Typically, Da Vinci drew Vitruvian Man in an artistic format."

"Back to Marcus Vitruvious Pollio. Rosslyn Chapel's ceiling depicts a galaxy of stars; one is off-set to the others and represents the Star of David. So by using the Vitruvian Man as a measurement of the ceiling and using the navel as the centre pin together with the measurement of twenty-three point five degrees, which is typically the natural angle of the earths tilt. Oh, and by the way this twenty-three point five degree tilt is officially used in Masonry. So we arrive back again at the exact spot on the floor below which lie the remains of Jesus and Mary, together with untold numbers of scrolls!"

"Fascinating! I take my hat off to you two, but how does Masonry get involved in this tilt? asked Harry.

"The twenty-three point five degree tilt should be officially used in Masonry by your Junior and Senior Deacons and Masters of Ceremonies when they're conducting their duties and carrying wands in the temple."
It's the angle at which the wand is carried," explained Clarissa.

"Clarissa I've got that call buzzing me, I've gotta go. You look after yourself, I'll be in touch as soon as I can," said Harry, angry that the phone signal was compelling an end to such engaging revelations. Harry switched Clarissa off without another word and opened the scrambled line to Jeremy Paxton-Smyth."

"Harry, I have Malik Ahmed's number. Also I've got some news about Morgan-Sinclair, he actually visits Italy a lot, apparently the bank in which he works has branches there."

"Any particular part of Italy, Skipper?" replied Harry.

"Definitely Rome and Naples, but I'll see what else I can find out."

"Skipper, is there any form of pattern to his trips to Italy? Like does he visit at specific times during each month?"

It took a few moments for Paxton-Smyth to reply. "Mm, according to this report it looks as if he visits Rome during the middle of the month and Naples towards the end… why, what are you thinking?"

"Nothing really, I just wondered if he might be attending Masonic lodges over in Italy."

"Interesting," replied Paxton-Smyth. "Tell me, where's all this going Harry?"

Harry reflected on the question for a moment before answering. "Everything seems to point towards Morgan-Sinclair and Ricardo Francini being involved in some mutual activity. When I mentioned Francini's name to Thor Olson in Trondheim his face went whiter than a ghost's. I'm convinced Morgan-Sinclair was behind Professor Thomas's death and - lets face it - two and two does makes four. How about if they're behind the financing of Al-Val Sinda?"

"I see your point… interesting. Okay, I'll start digging deeper. Now listen Harry, since the 'Wanted' sign went up for Lewis Ford the Americans have been continually on my back. They're naturally suspicious and I'm sure they think I know your whereabouts. Even the PM is barracking me with questions, because he's getting politely grilled by the White House.

"This is a manhunt, Harry, of massive proportions: the Americans want Ford dead at any cost and if we're not careful, you'll be next without a shadow of doubt. My hands are tied and even I'm being watched therefore I can't help you."

Harry's heart took a leap in his chest as he realised the substantial scale of the trouble they were in. "Skipper, how

The Knights of Black Chapter

about if you were to tell them that I had actually followed your instructions and Lewis Ford was now dead?"

"They'd want proof, but they'd be cock-a-hoop," replied Paxton-Smyth.

"Then let's give them some proof," said Harry, his mouth working faster than his brain. "Skipper if this bloke was any normal man he'd be dead by now anyway, from the wounds he sustained. The only reason he's still alive is because he's a stubborn bastard. I could simply finish him off right now, he means nothing to me and if it would get Uncle Sam off our backs I'm fuckin' sure that would be motive enough."

"Harry, I don't want to know. If the Americans find him dead then the heat will be off. You might even get the hero treatment."

"Leave it to me Skipper, I'll see what I can do." After taking down Malik's number, Harry closed his phone.

"Harry, can I have a word?" asked X-Ray as he took Harry by the arm and ushered him into a small tent. "Harry, the CIA are about to drop in on us, now whether that's just a couple of them or a couple of hundred is anyone's guess, but those bastards don't hang around."

"Can you hide us?" asked Harry, beginning to feel a little uneasy.

"I'm going to have to. We've had strict instructions from them to halt any movement outside of camp, so if we put a helicopter in the air they'll make us bring it down. I'm going to take you into Khorough, we have a place in town where you'll be safe."

"How soon can we leave?" replied Harry.

"Right now. We've hidden Ford in the back of a jeep under a pile of laundry. Get into these clothes, then just saunter out of the tent slowly... you'll see the jeep, it is over there no more than fifty yards away. Put this bundle of laundry over your shoulder, then when you get to the jeep casually throw it in the back and get in the passenger seat, but do everything slowly because I'm not sure if we've got a spy amongst us or not. If we have he's quite possibly working for the CIA, so I don't want to take any chances. Here take this..." X-Ray handed Harry a Sigsauer 9mm pistol "...but for fuck's sake only use this weapon if you absolutely have to."

"Thanks X-Ray," said Harry who was already stripping off and climbing into a pair of cotton trousers and a typical long shirt. He then placed a pre-wound turban upon his head, threw the large bundle of laundry onto his shoulder and slowly walked out of the tent.

Harry's walk to the jeep seemed to take forever. Every impulse that surged instinctively through his mind tempted him to quicken his pace as he felt as if eyes were watching his every step. Eventually he reached the jeep, opened the back door and casually threw the bundle inside. He then scanned the interior for any signs of Ford, but all he could see was the bundles of laundry that now filled the entire back of the jeep.

Harry followed X-Ray's instructions to the letter and climbed into the passenger seat where he sat for a few moments. Then he heard the familiar sound of rotor blades. Through the windscreen he saw a Puma helicopter approaching. Soon it began to drop lower and lower before eventually disappearing somewhere towards the rear of the camp. Harry then heard the driver's door being opened and in a flash the doctor slid onto the seat alongside Harry, followed by X-Ray who leapt behind the steering wheel. He started the Jeep and off they sped. Harry turned around to try and see where the helicopter had landed but it was still not visible.

"I gotta say that's some impeccable timing, X-Ray," said Harry.

X-Ray smiled. "You know, the Regiment taught me many things, but one thing in particular: practice makes perfect."

"You mean you actually rehearsed this?"

The doctor just sat with a broad grin across his face.

"You bet," replied X-ray. "Many times and soon you'll see why. That helipad the Puma has just landed on has been purposely built on the far side of the camp, away from the town. And yeah know it was built in a spot that's terrible for collecting lots of fine sand around its perimeter - not good when rotor blades kick up sufficient shit to kill visibility for at least a couple of minutes. Which means there's just enough time for us to get clean away. So by now we'll be seen as just a pile of dust in the distance. And by the time those CIA bums have walked to the admin tent, we'll be well out of sight."

X-Ray drove the jeep right through the town and almost right out the other end. He eventually slowed down so as to turn into a narrow alleyway. Harry could see two men directly in front of them; as the jeep approached they began to open a pair of large wooden doors. Without hesitation X-Ray drove the jeep right into the building. The doors were instantly closed behind them.

Without a word the two men opened the back of the jeep and began throwing the bundles of laundry onto the floor, eventually uncovering a rather hot and flustered Lewis Ford fastened to a stretcher. Despite his verbal protests, Ford was carried through a single door and into what appeared to be a factory.

"I didn't want you to see this Harry, but needs must. This is simply a packaging plant for opium."

Harry looked visibly shocked to see dozens of people working virtually at production line pace.

"Do the authorities know this is going on?" said Harry as they walked through the lines of workers.

"Harry, the economy here is shit, so officially they don't know, but unofficially they do. Khorough like many other towns in Tajikistan has very little official administration, so it's simple to run this operation without intrusion."

"How about the law?" replied Harry.

"We keep them and their families well looked after," said X-ray as he led them to a small room at the back of the building.

"Okay so you hang out in here for a while, where you'll be safe."

"Say doc' how can this bloke die for a while?" asked Harry.

Ford looked aghast. "Get these fucking ties off me!" he shouted.

"Be quiet," replied the doctor, "The name's Doug' O'Driscoll by the way, we haven't been formally introduced," he said, offering Harry his hand.

"Where're you from, Doug', Ireland?" asked Harry.

"Ireland be fucked, I'm from Canada."

"Look, I hate to break up this small talk bull-shit, but will someone unhook me?" bellowed Lewis Ford, struggling to free himself from the tightly knotted bandages tying his wrists and ankles to the stretcher.

"Listen Yank, the world and its posse are galloping across the planet trying find you. They want you dead. In fact right now they probably want you more dead than they do Abu Atif. If there was some way of killing you off for a while they'd be off our backs," shouted Harry.

"That's no problem," replied Doug' O' Driscoll, "I could soon mix up a concoction that would put him so deeply asleep his heart would stop beating."

"Bull shit, that could cause brain damage," shouted Ford.

"Be quiet, you're not Canadian, you're American so your brain's damaged anyway," replied Doug with a smile.

"Would it work?" asked Harry.

"Absolutely, no problem. I could trim up those lethal looking fuckin' hands at the same time."

Lewis Ford began to kick and roll about on the stretcher until his face turned purple and the veins in his neck threatened to burst through the surface.

"Look Mr Ford be a big brave boy, this could be the only way of keeping you alive," said Harry before turning his attention back towards Doug. "How long would it take to sort him out?" he asked.

"No more than a few minutes. In fact if he co-operates, I can have him looking like a corpse that has died of his injuries."

"Yeah can take a running fucking jump and when I get my hands on yeah you'll be the ones who's dead," shouted Ford opening and closing his hands like Venus flytraps desperate for food.

"Okay, so tell me Mr Ford… currently you're shot up pretty bad, which means a speedy get away would be nigh on impossible. You're in no fit condition to fight your way out of a paper bag right now, so what options do we have?"

Lewis Ford momentarily stopped struggling. "So if we do this what are my chances of recovery?" Ford eventually asked.

Doctor Doug' O'driscoll smiled, "About fifty-fifty, but that's if I was an average doctor. But me, I'm fucking brilliant so, seventy-thirty in your favour."

"Okay, I'm sold but if you fuck up I'll come back and haunt the crap out of yeah."

The men smiled at one another and shook hands.

"So, this is what we do. X-ray if you and I drive back to camp with Lewis, we'll head straight for the field hospital. I'll need a little time to prepare, then you can then bring the CIA agents over. I'm going to put him down for no more than ten minutes, after that his heart will need to be started again."

Lewis Ford lay on the stretcher motionless looking up at the man whose skills he was about to stake his life upon.

"I'll phone admin'," said X-ray picking up a landline phone. "Jim, this is X-ray, can you talk?"

"Hi Terry, good to hear from you. Yes, there are about five cans waiting to be collected."

The Knights of Black Chapter

"Okay Jim, I get the message. So you can't talk, then just listen - we are on our way back. Try and coral those five agents together somehow, we need a clear run to the field hospital."

"No problem Terry, the cans will be waiting for you near the mess tent."

"Thanks," replied X-ray and dropped the phone. "Okay, so let's go," he said then turned to face Harry. "You wait here Harry, we'll be in touch."

Harry bent over Ford and shook him by the hand. "See you later," he said.

"I'm not worried about you seeing me, it's me seeing you that's concerning," said Ford with a faint smile.

With Lewis Ford again ensconced in the back of the jeep, covered in bundles of laundry, X-ray and Doug drove back to the camp. The mess tent was a good hundred yards away from the field hospital therefore X-ray was able to drive between a number of tents without being seen.

He backed the jeep as close as he could to the field hospital and within seconds Lewis Ford had been carried inside.

Doug began to produce a cocktail of drugs from a number of bottles he took from the medicine cupboard. After which he tore the packaging off two syringes and carefully drew a small amount of the fluid he'd mixed from a test tube. He repeated the exercise only this time he almost filled the other syringe from a second test tube containing the antidote. He placed the second syringe with the antidote in a kidney bowl and covered it with a cloth.

"Okay, let's synchronise watches. This drug works within a couple of seconds, so if you go and collect our CIA friends, when I see you walking back, I'll administer the dose. X-ray, remember we only have one shot at this."

X-ray smiled. "I hear yeah, good luck buddy," he said, touching Ford on the shoulder, "Oh and if yeah get a chance to meet any long dead SEALS on your travels, say hi to them for me."

Before Lewis Ford was able to think of something sarcastic in response, X-ray had gone.

The agents were waiting in the mess tent.

"X-ray, this is Agent Labone, he's from the CIA and these four gentlemen accompanying him are looking for some American guy, what did you say his name was?"

"Ford, Lewis Ford," replied Agent Labone.

X-ray smiled casually and put out his hand in friendly gesture. His offer, however, was ignored.

"We have reason to believe this man is here in your camp," the agent said, showing X-ray a passport photograph of Lewis Ford.

"Well, he could be... we have a stiff in the field hospital, although he's got no ID. It could be the guy you're looking for."

"I'd need to take a look."

"Sure," replied X-ray, "Follow me, or do you want to finish your coffee first?"

The five agents were up on their feet and already walking towards the door of the mess tent.

"Was this guy some kind of criminal?" X-ray asked as they walked across the clearing.

"A murderer," replied Agent Labone as he turned to face X-ray with a look that showed a degree of sceptical suspicion.

"This way gentlemen," X-ray opened the door of the field hospital.

They were greeted by Doug' O' Driscoll, now dressed in a white gown.

"Doc, these gentlemen would like to see the body of the guy we picked up a few days ago."

Doug looked serious as he crossed the floor towards them. "Well thank god for that, you got my message then?"

"Message? What message?" replied Agent Labone with a frown.

"I called the Ministry of the Interior in Dushanbe to report this dead westerner. They said they'd get in touch with the authorities."

Agent Labone pulled a face and shook his head. "Where is he?" he said.

"Follow me," replied Doug', opening the flap of the tent's interior. He led them to a partitioned space in which a corpse lay covered by a sheet.

One of the agents went over to Ford's head and pulled back the sheet to expose a very grey and ashen face.

"Is this him chief?" asked the agent.

"Oh that's him alright," responded Agent Labone with a smile stretching from one side of his face to the other.

"Okay, thank you doctor, we'll take him off your hands now."

X-ray looked shocked as Doug' stepped forward. "Well gentleman, that's fine, but his body has already begun to rot away, see he was shot several times in the stomach and right now the body's what I'd call crawling."

The Knights of Black Chapter

With that Doug lifted the remainder of the sheet covering Ford's body to reveal his middle massed with dried blood and with a quantity of maggots crawling over it.

A startled Agent Labone quickly threw the sheet back over Ford as two of his agents rushed out of the field hospital with their hands covering their mouths. Agent Labone picked up Ford's limp hand and checked for any signs of a pulse.

"Dead as a fuckin' door nail as you can see, would you like him gift-wrapped?" said Doug, smiling.

"Burn it, I've seen enough," replied Agent Labone as he and the remaining two agents walked from the field hospital.

As soon as X-ray and the agents were clear Doug quickly found a vein in Lewis Ford's arm to administer the antidote.

After the Puma was safely in the air, X-ray rushed back to the field hospital to find Doug' attempting to revive the very limp, lifeless body of Lewis Ford.

"How is he?" X-ray asked, looking concerned.

"Yeah know I did say there'd be a seventy-thirty chance of him pulling through, well right now those odds have been reversed. I've pumped the antidote into him but it doesn't seem to be working."

"What can you do?" replied X-ray.

"Not a lot without the right equipment," replied Doug' with the end of his stethoscope searching around Ford's chest for any sign of life. "I got it, goddam it, I got a fucking start up," he shouted as he rushed over towards the oxygen mask, which he then placed over Lewis Ford's face.

Ford's body began to convulse as if a hundred thousand volts had just rushed through it, then slowly his eyes began to flicker and eventually they opened. When Doug thought Ford's breathing could continue without the assistance he slowly removed the oxygen mask from Ford's face and smiled.

"Hi, did you have a good trip?" he said as Ford glared back up at him.

"Head feels as if it has been kicked in," replied Ford. "What the fuck's happened to me, I've got a funny tingling sensation around my balls?"

Doug' smiled. "Oh don't worry, it's the special effects I used to convince the CIA you were dead and rigor mortis had set in."

"Feels like I got a bunch of worms takin' a nibble," replied Ford, with his faculties and strength returning to him. He began to raise himself up on one elbow and as he did so the sheet fell away to reveal the lower half of his body. "Shit I hate maggots, get them off me," he shouted in horror.

"Quick hold him down, I don't want him to bust those stitches again," shouted Doug'.

X-ray rushed over and pinned Ford down to the bed by his shoulders.

"Calm down, I'll get one of the local gals to bath your bollocks," Doug said, wiping maggots from Ford's testicles.

"The news that Lewis Ford was dead travelled at lightening speed across continents to reach the ear of the Director of the Central Intelligence Agency, who smiled. "Good stuff, you did great," said James Parker. "And just as a matter of interest how did he die?"

The line went silent for a moment before Agent Labone finally replied: "We took him out Mr Director."

"Well that's great work, your name will be given directly to the President," replied James Parker.

"Thank you sir."

"No thank you, Agent Labone."

*   *   *

"So you did it then?" Jeremy Paxton-Smyth said, after Harry finally answered his mobile.

"Skipper, I can hardly hear you. I'll call you back when I'm in an area with a better reception," said Harry with a beaming smile extending across his face.

The Knights of Black Chapter

21

After several attempts Lewis Ford eventually got through to Malik Ahmed, who was initially very cautious.

"Malik, I got shot in the guts by fellow Americans, can you believe that?"

"I know," replied the deputy head of SHILK, the Albanian Intelligence Service. "I had a call from the CIA looking for you. What have you been up to my friend?"

"Malik, I was set up, and framed for the murder of a guy who was officially appointed by the White House as an observer when I was hired at great expense to capture Mohammed Abu Atif."

"Interesting... great expense you say?" said Malik, sounding keen to learn more.

It was precisely Ford's intention to get the deputy head's undivided attention. "Yes, and I know you're always up for a deal so I'm calling you for some help."

"Very good, and how can I help you?" replied the Albanian.

"I've taken a hit in the guts, which means I'm not moving around too well at the moment, so I need a place to recuperate."

"That's no problem providing the finances are in order. Where are you?"

"Tajikistan," replied Lewis Ford.

"Where?" was the reply.

"Tajikistan." Lewis Ford heard Malik begin to laugh on the other end of the phone, which annoyed him intensely. "Look, I didn't laugh when I pulled your son out of that drug bust in Cairo did I? ... or have you forgotten? What was it you said? 'Call me anytime, I owe you a big favour'."

"My friend, I am an honest Muslim who honours his pledges. I need to sort out a few things that's all, no problem, I'll be in touch."

"Malik, I shall be travelling with a Brit, we'll need papers and passports."

"Naturally," replied Malik Ahmed before hanging up.

The Knights of Black Chapter

It took almost a week for arrangements to be made. Papers and passports were brought to the camp by special courier; they described Lewis Ford and Harry Blakemore as Canadians, under the names of Bill Pearl and James Johnson.

"Sounds like a double act," said Harry as he packed a few bare essentials for the journey.

"Thanks, X-ray, I'll be forever in your debt," Harry said after getting a bear hug from his old friend."

"You take care of this guy, walk as little as possible and dress that stomach wound frequently. Yeah know I'll think of you every time I go fishing," said Doug, laughing.

Purple Rain's helicopter took them over the Afghan border to Feyzabad Airport, where they caught a plane to Montenegro and finally went on to Tirane where Malik and his son were waiting for them.

What with the long journey, being held up at Montenegro airport for almost five hours and three changes of aircraft, Ford was left looking much the worse for wear.

"He needs to have his wounds looked at," said Harry after the familiarities were over and both he and Lewis Ford were ensconced in the back of an official looking black Mercedes, speeding through the streets of Tirane.

"So my friends... I, Malik, have ranged a good hotel for you. Top star."

"I didn't know you had such a thing," said Lewis Ford attempting to stretch his legs as much as possible to relieve the discomfort and pain he was feeling.

"We need to get this bloke a doctor, that wound needs looking at," exclaimed Harry as he watched Ford wince in pain.

Malik looked at his watch. "It's almost one in the morning; I will have my personal physician attend you first thing tomorrow."

Malik's promise was followed by a long silence as the car sped through the outskirts of Tirane. Eventually it was Malik who spoke. "My friends, Malik is a man of honour, I keep my word and fulfil my debts,"

"Okay, I recognise the intro. Now you're going to ask what we can pay you for such wonderful hospitality."

Both Malik and his son, who remained silent, smiled at Ford's remark.

"Lewis, my friend you know me so well. Naturally I am keen to be paid for my services and especially the risks I am taking. I believe you Westerners call it business. Now tell me, how much are you being paid to capture one so important as Mohammed Abu Atif?"

"Come on Malik, as if I'm going to tell you that. How much do you want for your continued generosity?"

Malik looked at Lewis Ford with a crafty grin on his face. He then began tapping his bottom lip with the index finger of his left hand as if trying to puzzle out a conundrum. "I would say the Americans will pay a high price for one so important. Maybe up to two million dollars."

Malik's dark eyes quickly scanned both Harry and Lewis Ford for any signs that he might have scored a direct hit.

"So how much?" repeated Ford, attempting to re-position himself to find a modicum of comfort.

"How does a hundred thousand dollars sound? And say twenty five now and the balance when you get paid?" Malik replied.

"Expensive," said Ford.

"Look, me I'm more generous than him, how about if we said a hundred and fifty thousand when we get paid but nothing up front?" said Harry.

A faint smile emanated from the short plump Albanian who looked well past his sell by date. "Your generosity overwhelms me, but you are asking me to put this entire deal on trust."

"You can trust Lewis," chimed in Malik's son, who spoke for the first time.

Malik gave his thirty-year-old offspring a paralysing glare. "Mm, Abdullah, my son will forever be indebted to Mr Ford for assisting him from – well - shall we say a difficult situation."

It was as if a ray of sunshine had suddenly burst into the car to produce the beaming smile that lit up Malik's face. "Very well, I'm not the kind of person who puts money above trust. You have a deal. Now my friends, how can I help you further? Let me see. We have a French man in custody; he is awaiting trial for murdering a Greek national. We believe this man is a disciple of Mohammed Abu Atif. Now Mr Ford I'm sure you'd like to have a little chat with this man?"

Harry and Lewis Ford looked at one another, and then Ford secretly winked at Harry before responding.

"We have a close angle on Mohammed Abu Atif right now, talking to one of his people might have some use but we're not that bothered," Ford said, again wincing in pain as he changed position on the seat.

The crafty old fox was fully aware of Lewis Ford's attempt to apply a nonchalant approach. "Oh very well, it was just a thought," he replied.

"Okay how much?" said Harry now getting the hang of the game.

Malik and Abdullah both smiled. Malik glanced over towards his son.

"Do you think we should help these Westerners my son?"

"I do father," came the reply.

"I am training my son, gentlemen," said Malik smiling.

"Then I'm sure he'll be very good, but you didn't say how much," replied Lewis Ford.

"Right and that is a very good question. Being a civilised country, naturally we do not practice the pagan ways of interrogation to make people talk, but I'm sure this man has a good tale to tell. I would say therefore that another hundred thousand dollar would be a fair price."

"Fifty... and if he gives us the exact location of Atif another fifty," Lewis Ford said in a categorical tone that sounded final.

"Very well. My friend I will arrange everything."

Eventually the car pulled up outside a typically run-down hotel. Due to the hour the place seemed completely devoid of anything that resembled life. Malik's driver knocked hard on the glass door after which a figure could be seen unlocking the door.

"Have a very pleasant stay, gentlemen," said Malik, making no move to get out of the car.

They all shook hands as Harry helped Ford climb from the back seat.

Standing proved almost impossible due to the excruciating pain he was suffering.

"Give us some help here!" shouted Harry as he wound Ford's left arm around his neck. The driver ran over to lend a hand at the behest of Malik. The man at reception gave Harry two keys whilst Ford was assisted into the elevator.

The rooms could best be described as basically adequate. Ford fell onto the bed and dropped into a pain-filled, restless sleep the moment his head touched the pillow. Harry covered him over and closed his door quietly before searching for his own room further down the dimly lit corridor.

The following morning, much to Harry's surprise, a doctor arrived at Lewis Ford's door - Malik had been true to his word. Without a word he began removing the dressings from around Ford's middle and shook his head several times as he dabbed the bandages over the unsightly surface. He then began speaking in his native Albanian tongue.

"What the fuck are you mumbling about? Speak in English," shouted Lewis Ford.

"This bad business," said the doctor.

"What the hell does that mean?" said Ford, sounding frustrated.

"You need hospital," replied the doctor.

"Impossible," responded Ford, "I spent a week in a hospital here once, suffering from food poisoning, the bastards almost killed me with the wrong drugs. You'll have to treat me here."

The doctor nodded as if he understood and keyed a number into his mobile phone. Both Lewis Ford and Harry heard the name Malik mentioned, but the remainder of the doctor's conversation was indecipherable.

"Dressings will come," the doctor said. Harry glanced down at Ford whose stomach looked a mess. A sort of yellow puss was seeping out from between two of the large stitches Doug had used to sew flesh and muscle together.

"That wound's infected, you need to go to hospital, like the man says," remarked Harry before biting into a piece of toast with orange marmalade.

"It's nothing a few antibiotics can't cure, " said Ford wincing from pain as the doctor prodded the surface around the infected area with his fingers .

Quite remarkably, after just three days Lewis Ford was back on his feet and walking around. And judging by the expression on his face, the pain he'd endured had virtually gone.

Late that evening Harry Blakemore's mobile began vibrating.

"Harry, Jeremy Paxton-Smyth."

"Evening Skipper," he replied.

"Harry, I've got some interesting news, but first tell me... How's the American?"

Harry thought for a moment before replying. "Did the Yanks not tell you about his fateful end?"

"Of course they did, but you don't expect me to believe such rubbish. I knew it was not your intention to close this man down, In fact a CIA Agent by the name of Labone has actually claimed the credit. So where is he?"

"Safe, Skipper," replied Harry.

"Okay Harry, thank you for that. In case you're wondering why I'm phoning you so late, it's because this call never existed. Even I have to be incredibly cautious. I've been doing some searching around. These chaps, Ricardo Francini, Father Macaroni and the inimitable Morgan-Sinclair are all members of Craft lodges in both Rome and Naples. Interestingly, Francini and Macaroni both have the same Mother lodge, the Santa Pudenziana Lodge. Named after the church in Rome. It was built on the site where St Peter supposedly lived and worshiped."

"Where's Morgan-Sinclair's Mother lodge?" asked Harry.

"Well that took some tracking down but I eventually discovered his name being first listed at the Niederroohrdorf Lodge in Geneva, Switzerland. After passing through his Third Degree, he was introduced to a lodge that bears the name of his father as a member, The John of L'Armagnac Lodge in La Rochelle. For some reason they all became joining members of the Dioscur Lodge in Naples."

"Do you know who proposed them as joining members?" asked Harry.

"No, at least not as yet," replied Paxton-Smyth, "Ricardo Francini was the first to join about fifteen years ago, then Morgan-Sinclair joined some two years later and then finally Father Macaroni about five years after that, so they have all been there for quite some time. These three characters also attend Royal Arch lodges and each one of them has passed through the chair of both Degrees. But - and this is the interesting part - Ricardo Francini is related to a very successful lawyer by the name of Gisseppi Francini, a man of power and significant influence. In fact he stood at the presidential elections a few years ago, but for some reason he withdrew right at the last minute."

"Skipper, I believe we're getting close to the target. How much help can you give me to see this job through?"

"Very little I'm afraid Harry," replied Paxton-Smyth.

"Is there anyone we can talk to at the Naples Lodge?" asked Harry.

"Not sure, I'll see if I can find out, but for God's sake make sure your Mr Ford sees the sense of going to ground and staying there. If the Americans ever suspect he's alive all hell will break loose."

"Skipper, if I'm to help Lewis Ford go to ground it'll cost a fair few bob!"

"Okay, I'll get money wired into your bank account, leave that to me.
I'll also speak to Captain Purdue in Hereford and ask him to assist wherever possible, but this must be kept under a blanket

of secrecy. So if Purdue is willing to play ball, I don't want you talking to anyone else at Sterling Lines, is that clear?"

"Absolutely, Skipper, replied Harry. "I presume we're talking about Squeaky Purdue?" he said with a smile.

"The very same, we need to keep this strictly in the family. Okay Harry, the money will be in your account by tomorrow morning, I'll call you."

With that the line went dead. Harry glanced at his watch. It was almost midnight local time, which meant it would be one o'clock in the UK. He debated whether he should call Clarissa for an update but decided to wait until morning, then changed his mind and called her. The phone rang several times and then eventually went to answer-phone. Harry didn't bother leaving a message. He closed the phone and settled down for the night.

He was just about nodding off to sleep when the mobile began to vibrate; its movement prompted the phone to turn several times on the bedside table.

"Hi Harry," said Clarissa. "Sorry, I was in the office."

"Do you mean our office?" replied Harry.

"Yes of course, we thought it best to leave Scotland, especially after almost being killed."

Harry sat up in bed and switched on the light. "What happened?" he said.

"Oh God it was terrible, we were supposed to be meeting Hugh McDonald in Slamannan. We were driving out there when Guy said that he thought the car some distance behind had been following us since we left Bathgate. We were on the B8022, it's quite a narrow road in parts but Hugh insisted it would be the best route to take. We got to a certain point when we saw a car heading towards us. Immediately the one behind began to increase its speed and came right up to within inches of our bumper. The car in front was heading straight at us. Guy said it was like being on a chicken-run back in high school. He was so brave. I climbed over into the back seat and lay down, too frightened to move. I was waiting for a huge crash any moment. Guy just pointed the car in a straight line and kept going. The car coming for us in front eventually chickened out and veered off the road."

"What happened to the car behind you?"

"It stopped and two people got out then began shooting bullets at us. Guy said they were probably aiming for our tyres."

"Did you make it to your meeting with Hugh McDonald?"

"You must be kidding? Hell no. We drove to the airport, handed in the hire car and flew out on the first available flight back to Manchester. I have tried calling Hugh but his phone seems to be permanently switched off."

"Is Guy there with you?" asked Harry, now feeling really concerned.

"Of course, he's in the flat asleep. I'm in the office trying to keep our business together. I wish you'd never found that bloody scroll. We were just building up this business quite nicely, the Professor would still be alive and we wouldn't have almost got ourselves killed."

The tone of Clarissa's voice rose an octave with almost every syllable until eventually she began to cry. Harry didn't speak; he thought it best to wait for Clarissa to come around in her own time.

"I'm okay, I'm okay really... Sorry about that," she said.

Harry relayed the information he'd received from Jeremy Paxton-Smyth and told her he'd make sure that both her and Guy would get some protection. "Look Clarissa, it's late, you get some sleep and we'll talk tomorrow."

Harry closed his phone and settled down, feeling a heavy weight of guilt on his conscience.

Meanwhile, down the hallway, there was activity taking place in the form of a blond, tanned Frenchman being ushered into Lewis Ford's bedroom by two uniformed prison wardens. The man's wrists were handcuffed in front of him and a wide strip of plaster covered his mouth.

Lewis Ford told the wardens to sit the Frenchman down on a chair he'd placed close to a folded two-leaf table. "Okay, you can go now," he said waving them away.

One of the wardens, who spoke a smattering of English, shook his head. "We must wait," he replied.

"Okay then, wait out in the hallway, this won't be a pretty sight." Ford noticed the Frenchman's body tighten on hearing the words Ford had purposely used to see if he understood English.

Ford ushered both wardens outside, he then hung the 'Do not disturb' sign on the knob of the door before closing it.

"Right my friend, you are Pier Duvall, a buddy of a guy by the name of Mohammed Abu Atif, am I right?"

The Frenchman made no attempt to reply.

"Okay smart arse, according to the authorities you're charged with the murder of a Greek national over an aborted arms deal. It seems you are a member of Mohammed Abu Atif's Albanian network."

The Frenchman remained silent and sat rigidly upright facing the wall.

"Do we do this in English or would you prefer it if we *parlez vous* in French?"

Still the Frenchman sat in stony silence. Lewis Ford walked slowly over to a small bedside table and opened the drawer. He took out a large pair of pliers with pale blue insulated grips, a hammer and two long nails. He then approached the Frenchman, placed the tools down on the table and drew up a chair.

"Yeah know, I respect loyalty, but bearing so much pain for the sake of it is plumb stupid," said Ford, taking Pier Duvall's right hand in his vice- like grip. Duvall attempted to struggle away, but Ford was far too strong and soon the Frenchman's right hand had been pressed flat down on the table.

"Okay are we sitting comfortably? Good then I'll begin. See, I have a very low boredom threshold and I lose my patience really quickly, so I'm going to commence the task of extracting fingernails, first we'll start with this little piggy," Lewis Ford pointed to the Frenchman's small finger,

"Then we'll just progress up the hand having a whale of a time, slowly ripping off one nail after another. Now by the time I've reached the thumb, holy fucking Mary it'll hurt: your hand will swell like a balloon and the ends of your fingers will start pumping blood. Yeah know, for me it's orgasmic. Now I bet you're wondering what these long nails are for, well as I'm in a really good mood, I'm going to tell yeah. The first one, I'm going to drive right into the back of your hand, pinning you to this table so to speak. Then I'll remove those creepers you're wearing and nail your feet to the floor, god I love my work. And that's when the fun really gets going. See by then you'll be in so much fuckin' pain you'll crap yeah pants. It's such a funny sight. By then we'll have twenty bits of Frenchman piled up on the table. Then if you're still not singin' my kind of song, this last nail will be driven into your eye. Then just one extra strike with the hammer will skewer yeah brain."

The Frenchman made a desperate attempt to kick and buck his way off the chair in an attempt to pull his hand away from Ford's grip, but his attempt was thwarted by sufficient pressure to drain the blood from the his hand, turning it white and numb.

"Now yeah see why I've brought this hammer and eight inch nails along just in case you struggle." Ford picked up the hammer and slammed it down right in the centre of Pier Duvall's hand. The Frenchman gave a scream muffled by the tape, and then literally shook with pain. "Oh silly me, how on earth can you answer my questions when your mouth's still taped up?" Ford picked the corner of the tape from the Frenchman's cheek and then simply tore it away from his mouth. "Now that's better isn't it? So are we going to have a very co-operative chat? Or shall we re-decorate the room with blood... yours?"

The Frenchman shook his head.

"Oh good. Yeah know I hate it when people just capitulate. I'd have been really disappointed if you'd begun telling me really good stuff before I've even made a start."

The smile on Ford's face instantly disappeared when he picked up the pliers. He looked straight into the Frenchman's pale, tear-filled blue eyes, then picked up the first fingernail and the fleshy bits of the finger between its claws.

"Last chance buddy boy," said Lewis Ford with a faint smile returning to his face. "Nothing? Okay here we go." He gave an almighty tug. Both nail and some skin gave way leaving the end of Duvall's finger visible like a piece of raw meat. Ford opened the pliers to allow the particle to drop onto the table. "Right that's one, now let's move up the branch a little and see just how big a pile we can make, shall we? Won't that be fun?"

"Wait," shouted Pier Duvall, his face contorted with pain. "I'll talk, I'll talk." "Of course you will, but later," replied Ford taking a grip of the second nail.

"Please Monsieur, I will tell you what ever you want to know."

"But do you have a lot to tell I wonder? And how much will be bull shit?"

"Non, non, Monsieur, I will tell you exactly the truth."

"Okay," said Ford, loosening his grip and placing the pliers down on the table. "I'm going to take my hand away now and you're going to talk, and answer all my questions. If you fuck me around or if I think you're giving me shit, we'll resume, do I make myself clear?"

The Frenchman nodded in acknowledgement.

"Okay, how long have you been working for the Al Val Sinda?"

"I don't work directly for the Al Val Sinda, I represent a syndicate associated with a network across the globe."

"What's this network called?"

"Monsieur, I believe it's called the Salafist Preaching and Combat Group."

"Where are they based?" asked Ford.

"Here in Albania, but I'm only an arms dealer monsieur, I have nothing to do with anyone."

"Now that sounds like bullshit to me," said Ford picking up his pliers.

"Non, please Monsieur."

"No *please Monsieur* smarmy bullshit... you people make me sick, these terrorist groups wouldn't be able to buy arms if guys like you weren't around - and that would seriously fuck up their operations. Okay, when was the last time you were out in North or South Waziristan, you know the Pakistani enclaves on the border with Afghanistan?"

The Frenchman looked sullen faced as he shook the hand that was throbbing with pain. "I was there about six months ago Monsieur."

"And you met Mohammed Abu Atif?"

"Oui, Monsieur."

"Okay, so you were there to meet Abu Atif to discuss an arms deal, right?"

"Oui," said the Frenchman, whose eyes dropped to the table.

"And when was the last time you met him?"

Pier Duvall hesitated before answering. "Just before I was arrested."

"How long ago was that?" asked Ford.

"Maybe three weeks."

Lewis Ford's expression brightened substantially. "Just three weeks ago, okay so where was this meeting?"

"The first time was in Algiers, then I met him two days later here in Albania."

"Well you sure do clock up the air miles. Who else attended these meetings?"

The Frenchman shrugged his shoulders in a nonchalant gesture, "An Italian by the name of Francini, a representative from Al Val Sinda, and of course Mohammed Abu Atif. We discussed the supply of arms to a number of groups, and the transfer of young Muslims into Europe and America."

"So this was about trafficking young Muslims to the West, trained in terrorist activities," said Lewis Ford. "You're one sick bastard. So what's going on now?"

"Monsieur?" replied Pier Duvall, not exactly understanding the question.

"Who is this Italian guy?" went on Lewis Ford.

"I'm not sure exactly, but his organisation is involved in the trafficking."

"Do you know where Mohammed Abu Atif is right now?"

Again the Frenchman shrugged his shoulders. "I do not know Monsieur. However I did overhear the Italian and Mohammed Abu Atif talk about another meeting being planned."

"Did they mention where?" asked Lewis Ford, returning to the chair close to the Frenchman's side.

"I heard them talk about Italy and I believe Capri was mentioned."

"Did they talk about when?"

"Non, but the way they spoke it sounded as if it would be quite soon."

When he was reasonably convinced he'd extracted all the useful information from the Frenchman that he could get, Ford slowly made a fist. He then bent the middle finger so that it protruded above his knuckles, and in a flash he aimed it at a target to the righthand side of Duvall's neck.

"I've just administered what's known as a kill. The particular artery I've chosen will begin to form a blood clot real soon; it will then take about three hours to reach your brain. You'll be dead within six hours."

Ford didn't wait for Duvall to say anything. The Frenchman just sat quietly in the chair transfixed and bewildered by the experiences he'd encountered, and by the startling statement Ford had just made. Ford re-applied the tape across Duvall's mouth, without the merest sign of resistance. He then went to the door and called the wardens, who simply dragged Pier Duvall off the chair and carted him away.

The Knights of Black Chapter

23

At breakfast the following morning Ford related the information he'd received from the Frenchman the night before to a very disgruntled Harry Blakemore.

"Why didn't you call me in? I would have loved to be privy to that meeting. Can we get this bloke back?"

Ford glanced at his watch, "I wouldn't think so, he'll be dead by now."

"What the fuck do you mean, dead?" responded Harry, slamming his fork down on the table.

"We couldn't afford for this guy to start singing like a canary when he got back to prison. If anybody gets a sniff I'm alive, I'm dead if yeah get my meanin'. It was done in a very humane way, he'd have just keeled over about three or four hours ago."

When Ford mentioned that Duvall talked about an Italian by name Harry perked up.

"He actually mentioned Francini being involved in a meeting with Mohammed Abu Atif?"

"You got it in one. Why, have you heard of this guy Francini?"

Harry related what knowledge he had, both about him and the escapades that had led to such knowledge.

"So the guy might be a senior player in this Incanda organisation. Pretty powerful stuff. Are yeah sayin' yeah think Freemasonry's in some way responsible for these Incanda activities?"

"No, of course not. At least not Freemasonry as we know it," replied Harry. "I believe they simply use lodges as meeting points and possibly as a way of communicating with one another. And I'm sure the Knights of Black Chapter do likewise."

"Look, I'm not really interested in saving the world from a major force, I'm only interested in seeing out my days tucked away some where in the Grenadines. I'm going to buy me a sailboat and just float around the islands."

"Great, because we need you to disappear as soon as possible to give me a clear run at the target."

The Knights of Black Chapter

"You mean you expect me to take a hike while you finish off the job? How will I know when the loot's been paid?"

"As soon as the deal's done," replied Harry. "I'll get your share paid into a Swiss bank account," he continued.

Ford looked hard, right into Harry's face, as if searching to unearth any signs of mistruth. "Yeah know Limey, fuck knows why but I'm goin' to trust yeah, especially as I'm clean out of alternatives right know."

Harry smiled. "My Skipper will be wiring me sufficient funds to keep you in hiding until the deed has been done. I'll get you the money later today. Where will you go?"

"Is that a need-to-know question?" replied Lewis Ford.

Harry smiled. "No, not at all, only it would be comforting to know that you'd be far enough away from Europe not to be in the frame."

"Okay then Harry Blakemore my old buddy, let's just say that you can leave mail for me at Roots Bar in Port Elizabeth - that's in Bequia by the way - yeah know the cheaper island next to Mustique. And if you fuck me Harry, I'll come looking for yeah."

"Oh, I know you will, trust me," said Harry with sincerity in his voice as they shook hands.

Later that day Harry broke the rules and called Jeremy Paxton-Smyth.

"Hi Skipper," he said, waiting to receive an avalanche of abuse,

"Sorry to call but I've got breaking news."

"I'll call you back," said a stern sounding Paxton-Smyth and instantly closed down the security line. It was over an hour later when Harry's mobile vibrated.

"Harry, I said under no circumstances were you to call me."

"Sorry Skipper but this is really important. We have spoken to a bloke who actually had a meeting with the target no more than two or three weeks ago. The man called Francini was also at that meeting, only trouble is I'm not sure which Francini."

"Giovanni Francini, almost definitely," replied Paxton-Smyth,"I've spoken to the Italian authorities about this chap. He has significant connections with the Camorra, the Naples Mafia but they say his main involvement is with the Sicilian Cosa Nostra and the Ndrangheta, which is a hierarchical structure. Apparently, about two years ago he was the instigator of an amnesty approved by the Italian parliament to release almost three thousand prisoners in Naples in an attempt to relieve prison overcrowding. The official view was that these were minor criminals but many were in fact Camorra members. Then, with these ex-prisoners in his pocket, a new highly sophisticated Mafia family was born."

"Don't the police have enough on him to bring him to justice?" asked Harry.

"Well you'd think so, but he seems to be blessed with substantial influence over the hierarchy. He's been able to slip away from prosecution many times."

"He's Incanda, I bet?" remarked Harry.

"Well, that's a strong possibility, at some level. I'm sure the Camorra and its offshoots see themselves almost like Robin Hoods, especially with unemployment running at around thirty per cent across the country and especially as over sixty per cent of people below the age of thirty have never had a job. So these groups provide attractive alternatives, especially for the poor from the Naples slums. A *capopiazza* who's appointed the head of a cell can earn up to thirty thousand US dollars a month and apparently a drug pusher will be earning about five thousand a month; even a lowly lookout standing on a street corner collects around three thousand. So I suppose there's a never-ending stream of candidates ready to sign their lives away."

"So this bloke Giovanni Francini seems to be above the law, and quietly creating havoc," said Harry.

"That would appear about the size of it," replied Paxton-Smyth. "The whole Italian infrastructure seems geared around these powerful groups. Even the Italian government's constitutional and structural policies seem to favour the Mafia in so many ways. For years now Rome has been devolving power to local governments but they are so open to corruption and domination it's unbelievable. The government in recent years has brought in so many spending cuts that have naturally restricted any efforts to resist Mafia influence, so naturally they continue to grow from strength to strength unabated."

"Skipper, have you been able to get me a useful name of a Freemason from that Naples lodge?" asked Harry.

"Well as a matter of fact I have," replied Paxton-Smyth, "a chap by the name of Tony Ricardo. He was until recently working for the Polizia Ferrovaria's special unit, but was forced to retire after being injured in a Camorra shoot out. I've had him checked out and as far as we can see he's had no dealings

The Knights of Black Chapter

with any of the Mafia families, so it's pretty safe to say that he has no association to Incanda either."

"Sounds like the ideal man to talk to!" replied Harry optimistically.

"What's happening with the American? The money has been wired into your account by the way,"

Harry thanked the head of MI6. "He's agreed to go to ground, well out of harm's way. "

"And are you going to tell me where that is?"

"He thinks it best if he just disappears without anyone actually knowing. I've got a point of contact so as to communicate with him when the assignment has been completed," replied Harry.

"Well make sure it's not on Italian soil - that would be a political incident we don't want to be involved in."

"Quite right too, Skipper," said Harry with a smirk across his face.

* * *

Harry Blakemore arrived in Italy via Athens and Catania. The last part of his journey took him to Rome where he spent the night in a moderately priced hotel just outside Fiumicino airport. The following morning he took a taxi to Stazione Termini, the railway station where he purchased a single ticket to Naples.

Tony Ricardo now lived a much quieter life immersed in the family business, growing olives upon the steep, fertile, volcanic slopes near Castellamare di Stabia.

The number Jeremy Paxton-Smyth had given Harry failed to connect with Tony Ricardo. However, after speaking to the Grand Master of the Naples lodge, Harry was advised that Tony had now joined a lodge in Sorrento. A brief conversation prior to Harry's departure concluded that Tony Ricardo would meet Harry off the train at Sorrento station.

The man who introduced himself as Tony Ricardo was nothing like Harry had imagined. He was much older, well into his mid-fifties and virtually bald-headed except for a modicum of black hair cut like a laurel leaf just above the ears, encircling both the back and sides quite inconspicuously.

"I have booked you into a small private hotel, not far from here, just on the outskirts of Sorrento. We will go there now, you can check in and I'll collect you around six o'clock. It will be my pleasure if you will dine with me and my family this evening, there we can talk freely," Tony said in virtually perfect English, which Harry complimented him upon.

For the first time in ages, Harry felt relaxed. He was in a country that had always appealed to him, especially with his love for antiques and works of art. The outlook from the hotel was simply spectacular. The panoramic view from Harry's balcony over the bay of Naples was literally breathtaking, whilst over to the right the renowned Mount Vesuvius was a commanding spectacle, overshadowing Pompeii and Naples. To the left lay the bay and town of Sorrento, gradually sloping down from its high cliff protectorate to the blue calmness of the sea below where lay the Punta del Capo and the remains of Pollio Felice, dating back to the Roman Empire. Directly in front of Harry the islands of Ischia and Capri were dressed in a slight haze.

Harry was determined to make the best of this free afternoon and therefore took the bus to the Piazza Lauro. He then strolled down the Via San Cesareo towards the Marina Piccola where he had a long relaxing lunch at Vela Bianca, tasting the delights from their extensive fish menu; the chilled bottle of Biancolella rounded the lunch off perfectly.

Challenging the substantially steep incline back into town on foot was not in Harry's game plan, especially on a full stomach. He therefore took a taxi which dropped him off outside the Villa Garden Hotel, where he sat in a comfortable, cushion-filled wicker chair on the cliff terrace, drinking coffee and contemplating just what might transpire over the next few days.

The Knights of Black Chapter

The Knights of Black Chapter

Tony Ricardo's younger brother Marco tooted the horn of the old dark blue Fiat 500 as he arrived outside the gates of the Villa Garden Hotel. Harry was waiting as instructed in reception, and ready to make a dash to the car as the heavens had literally opened and rain was falling like stair rods.

The initial part of the drive was through the streets of Sorrento, awash from the torrential rain. At one point Harry was forced to put his feet up on the dashboard to avoid paddling in several inches of water that suddenly washed into the foot well. It was amazing how the tiny car's engine kept going, as Harry remarked to the young man with a magnificent mop of curly black hair.

"It is good she has her engine in the back!" exclaimed Marco, with an unconvincing expression on his face.

Fortunately they soon turned off the straight and proceeded to climb slowly up the hillside, allowing the water to drain out from the back of the car. It took them the best part of half an hour to reach Ricardo's, and at least a third of the journey was spent winding up one incline after another, a task that proved exhausting for the little car that was well past its sell-by date.

"My car, she has been handed down three times now by papa - originally it belonged to my grandfather," said Marco who was now feeling sufficiently confident to speak positively about the car, especially as the rain had abated to no more than a drizzle and the engine was still going despite the odd stutter. Marco described the finer points of the car's history as if discussing a priceless family heirloom.

Eventually the Fiat came to a juddering halt with its bonnet almost touching a pair of heavy metal gates. Marco scrambled from the driver's seat and opened the gates to their full extent. He then returned to the car and drove it far enough into what appeared to be a private driveway to be able to close the gates again behind them.

The drive up to the house took all of five minutes, passing through row upon row of olive trees, draped in fine black nets to prevent the precious fruit from falling to the ground.

The Knights of Black Chapter

The modestly furnished house seemed to be bustling with people. Tony Ricardo ushered Harry inside and began introducing him as a fellow Freemason visiting Italy to learn the Italian ways of the craft. Unfortunately hardly anyone could speak a word of English and therefore they just smiled at him politely. Tony escorted his guest to a long narrow dinning table that was laid as if ready for a banquet.

It was the first time Harry had experienced the treat of actually dining with an Italian family and although Tony advised him that the spread in front of him was their normal family meal, Harry was convinced it had really been prepared in his honour.

After spending the best part of two hours consuming large helpings of wonderfully prepared local delicacies, Tony escorted Harry onto the porch, which commanded a terrific view down through the olive groves to a sunset backdrop of striking red and crimson flames, dashed sporadically across the sullen sky and tranquil sea. The rain now had virtually stopped, leaving a view of such crystalline freshness and clarity, that it was as if an artist had varnished the picture.

Tony poured generous measures of cognac into two huge balloon glasses and presented one of them to Harry, he then invited him to sit in a comfortable looking, floral patterned armchair.

"This is quite a place, I've always loved Italy," said Harry, feeling full, comfortable and relaxed.

"Have you ever been to this part of Italy before?" asked Tony. Harry shook his head and took a sip of cognac. "Sorrento is considered one of the pearls of Italy. It stretches right across the Tufa Plateau, formed by a volcanic eruption of the Flegreian Fields in the northern part of Naples, and that was over thirty six thousand years ago," said Tony proudly.

"In case you are interested," he went on, "the name Sorrento derives from the legend of the Sirens. In Roman times it was a place favoured by the Patricians. The Goths and Byzantines dominated Sorrento for many decades... and it was the home of Torquato Tasso, the great poet. He was born here on the 11th of March 1544. Tasso was an active Freemason for most of his life."

"Well you sure know your history," said Harry, impressed by Tony's ability to provide him with a snapshot of local knowledge.

"So Harry, you are apparently here in an unofficial capacity, but you seem to have very powerful allies. There was, it appears, a thorough check made of my credentials before we met today." The expression on Tony Ricardo's face had changed to cold and enquiring, as if he was back working for the Carabinieri.

"Tony, I am on a very delicate job, I've been unofficially appointed to track down a bloke by the name of Muhammad Abu Atif. My search for him has led me here. We have it on good authority that he has an important contact in one Giovanni Francini, no doubt you have heard of him."

The expression on Tony's face changed again the moment he heard the name Giovanni Francini. "The man of whom you speak is very powerful," said Tony, turning his gaze towards the olive groves as if to reflect upon a period of history he'd rather forget.

"What can you tell me about this bloke?" asked Harry, sensing Tony and Francini's paths had significantly crossed at some stage.

"What do you know about the very deep Orders of Freemasonry?" asked Tony after taking a sip from a glass of water.

"Well, of late I've learnt quite a bit," replied Harry.

"Then you probably know that the Degrees of Masonry reach to incredible depths - the lowest Degree holds the power of Man's entire existence. The destiny of mankind ultimately rests in the hands of two opposing families, Incanda and the Knights of Black Chapter. Incanda was initiated from religious belief, their objective has always been to destroy the Knights of Black Chapter and thereby gain supreme power above all things."

"And they've been taking pot shots at each other ever since," remarked Harry, who was excited to think everything was materialising, virtually in front of him.

"For centuries the deep-rooted belief in religion held the keys to obedience and power. Incanda have always capitalised on this, but now, behind this shield of belief, lies terrorism on an immense scale."

"Tony, I am aware of these two Degrees," replied Harry, "we believe Muhammad Abu Atif is in some way connected to Incanda."

"Muhammad Abu Atif is a Cardinal of Incanda," interjected Tony, "and so is Giovanni Francini. A Cardinal is a high position within Incanda; the equivalent is that of a Grand Superintendent's Degree in Freemasonry.

Giovanni has a cousin called Antonio Francini. He's younger than Giovanni. Antonio was born into a Mafia family with long standing affiliations to the Incanda brotherhood. Antonio was very bright, but a rebel in his youth. The family sent him to America where he attended Harvard. He read accountancy and eventually succeeded his father in the position of Stalker in the Incanda Degree. A Stalker is the equivalent to a Grand Superintendent of works in a Provisional lodge. The Chapter he's a part of is quite high in the pecking order; I'd say about five Degrees below Incanda."

"Do you know where this Antonio bloke is now?" asked Harry.

"Yes," replied Tony, "he's in Chicago, where he's the senior partner of a successful accountancy business. He comes over to Italy now and again. We've been watching him closely for years... that is until the Italian Government wanted to reduce the investigation budget and gave us an ultimatum: get proof and make arrests or stop chasing shadows."

"Do you think this decision was influenced by Incanda?" asked Harry.

"Definitely," replied Tony.

"You seem to know quite a lot about Incanda," said Harry cautiously.

"My understanding, Tony, is that Incanda is controlled by just nine people. So are you saying that Abu Atif and Giovanni Francini are two of these nine?"

A broad grin spread across Tony Ricardo's face. "No, unfortunately, if they were a contract killing would have been instigated years ago. Maybe executed by a person like you!" said Tony, giving Harry an enquiring stare, but Harry remained expressionless and was not going to get drawn. "They are no more than servants to Incanda," continued Tony, "but they sit on the Grand Council. The followers of Incanda are positioned in different Degrees, some closer to the Incanda Degree than others. I'm sure the Grand Council, if not the very next to Incanda, is very close. Many of these, let's call them servant Degrees to Incanda, are almost as old as Incanda itself.

"Giovanni Francini was born in Trondheim Norway, the son of an Italian immigrant, probably sent to Norway by Incanda. The mantle of Cardinal would have passed to Giovanni as the oldest son. He moved to Italy about twenty years ago. As a Cardinal of the Grand Council we believe he's one of the most influential heads of the Cardinal Degree. Francini was married by arrangement into a significant Sicilian Mafia family.

Unfortunately his wife suffered a horrific skiing accident, she lost the child she was carrying and almost died herself. The accident meant she was unable to bear any children, which presented Francini with the problem of no heir. A disposable prostitute was hired from Rome, employed to conceive the continuation of the bloodline. Nuns kept the prostitute under close supervision at a convent near Positano until the boy was born. The prostitute was promised substantial wealth for her services but after she conceived she was never seen or heard of again."

"The child is now fifteen years of age. His instruction will have commenced when he was ten, in preparation so that one-day he will follow his ancestors in the service of Incanda - and so the cycle continues."

"So if this bloke Giovanni Francini was to unfortunately die prematurely, his son would not be completely versed in the teachings, I presume?" said Harry.

"There's obviously something in place to overcome such a situation, but the line would definitely be weakened, especially one as important as the Francini dynasty. It would probably be demoted in some way - from Cardinal of the Grand Council to that of Stalker for example."

Harry sat back in the armchair, sipping his brandy, deep in thought. Taking out Francini as well as Muhammad Abu Atif would rid the world of two significant members of the Incanda movement and maybe earn him an extra bonus into the bargain.

"Tony, I'm sticking my neck out here... would you be prepared to help me to achieve the objective the British and Americans have hired me to accomplish?"

Tony Ricardo walked over and sat in an armchair next to Harry then looked out across the olive grove. He sat back in the chair and turned towards Harry. "This olive grove has served my family for generations. But from a young age I had no desire to grow olives, I wanted to become a policeman. My family accepted this and so I left the olive grove and become a policeman in Rome, then eventually in Napoli. Two years ago I took four bullets in the trunk of my body, which almost killed me. Now I have difficulty walking very far and with only half a lung I get very short of breath. This new wave of Camorra was responsible for the shooting; their Godfather is Giovanni Francini. The pension I receive is not sufficient to live on, therefore I have been ensconced in the business; my family have accepted me as if I had worked the olive grove all my life. Now my wife and two children live here, they are happy in the bosom of the family."

"And how about you?" asked Harry, detecting that Tony had a more restless spirit.

"Me, I'm a broken man. I'm angered to think my career, one that I loved so much, has been swept away by a hail of bullets." Tony then turned towards Harry to look him squarely in the face. "How can I help you Harry?"

"Be my eyes and ears," replied Harry smiling. "This coastline is your home, you know it and I don't. Tony if you help me, I'll see you and your family right, money will never be a problem for you again."

Tony Ricardo had a tear in his eye as he leaned over to shake Harry by the hand.

25

Harry raised the shutters onto a fine morning and, as he opened the French doors, sunlight literally streamed into his bedroom at the Villa Garden Hotel. He strolled onto the balcony and looked out across the peaceful sea towards Capri, which was barely visible through the early morning mist. Harry leaned upon the railings around the balcony and took a few deep breaths, then just stood for a while soaking up the splendour in front of him.

He had already decided that once this job was all over and the dust had settled he would definitely return to Sorrento for a long holiday. His thoughts on such a trip were interrupted by his mobile that began to vibrate in the waistband of his boxer shorts, providing him with a rather pleasant tingling sensation.

"Harry, for god's sake where are you? I've been trying to get hold of you for ages," remarked Clarissa.

"Sorry, love I've been otherwise engaged," replied Harry, dodging the question as to his whereabouts.

"Harry, we've had a significant breakthrough," said Clarissa, sounding like an excited child. "Briefly - Rosslyn Chapel also holds the remains of a man that for generations was hailed as the second Messiah. His name's Jacques de Molay, he was the Grand Master of the Knights Templar. The French and the Pope burned him at the stake."

"Yes I know. I've read all about him," replied Harry.

"Well good, because after he'd met his end, his remains were smuggled out of France and secretly interned under Rosslyn along with those of Jesus and Mary Magdalene. But putting that to one side for a moment, the breakthrough has come from the notes the Professor took from the Scroll. We have now discovered far more about the Knights of Black Chapter. Listen to this…" there was a slight pause whilst Clarissa seemed to be unfolding a piece of paper "…The way of the Knights of Black Chapter has always been through royal lines as we discovered. Unfortunately for them the power of royalty has been eroded over several generations. Right, now listen to this."

Harry took the phone into the bedroom and sat down upon his bed in anticipation of this being a long call.

The Knights of Black Chapter

"Right," continued Clarissa, "George II was a Hanoverian who succeeded his father as the King of Britain. Eighteen years later a Jacobite uprising took place... we're talking around about 1745 here. Charles Edward Stuart, known as Bonnie Prince Charlie, decided to challenge the succession to the throne by these Germans. The Scottish church was a great supporter of the challenge and in the Abbey at Holyrood House they symbolically crowned Prince Charlie as King Charles III, in the presence of the Catholic and Presbyterian churches who both agreed to the crowning. Of course James III was still living, but in a declaration on the 23rd of Dec 1743, he had transferred everything over to his son. The declaration announced that James was appointing his son Charles Prince of Wales to become the sole Regent of the Kingdoms of England, Scotland and Ireland together with all James's other dominions during his absence.

Prince Charles restored Parliament and issued a decree saying that the English should have equal rights with regard to religious and political freedom. This was proclaimed in Edinburgh in 1745. At around the same time, Bonnie Prince Charlie was invested into a very high Freemasons Lodge as Grand Master; I think it was called the Order of the Temple of Jerusalem. In fact he declared in a speech that he would restore the Order of the Lodge back to its former glory, as enjoyed during the time of William the Lion."

"When a significant Scottish army marched south as far as Derby, London went into panic mode. Even George II gathered all things precious including the crown jewels and loaded everything onto barges ready for a quick exit to Germany. Propaganda was circulated proclaiming that Bonnie Prince Charlie would never reach London, it was bullshit but it worked. The re-enforcements Charlie was banking on therefore never actually arrived. Lord George Murray persuaded the chiefs of the clans to retreat then re-group to meet the Duke of Cumberland's army. They met Cumberland's men on the 16th of April 1746 at Culloden Moor near Inverness."

"By now the Scots were tired, half starved and making many big mistakes with regard to their battle strategies, and subsequently they lost the fight. If the propaganda had not been put about when the Scots had reached Derby they would have successfully taken the capital with ease. A Stuart would then have officially become the King of England and Scotland, with each country having its own Parliament. It's remarkable but that's exactly where it's heading today through devolution, promised by the Labour Government's mainly Scottish hierarchy. So you can say that the Scots are at last getting their just desserts!"

"Now we come to some very strange happenings in Royal circles. James VII instigated religious freedom, which was a popular move in the eyes of the British people. The Whigs, however, needed to secure their own domain, probably at the instigation of Incanda. To do this they needed to get really personal and they began desicrating the memory of the Stuarts and King James in particular. They launched personal attacks upon James's wife, Queen Mary d'Este. Queen Mary was the daughter of Alfonso IV, the Duke of Modena, by the way."

"The Hanoverians did a character assassination by saying she was the illegitimate daughter of the Pope. They also looked deeply into the Cromwellian archives in an attempt to find critical things to say. James VI was regarded as the British Solomon, but these Whigs called him the wisest fool in Christendom. The intestinal illness he suffered from was cruelly used to portray him as a vulgar glutton. A witch-hunting charge, commonly used by the Puritans, labelled him as sexually deviant.
Despite all this Prince Charles Edward Stuart's popularity was widespread. Bonnie Prince Charlie was proving a threat to George II."

"Charlie was made out to be a treacherous warmonger. Another successful character assassination took place when he was described as a drunkard and a woman beater. All Charlie's children except for Charlotte of Albany were excluded from any historical record of British history. Likewise with Charlie's many other lady companions, except for the one childless marriage he had with Princess Louise de Stolberg, and of course Charlottes mother, Clementia Walkinshaw. Charlie suffered bad attacks of both epilepsy and asthma; these were portrayed as drunken fits. Charlie died in 1788 and after his death writings about his life were made from Hanoverian recordings. Most history books and biographies available today still portray Charlie in the way the Hanoverians' character assassination machine depicted him, which, Harry is grossly unfair."

"At this rate you'll be looking to become Scottish," said Harry with a snigger.

"No way, I'm Welsh and proud of it. If I were English I'd consider changing though! Now where was I? Oh yes, quite a

The Knights of Black Chapter

number of people in Scotland today still view Bonnie Prince Charlie as King Charles III and naturally hold that view with a great deal of pride. In the registers of Europe, Charlie and his legitimate descendants are clearly recorded as a royal bloodline. Unfortunately for the Scots the British Government smothered these records and information from the people. Now we come to present times and await HRH Charles the Prince of Wales of the house of Windsor, to become King Charles III. The Scots are pursuing, through devolution and the Scottish National party, a re-instatement of the Scottish parliament. Okay, at the moment they are still under the rule of Westminster, but for how long?"

"The Scots also have a Written Constitution in readiness for full independence. It will give the nation the rights to reject the overlords of England and to choose its own monarch. If Charles Prince of Wales does eventually become King Charles III of Britain, the nationalistic Scots almost certainly would not recognise him as the second Charles III. When Charles's mother was crowned Queen Elizabeth II, the Scots protested because they never had an Elizabeth I. You see Elizabeth Tudor reigned over England only. Right up until 1917 the Royal family's name was Saxe-Coburg-Gotha. They only changed their name to Windsor to appease the British people during the First World War. A name change might have to be arranged again, this time for Charles if he's to be made King. A name change was actually carried out for his grandfather Albert, Duke of York who became King George VI."

"So, in my opinion, Charles will never be crowned Charles III. Parliament has the full hand of cards and it's clear Charles will never be crowned King in his or any other name especially if the present government are still in power. In fact the government has already prepared a character assassination paper to discredit the Queen upon her death. The BBC has been charged to deliver it to the people."

"Fascinating stuff, Clarissa but where is this all leading us too?" said Harry, fidgeting on his bed to find a more comfortable position.

"Don't you see, if Charles, Prince of Wales does not rise to the throne the likelihood is that the British monarchy will die and that could present a huge problem for the Knights of Black Chapter, much to the delight of Incanda. From the notes the Professor took from the Baton Scroll, Guy has been able to roughly calculate that a gathering of the Nine is due sometime very soon; so we're leaving for Crete tomorrow to research the possibilities. Oh, and by the way we're now convinced that Princess Diana was not killed by accident. We are convinced her death was instigated by command of the Knights of Black Chapter: clearly she was pregnant and about to agree to become the wife of a Muslim. Can you imagine the repercussions that would have had, the heir to the throne having a Muslim step father?"

"Surely that's mere speculation?" said Harry.

"Not from the information we've got. Harry I can't explain things to you right now on the phone but I will when we eventually meet again. Our investigations have revealed such a lot of things. We have actually spoken to the person who was the principal who arranged President Kennedy's assassination. Harry you'd be amazed at the number of people who've been put to death in order to protect the Knights of Black Chapter."

Harry was tempted to tell Clarissa of his present location and what he was doing, however he thought of the possible consequences and simply wished her a good trip and promised to keep in touch.

In a strange way the revelations Clarissa had related about Princess Diana had saddened Harry. He had built up this image of the Knights of Black Chapter as being the really good guys, championing the cause of freedom, but then he reflected on the cost that often has to be paid, and felt a little easier in his mind.

"Harry, good morning! I have a person who I think you should talk to," suggested Tony Ricardo, following Harry's call to him.

"Okay," replied Harry, "Who is he?"

"He was the source of a lot of information I used to obtain about Giovanni Francini," replied Tony. He and Harry arranged to meet outside the small church in the Viale dei Pini just around the corner from Harry's hotel.

No sooner had Harry closed his phone than it began vibrating again. Harry opened it and saw the now familiar formalities and procedures that asked for the security code, which he dialled. To his surprise they revealed that Lewis Ford was on the other end.

"Good day, I trust by now you'll be fit enough to set off for never- never land?" asked Harry with a degree of sarcasm.

Ford ignored the remark. "I'm about to leave Albania, my friend, I'll do the Peter Pan stuff when you get this deal done, until then I'll be in your face."

"Very good, so is this call to flex those muscles of yours or have you got something useful to say?" replied Harry.

"Malik Ahmed's guys have just brought in a member of Al Val Sinda who's been singing like a canary."

"What did you do this time, choke a confession out of him with bird seed?"

Lewis Ford ignored Harry's wit. "This guy reckons Mohammed Abu Atif is currently en route to Sicily in a private jet."

A broad smile lit Harry's face. "Fantastic, getting him out of the Middle East will leave him far more exposed. And did this canary sing about anything else?"

"No. Say, what more do yeah want? Abu Atif is flying right in your goddam direction. I hope you're not going to let me down limey, there's only one future for this guy Atif, a very short one."

"Don't you worry, you just lap up the sun in the South Seas and leave the rest to me." Harry closed the phone.

Precisely at eleven Tony's Alfa was parked under the Maple trees outside the church in the Viale Dei Pini.

"Good morning. We go to Napoli," Tony said as Harry climbed into the passenger seat.

Neither man spoke much until Tony turned onto the Corso Italia that took them out of Sorrento towards the steep winding road of the Golfo de Napoli.

"Who are we going to meet?" asked Harry, still reflecting on Ford's information.

"Someone called Marco Tippett. Marco is Giovanni's gardener and brother-in-law, although Giovanni never treats him as such. Marco, to a degree, is a simpleton, he's treated quite badly by the Francini family. But he plays on his condition and acts far simpler than he really is. I first met him when I was sent to interview him in hospital after he'd been beaten within inches of his life. Nobody ever bothered to visit him. I felt really sorry for him so I used to visit him, often; he began treating me as if I was a friend, and for years after he provided me with useful information about Francini."

Eventually they drove into central Naples and parked the car close to the Napoli Centrale railway station in Piazza Garibaldi; they then walked down toward the harbour where they were to meet Marco Tippett in a small café just off the Via Nuova Marina.

The café was very plain and according to its décor did not cater for tourists. The chairs were stripped pine and the tables had plastic cloths covering them. They had been wiped so frequently the pattern had almost worn away.

"Not exactly the Café Royal!" exclaimed Harry.

Tony smiled. "This is the real Napoli, people here are very poor but the food they prepare is magnificent. Sophia Lorraine actually worked in this very café when she was no more than a little girl."

"And every other café along this part of the coast, I'll bet," replied Harry.

Tony smiled and with his thumb and the first two fingers of his right hand placed to his pouted lips, he kissed them dramatically in a gesture of perfection. "Molto bene," he said with a smile just as a large, well-endowed lady with a floral patterned apron appeared from around the kitchen side of the tiny counter. She raised her arms and expressed a smile that literally shone out from her attractive face.

"Hi Toni...! Papa! Toni!" she shouted, wrapping her arms around Tony's neck. Tony eventually alighted from this frenzied attack of friendship with a reddish beam upon his face. Papa stood to wait his turn, a small looking man with a substantial number of wrinkles across his face. He ninety if he was a day!

"Papa!" exclaimed Tony, embracing the old man who began to grin broadly, as if in pain from suddenly being gripped in a bear hug. "Harry I'm sorry. This is my wife's family, Maria my wife's elder sister and my father-in-law Alfonso. Maria's café makes the finest truffles in the whole of Italy."

Maria smiled enjoying the accolade as she shook Harry's hand.

"This is where Giovanni Francini comes when he wants truffles," said Tony, at which the expression upon Maria's face changed to one of contempt. She began exuding words like a machine gun until Tony stopped her with a gentle smile and a touch upon her lips with his finger. "Maria, hates Giovanni with a passion. Come, we sit over there, Mario will be here in a moment."

Maria brought them espressos and a small white plate with two huge chocolate balls rolling around upon it.

"Here, try one of these," said Tony picking up the plate and holding it in front of Harry. Harry was not particularly a lover of chocolate; however after biting into the crisp outer shell covered in vermicelli chips, even he had to admit the flavour was sensational.

The Knights of Black Chapter

"Maria says Giovanni Francini calls in here almost every day and eats at least six truffles. And when he entertains at home he orders them by the bucket full." Tony glanced over Harry's shoulder towards the door and smiled. "Ah, here's Mario," he said, standing.

A quite small, plumpish man, bent slightly in the middle over an ample stomach, smiled upon seeing Tony. The smile seemed to lean to the left of his face as if he'd suffered a stroke at some stage in his life.

"Come let's go into the back parlour," said Tony after the formal introductions were made. Maria kissed Marco on both cheeks en route through the kitchen into a small living room with four easy chairs covered in floral throw-overs.

Within a trice Maria appeared with a tray bearing three tiny cups and saucers containing thick sweet espresso coffee.

"So we talk," said Tony.

"Giovanni, he a bad man. I Marco he treat very badly, Toni he my friend. I tell him things."

With that Marco stopped as if waiting for a reaction. He then took an undignified slurp of coffee.

"Hey Marco, tell my friend Harry what's going on."

The middle aged Italian with the mop of jet-black hair and cheap looking clothes turned to Harry. "Marco, I am gardener, I hear things for Toni."

"What have you heard just lately Marco, tell me and Harry, Harry's my friend," said Tony, reiterating his earlier remark.

"Big boat coming with man for meeting."

"Big boat coming from where?" asked Harry.

"Big boat coming from Sicily with man."

"Do you know this man's name?" replied Tony.

"Man with funny name," said Mario, as if the words he was extracting were causing him a certain amount of pain.

"Was his name Mohammed Abu Atif?" asked Harry, gripping his hands together in anticipation of the right answer. From the expression that flowed across Marco's face it was clear he recognised the name. He simply turned to Harry and nodded.

"Bingo," responded Harry clapping his hands together.

"Mario, listen to me carefully. Do you know when this man is coming in the big boat?" Tony asked, with Harry waiting intently for the response. But Mario shook his head.

"Mm pity," responded Tony with a frown. "I'll try to find out, he won't be coming on the public ferry service that's for sure. If it were me I'd be travelling on a luxurious yacht of some kind."

"Capri," said Marco without a prompt.

"Capri, this man in the big boat is going to Capri?" said Tony holding Marco's arm. "So that means this meeting's been arranged on Capri maybe even at Giovanni's summer villa," said Tony with a slightly puzzled expression upon his face. "So in that case it would make sense if he flew into Sicily, possibly by private jet. That means the boat he'd come over in would probably leave Palermo, there's a large number of Mafia family owned yachts in the marina. I see the sense in meeting on Capri. Luxury yachts sail in and out of there every day and it is just that bit further from the mainland, which means a fast craft can be miles away before any coastal patrol vessels can be scrambled. I'll see what I can find out from some of my contacts in the Cosa Nostra."

Tony sounded excited at the prospect of undertaking some investigative work. It had always been a part he particularly enjoined in the Carabinieri.

"Thank you Marco, you have been very helpful. Now Maria is going to give you lunch," said Tony.

Marco's face lit up at the prospect. As if right on cue Maria appeared from behind a bead curtain and ushered Marco away into the kitchen.

"Tony, I need to assemble some bits and pieces to instigate a hit," said Harry, glancing at Tony for a reaction. The response was non- committal.

"Can you help me?" asked Harry.

"It depends on what you want, if it's a high velocity sniper's rifle there might be a problem," said Tony with a smile.

Harry shook his head. "Do you know of any Varnish manufacturers around?" he said, returning the smile.

The Knights of Black Chapter

"Can I speak to Captain Purdue please?" asked Harry after phoning the number Jeremy Paxton-Smyth had given him. Harry was surprised to hear someone other than Squeaky Purdue answer the phone.

"Is that Harry Blakemore?" asked the voice.

"Absolutely," replied Harry.

"Duke Wellington, here Bob, or do I have to call you Harry now?"

"Afraid so Duke."

"Oh well, Squeaky's in the 'house' right now putting a few of the new guys through their paces. He said if you were to call I could either take a message or help, whichever."

"Duke, I need a few bits urgently," said Harry.

"Bits?" responded Duke.

"Yes, I need some shock energy detonation transistors," replied Harry with tongue in cheek.

"Hello, what the hell are you up to?" replied Duke, ending his question with a chuckle.

"Trying to do my job, Duke, and that's as close as you'll get to an answer."

"Okay, fair enough... what size transistors?"

"Pin head," replied Harry.

"Anything else?" said Duke.

"You sound like a shop keeper. Oh but I forgot you're working in the shoe department at Rackhams in Birmingham, how's it going?"

"History, the store manager was a complete arsehole, although the main board of directors knew I was only a plant, under these wonderful new terrorist rules. I was seconded to the department without the normal formality of being interviewed by the store manager, which didn't go down very well, so naturally I wasn't flavour of the month. Although he *was* told I would only be there as and when, and that other work would take priority, which to him was like red rag to a bull."

"So you hit him!" exclaimed Harry, knowing the fiery little Black Country man of old. Harry heard a roar of laughter followed by a few coughs down the other end of the phone.

"Ah well, you know me! Anyway, I'm at Asda as floor detective, much more interesting."

"Yes, well, each to their own," said Harry. "Right, now what else? I need two books, *Verlag Chemie* by Doctor Rudolf Meyer and the *Merck Index*, the twelfth edition."

"Fuck me stupid and I thought you were into Harry Potter. I suppose you have special library tickets for the rare editions?" replied Duke laughing.

"You bet," said Harry participating in the banter.

"You do realise the fines are pretty horrendous if you get them back late."

"Tell the librarian to charge all fines to Paxton–Smyth," said Harry.

"Christ, so you're working for our old Skipper, that must be MI6 then?"

Harry ignored his old friend's question. "I need these couriered to Italy and I need them by tomorrow."

"Not a problem," replied Duke. Harry related the address of his hotel where he wanted the package to be delivered.

"There's a varnish manufacturer in Sorrento," said Tony, curious to learn why Harry was so interested in such a thing as varnish.

"Do you think your sister–in–law would teach me how to make truffles?" asked Harry.

There was a pregnant pause whilst Tony frowned and reflected upon the question.

"I'm sure she'd be delighted," replied Tony. "Why?"

"Well I'd like to make a very special variety of truffles, the sort Francini Giovanni would have a painful time forgetting."

Although Tony was a little unsure of what Harry was actually talking about, he concluded that if it was going to be an unpleasant experience for Giovanni that was okay by him.

"I also need to find a good chemist, an industrial chemist ideally," said Harry with a non-committal expression on his face.

"I know one who may do, we buy insecticides from them. They're along the coast at Castellammare, I could take you there now if you like."

"Let's go," said Harry jumping into Tony's Alfa without another word.

"I need a bottle of organic peroxide and do you have any pentaeythrol tetranitrate, nitropenta and tetranitrate de pentaerythrite?"

Both Tony and the chemist looked closely at Harry, for completely different reasons.

"What do you want to use these for?" asked the chemist in very poor English.

"Being a marine biologist, employed by the European Union, I'm conducting experiments to discover the best materials for controlled coral destruction, we have a rogue coral that is affecting marine life, I'm looking to eradicate the problem. "

A slightly open-mouthed Tony looked dumbfounded at Harry's response. However the answer must have done the trick with the chemist as he scooted off without another word.

"I presume you're well versed in ad-libbing?" remarked Tony.

Harry looked at him and winked as the chemist returned.

"I will require a signature for these and an address," said the chemist placing a small box with the relevant materials down on the counter. As the chemist uttered the request in Italian, Tony looked at Harry.

"He wants your name and an address."

"Fine", said Harry taking out the passport Malik had provided so that he could leave Tajikistan, issued in the of David Johnson. He showed the appropriate page with his photograph and signature and then he mimicked the scribble on the official form the chemist put on the counter in front of him.

"David Johnson?" said Tony reading the name on the passport upside down. "Who are you really, Harry?"

"God knows, it's been so long now I've almost forgotten," replied Harry.

"My current address is Apartment 4, 1140, Via Pieta Sorrento," he said with a smile. "A good tip, always find an appropriate address, you never know when you might need one... And always make sure it's an address you can easily spell," he said, filling in the box where the chemist was pointing.

"Harry you'll either make me a wealthy hero or a convict. Right now I'm not sure which," said Tony as he opened the boot of the car for Harry to put the box inside.

Harry just smiled. "Look Tony, you're a great guy and I realise the world in which I live might seem unorthodox to you, but when you're dealing with the likes of Mohammed Abu Atif you have to use unorthodox methods otherwise you lose."

Tony looked uncertain but accepted Harry's offer of a handshake across the now closed boot lid of the car.

"Trust me, Tony, Abu Atif has a big bounty on his head, some of it will wend its way into your bank account, I'll make sure of that."

"Well any money at the moment would be very helpful," exclaimed Tony as he got into his car.

"I need a few more things," said Harry during their drive back to Sorrento. "I need some skin-diving gear, a single tank will be ample, a small workshop, oh and a boat?"

"A boat," repeated Tony.

"Yes, it would be my guess that Mohammed Abu Atif won't just sail into the Marina, it'll most likely moor off the coastline to enable a quick get away. So I need a boat."

Tony thought for a moment. "Well my cousin is a fisherman; perhaps you could borrow his boat."

"Perfect," replied Harry.

"It would mean he'd need paying though, because he uses it every day."

"Not a problem," said Harry with a smile. "Where is it?"

"Moored at the Marina Grandee," replied Tony.

"That must be the small marina in the centre of town and what about a workshop?" said Harry.

"We've got workshops in the olive grove, you can use one of those," Tony said without a second thought.

Harry decided to hire some transport from a local vehicle rental office in town, then bright and early the next morning he set off for the olive grove in a bright yellow Fiat Uno. He'd not gone far before his phone began to vibrate.

"Harry, I've just been speaking to Captain Purdue, he tells me you've asked the Duke to send you a number of detonation transistors. Under no circumstances are you to take out Mohammed Abu Atif on Italian soil, do I make myself clear?" said Jeremy Paxton-Smyth in a voice uncharacteristic of his normally quiescent tone.

"Perfectly, Skipper, I have no intention of doing anything like that honest," said Harry. "So you've heard about Abu Atif arriving here on Friday?" continued Harry, changing the subject in an attempt to deflect the conversation away from the detonation transistors.

"No, I'm told Sunday," replied Paxton-Smyth, then suddenly realising he'd fallen right into Harry's trap, "You cunning sod, you used Friday as bait for me to tell you the day!"

"Me skipper? That's far too intellectual, it sounds more like an MI5 tactic."

"Well it worked, but Harry I'm deadly serious. Follow him by all means and pick your spot but not in Italy."

"I hear you skipper, don't worry. So I presume Squeaky Purdue has blocked the transistors then?"

There was a brief silence before Paxton-Smyth answered. "Well, actually no. The Duke had already sent them."

A beaming smile lit Harry's face. "Oh what a shame," he said sarcastically.

"Are you going to tell me what you're planning to concoct using those chemicals?" asked Tony whilst directing Harry towards a small old wooden workshop on the northern edge of the olive grove.

"Okay, let's get this box of goodies inside first," said Harry ignoring Tony's question. "Tony, this is perfect," he said, turning on a switch close to the door, which activated the single light bulb hanging from a cobweb matted flex over an empty workbench. Harry placed the box down and turned to Tony.

"Let me explain. I'm going to make a substance known as PETN, which you might know by its more common name, semtex. In fact its true title is semtex 'H'. PETN is the acronym used to describe Pentaeythrol Tetranitrate Nitropenta. The mixture is quite stable and pretty safe so don't worry, I'm not going to have an accident and blow up your family's olive grove. The substance is insoluble in water, which is very useful for our purposes."

"So to prepare it, I'm going to introduce pentaeythrol into concentrated nitric acid. This stirs the substance up and induces a cooling effect. A substance known as tetranitrate has now been created which basically means the mix just crystallizes out of the acid. The solution is then simply diluted by about 70% from its original mass. The product can then be washed in acetone and then hey presto! PETN! Just about the most powerful explosive of its kind."

"Do you remember in 1988 when the American aircraft, flight number AM103 exploded over Lockerbie in Scotland? Well that was brought down using PETN. It has a whole bunch of uses."

Tony looked nervous. "How do, you intend using it?" he asked.

"Well that's the sixty four million dollar question, Tony. Not to varnish you're dining room table or produce hair lacquer for your wife's *bouffant*, that's for sure, although PETN is present in both those everyday materials. I needed the varnish manufacturer because I had to get my hands on a small supply of acetone. See, once this product is made it can be used in several ways. Incorporating a small amount in a wax carrier can make a very effective limpet device."

Tony suddenly smiled. "So that's why you need the boat," he said.

Harry returned the smile. "Got it in one, you catch on fast my friend," he said, patting Tony patronisingly on the shoulder. "Of course, just a small amount of this stuff could shoot any size boat into orbit. But I intend to use it first as the filling for some very special truffles."

Harry then took from his pocket a thin strip of white card, no bigger than a bookmarker. One surface of the card contained two rows of tiny black dots, barely more than a spec of dust in size; each one was individually suspended under a clear plastic film.

"These little babies are shock energy detonation transistors. One of these in the PETN mixture and another at the detonation trigger end will induce a shock wave between the two poles, which then builds up to a certain pitch - then boom, it's goodnight Vienna."

"What's the wax for?" asked Tony.

"With any crystalline explosive, there's a certain impact and friction sensitivity, so the Hexogen and PETN mixture can be altered and made more safe with the addition of what's called a phlegmatizer, and wax is probably the best one to use. You've heard of the term plastic explosive?
A common product like Vaseline is often favourite as a gunpowder stabiliser because it's got unsaturated hydrocarbons in its composition, which is very suitable as a binding agent."

"When are you going to make a start?" asked Tony still quite nervous at the thought of having the workshop turned into an explosive making facility, perched right at the centre of the family's olive grove.

"No time like now," said Harry. "Today's Tuesday, and according to some pretty accurate information I've received, Mohammed Abu Atif should be gracing the waters of Capri on

Sunday, that gives us four clear day's to prepare. If you can talk to your cousin about using his boat and get me some diving gear, I'd be forever grateful."

Harry leaned casually on the bench and looked at Tony full on, as if giving him the cue to leave so that he could begin turning the workshop into a laboratory. His body language was message enough.

"Well I'll leave you to it then," said Tony walking towards the door.

"Thanks," replied Harry closing the door behind him. After washing down the workbench he commenced the delicate job of formulating a number of chemicals into explosive compounds.The two books Duke had sent were fundamental to achieve the exacting calculations required to successfully produce the colourless micro crystals. The molecular weight had to be exactly at 316.1, as did the energy formation and oxygen balance, which could accurately calculate the volume of detonation gases and specific heat for the explosion requirements. The velocity of detonation could then be calculated out at 8400m/ equalling 27,600 ft squared. A deflagration point of around 202 centigrade or 396 Fahrenheit needed to be achieved in order to produce the required impact sensitivity.

Gowned in a heavy-duty apron and black rubber gloves up to his elbows, Harry worked late into the night to achieve the objective. He then needed to test the material he had created and so just before five o'clock the following morning Tony and Harry chugged out of the harbour in the old brightly painted red and yellow open fishing boat.

"You know there's something about boats that's calming," said Harry sitting in the centre of the small craft with his back to Tony who was perched at the rear steering by way a long wooden tiller, guiding the boat out towards the open sea.

Within about half an hour Capri became quite visible out of the morning mist. Other fishing boats of roughly the same size had already staked claim to their particular spot in the water and could be seen trawling for fish, which meant Harry and Tony were forced to travel out to sea much further until eventually they were sure no other fishing boats were in close proximity. Harry raised his hand, instructing Tony to stop.

"Okay this will do. We'll drop this small device over the side and see how far we can lift a few litres of sea water into the air," said Harry.

The Knights of Black Chapter

It had been a number of years since former Sergeant Bob Richardson had developed such an explosive device, and at that time he composed the substance in well-equipped laboratory back in Hereford, not a bedraggled old wooden workshop on the slopes of an Italian hillside.

"Right, now this will gradually sink to the bottom," Harry said taking a desert spoon from the canvas bag he had next to him. The dish part of the teaspoon had been filled with the substance. An old piece of rag had been carefully bound tightly around the spoon and held in place by several lengths of sticky tape. Harry held the spoon aloft so that Tony could see, he then threw it as far as he could into the water. Harry then dived back into his bag again.

"This was a transistor radio which I've modified," said Harry showing a very nervous looking Tony Ricardo the small red plastic radio with an aerial extending from its case. "Inside here I've installed one of those tiny detonation transistors I showed you, let's call this the male. I've put the female part into the mixture suspended in the wax which at this precise moment is sinking down to the seabed. Now as soon as the radio is turned on and tuned into a specific frequency a wave impulse will be created, this builds up to a crescendo and then hopefully it will induce the explosion." Harry's voice trailed off into a slight stutter.

"I trust you've done this before?" said Tony who began to wish he were somewhere else.

"Well, naturally, replied Harry. "Although I had better kit to work with and a purpose built trigger unit, not a cheap crappy radio made in China, but hey ho, where needs must!"

A slight build up of sweat began to form on Harry's forehead. "Okay start the engine," he shouted a little nervously. "Let's move a bit further away before I tune this thing into the pop channel."

Tony didn't need to be asked twice, he pressed the start button on the small column in front of him, and then put the tiller hard over. The old fishing boat seemed to moan and groan abjectly as she slowly turned back to face the mainland.

"Okay that'll do," said Harry after they had travelled no more than a hundred metres or so. They both sat for a few seconds whilst an unexpected swell in the sea gently raised them up onto a crest before gracefully tilted them back down again. Harry switched the radio on then turned the tuner to the frequency. They then waited, and waited, but nothing happened.

"Oh silly me, I've got the volume turned down," he said adjusting the knob which, after a few seconds had the desired effect. A muffled rumble could be heard, followed by a fountain of water that rose about three metres above the surface. Harry punched the air and Tony clapped vigorously to expel the nervous tension he'd been suffering from the start of their boat trip.

The following morning, just as Harry was taking breakfast in the hotel's conservatory, his phone began its usual silent dance in his breast pocket. As there was no one else taking breakfast at that particular time Harry took the call.

"Hi, it's Tony I've just spoken to my good friend of the Cosa Nostra in Sicily. A Sunseeker Portofino 53 by the name of *Angelina*, will be used to transport our friend to Capri. Apparently the boat is registered in France and has been chartered by someone called Bernard Weigner?"

"Any idea what time she's due to make Capri?" asked Harry.

"My friend could not be precise but he'll call me the moment she leaves. She'll have to report to the coastguard on her approach into these waters anyway."

Having been assured that Giovanni Francini never failed to visit Maria's café on Sunday mornings; Harry took the late train from Sorrento to Naples and stayed in a small hotel close to the Piazza Garibaldi so that he could present himself bright and early for kitchen duties the following morning. The smell of freshly ground coffee and baked bread made Harry feel quite hungry. As Maria spoke virtually no English, Tony stayed with the family the night before so that he could act as translator in the morning.

"Ask Maria how many truffles does Francini normally eat when he comes into the café?"

Tony repeated Harry's question to Maria who listened carefully.

"If he comes weekdays, about two or three but on a Sunday he'll gorge himself with at least two cappuccinos and anything from four or even as many as six truffles. Maria say's he normally arrives around nine; his wife and maid usually go down the market to buy fresh vegetables and cheese. Sometimes Francini has a couple of minders with him and sometimes his son comes along also."

"And do the minders and his son eat truffles?" asked Harry, wondering just how many he'd need to prepare.

"Oh no, Francini egotistically thinks Maria makes them exclusively for him. If his son comes he just drinks coke."

"Well, we'll be massaging his ego with a very exclusive variety this morning and that's for sure," replied Harry with a smile.

Melted chocolate had been mixed with a rich cream and a generous amount of cognac, producing a sticky alcoholic substance. Maria took a wooden spatula and drew a portion from the bowl. She then began to turn it into a round ball whilst Harry watched intently.

Now it was his turn. Following Maria's example he took an amount of the thick chocolate but then added a pre-determined quantity of the crystal substance and the minute detonation transistor, then came the difficult part, turning everything into a neat round ball. Unfortunately all he achieved was a mess with more chocolate sticking to his fingers than creating the desire effect.

Maria gently but firmly pushed Harry to one side and began working the mixture into the required shape.

"Maria says it's all about having cool hands, hot hands are no good for chocolate truffle making."

Maria looked up from her table towards Harry and smiled as if she had understood every word Tony had said.

Within no time a dozen large balls of the chocolate with the deadly PETN mixture had been placed in two neat rows upon a stainless steal tray, which Maria then put into a refrigerator to cool. A small liquidiser was then used to whip more chocolate that would be used to form the outer shell. Everyone had coffee with crisp, freshly baked bread and goat's cheese whilst the balls cooled sufficiently so that they could then be dipped in the chocolate coating.

Again Harry was shown how to pick up a ball and physically dip it into the liquid chocolate, but the mess he created was even worse than the first attempt and again Maria took over. Each ball was then carefully placed onto a tray that had first been covered with greaseproof paper. Harry was given the job of sprinkling icing sugar over the surface of each truffle, a task he finally excelled at, much to his pleasure.

"We could patent these and flog them, they could be called *Chocosem*. I can see the caption now that says, 'The truffle that blows your mind'", said Harry laughing.

The finished truffles were then put back into the refrigerator for a final cooling.

It was around eight thirty when the plump, well-dressed figure of Giovanni Francini entered the café, accompanied by a tall wisp of a lad with a multitude of black curls and a large Roman nose, unlike his father who had no hair at all and a nose that was virtually flat to his face. Giovanni had a large white handkerchief in his hand, which he constantly dabbed across his forehead. A smell of expensive cologne wafted through the café and into the kitchen where both Harry and Tony were sitting.

Maria went out to greet Francini in her usual welcoming manner and then returned moments later with an order. She looked pensive and spoke to Tony in rapid Italian, then made some flamboyant gestures with her hands as if to emphasis her point.

"What's wrong?" asked Harry as he watched the expression change on Tony's face.

At first Tony ignored Harry and carried on a brief conversation with Maria, after which he turned to Harry. "He does not want truffles this morning. He's asked for two panini, a cappuccino and a coke."

"Fuck," responded Harry.

"Ask Maria to say that she has just prepared a very special batch in his honour," said Harry.

Tony repeated Harry's suggestion, which met with an exaggerated shrug of the shoulders and a negative expression. Maria took the truffles from the refrigerator and placed them carefully upon a large plate covered with a paper doily. She then disappeared into the café, returning moments later having placed the plate of truffles on the counter.

After serving Giovanni Francini and his son with their order, Maria returned to the kitchen and peaked through the tiny hatch watching them both tucking into their breakfast. Giovanni consumed his panini in just a few mouthfuls, whilst his son ate his with the delicacy of a young woman.

The Knights of Black Chapter

Harry couldn't resist joining Maria to have a crafty look through the hatch.

"He's eyeing up the truffles," said Harry in a loud whisper, almost willing the Italian to walk over to the plate. "He's standing up," he said, continuing the running commentary excitedly, willing him to oblige. "Come on you big fat bugger."

It was as if Harry's words had been picked up telepathically, as Francini stood up from the table and strode the few paces towards the plate. Giovanni peered for a moment at the array of large enticing chocolates. He then moved a particularly large specimen with a chubby finger, just like a cat would cruelly play with a mouse. Then, like a naughty schoolboy, he quickly looked around to see if anyone was watching and then devoured the truffle, swallowing it almost whole.

"Ha, Maria! Uno cappuccino," shouted Giovanni, now with the plate firmly in his hand returning to his seat.

"One gone," said Harry directing his comment to Tony who by now was leaning over his shoulder to get a look through the hatch.

Giovanni wafted the plate in front of his son as if gesturing him to take one, to which the lad shook his head and pulled a face before continuing to eat the remains of his panini.

Both Harry and Tony watched as one truffle after another was consumed and by the time Maria was serving the pair with more drinks, three more giant truffles had gone down the hatch.

"Blimey that's four," said Harry as he watched Giovanni Francini unwittingly conclude his fate.

By the time the Francinis departed only three of the dozen truffles remained on the plate.

"He's eaten enough to blow half of Capri out of the water," said Harry.
Tony looked pensive as Harry's phone started to vibrate.

"Hi limey, that's one motherfucker of a meeting about to happen there," was Lewis Ford's opening line.

"Where are you?" asked Harry, surprised to hear from his American counterpart.

"I'm still in Albania and it's a good job I am, because that canary I told you about has told us this meeting is going to involve a serious arms deal. The aim, apparently, is to blow another great hole in New York and London, and that's just the start - bombing campaigns have been planned in a number of major cities across Europe. This meeting is to co-ordinate plans and financial arrangements. This is major league stuff involving a bunch of geurilla groups like the Basque Separatists and the IRA, as well as the Taliban and Al Val Sinda. Yeah know there just might be a whole bunch of ransoms around for the taking, so go to it buddy boy."

"I'll do the best I can, now for Christ's sake get the hell out of there before my governor finds out and goes completely mental," Harry said sternly.

"Okay, okay keep your shirt on, I'm leaving tomorrow."

With that the phone went dead. Harry related the information to Tony Ricardo who in turn called his friend in Sicily.

"The *Angelina* has sailed," he said. "In fact she sailed yesterday morning."

"Yesterday morning," repeated Harry, showing some anger in his voice.

Tony put out his hands and gave the typical Italian shrug of the shoulders, which angered Harry even more.

"Come on we best get motoring, fast," he said as he strode towards the door.

The journey from Naples to Sorrento was completed virtually in silence whilst Tony drove the Alfa at full speed; fortunately the traffic was quite light and the journey took less than forty-five minutes. They parked the car and climbed into the boat just as the clock in the marina showed ten o'clock. Tony jumped onto the helmsman's seat and started the engine whilst Harry dived into the locker where the diving equipment and wetsuit had been stowed.

As Tony steered the boat out of the marina, Harry stripped off and began struggling into the wetsuit.

"I'm not quite sure which villa belongs to Francini, it could be any one of about half a dozen," said Tony.

"Don't worry, when you hear a big fuckin' bang, that'll be the one," replied Harry with a broad grin.

Once the fishing boat was no more than a few hundred yards off the Capri coast, Harry asked Tony to cut the engine and handed him a pair of binoculars. "Here have a look through them," he said.

Tony put the powerful binoculars to his eyes and began to scan the hillside, first moving one way and then another. Eventually he handed the glasses back to Harry and pointed up to a handful of stark white villas positioned in comparative isolation upon the hillside, their balconies precariously hung over nothingness with a sluggish, aquamarine sea many metres below.

"I have been to Francini's villa just once. I secretly collected Mario, he'd been clearing up after a party and wanted me to travel on the ferry with him, he is fearful of water. The highest point is Monte Solaro," Tony said, pointing in the general direction.

"So you reckon it's one of those?" said Harry. He then turned the binoculars to scan beyond Capri towards the open sea.

"Yes," said Tony. "Unfortunately, from here it's impossible to tell which."

"What the hell does a 53 foot Sunseeker look like?" asked Harry as he watched a craft at anchor swing casually on her mooring no more than a quarter of a mile from the marina. He passed the binoculars to Tony who soon concluded that the vessel was indeed a Sunseeker Portofino 53 and, as she swung slowly around, the name *Angelina* could be seen upon her stern.

"Fuck, now we don't know if Mohammed Abu Atif is on board or in one of those bloody villas," said Harry, putting his arms through the harness of his single tank of air. "Tony get us a bit closer to the *Angelina*, I'm going to fit these little buggers to her hull." Harry took two homemade limpet devices from his canvas bag and placed them in a plastic bag he had swinging from his belt. "These little beauties might not look much, but I'll guarantee they'll do more than take the gel coating of that gin palace."

Harry dropped into the water and then held onto a rope so that he could be towed behind the fishing boat that proceeded cautiously towards the *Angelina*.

After going as far as he felt able, Tony killed off the engine and began dropping a net into the water as if he were preparing to fish. Harry covered his face with a mask and fitted his mouthpiece after turning on his air bottle. He then checked the gauge, co-ordinated the time on his watch and dived below the surface.

He soon began to realise how unfit he had become following his transition out of the army, and had to slow his swim down considerably. Eventually he passed the stern of the vessel on her port side. Harry decided to fit the first limpet to the bow thrusts, which lay idle at the sharp end. He lashed the device to the thrust propeller with a cord and then with some difficulty proceeded to swim towards the rear.

The rudder seemed the most suitable place to secure the second device and soon Harry had convinced himself that the limpet was sufficiently secured to reduce the craft to scrap metal.

No more than twenty minutes later Harry was back on the boat, struggling out of the air tank harness.

"I'm convinced the middle villa is the one," said Tony, offering the binoculars to Harry who aimed them in the direction Tony was pointing.

There was definite movement on the balcony, with more and more people appearing. Harry strained his eyes to gain a better view.

"There's an old bloke who looks a Brit or American ... I'd say a Brit by his clothes. There are also two suited and booted characters with drinks in their hands. Oh, and that's interesting! Mr Morgan-Sinclair Junior. Well, well, well. He's the bastard responsible for the Professor's death, which I told you about."

Harry then saw the familiar frame of Giovanni Francini accompanied by three Arabs. Unfortunately it was impossible to tell if either one of them was Mohammed Abu Atif, especially as Harry had only seen a blurred photograph of him.

Tony's heart was beating at such a pace he thought it would burst from his chest as Harry pulled the red plastic transistor radio from the canvas bag. First he switched it on and then turned the volume control up to maximum. Tony gestured the sign of the cross in front of him as Harry began to slowly turn the dial.

At first there was no visible reaction, then suddenly Giovanni Francini dropped to his knees clutching his stomach. Harry lost sight of him behind the ornate marble balustrade; but presumed that by now the fat Italian would be rolling on the floor in excruciating pain as the acid within the mixture began to separate. Then it happened: the entire balcony exploded into minute fragments. Particles of stone and marble were blasted several feet into the air. Harry and Tony watched as a whole chunk of balcony gradually broke away from what was left of the villa and then - almost in slow motion - gradually toppled down into the sea.

The impromptu explosion resulted in a number of people on board the Sunseeker scurrying around as if to prepare the boat to weigh anchor. Harry then heard the props burst into life and simultaneously the automatic winch began hauling up the anchor chain. The moment she was free from the sea bed, the powerful jet turbines lifted the bow out of the water and within seconds she was gathering pace. Harry turned the radio to the predetermined frequency. But unfortunately the explosion that followed simply sent a huge spray of water high into the air.

"Bollocks!" shouted Harry, throwing the radio down in anger. Just then they saw an Italian Command Vessel appear out of nowhere. It began to turn rapidly with the clear objective of intercepting the Sunseeker.

"Ahoy *Angelina*, this is the Italian Coastal Command. Slow down immediately and be prepared for boarding," said a voice in broken English through an electric tannoy system.

Gunshots broke out from the Sunseeker as she heeled over, away from the Command vessel in an attempt to escape. She increased the thrust of her engines, which by now were screaming at maximum revs. The Command Vessel turned in pursuit and again tannoyed instructions, only this time the Sunseeker was ordered to stop her engines otherwise she would be fired on. The instruction was again ignored as the Sunseeker attempted to head further out to sea. But her passage was thwarted by a second control vessel approaching directly bow on, steaming across the bow to trap the yacht in a pincer movement that permitted little manoeuvrability. The first Command vessel then opened fire with a volley of bullets from a 7.2mm machine gun positioned strategically on the bow. The rapid volley was delivered with deadly accuracy, ripping along almost the full length of the Sunseeker's port side. This was quickly followed by a second attack directly aimed below the yacht's water line. This final sweep had the devastating effect of stopping the Sunseeker in her tracks. Within a few moments she lay idle in the water, crippled and sinking. The two Command vessels quickly sandwiched the dying yacht, coming up on either side, and as Harry and Tony watched a handful of men could be seen standing on the afterdeck holding their hands above their heads.

Harry counted four men who all looked European, then Mohammed Abu Atif appeared from out of the saloon, dressed all in white. Two officers from one of the Command vessels jumped on board the Sunseeker and assisted Mohammed Abu Atif onto their craft where he was instantly taken below.

"Bastard, fucking stinking bastard!" shouted Harry Blakemore, "No wonder my Skipper said not to take the swine on Italian soil, your lot were lying in wait." He picked up his facemask and threw it into the bow of the boat, each flipper followed in quick succession.

"Men died up there Harry, you killed them but missed the man you were aiming for," said Tony gruffly as he made the sign of the cross before starting the engine.

"Don't go righteous on me now, Tony. Listen, those bastards up there were no better than Abu Atif. They were not up there to marvel at the view yeah know; they were there to cut a deal that would have brought death and destruction to possibly hundreds or even thousands of people. And don't forget the fat git who fucked up your life, not to mention that bastard Morgan-Sinclair who was instrumental in the killing of my partner's good friend. What we've done is fuck up Incanda's plans and get rid of a few of his servants along the way, so don't go all holy now for fuck's sake."

The mere glimmer of a smile flickered across Tony's face. The men travelled back towards the Marina Piccolo in total silence. Harry unbuckled the harness on his air tank and looped his canvas bag containing the radio, his flippers, mask and weight belt, through the strap, then buckled it back up again. He then flung the entire package over the side.

"I'd call that mission accomplished, except for one thing... where do you think they'll be taking Mohammed Abu Atif?"

The Knights of Black Chapter

That afternoon Harry rang Jeremy Paxton-Smyth but was forced to leave a message. He then tried Clarissa, who answered her phone after just two rings.

"Hi, it's me," said Harry, "How's it going in Crete?"

"Oh Harry we are so close, in fact we're now pretty certain the nine Knights of Black Chapter are planning a gathering really soon."

"Do you know where?" replied Harry.

"In Greece, either right here in Crete or on Corfu."

"Why one of those islands? Surely there would be more appropriate places, a Golden Castle or even a ten star hotel perhaps?" said Harry sarcastically.

"Because, we're convinced that Prince Charles is of the Nine and so is his father Phillip. See, Prince Phillip was born into the Greek royal family. His father, Prince Andrew, was brother to the deposed King Constantine who went into exile. Phillip was shipped off to England where he spent his formative years. In so doing his royal line was severed and he became simply Lieutenant Mountbatten when he joined the navy. But you see his destiny had already been mapped out for him. All pointers lead us to be quite sure that Prince Andrew, Phillip's father, was from the direct line of Rex Deus. When the break occurred his line became one of the Knights of Black Chapter."

"But I thought the mantle is only handed down from father to son upon death?" interrupted Harry.

"No, a father may pass his position on to his son or daughter at any appropriate time, providing there is sufficient reason and an agreement with the other eight has been verified. But there was no need to carry out such an arrangement in Phillip's case, I'll explain why in a minute.

"Edward, George's elder brother, was a nightmare in royal circles, and did his own thing most of the time much to the annoyance of the King. And like the King, those in powerful positions were not in favour of Edward becoming the future King. His father was also uncomfortable with him taking the mantle and becoming a Knight of Black Chapter. So this first-born and heir apparent was abandoned in favour of George."

The Knights of Black Chapter

"But a cunning scheme needed putting in place; a scheme that would slowly manifest in favour of George becoming King and a knight of Black Chapter. Mediators in both royal and political circles also saw a wonderful opportunity unfold by announcing the engagement and, later, a strategically planned marriage, with the Earl of Strathmore's daughter. A marriage they thought would kindle and unite the two countries of England and Scotland. A lady with pure, noble Scottish blood would therefore become Queen."

"In 1923 Prince George married Elizabeth Bowes-Lyon. They had two children, Elizabeth and Margaret. It was deemed that Elizabeth would one day become Queen and, for protocol, would indeed become Elizabeth II and therefore rule over both England and Scotland. In their wisdom they thought surely the Scots would be jumping for joy at having a Queen on the throne with such a significant amount of Scottish blood running through her veins."

"The rest is history; Edward actually became King Edward VIII, but his previously contrived abdication took place soon afterwards in 1936. The deal was that he would live out a comfortable life in France as the Duke of Windsor under the close watchful eye of the Knights of Black Chapter."

"I'm digressing a bit, but we have stumbled on someone else who Guy is convinced might well have been a high ranking member of the Knights of Black Chapter - a man who met King George both privately and in sight of the public on several occasions. His name was Franklin Delano Roosevelt. Guy has studied him in detail. This was the man who was to become President of the US on no less than four occasions, two times more than any of his thirty predecessors. He was a man crippled by infantile paralysis at the age of forty, and was a lawyer by profession but it seems the Knights of Black Chapter deemed he should become a politician. He was made governor of New York State and in 1932 he became the elected President of the United States for the first time."

"It was at a time when the US was going through a major crisis in its history. Banks were going bust. Every day more and more of the rich and powerful were being made bankrupt. Incanda must have been having a whale of a time! Unemployment had reached a record level and continued rising right across the USA. Roosevelt uttered just a handful of sterling words that changed the thinking of America forever. He said; *'The only thing to fear is fear itself.'* He brought sweeping reforms to industry, business, and agriculture, and especially in the administration of justice. He inaugurated schemes of aid from the federal government for housing and the relief of unemployment and also children's welfare. Against the odds he made the federal government more accountable and directly responsible than it had ever been before. Guy reckons the power of the Knights of Black Chapter must have played a significant part in this accomplishment."

"Roosevelt was re-elected back into power in 1936 by a sweeping majority. With the outbreak of the Second World War in 1939 the people of the USA built up this significant hatred for Hitler's Germany; and of course we know Hitler was a senior ranking member within Incanda. There was, however, a determination to keep America out of the war. Roosevelt made it quite clear where his feelings lay, he secured an amendment of the two American Neutrality Acts because as it stood they favoured Germany not England. Incanda must have been furious."

"Guy reckons his close association with King George VI instigated the transference of a significant number of weapons to Britain in 1940, after the fall of France. He instigated a policy to provide all aid to Britain, short of troops for outright war. Despite a lot of opposition, Roosevelt achieved the unprecedented feat of becoming President for the third time. He developed a very business like arrangement to thwart those opposed to his determination to help Britain. He called it 'lease-lend' - by which Britain and others who fought the 'Axis' powers could borrow or hire from America anything needed for the prosecution of the war. This was an exact repetition of Pope Urban II's pledge at the council of Claremont in 1095 - to help equip, not just one army but many armies for the first crusade."

"In August 1941 Roosevelt met Winston Churchill, who we all know was a Freemason but Guy is convinced was a senior officer in the service of the Knights of Black Chapter. This was a memorable meeting at sea, the safest place to discuss the significant pathway for the future. Together they drew up the Atlantic Charter, which was to become the basis of the United Nations. It was specifically designed to clip the wings of Incanda. We are also convinced the Japanese invasion of Pearl harbour on the 7th of December 1941 was instigated by Incanda flexing its muscles, but it was just the excuse Roosevelt needed, especially with a country already attuned to the idea of getting fully involved in a war to the bitter end. So as Commander in Chief, which was Roosevelt's title as president, he led the American people into the war to fight alongside the British and Commonwealth armies against Germany, Italy and Japan."

"Now we come to 1948, the year Phillip and Elizabeth were married. I'm not sure about historically, but certainly in modern times at least this must have been quite a unique marriage. Not only was Elizabeth heir to the throne could also have held an association with Knights of Black Chapter. Of course we are guessing but if this were true two members of the nine could be joined in wedlock. This is the reason we think Charles could never become King."

"Hang on a minute," interrupted Harry, "Surely the great and good would have realised that calling their first born son Charles would cause all kinds of problems, remember you told me about Bonny Prince Charlie being Charles III."

"Correct Harry, but it's our belief there was an even more powerful reason why he will never be put on the throne. We believe he was destined to become the Grand Master and Eminent Prior of the Knights of Black Chapter."

"So are you saying that the Duke of Edinburgh and Prince Charles are both Knights of the Black Chapter?" Harry said, his attention now fully fixed on Clarissa's revelations.

"Perhaps, and that might explain the problems that were emerging. It's my guess Princess Di secretly announced that she was pregnant and marrying a Muslim. Who knows, it might be a possibility that this Muslim's family is associated with Incanda in some way? It's also possible that the Knights of Black Chapter stepped in and put a halt to proceedings. As I mentioned before, an heir to the throne and Knight of Black Chapter having a Muslim step dad might be tricky? Crusaders would turn over in their graves!"

"We've taken a small apartment Harry. It belongs to a friend in Chania, down by the harbour. It would be great if you can join us."

"I promise I will as soon as I've finished what I'm doing. You take care I'll talk to you soon." Harry closed the line down before Clarissa started asking him questions that required lengthy explanations.

Harry was then about to try Jeremy Paxton-Smyth for the second time when the phone started its familiar vibration. He prayed it would not be Lewis Ford.

"Harry, I hear you've been busy blowing up half of Capri!"

The Knights of Black Chapter

"Hi Skipper, why on earth should I get the blame for that? Do you think I'd attempt something so rash?"

Paxton-Smyth laughed. "It had your name all over it. You certainly did a job on the place. As far as we can detect, six people were killed, but not Mohammed Abu Atif. Harry you ignored a direct order and I'm really pissed off about that."

"Er... your precise words were 'on Italian soil'. Capri is not exactly Italian soil. And besides I tried to blow up the yacht but my devices fell short. Tell me Skipper, where's the target being taken, I presume he won't be staying in Italy for long?"

"I have no idea," replied Paxton-Smyth. "The longer he lives the greater chance he'll have of escaping. Incanda will never allow such an important member to go on trial."

"So you're saying the deal's still on?" said Harry with an ear-to-ear grin across his face.

"How you accomplish the job is up to you, but again I stress don't make an attempt on Italian soil or its islands, waters or airways. If this ever gets out the Americans will kill you and I'll make doubly sure you're dead, is that clear."

"Oh, absolutely. Like crystal," said Harry.

The destruction and carnage on Anna Capri captured the headlines across Europe. *Il Mattino* dedicated almost all of its pages to display pictures and a graphic account of the remains of the villa and balcony as did the *Giornale di Sicilia*, Sicily's largest circulated newspaper.

However no paper mentioned specific names of those killed, except to describe them as international business people, some of whom it was believed had Mafia connections. One paper intimated that the bomb had been the result of a significant long-standing feud between two Mafia families. Every newspaper reported that the explosion had obliterated the bodies to such an extent that they may never be individually identified.

However the capture of Mohammed Abu Atif failed to even get a mention, much to Tony's surprise. The two men sat around the pool of the Villa Garden Hotel with a mound of newspapers spread over a tabletop.

"Try one of your mates," said Harry. "Surely by now there'll be some news about Abu Atif and where you lot are holding him!"

Tony picked up his mobile and after getting a connection began jabbering away in Italian. Eventually he switched off the phone and shook his head. "Everybody denies they are holding him, even one of my closest friends, who I've just spoken to, knows nothing."

"Think logically, go back in your police days. If you were in charge of one of those patrol vessels and captured someone, where would be the best place to take him... to keep him away from the world so to speak?"

"Well for starters those were coast guard vessels, run by the navy. Of course, Elba, that's where they must have taken him. Straight to Elba that's where those Navy boats must be stationed."

"I suppose it's too much to ask if you know anyone on Elba?" said Harry.

"I do, but I doubt if she'll know anything," replied Tony who then looked as if he'd gone into deep thought for a moment. He picked up his mobile and within a few seconds was again rapidly speaking in Italian. "Apparently he's being flown to Turkey," said Tony after switching off his mobile.

"What, how do they know that?" shouted Harry.

"I have a cousin who works in the ops room at Coastal Command on Elba and that's what she's just told me. He's currently in isolation awaiting departure. I suppose they'll take him to the military airbase on the outskirts of Naples."

"Turkey, that's crazy, he'll be free within twenty four hours of landing," said Harry, kicking over the table full of newspapers in total frustration.

"Hello is that Malik Ahmed?"

There was a lengthy pause before the head of the Albanian Intelligence service answered. "Mr Blakemore, what a welcome surprise. I presume you are calling to advise me when my money will be in the bank account?"

"Malik we were so close. Mohammed Abu Atif is currently being held in Italy awaiting deportation. They are flying him to Turkey."

The chuckle that erupted into full-blown laughter was somewhat of a surprise to Harry. "Of course I know this, in fact we are aware of every flight that encroaches on our airspace, especially military aircraft."

"So could you insist the plane lands in Albania en route?" asked Harry.

"Of course my dear friend, but that would mean I would collect all the reward money for myself, yes?"

"No," replied Harry getting prepared for some rapid thinking. "Look Malik, you need to distance yourself from this, especially in your present position. If you had the plane brought down and somehow removed Abu Atif from the planet, there would be massive diplomatic repercussions, and you'd be right in the firing line. It would all come out, that bloke Pier Duvall that you smuggled out of jail and put back later and then he died… everything would come out. You'd never see a penny of the reward plus you'd have cheated Lewis Ford into the bargain. And you know he'd come looking for you, that man would not rest until you were dead. Now on the other hand if you continue to help us, you'd be able to retire with even more money and live in comfort for the rest of your life."

"My friend, I, Malik, was joking, I do not wish to dirty my hands in such a way, I will leave that to experts such as you."

"Good, now can the Albanian authorities insist the aircraft lands at Tirane?"

"It is possible, but it will be difficult."

"How much difficult?" replied Harry.

"A million on top of what you already owe me," said Malik in a very matter of fact way.

"Impossible, three hundred thousand extra," Harry said.

"Mm my friend you have a very low bargaining power at the moment but I'll be generous because I like you. Six hundred and fifty thousand."

"No chance," said Harry half laughing. "Look, four hundred thousand or forget it, I have some good contacts in Turkey, we'll get him there."

"Mr Harry Blakemore, you drive a hard bargain. If we insist the plane lands at Tirana what next?"

"Leave the rest to me," replied Harry. "Do you know when the flight is due in your airspace?"

"Tomorrow morning, I do not have the precise time but I can get it."

"Good, call me when you know, and think of a good reason why you are bringing the aircraft down then be prepared to hold it there."

"Our paperwork is very complicated; we can hold an aircraft for twenty four hours."

"Good, let's talk soon." Harry closed the phone and dialled down to hotel's reception. "Can you make up my bill please, oh and I need to get the next available flight to Albania, landing at Tirane."

The receptionist obligingly offered to make the reservation. Harry packed, called Tony to explain and promised to call again as soon as possible.

The Knights of Black Chapter

29

The only direct flight Harry could take was from Rome International. That meant taking an internal flight from Naples first, which was frustrating as time was of the essence. Two calls to Harry's mobile, one from Clarissa and the other from Jeremy Paxton-Smyth, were both ignored and instead he called Malik.

"My friend the flight, it arrives here in approximately two hours time. It seems the Turkish authorities are very unhappy to hear that an Italian military aircraft hopes to land in their country because only a civil diplomatic clearance has been agreed; military clearance would have taken at least twenty four hours longer to organise."

"And I suppose the Italians didn't know that until they were airborne!" said Harry.

"Correct my friend," replied Malik with a childish titter. "Albania has provided diplomatic clearance for the aircraft to land here at Tirana, the flight will land directly into our military airbase. Mohammed Abu Atif will be retained in a security cell on the complex. I presume you will want a weapon of some sort?"

Harry thought for a moment. "What do you have for rats? he asked.

"Rats?" repeated Malik.

"Yes, a very strong poison that snuffs them out in seconds."

"Okay Harry Blakemore I understand, I'll see what I can do," replied Malik.

"And can you please make sure it can be injected, I need the stuff in a syringe."

"Yes, yes of course, now do you have your flight number?" replied the Albanian.

Harry looked at his ticket. "AL221," he replied.

"Good, call me when you have cleared customs. Tell me is your name still David Johnson?"

The Knights of Black Chapter

Harry felt himself foolishly nod, he then replied, "Yes no change."

"I will have my son, Abel meet you, he will be holding a sign that says Raja Hotel on it. Don't speak to him, it's too dangerous. Just follow him to his car."

The Albanian aircraft was not exactly worthy of any comfort ratings; its seats were both worn and badly stained, a number were even broken. With only two stewardesses the service was appalling. By the time it was Harry's turn to be served dinner virtually everything had gone except a rather strange looking substance, described on a label stuck to the tin foil lid as curried mutton, which even the Albanians on board had all turned down. Harry settled for a cake and black coffee.

Customs were an unhurried affair with a tired looking official sat in a metre square box with cigarette burns across the top. He sported a huge, badly kept moustache that hung from his upper lip like wire wool. The black thicket had been allowed to grow uncontrolled over his mouth. His unemotional expression typified the complete and utter boredom he obviously felt as he took a fleeting glance at Harry, then Harry's passport and then back to Harry again. It seemed every movement was carried out with great effort. He raised his hand and waved Harry away.

The reception at Tirane airport was best described as bustling. Eager cabbies and hotel minibus drivers were clamouring outside the arrivals area, with chalked on notice boards either offering Limo services or hotels. Harry read all the names on every board. The one that said Raja Hotel was held by a frail looking character who didn't look as if he'd last the night!

Harry waited as the arrivals hall began clearing of his fellow passengers from the flight, and within minutes the place was virtually deserted. After almost half an hour Harry was getting concerned. He attempted to call Malik but the phone just rang and rang. Something told him to move to a less conspicuous place in the hall. He therefore pushed his trolley to an area with subdued lighting. Just then four uniformed police officers walked casually across the floor. Harry slipped behind a large pillar until they had passed by.

"Hallo Mr Harry, sorry to be late," said a voice that startled Harry into suddenly turning around - to see a hot and quite bothered Abel standing with a board that said Raja Hotel.

"Well as there's only you and me in this entire place, I'd say that board's fuckin' redundant, wouldn't you?" shouted Harry.

"Mr Harry, there has been complications about our guest."

"Complications, what do you mean complications?" replied Harry sharply.

"He is ill and has been transferred to hospital."

"Shit, what has your father said?"

Abel began to push Harry's trolley as they walked at a rapid pace from the hall towards the exit. Abel waited until they were at his car before answering Harry's question.

"My father, he said you are to be driven to the hospital. Please put these clothes on."

Abel handed Harry a bundle of off-white clothes from the back seat. The clothes, which consisted of a t-shirt, a short jacket, trousers and a disposable surgeon's pillbox hat, smelt strongly of detergent and starch. A facemask, stethoscope and a security tag with Harry's photograph on it, made up the outfit. Harry felt much happier as he got changed in the back of Abel's car, as they drove from the airport compound.

"Mr Harry, I am to drop you at the rear of the hospital, it is where the kitchens are. Here this is a plan of how to find our guest."

Abel offered Harry a crumpled piece of paper. "He's in an isolation ward," he continued.

Just then Harry's phone began its familiar dance in his breast pocket.

"Mr Harry Blakemore, I trust my son has collected you?"

"Yes Malik, I'm well and truly collected. And dressed up like a brain surgeon, what's happening?"

Malik let out his usual frustrating chuckle before replying. "Well, my friend it would seem Mohammed Abu Atif has a perforated duodenal ulcer. He would have died on the plane if we had not agreed to the landing."

"God your shit must smell of rose petals?" replied Harry.

Malik roared with laughter. "Oh my friend, you do say the most complimentary things. Now please listen. There are security guards posted at the door of his room."

"Hang on, has he been operated on yet?" asked Harry.

"Why of course not, what a waste of time and expense that would be, especially as his fate awaits your pleasure."

"So, if he doesn't receive medical help he'd die very soon anyway?"

"Precisely, and the reward would die also I presume?" said Malik. "Now when you go into the room you will find a trolley.

On the trolley will be a dish with a syringe in it, exactly as you asked. Malik has done a good job, yes?"

"I'll let you know that when the job's done. I presume you'll book me onto a flight from here afterwards."

"Naturally, where do you wish to go?"

"Crete," replied Harry without a second thought.

Harry followed the directions on the paper Abel had given him and was soon at the top floor where the isolation wards could be found. The floor was fairly quiet which surprised Harry. Dressed in his hospital attire he strode purposefully as if he knew exactly where he was going. He eventually found the room described on the piece of paper as number 205. And, just as Malik had said, two guards were stationed, one either side of the door.

Harry marched boldly up and showed one of them the badge he was wearing but all he received for his effort was a nod. He then opened the door and entered the dimly lit room. He then set eyes on the very man both he and Lewis Ford had gone to extraordinary lengths to apprehend.

Mohammed Abu Atif simply lay there motionless with his eyes closed. Harry was taken aback by his almost boyish good looks. Were it not for his long, wiry, unkempt beard, his face could almost be described as effeminate. At first Harry found it difficult to believe this was the perpetrator of so much death and destruction.

Muhammad Abu Atif was dressed in a surgical gown with both arms resting at his sides. His hands were slender, with long fingers and immaculately manicured nails. A black watch with a wide strap was buckled to his right wrist. But it was the gold ring on the small finger of his left hand that made Harry's blood run cold. The ring bore an engraved column on its face identical to the one that Professor Thomas had shown both him and Clarissa back in Aberystwyth. Even the modicum of compassion Harry felt for this baby-faced man who lay there apparently helpless and unconscious and at his mercy, soon evaporated with the sight of this ring.

"Well, we'll soon put another dent in Incanda's armour. You are going to die, mate and I hope those who you have directly and indirectly killed will rest peacefully knowing you'll not harm anyone ever again," Harry said, moving with purpose towards the trolley.

The Knights of Black Chapter

There, sure enough, just as Malik had said, was the syringe fully charged, lying in an enamel kidney bowl. Harry picked the syringe up and squirted a few drops through the needle, just as he'd seen doctors do on the television. He walked the few paces towards the bed and pulled up Abu Atif's sleeve, then turned his arm over to seek a vein close to the surface. Harry then carefully began to insert the needle into the soft skin. But it was as if the sudden prick from the needle had brought the well-nigh corpse back to life. Mohammed Abu Atif shot bolt upright and opened his eyes. Then he saw Harry and a look of fear suddenly appeared on his face. He began to struggle with a surprising degree of strength for one who had looked virtually dead only seconds before. But now the needle was firmly embedded into his arm and Harry's thumb hovered against the plunger. Mohammed Abu Atif grabbed Harry's wrist and then stared at him almost righteously.

"Do you honestly think my destruction will halt my overlord's objectives?" he said softly but with a penetrating engagement. "We are mobilising the masses, the wheels are turning in an unstoppable direction. The successful attack upon your country and America has galvanised undecided Muslims to our universal cause. I applaud Incanda's strategy to strengthen the co-religionists, enlisting them in one Islamic universal state is to create an irreversible machine that will ultimately reach its objective. Soon we will crush Israel's military arsenal and take ultimate control of the Middle East. The inner feelings of all naturalised Muslims will be provoked in a world wide Jihad. Our infiltration into the workings of the West will continue unabated, even helped and assisted by the blinkered greed and ignorance of your politicians."

Harry had heard enough; his anger was fuelled by this highhanded statement carefully chosen and executed by a man committed beyond life for his cause. His words had invoked such a great fear and realisation that Harry simply pushed his thumb as hard as he could against the plunger.

Mohammed Abu Atif suddenly dropped flat on his back and then began to convulse to the point where his entire body seemed to rise completely off the bed. It then violently shook before, eventually, all life had drained completely away, leaving a shocked expression and an open mouth that emanated a vile stench. The eyes of the Al Val Sinda leader bulged, staring up at the ceiling as if his very soul was experiencing the horror and shock of death.

Harry knew from old that the sight of death now in front of him would be automatically added to the picture catalogue of night demons that often intruded into his mind at the low ebb of his being: uninvited, haunting, returning him in his mind to places and situations he desperately wanted to forget. The times he'd been bathed in a blanket of sweat crying out to be left in peace. He was reminded of the wish words of an old soldier, uttered just after Harry had completed his selection course for the Regiment. *"Every life you take will be a gallery of memories that will live with you forever!"*

Harry went to the small sink in the corner of the room, with tears rolling down his face. He broke the needle from the syringe and poked it down the plughole. He then put the harmless remains of the syringe into his jacket pocket.

After closing Mohammed Abu Atif's mouth and making the body look as comfortable as possible, but still with its eyes wide open, Harry took the newspaper he'd obtained from the airport in Rome and placed it alongside Atif's head, appropriately folded to show the date clearly at the top of the page. Using the camera on his phone, he then took a number of pictures of the dead man and, without hesitation, sent them straight to Jeremy Paxton-Smyth. He then opened the door and casually walked out into the corridor where he was completely ignored by the two bored looking guards.

Harry was just passing the kitchen when two men suddenly set upon him, one brandishing a large knife which he immediately attempted to thrust into Harry's chest. The second was now behind Harry attempting an arm lock around his neck. Fortunately, he saw the knife coming, and was able to parry the blow by kicking his attacker directly between the legs, which instantly dropped him to his knees clutching his testicles. Harry then took hold of the man behind him by gripping both his ears. He then literally bent forward and pulled at the same time. The effort lifted the man completely off his feet and rolled him over Harry's head, where he fell uncontrollably into a heap on top of his accomplice.

A number of people then appeared from the kitchen just as Abel arrived. The young son of Malik immediately took charge and ordered the kitchen staff to hold both of the two men at knifepoint.

"What should we do with these two Mr Harry?" asked Abel.

"Throw them into the bloody incinerator," replied Harry, catching his breath.

Abel looked at Harry in horror.

"Look these men are evil, they will make things very bad for your father, they may well even have killed him!" said Harry adjusting his dress.

Abel had heard enough, without another word he instructed the kitchen staff to take them next door to where corpses were usually incinerated. Four of the kitchen staff smiled and another third giggled as they took the attackers away.

31

The address Clarissa had given Harry in Crete was for an apartment in Chania, the second largest city on the island. Harry flew into Chania International via Athens and took a cab to journey the 15 kilometres into the beautiful old city, designated as a conservation area. The cab dropped Harry off in a square next to the long sprawling harbour, where ouzo shops, fish tavernas and a multitude of tourist shops are located throughout the narrow alleyways that spread like a spider's web from the quayside, with their Venetian influenced buildings.

Harry walked the hundred or so metres around the quay and up the tiny narrow cobbled street until he reached number 21 Theotopoulou, off the old harbour. He then knocked on the brightly painted orange door that, according to the address, was the apartment where Clarissa and Guy were staying. There was no reply; he knocked again, only this time very much harder and then directly afterwards tried the doorknob which turned and opened. Harry cautiously walked inside. The darkness of the interior was a stark contrast to the bright sunshine outside.

Harry closed the door behind him and switched on the light. He was standing in a sort of living room with a well-equipped kitchenette and a large pine table upon which books were neatly piled; their subjects provided Harry with sufficient evidence to conclude that he was definitely in the right place. Further investigation took him into two modestly furnished bedrooms; in one he recognised some of Clarissa's belongings. Harry therefore presumed Guy would be using the other room.

Harry was exceptionally tired and hungry. He therefore decided to eat first and then use Guy's room for a well-earned nap. After leaving the apartment he was completely spoiled for choice with at least ten restaurants within a stone's throw. He chose the one almost directly opposite which seemed the quietist, tucked up in the corner of the harbour. From under Harry's parasol covered table he had an excellent panoramic view across the historical harbour towards the old Turkish quarter. Harry glanced over towards the breakwater and the old sea wall that for centuries had encircled the harbour like a long bent finger protecting it from winter seas. At the end of the wall was the 16th century lighthouse.

On the wall close to him, Harry noticed a sign in English with an arrow pointing towards a museum that apparently had been dedicated to the British for liberating Crete from the Germans during the Second World War. He promised himself a visit some time, just as his Greek salad arrived together with a bottle of chilled, local white wine.

After the moussaka and a nibble of the hard Anthotyros cheese, a Cretan specialty, Harry felt quite relaxed for the first time in ages, especially with the warm sun on his face. Over coffee, he reflected upon life back in Wales. How he longed to re-capture those times, dealing with antiques through the good times as well as the bad. He thought of the support he and Clarissa gave each other when either were going through a rough trading patch. Now, with the anticipated healthy off-shore bank balance, that all might change for the better - or even perhaps the worse, who knows? How different would life be? And what about the Lodge? Would being a Craft Freemason ever seem the same to him again? Would he attempt to gain extra Degrees, even aspire to the chair as Grand Master, or would he not bother and leave Masonry altogether?

Within seconds of his head touching Guy's pillow, Harry had dropped into a sound sleep. When eventually he did awake he felt as if he'd been struck by a paralysing affliction that had rendered him unable to move. He was sitting upright in pitch darkness. His wrists seemed to be tied to the arms of a chair of sorts. More binding encircled him around the chest; even the movement of his legs and feet were heavily restricted.

Harry strained his eyes in an attempt to see and then instinctively began to struggle. Just then a crack of light beamed down onto him, the light glowed more intensely as a shutter across a window was opened by a figure dressed in what resembled a monk's habit. A large hood completely covered the figure's head.

"Where the fuck am I, and who the fuck are you?" shouted Harry, resuming his fruitless struggle against the bindings.

His head began to ache from the strain of his actions and the drug someone had obviously administered. The figure turned towards Harry and then walked slowly across the bare stone floor.

"You are in the Commandery's Ante room at the Palace of Minos in Knossos. Do not be afraid," said the figure in perfect Oxford English.

"What am I doing here, who are you?" shouted Harry.

The figure stood in front of Harry. He could now see him more clearly. His dark brown habit hung open at the front to display a white mantle, which bore the curved Templar Red Cross. A large buckled belt encircled his waist, upon which a frog supported a sword that hung from his right hip. The hood remained over his head, completely covering his face.

"I am called a Casal. In olden times my forefathers were responsible for the daily business of various estates. I am a Knight but for centuries the family rank of Casal was at the level of a sergeant. My family have served Grand Masters for over five hundred years."

"Then you are from the Knights of Black Chapter or does your allegiance lie with Incanda?"

The figure refrained from directly responding. "Mr Harry Blakemore, alias Sergeant Bob Richardson, you have been chosen to present yourself at this Grand Priory lodge of the Knights of Black Chapter who last met as a gathering exactly one hundred and twenty five years ago.

"As Deacon of this Grand Priory lodge, I have been appointed to instruct you. Do you recall your time as an entered apprentice and following that when you were initiated as a fellow Craft Freemason?"

Harry nodded.

"Very well," replied the Deacon. "As an initiate, to govern your admission into the Three Degrees of a Master Freemason you would have learned more and more about King Solomon's Temple and its builders. You would have also then discovered there were two grades of Mason, an Apprentice and a fellow Craft. The ritual you undertook for your second Degree will be very similar to that of which you will experience later.

"During the time of King Solomon, around 950 BC, the three Degrees would have been presided over by three Grand Masters: King Solomon himself; Hiram, King of Tyre; and Hiram Abif, the master architect. Three men were responsible for the murder of our master Hiram Abif, the deed re-enacted during the third Degree. They were Jubela, Jubelo and Jubelum. The direct descendants of these three contributed to the ultimate break up of Rex Deus and played a significant part in the forming of what eventually evolved as the Knights of the

Incanda, to give them their full title. Their direct line is now part of the principal Nine."

"Can I ask you a question?" asked Harry, now feeling a little more relaxed.

"Ask away my dear fellow," replied the Deacon.

"How did this really all start and how did Rex Deus start in the first place?"

"That's a very long story; the origin of the nine Rex Deus is as old as mankind itself. But they really evolved as a ruling power during the time of Enoch, the seventh of the Hebrew patriarchs of the Old Testament and the great-grandfather of Noah. Enoch initiated and promoted the craft from which the eternal truths of Freemasonry were revealed by way of emblems, symbols, and mysteries. Many of which you will see later. Such as the wooden chest, known as the Ark of the Covenant, that contains the tablets on which the Ten Commandments were presented to Moses in the wilderness. These were housed in the innermost sanctum of King Solomon's temple."

"And what of the Holy Grail?" asked Harry, almost speechless from the revelations.

"The Gradalis will also feature in the Temple."

"Gradalis, what's that?" asked Harry.

"Simply a word in Latin that describes the covered dish containing the ashes of Mary, mother of Jesus Christ."

"What, you mean you actually really do have the Holy Grail and that it contains the ashes of the Virgin Mary?" said Harry, astounded by the proclamation.

"The Gradalis has had many resting places since the split of Rex Deus.
One such place is not that far from where you now live: the Castle of Dina Bran, which is now nothing more than a site on a hill in the Dee Valley near Llangollen in mid Wales. The Gradalis and the Ark of the Covenant have been in the possession of the Knights of Black Chapter since the 1300's."

"Whilst you are here you will be called by your God given name: Brother Richardson. The gathering here at Knossos follows an enactment through the three Degrees. The last Degree has just the Nine in attendance. This is a very special time for those of us who are a part of the Order. My great, great grandfather attended the last gathering. Every generation practices in preparation, through a Lodge of Instruction, for the possibility of being called upon to participate in such a great honour. The Grand Master has called this gathering for a specific reason that only the Nine are privy too."

"And is the Grand Master actually Prince Charles?" asked Harry.

There was a long silence before the Deacon answered. "The everyday outwardly functions of any member at any grade, from the Grand Master down the ranks to that of Serf, has no bearing on the gathering. This Chapter has supreme command over the policies of World affairs. Members of the Order of differing ranks are spread throughout the power bases of governments, industry, science, banking and the law. Only Incanda go some way to reach such an ultimate power."

"Why me? Why have I been chosen to attend such a historical gathering?"

The Deacon stood to the one side of Harry, still bound in his wheel chair.

"Brother Richardson, the Nine Knights of Black Chapter choose one person to witness the first part of the ritual. You have been chosen because of the deeds you undertook and succeeded in accomplishing against Incanda."

"You mean with the death of Muhammad Abu Atif and a couple of blokes on Capri?" replied Harry.

"No, there was one who ranked far higher than all the others. His name was Bernard Weigner. Bernard Weigner was the Knight Commander of the Bulla or seal of Incanda. He was the direct descendant of King Ahaz of Judah, who reigned in 678BC. The epic journey of his forebears was drawing to a close with the reversal of the Sun Dial of Ahaz. This reversal would have brought eventual darkness across the world and have taken mankind into oblivion. His quest was to conclude the task, a mission that he may well have accomplished had it not been for you blowing up that villa on Capri, killing this highly protected Knight Commander."

"So I've inadvertently killed one of the top blokes of Incanda? Well I bet they're pretty pissed off with me right now. That means my life's not goin' to be worth a penny!" Harry said, now feeling his heart begin to race in his chest at the consequences.

"All traces have been eradicated, Brother Richardson, fear not."

"But there was this bloke called Tony Ricardo, he was with me on the boat?"

The Knights of Black Chapter

"Brother Ricardo was selected to help you because he is a Serf of Black Chapter."

"You mean, Tony is an actual member of The Knights of Black Chapter?" said Harry in disbelief.

"Of course, as indeed his line has been for many centuries."

Taking a knife from beneath his cloak, the Deacon walked towards Harry and began to cut the bindings.

"It is almost time, you will wait in the Commandery under the custody of the Outer Guard, who will be armed with a drawn sword just like any Freemasons lodge. I will summon you at the appropriate time and then lead you into the Temple. In the centre of the Temple you will see the Sepulchre around and upon which ancient relics are laid, these include the Ark of the Covenant, the Gradalis and a crucifix, made with the wood from the cross upon which Christ himself was crucified. A Lamb, a Cockerel and a Dove will also be there; these living things will be the offerings for sacrifice. All will be displayed."

"In front of the Sepulchre you will see a kneeling stool. Each side of the Temple will be two rows of Knights representing the North and South columns; their positions stretch the full length of the Temple. At the top of the Temple is the altar, behind which sit the eight Grand Knights of Black Chapter and in the centre between them will sit the Grand Master making the Nine. Upon the wall behind each Knight will be a shield bearing their respective Heraldic devices. Their broad swords will be placed upon the altar directly in front of them, pointing up the Temple towards the Sepulchre. Directly in front of the altar will be another kneeling stool this will be used for the accolade."

"All Knights at the North and South columns will show their devices upon pennants behind each of their station chairs. The further they are seated up the columns towards the altar, the higher rank they hold. The Grand Knights will each wear Heraldic Helmets, save one who will be hooded. The Helmets are called *Pranker-Helm*, the visors have just one narrow slit."

"Why is one of the Nine not hooded?" asked Harry.

"A female does not wear a Heraldic Helm, instead she is hooded but the helm of her forefathers is displayed upon a plinth. Now, unless you are asked to do so, you will not speak except for repeating words after me. In the Temple you will be referred to simply as 'Pilgrim'. We have a few moments longer. So, you may well ask, why do the Knights of Black Chapter hold their Grand Priory Lodge here at the Minos Palace at Knossos? The Minos were the first judges of the world and presided here in Crete, which formed the very crossroads of Asia, Africa and Europe during the 5th and 6th Centuries BC."

"Rex Deus evolves from the pre-Neolithic period of 6,000-2600 BC. The Minoan period commenced with the Pre-palace period 2,600-1900 BC.
But it was the First Palace period 1900-1700 BC, when the centralised power evolved, centralised in the hands of Kings. The direct lines of the Knights of Black Chapter go back to these periods."

"In the Second Palace period 1700-1350 BC, Minoan civilisation reached its zenith. New palaces of even greater magnificence were built upon the ruins of the old. The cities around them expanded and literally buzzed with life. A large number of rural villages evolved, the residences of local governors managed and controlled vast areas long before the feudal castles of the Middle Ages. Roadways grew like a spider's web, harbours were developed and sophisticated ports where fast ships were moored that carried farm products and Cretan art across the whole of the civilised world."

Free now from his bindings, Harry was allowed to stand. "So you're saying that this tiny island was the heart of world power in those days?"

"When a gathering takes place, it still is!" replied the Deacon, who walked over to an old oak table where lay a long brown Mantle. He held it for Harry to put his arms through. "You will wear this mantle," he said, buttoning the heavy cloth down the back. He then took a rough hemp rope and tied it around Harry's waist. "A number of Knights will form what is called an Arch of Steel in the West. That means that two columns of five Knights in each column will hold drawn swords aloft to form an archway. You will be directed through the archway by the Marshall of the Temple, after which I will act as your companion throughout the proceedings. Now wait here."

The Deacon slipped through a doorway and returned just moments later.

"Right, follow me," he said beckoning a very nervous Harry Blakemore, alias Bob Richardson and now about to become alias Pilgrim.

The chamber in which stood the Deacon and the helmeted outer Guard was very dark; it therefore took Harry's eyes a few seconds to adjust to the light. The Deacon drew his sword from its scabbard and used the hilt to bang three times on the door. A few seconds later the door opened.

The Knights of Black Chapter

"Who is there?" asked a voice from within.

"I, the Deacon on the Grand Priory Temple seek admission."

"Hold whilst I seek permission," replied the voice.

Moments later the door was opened. "Enter, Sir Deacon and welcome," said a voice.

The Deacon entered as instructed with his drawn sword at the carry position. Harry was now left with the outer guard standing in front of the door.

"Nice day?" said Harry, feeling the need to utter something. "You must be very proud?" Harry continued.

The outer guard simply raised the index finger of his gauntleted hand to indicate silence. Then Harry heard the distinctive knock upon the door from within. His heart began to beat at a hundred miles an hour in nervous anticipation of witnessing and becoming a part of such an historical event. The outer guard replied to the knock by repeating it with the hilt of his sword. With this, the door opened.

"Who have you there?" asked a Knight. He was cloaked in black with a large insignia upon the right shoulder showing an emblem of the Grand Constable, depicting a drawn sword crossed by its scabbard, within an encircled buckled belt of gold braid, inscribed with the words 'Grand Priory' around its circumference.

"A Pilgrim who seeks council," replied the inner guard.

"Pilgrim, enter the Temple but be aware that you enter this holy lodge through an Arch of Steel and that in so doing you will comply to the conditions as scribed by our ancestors. Should you fail in this endeavour or pose any threat to this Temple or its brethren, the Arch of Steel will cut you down and without mercy your body will be hung drawn and quartered. Now fully aware of these conditions do you still wish to enter?"

The inner guard leaned towards Harry. "Repeat these words after me. *I do, Great Constable of Black Chapter'.*"

Harry repeated the words in as determined a voice as his nerves would allow.

"Then enter," said the Great Constable.

Harry was guided into what was almost pitch darkness, save for the light of a single candle flickering some distance away.

"Pilgrim, you are honoured to be given the opportunity of becoming a member of the Knights of Black Chapter, how say you?"

The inner guard again lent forward toward Harry. "Repeat after me: *I am a Master Mason and have acted well. I have served this chapter against its foes and therefore beg council to prove the point of my entrance."*

Harry repeated the words verbatim. With that he could just make out the Deacon approaching him through the Arch of Steel, his sword was now reversed, and he was holding its blade in his hand with the hilt in front of him in replication of a cross.

"Pilgrim, follow me."

He turned and, as instructed, Harry followed. The Deacon led him towards the kneeling stool in front of the Sepulchre.

"Kneel upon both knees," instructed the Deacon. Harry did exactly as he was told; he raised his Mantle at the front sufficiently to kneel and then knelt down.

"Pilgrim where were you made a Mason?" asked the Deacon.

"*In my heart,*" replied Harry, not waiting for the Deacon's prompt, having remembered the words from his second Degree.

"Where next?"

"*In a convenient room adjoining the lodge,*" replied Harry again.

"Describe the mode of your dress," asked the Deacon.

"*I was devoid of all metal and hood winked. My right arm, left breast and knee were made bare. My right heel was slip shod and a cable tow was placed around my neck,*" said Harry, feeling quite proud that he had remembered the words without the need for prompting.

"And where were you made a Mason?" continued the Deacon.

"*In the body of a lodge just perfect and rectangular,*" responded Harry.

"And when?"

"*When the sun was at its meridian.*"

"Why are Freemasons lodges held in the evening?"

"*The earth, constantly revolving upon its axis in its orbit round the sun and Freemasonry being universally spread over the surface, it necessarily follows that the sun must always be at its meridian with respect to Freemasonry.*" Harry was able to get this longer sentence out with just one little prompt. But the revelations described by Professor Franklin Thomas, Hugh McDonald and Thor Olson provided so much meaning behind these words that they now made perfect sense.

"What is Freemasonry?" continued the Deacon.

The Knights of Black Chapter

"*A peculiar system of morality veiled in allegory and illustrated by symbols,*" Harry said, his voice gaining a stronger pitch as he proceeded.

"Name the grand principles upon which the Order was founded?"

"*Brotherly love, Relief and Truth,*" said Harry without faltering.

"Who are fit and proper persons to be made Masons?"

"*Just, upright and free men of mature age, sound judgement and strict morals,*" Harry said with pride in his voice, as indeed he had done his best to follow these words since becoming a Mason.

"How do you know yourself to be a Mason?"

"*By the regularity of my initiation, repeated trials and approbations, and a willingness at any time to undergo an examination when properly called upon.*"

"How do you demonstrate yourself as being a Mason to others?"

"*By signs, tests and the perfect points of my entrance.*"

After Harry had answered this last question the Deacon placed a hand upon his shoulder. "Grand Master and Grand Knights of the Nine, I have asked the questions associated to a Freemason's second Degree. Do you wish me to ask the Pilgrim any further questions?"

"Star Knight Commander of the Grand Order, ask the Pilgrim what he now seeks?" said a voice from somewhere within the darkness.

Another Knight appeared at the end of the Arch of Steel. He was draped in chain mail over which a mantle hung bearing the insignia of a lion's face, holding in its jaws an amulet, the base also was argent, charged with two sable bars. Upon his helmet, rising as a crest, were two buffalo horns. Around his neck was a wide red ribbon from which hung a cross representing the Grand Cross of the United Orders. In the centre circle of the cross was a Patriarchal Cross and within it, the words *in hoc signo vinces* lettered in gold. His sword hung at rest in its scabbard as he was carrying a baton in his right hand signifying that he was the Knight of the Grand Cross. From his portly build Harry gauged him to be of middle age.

The Deacon leaned toward Harry: "Repeat after me: *I, a Pilgrim beg light*"

Harry repeated the words and as if by magic the entire Temple became lit to the point where he could see a wonderful spectacle in front of him. He was gazing upon an event that no-one else in the Temple, irrespective of rank, had ever actually witnessed before. The Temple must have been full, with at least two hundred people. They sat in silence. Harry could now see he was kneeling about a foot away from the Sepulchre. He didn't quite know what to look at first, but then his attention was drawn to the Deacon.

"Pilgrim, you are to advance forward towards the altar. There you will kneel upon the stool for the accolade. You will now proceed to follow my lead."

With that Harry was raised up to onto his feet and ordered to turn to the left. The Deacon then took him around the Sepulchre. The distance from the Sepulchre to the next stool was exactly ten paces. Upon reaching the stool the Deacon bid Harry to kneel. The Deacon then stood just behind and to the left of Harry who by now was looking straight at the Nine Ultimate Masters of the world. Which one was the direct descendant of Jesus, he asked himself.

The Grand Master spoke, his words seemed a little husky from beneath his visor; however Harry was certain he knew the voice. A voice he hadn't heard directly for a number of years, but one that was distinctly recognisable to him, having been on Royal protection duties as bodyguard to the Prince of Wales on one of his inaugural visits to America.

"Pilgrim, you have shown yourself to be a man of sound standing, it is therefore the bidding of this Chapter, of which I sit as its Grand Master, to initiate you into the Order. You will therefore become a squire of Black Chapter. How do you say?"

The Deacon answered for Harry to repeat: "*Grand Master, I pledge myself to this your order.*"

Harry repeated the words willingly.

"Pilgrim, I am sure, like many within this Temple here today, you feel the impulse to immerse yourself in the true legends, and marvel at the relics that adorn the Sepulchre. Legends are but history and these relics are from the bygone ages of our forebears. Let us all therefore use this auspicious occasion to feast our eyes upon them, for we are but a speck upon the soul of life eternal. It is now our time to pick up the gauntlet to carry on in the perseverance of life and continue the fight against human oblivion."

The End.

The Knights of Black Chapter

AUTHOR'S NOTE

A note from Joyee:

As I've mentioned at the beginning of other books in this series, I didn't foresee having three series in one world when I wrote *Micah*. Things got a little complicated. Now that *Virgil* is here and *A Bevin Hero* coming up, two parts of the world will be completed. *However* that in *NO WAY* means the stories are over, nor is the Mariuses' world and all those they love. There will be many, many more books to come, simply all of them under the Beyond the Marius Brothers series. I have a long list of rural Virginia most eligible bachelors that need their Happily Ever Afters. But with all the different series in one world and the fact that these next four books coming make the grand total to twenty one books, that's a lot of main characters and their mates, and more minor characters to keep popping up. So I've put a character chart on my website with some basics of who is mated to whom, what species they are, current jobs, and a few key points like their special gifts. It's downloadable, printable, and snuggleable if someone should really want, though probably not something I'd recommend because of those pesky paper cuts. http://www.joyeeflynn.com/book-series/the-marius-brothers/ I truly hope everyone has enjoyed the ride of all seven brothers and is excited for which of their friends will find love next in the future.

All my best,

Joyee

VIRGIL

Marius Brothers 8

JOYEE FLYNN
Copyright © 2013

Chapter 1

Virgil

"Your *highness*, good to see you," Stefan ribbed Caleb as he hugged one of our family's oldest friends. He might have been Micah's best friend, but he was like a stepbrother we actually liked to the rest of us. Caleb laughed before pulling away and giving me one of his bear hugs.

"You're so high because you're so tall," I mumbled in his ear. "Good to see you, man."

"You will address the King as his *majesty*," one of the warriors who escorted us from the airport growled menacingly.

"Dude, Evander, take it down a notch," Caleb chuckled as we parted. "Friends of mine, remember?"

"Sorry, your majesty." The man bowed and stepped back, looking properly chastised.

"Wait, did we do it wrong because you're a guy?" Patrick asked while hugging Caleb as well. "We called Queen Magdalena *your highness* all the time. Is it different for women and men?"

"Don't feel bad, we had to explain the difference to our mate as well," Liam answered with a snicker.

Micah had told me that since Caleb's mates were identical twins, there was an extra security risk if they couldn't keep them straight. Since then, Liam always wore something with the shoulders cut out so his birthmark showed, distinguishing him from Lorcan.

"The fae Queen keeps things informal or she doesn't like to have everyone treat her so differently, but she should be called her majesty as well. Ruling King or Queen get majesty. Anyone else in the ruling royal family gets your highness."

"Okay, so you and Lorcan get your majesty because you're Caleb's mates, but you're both still Princes because you can't be Queen since you don't have boobs," Patrick surmised. I bounced my head along with that one and then snickered. My brother's mate had such a way with words.

"I love how Americans know how to turn a phrase," a deep, loud voice chuckled from behind Caleb. I saw him before his scent hit me and I almost fell over just from how handsome he was. There were too many flowers in the throne room where we met up with Caleb after a meeting of his for me to have caught his scent sooner. But when I did, I froze… Except my fangs. The stranger's eyes met mine and he saw them come out, schooling his reaction carefully.

"I don't know if he's picking on me or not," Patrick said to his mate, getting the fae's attention.

"No, not at all," the man replied gently, shooting me another look quickly. "I honestly do love it. I appreciate bluntness. And his majesty, Prince Liam, is correct, our Queen smacked one of us once for calling her by that term. She said she was more mother to us all than ruler to be put up on a throne away from her people. We call her the term *highness*. She couldn't make us stop so she gave up."

"This is Foma, one of the new additions to our security," Caleb said as I stared at the god of a fae man. His scent was confusing me though because it wavered almost as if there were two of him. Then again I was desperately trying to get my fangs to retract so I was slightly distracted. "And this is his mate, Mareo." Caleb gestured to the other side of him and I locked eyes with the deepest midnight-blue eyes I'd ever seen. And I knew Mareo had seen every second of my reaction.

Did they know they were my mates? Fuck!

Stefan reached for Foma's hand. "Nice to meet you. We didn't get a chance to when the fae crossed over."

"We crossed over a couple of centuries ago in search of our mate," Foma explained, staring at me again. I felt the blood drain from my face, knowing he'd busted me, and glanced away… And met Mareo's gaze. *Shit!* "When we heard that the Queen and the rest of our people crossed over to this plane and some were coming to Greece, we made ourselves known to Caleb and offered our services to help acclimate the fae."

"Very nice of you," Patrick said as he shook the man's hand next. "Damn, you're just huge in a whole new way, man."

"So I've been told," Foma drawled and then snickered. "I've almost got two feet on you. I'm seven seven."

"Five eight," Patrick chuckled. "Just call me *shorty*."

"Virgil, are you going to come meet Caleb's people or stand there?" Stefan asked jokingly but I could hear the slight concern in his tone. "Dude, you okay?"

"Yeah," I answered, clearing my throat. "Just weird seeing Caleb like this with all the grandeur." I gestured around, lying through my teeth. "That and the flight." I shrugged. "Sorry. Just kind of spaced out."

"Then we should show you to your rooms for some rest," Mareo said as he moved closer to me. "I didn't catch your name."

I swallowed loudly as I stared up at the massive man. Yes, *I* had to stare up at him. He was maybe an inch shorter than Foma but at least seven and a half feet tall. "Virgil Marius."

"Nice to meet you, Virgil," he said in a slightly husky voice. We shook hands and I noticed that Stefan and Patrick were talking to

Liam and Lorcan again, everyone else distracted. They wanted to see their new baby before we settled in.

"Same," I mumbled, trying to get back my hand and not breathe at the same time. If I took in his scent with how attracted I was to him, my fangs would come right back out and I'd be busted.

"Virgil did you say?" Foma asked, suddenly right next to his mate, both of them practically surrounding me but keeping a polite distance… Technically. To everyone else it might have looked as if we were just in a private conversation. "Lovely fangs you have."

"Thanks, I'm, um, th–thirsty," I lied. "Tired and thirsty."

"Hmm." Foma glanced at his mate and I had a feeling they didn't believe me. "Then we should check on you during your nap."

"Maybe keep an extra close eye on you," Mareo agreed as he let go of my hand only for Foma to take it in his massive one. I stared into his light brown eyes and found myself twenty seconds from swooning. I swear he had gold flecks swirling around in them or something. It was hypnotic and alluring all at once. "Like as you're lying naked and sated in our arms."

I felt a thrill of desire go through me and my fangs, the fucking things, popped back out. I shook my head and pulled my hand back as I got them to retract. "I'm sorry, no thank you. I appreciate the offer but I'm straight."

Mareo leaned in until his shoulder-length black hair brushed against my ear. "The erection you're sporting would suggest otherwise. Why do I get the feeling most everything you've said is bullshit, Virgil?"

Because you're smart. But I couldn't say that. "If you'll excuse me, I want to meet my nephew." I cleared my throat and went to step around them.

"Running won't stop us from pursuing," Foma warned. I glanced at him, noticing a blond curl had fallen out of his tie. He had it bundled at the nape of his neck and it looked so soft I just wanted to bury my face in it.

I shook almost at the threat and promise rolled into one, his deep, commanding voice doing a number on my already-melted brain. Stefan shot me a look as I joined their group. "What was that about?"

"They thought they knew me," I lied again, giving him a look that clearly said none of his business though. He nodded, knowing I wasn't telling the truth because it wasn't for mixed company. "Oh, he's so cute!"

"This is our son, Prince Nicholas Michan Kyros," Lorcan announced proudly as he handed me the baby. He wasn't even three months old yet and it was always scary to hold a child that small, but I'd gotten lots of practice with Micah and Riley's daughter.

"You look like you know what you're doing there," Foma said as they joined us. I flinched but focused on Prince Nicholas.

I glanced at my mate, a need to be honest with him when I'd told him lies already filling me. "My brother has a daughter and I've sat with her many times being the only single one left in our family. Plus, she's just fun."

"And there's another on the way we hear?" Liam asked, a huge grin on his face.

"Yes, our surrogate, cool Aunt Sydney, is pregnant," Patrick practically squealed. "With the six-month gestation period vampires have, and that one threw me because no one told me that until after we found out she was pregnant in March, she's due end of September."

"Congratulations," Caleb said as everyone started hugging again. I smiled as I looked at them. They were so excited to have a family. I wanted that. I cooed at the baby as I snuck glances at my mates. And yet, I found them so why wasn't I saying anything?

That's right. I was stupid in the head and fucked up. I had always planned on my mate being a woman and now I had two mountains of fae warriors that were actually who fate gave me. So it seemed my phase of wanting ménage gay sex wasn't really a phase.

I didn't know what to do with that. I really, truly, didn't. I just needed time.

Prince Nicholas smacked my face with his chubby hand and I stared down at him. *Not a bad idea, kid. I could use a few more good cracks though.* When Liam looked ready to bust open with need to have his child back, I handed the Prince over.

"Sorry, it's just we're new to this and we be so scared of the dangers," Liam explained.

"Does this have anything to do with why Caleb suddenly wanted to be King and be officially sworn in? I wondered why he hadn't over the past two years but now did before the baby was born," I said quietly.

"It's complicated and something he wantin' to discuss with ya tonight when no one be listening," Lorcan mumbled under his breath. "But let's get ya to your rooms. We've got a few meetings and then we'll all have dinner, relax, and catch up."

"Anything you guys need, we're here for you always. Never doubt that, Lorcan," I assured him as I wrapped a comforting arm around his shoulders. He leaned into it and sighed, nodding his head. Wow, there was really something going on here then. That was never good.

Then again, when was there *not* drama and shit hitting the fan in our lives?

* * * *

Foma

I watched as the man I suspected was our mate comforted the Prince as we left the throne room. Their bags had been brought to their rooms by the staff so it was just a matter of showing them where they were. I was shocked when Caleb had made a point to say his visitors were going to be staying in the royal residence wing instead of in the guest wing. But now that I saw how close they were, I understood.

Caleb and his mates treated these men like family. I was glad for him because while the O'Hagans were a big family, Caleb mated into that clan, though really having no family of his own so that had to be hard for him. I now saw that wasn't really true since the Mariuses seemed to be Caleb's family. Caleb pointed out Virgil's room and when the man broke away from the group, I shared a glance with Mareo and we did the same.

"Are you sure you won't take us up on our offer?" I asked as I let my fingers graze his hip as he reached for the doorknob. "We could be so good to you, Virgil. Show you so much you've been missing out being straight. There's nothing wrong with just sampling what else is out there." I saw the slight shiver even as he shook his head.

"I'm sorry, I didn't hear what you said," Mareo purred as he leaned in closer and kissed Virgil's neck. The man tilted slightly to give him more room and then realized what he was doing and flinched, turning to face us. And that's when we saw his fangs were out again. "Did you say *yes, please come into my room and ravage me*?"

"No. Please leave me alone," he whispered, shaking. "I can't do this."

"Do what?" I asked gently, seeing the fear in our mate's eyes. "What's the big deal? It's not like we're mates or something, right?" Virgil flinched as he went pale. I opened my mouth to specifically ask the question, forcing him to answer, but he opened the door and darted into his room before I could, locking it behind him.

"I knew it," Mareo whispered as he ran his fingers over the door. "He's ours. I'd bet all our savings that he's ours. Why wouldn't he tell us? What's happened to our poor mate that he looks so scared?"

"Closet case?" I guessed, shrugging.

"No, something more than that." He shook his head and then gave me one of those soulful looks that made me always melt at how intense my mate was. The man saw *everything*. "Let's go talk to Caleb. He'll help us."

"But he's Virgil's friend," I hedged even as I trailed after my mate.

"*Exactly*," he chuckled. "He'll know all we need to know about our potential mate and how to get him into our arms." I hoped Mareo was right. I felt intensely attracted to Virgil. He was gorgeous and all but it was more than something shallow. The only other man I'd ever felt that draw to before was Mareo. It just seemed all the signs were pointing to Virgil being our mate so why would he not be glad and instead look scared?

I knocked on the door to King Caleb's study, knowing he had a meeting in a bit. "Come in."

"Sorry to interrupt you, your majesty," Mareo said as we entered, both of us dipping our heads in respect.

"Guys, seriously, if it's just us, call me Caleb," the King drawled yet again. "Or I swear I'm going to think we're not friends."

"Yes, Caleb," I said quickly before Mareo could argue. He was very stuck in his ways and sometimes I had to snap him out of his ruts. Caleb was awesome and our friend. I didn't want to lose that. My mate gave a slight nod, letting me know he understood what I'd just done.

"Cool. So what's up?" Caleb glanced at us from what he'd been looking at.

"We were wondering about what makes a vampire's fangs come out," Mareo said smoothly. "There's been some rumors among our people and we felt it was best to come to our most trusted source to get answers so we didn't have the wrong ideas running rampant."

"I hate rumors but I can understand why the fae would be gossiping about vamps, especially with this blood thing," he grumbled as he rubbed his hands over his face.

"You mean that's *true*?" I gasped, not being able to hide my shock in time.

"Yes. I thought everyone knew that now." Caleb swore under his breath and got to his feet. "Please press upon the fae staying here that it's not a rumor. Your blood, if not despelled by your Queen, pretty much drives a vampire mad. And not the good kind of crazy shifter blood can do."

"Okay, give us the short version on that," Mareo sighed. Yeah, I wasn't up to date on all of this either. Caleb quickly went over what fae blood did to vamps, and then how shifter blood worked.

"So your kind isn't specifically drawn to fae or shifter blood? Your fangs won't just pop out when you smell one of us?" I asked, trying to get the answers we needed.

"No, not at all," Caleb said firmly. "Unless a vampire is severely thirsty for blood, they should have complete control over their fangs."

Mareo nodded as if this conversation was no big deal. Damn, my mate was smooth. "What else would make them come out? Aggression of course. I've seen yours descend when you're sparring."

"Yes, but normally when it's aggressive our eyes change to like a gray or black and our hands to claws if we're threatened," Caleb clarified. Good, so it wasn't that Virgil had been threatening us. "They pop out when we're turned on."

"So every time you see a man you're attracted to your fangs come out?" I asked. "Have they ever come out for women since you're gay?"

"No, nothing like that," he snickered. "I was never with a vampire woman, but most of us don't bite other vampires than our mates. Micah used to tell me of the human women he'd bed, his fangs would pop out as they'd climax, he'd drink, lick the wound closed to heal as they finished, and most times they'd never be the wiser he just had a pint."

Mareo nodded and I was out of questions so I deferred to him. "But he had control no matter how turned on he was? Ever a time when vampires can't control them besides severe thirst?"

"When I say severe thirst, I don't just mean we've gone without all day. I'm talking like getting over injury and need to replenish big-time," Caleb explained. "Other than that, the only time I've seen vampires not be able to control them is when they smell their mates. My situation was a little different because I was frightened of hurting Liam and Lorcan but they still popped out when I smelled them."

"I think that gives us enough to answer any other questions we might get," I said, nodding my head as I took in what Caleb said. He basically just confirmed what we'd thought. Virgil was our mate and he didn't want to admit it.

"Anything else then?" Caleb asked as he walked back towards his desk.

"You said we're friends, right? We can ask you something personal?" Mareo hedged as he shot me a glance.

"Of course but we have to make it quick. I have a meeting and I don't want it to run long because I really just want to take the night off and visit with my visiting friends. I know it's Stefan and Patrick's belated honeymoon, so they won't be staying with us too long. They're going to want lots of alone time." He wiggled his eyebrows as if we hadn't already known what he'd meant.

"We were wondering if we'd step on any toes if we asked to spend time with Virgil Marius while he was here."

I held my breath as Mareo's words hung in the air, hoping Caleb didn't see the question as crossing some line.

"You can try but Virgil's straight," Caleb chuckled. "Then again, I thought I was too before I met my mates. Or maybe I didn't. Who knows." He bit his lower lip and stared off at the empty fireplace as if wondering about his past.

"Virgil?" I hedged.

"Oh, right, sorry. Yeah, I've really never known him to date much or talk about anyone he's been with. He's kind of closed-mouthed about his personal life. He's a great guy though. He's not a bigot and won't freak if you ask him. Just don't be offended if he says no. I'm pretty sure he's never crossed the fence. He's been looking for his mate for as long as I've known him, always saying he's ready to make a life with her." Caleb shrugged.

I felt my heart drop into my stomach. That could explain a lot. Depending on how old Virgil was, he could have spent hundreds of years waiting for a female mate only to find out he was mated to *two* male warriors who towered over his six-three frame. Ouch. Yeah, that would make anyone flip.

"How long are they staying?" I asked, trying to keep the panic I was feeling out of my voice.

"Only two nights, though I was hoping to talk them into a third. There's a lot I need to discuss with them at dinner tonight that I couldn't over the phone or e-mail. You'll be there, right? I trust your input and with some new developments I was thinking of sending you to discuss what's been going on directly with your Queen."

"Of course. We'll leave you to your meeting," Mareo agreed. We excused ourselves and left his study.

"We only have two nights?" I whispered in horror. "He looked so scared and was so quick to push us away. That's not going to be enough time to change his mind, Mareo."

My mate scratched his chin as he nodded. Then he got a feral smile on his lips and that mischievous twinkle in his eyes. "Not without help, it's not."

Oh shit. He was up to something. That could either be really good for us, or really bad. With Mareo it was a fifty-fifty shot if his plans worked or if it made things worse for us.

I prayed to the gods it was that the plan worked this time. We couldn't lose our mate.

Chapter 2

Mareo

I knew Foma had questions but we didn't have much time. Dinner was in a few hours and for this to work we needed to hurry. I gave him a wink as we jogged along, trying to reassure him I had everything in hand. To be honest, I didn't. This would either epically work or epically fail.

I was praying for the first.

"Jordy, we need a favor," I said as I found the man we'd been looking for.

"Are you sure about this?" Foma hissed at me, figuring out the plan.

"I'm open to suggestions if you've got another idea," I shot right back before focusing on our cute little friend and sometimes bedmate. "We need your help, sweetness."

"I have some work I need to do but then I can help you," Jordy replied shyly, his eyes filling with lust.

"Oh, hun," I whispered. I pulled him out of the main hallway and down a deserted corridor, Foma following. I cupped Jordy's cheek, wincing when he pursed his lips. "No, Jordy. I'm sorry. We need your help because we think we've found our other mate."

"Oh, congratulations," he mumbled, hurt filling his eyes as embarrassment heated his cheeks. "What do you need from me? What can I do to help? I'm just liaison to the local wolf pack."

"Yes, but we found out that wolf blood can help us open up a vampire and drive up their lust," I hedged as I ran my fingers through

Jordy's soft black hair. "We need your help. The man isn't staying long and something's holding him back. We need to spur him past the fear into need and desire mode so he'll admit everything to us. He won't go to another for his needs if his mates are here. No man of honor would do that."

"You want me to help you get your mate drunk with my blood?" Jordy gasped, pulling away from me. "No, I won't do that."

"Please, Jordy?" Foma begged quietly. "I'm not a fan of this either but we're desperate. We can't smell our mates like you guys can. He's given us every sign he is but we can't just call him a liar. He's good friends with the King. We're just going to give him a little bit to help loosen him up."

Jordy worried his lower lip for a moment, glancing between us. "You said this man isn't from here. Is he one of the visitors from America?"

"Yes and they're only staying a few days," I answered.

"I'll help you but will you help me?"

"Of course. We would have even if we weren't asking this of you. You know that, Jordy," Foma said gently. "What's going on?"

"You weren't in a position to help me before," he explained, shaking his head. "I want out of my pack and far, far away from here. Being liaison is the only thing that's helped but I want out of Greece. If you end up with your mate and go back to America, will you help find an Alpha who would accept me into his pack? Mine won't let me leave and no one wants to go against him around here. But that far away, they might not care."

"You have our word we'll help. We can ask our Queen either way, Jordy. We'll figure out something," I said firmly. I didn't know what was going on and it wasn't my place to ask for the full story, but Jordy was a sweetie and wouldn't ask for assistance lightly. I might just put in a call to Magdalena anyways.

"Thank you," he sighed in relief. "Yes, you can have my blood. Just don't tell anyone you got it from me. I don't need to be in any more trouble than I seem to always be in."

"Why didn't you tell us, Jordy? We could have given you sanctuary," Foma asked gently.

"Wolf business is supposed to stay with wolves." Our little friend shrugged.

"Fuck that," I growled, cupping his cheek. "We take care of our friends. Go with Foma. He's trained as a medic and can take the blood we need. I'm going to call our Queen right now and ask about the pack that's in her coven. We'll get you out of whatever's going on, Jordy."

"Thank you," he whispered as he stood on his toes and kissed my cheek. "I wish I had gotten mates like you. Your man is very, very lucky."

"I hope he feels that way one day," I admitted sadly.

"Hey, life is scary. Maybe he's just reeling and would come around on his own," Jordy said gently. "A little of my blood and he'll be begging for the pleasure I know you both can give. Then you'll show him how big of hearts you both have. He'll see how loving, kind, and wonderful you both are."

"Thanks, sweetness." I rubbed his hair affectionately before he hurried off with Foma. I quickly called the Queen but she was in a meeting. Baylor was currently working as her personal guard and message taker I guess and said she'd call me back as soon as she could. Feeling I'd done what I could for right then, I headed to medical where I knew Foma would be.

Time to get our mate into our arms, our bed, and into his heart. We'd help Jordy as soon as the Queen called me back.

* * * *

Virgil

After I had calmed down from my mini-freak-out over finding my very male, very massive mates, I called my only really close friend Ferris Braden. He was busy so I didn't bother leaving him a message. What would I have said anyways?

"Hey, Ferris, I know we've never talked about this kind of stuff, but I thought I was addicted to werewolf blood and that's why I liked to have two men fucking me but apparently I was wrong. I just wanted to see what being with a guy was like and I had two offer, but then I kept going back. I thought it was their blood so I told them no more. Then it seems fate just wanted to fuck with me because I'm mated to two massive fae warriors.

"So am I a recovering addict or am I just gay? If I'm gay, then why have I never been attracted to men over my three hundred and ninety years until recently? I thought maybe after that mission six months ago when I hit my head I jarred something loose in me that made me wild and wanted to try something new. But apparently not and maybe I'm just losing my mind. Can that happen with a vampire?"

Yep. That sounded good. It gave me another idea though. I quickly found Riley in my contacts and connected the call. I didn't even greet him. "Can a head injury change what someone likes?"

"Hey, Virgil, how are you?" he drawled. "You have to be more specific than that for me to answer you. Are we talking about a vampire?"

"Yes." I racked my brain as to how to ask the question without really asking it. "Say a person never really liked strawberries, or just never would have wanted them, asked for them, or craved them. Could taking a blow to the head make them all of a sudden crave strawberries? Or say affect their sense of smell to where they think they smell something that's not there?"

"Virgil, what's going on?" he asked gently, but very quietly. I heard some shuffling and then a door close. "Does this have something to do with when you got hurt several months ago? What are you wanting that you didn't before?"

"Strawberries?" I tried, knowing that it sounded a question instead of a statement.

"Brother, talk to me. You know I can't tell anyone as your doctor. You know I don't judge. I respect that you're a private man and you like to keep to yourself but that's not healthy if something's going on. Obviously you're not sure or confused. I mean, why would you need to know about wanting something you haven't before and your sense of—" He gasped and I winced. "Virgil, did you find your mate?"

"Mates," I admitted in a choked whisper. "I've always wanted women, Riley. But I don't know who I am anymore. At the Halloween party I was flirting with this sexy wolf, and I thought he was a girl with the way he was dressed up. We went off alone and I realized he was a guy when we were making out but it was fun and all my brothers are gay and it's not like I was disgusted so I thought I'd just try some wild times. Sow my oats."

"Sure, that's completely normal," Riley said supportively.

"And then his friend came looking for him and next thing I knew I'm drinking from them and they're, we're, um, both of them, me, yeah."

"They took you together," he hedged, trying to help me.

"Yes," I whispered as I felt my cheeks heat up. "I thought it was the wolf blood. Maybe it made me a little too wild. Then I wondered if it was the crack to my head I took. It was like I couldn't stop though. But I did a few months ago, thinking I'd become addicted to werewolf blood or something and it made me want things I wouldn't normally want. I've never wanted that before."

"I've never heard of that side effect of shifter blood, Virgil." I could hear they sympathy in Riley's tone, but knew he was telling me the truth. "And I scanned your brain weeks after you were hurt. You healed just fine. There's nothing to suggest a personality change and a hit to the head wouldn't leave you with just *one* change like this. And shifter blood really isn't addictive. They just tell vampires that to prevent us from ever trying to keep them like food."

"Maybe it could be addictive to just someone though, right? I'd crave it, Riley."

"I wouldn't rule it out then," he hedged. "I'd need to run some tests when you get home. I think the more likely answer is you equate wolf blood with the excuse to be free to do as you want which is experience two men in bed like that. There's no shame in that, Virgil."

"I know. We have friends who are in ménages. Damian likes to bottom for Cyrus and they're into all kinds of kink."

"Then what's holding you back?"

"There was a plan, Riley," I whispered as I felt my eyes burn. "Someone doesn't just change from being attracted to women after over three centuries of it to men. And it's not like I want a man. I want two men on either side of me. It's freaking me out. I've never looked at a man and now that's what I crave."

"Just breathe, Virgil, okay? Nothing needs to be decided today."

"Except I met my mates in Greece. I think they know because of my reaction when I met them. They're two *massive* fae warriors, Riley. That *so* wasn't the plan. The plan was to mate a nice woman, have lots of babies, be a warrior, be happy, and live my life."

"Virgil, I say this because I love you. If vampires could be OCD you would. You're too rigid and a little boring. You don't do well with people, you keep to yourself, and you barely have any friends. You seem lost in yourself most times. I think fate gave you two men because it will blow open that little box you see yourself and your life fitting into or what it should be."

I just blinked at the phone for a few moments in shock. "And people wonder why I don't let them in? So you love me because you're mated to my brother and family now but you obviously don't like me or respect me. Thanks, Riley."

"No, Virgil, that's not what I meant!" he shouted as I hung up the phone. Ouch! That just, *wow*, hurt! When he called right back I ignored the call and sent it right to voicemail. I got the answers I wanted and a lot more. Now I had a whole new list of reasons not to want to acknowledge my mates… They wouldn't like me. Riley knew me pretty well and obviously he didn't.

I couldn't take my mates not liking me and just being stuck with me.

I lay down on the bed in the room Caleb had given me for our stay, tired down to my very soul. Now I wondered if vampires could get depressed. Did my family feel this way about me? Yeah, I knew they pitied me being the last of us who wasn't mated, but maybe it was more than that? Maybe they pitied me because I was *me*.

Yup, that was depressing.

I didn't even realize I'd fallen asleep, waking when Stefan knocked on the door and told me it was time to go down for dinner. I called out I'd be down in ten and jumped up. I needed a shower after the long-ass flight. Grabbing my toiletries bag, I hurried into the bathroom, showered, dried off, dressed, and was making my way through the palace a little while later.

"Lost?" Mareo asked as I turned the corner.

"Yes," I admitted, remembering all my training and the tough situations I'd been in before. I could handle myself. Just because they were my mates and had thrown me the first time didn't mean I'd act like a child. I was a fucking warrior. I could control my reactions and emotions.

"We'll escort you to dinner," Foma offered as he held out his arm for me.

"Thanks. Lead the way." I gestured for him to go ahead, ignoring the arm. I saw hurt flash in his eyes before he walked away. He wouldn't have been hurt unless he knew. *They knew*. Had I been that see-through earlier? I didn't know but I still didn't grasp what to do about them, feeling less inclined to tell them we were mates than I had been *before* talking to Riley.

"Hey, I got a couple messages from Riley asking me to please have you call him," Stefan said as we joined them for dinner. It wasn't what I'd expected for a dining room in a palace so I had a feeling this was just a smaller one in the residence wing for normal, everyday meals. "What's going on? He sounded upset."

"Doesn't matter. I'll have to talk to him when we get home," I responded, not bothering to hide my annoyed tone. Stefan blinked at me in shock as we all sat down. I know, I know, boring Virgil didn't ever bitch or say anything bad about anyone. Apparently that was part of what made me unlikeable. So screw it. And it didn't help that Mareo had sat to my right and Foma on my left. How the fuck had that one worked out like that?

Caleb gave me a funny look when I met his gaze so I quickly focused on my water glass. "The reason Michan, Manus, and Brighid aren't here is because they're in Paris fighting for their High Council seats. Their Barnabas for that area is Councilman Dubois and I guess that there's bad blood there so Michan and Manus living here, out of the Eastern European High Council's territory, is what he's saying is the reason that he's going after their seats."

"That man be a bastard," Liam bitched as our salads were served. I had my suspicions he was right and a lot more but I'd kept quiet, waiting for someone else to connect the dots. I didn't like taking center stage and every time I seemed to open my mouth, most looked at me like I was dense… Which was really the opposite.

But it also made Riley's words ring in my head. I kept to myself because, unlike my genius brother-in-law, my intelligence wasn't accepted as a gift. Normally everyone just glanced at me as if wondering why was I wasting their time and moved on. A few centuries of that and I started to become resentful so I started avoiding them too, not interacting with them well. So much so that Riley was correct and I knew that. I just loved how it was my fault of course.

Caleb snapped me out of my thoughts when he confirmed my earlier suspicions.

"Look, one of the reasons I moved from being heir apparent as I was when I found out who I was to being sworn in as King is it gives me more leverage, protection, and a louder voice once I have that title. Plus, it's more security for my family and prestige that our son brings because I have an heir and a line. It wasn't just my mates and son I was looking out for by doing this."

"We've heard that other High Councils might be pacing in the wings that we've got fae, margays, and wolves in our coven now along with a good percentage of the East Coast covens," Stefan hedged.

"Aye, ya got that from Finn and Fergus," Lorcan agreed. "We know. Our das be the ones who told us what the Eastern Europe High Council be discussing. Caleb confirmed it with the Central one along with the Russian providences High Council. They're nervous. We don't have as many contacts in the Americas or Asian ones but the ones we do know be riled up."

"It's just odd," Stefan grumbled. "Why make such issue with this? We've been telling everyone what's been going on. You know our High Council's been communicating about our attacks."

"But nowhere else is getting as many attacks as you are," Caleb said quietly. "They wonder if you're making it up to justify building an army." I sighed and he glanced at me. "I know this is frustrating but we have to come up with a strategy as to what is the next move. Otherwise the Western Europe High Council could declare war on the East Coast High Council or something. They might require you get rid of the margays and fae."

"And this isn't something you can just call Father up about. So you wanted to discuss this while we came to visit," Stefan surmised, nodding. "What do you think is the best plan to ease their minds?"

"I've had a request from the head of the Western European High Council to have some of his liaisons observe how things are going at the palace," Caleb answered. I felt a rush of adrenaline and fear fill me. Shit. I might not be able to stay quiet much longer. These circumstances were too severe to let someone else figure out the answer as I normally did. "They want to see how having the fae in our coven along with displaced shifters works. Also our alliances with the local shifters."

"And let me guess, he's hinted he wants you to smooth the way for the same at our coven?" I said, swallowing back my nerves at jumping into the fray. In a fight as a warrior, I never had a problem. But after centuries of people looking at me like I was stupid or should just shut up most times I spoke, it was hard for me to communicate.

Then again, apparently the way I'd been made me unlikeable, according to my brother-in-law, so fuck everyone and I was just going to be who I wanted.

Caleb blinked at me in shock as if remembering I was there or something. "Yes. He wants his own people to see what's going on in your coven to reassure that there's no army being built."

"Oh I bet he wants to see what's going on, but not because he thinks we have an army," I drawled. "You have a map of Europe or projector? I want to show you what I've been working on."

"Virgil, this really isn't the time for—" Stefan started to say, giving me a confused look.

"I always fucking listen to *everyone* else all the fucking time about everything. Just this *once* would someone listen to me without giving me shit or basically telling me to shut it and go away?" I bellowed, letting out years of pent-up aggression. I guess what Riley had said to me really got to me worse than I thought. "I know the answer. Jesus. Just shut the fuck up and listen before we all end up dead."

"Yeah, sure, Virgil," he whispered, his eyes practically popping out of his head… As were everyone else's in the room. Fuck them. I was tired of blending in with the scenery now that I knew Riley saw me that way. Because in my heart I knew if Riley felt that way, most others did.

"I'll get a projector brought in. Do you need a laptop too?" Caleb finally said after a few moments of silence.

"No, I just need my tablet." I practically raced out of the room, not being able to take their stares. I remembered the way back to where I was staying, grabbed it, and made my way to the dining room again.

"I don't know what's going on with him, Caleb," Stefan muttered as I got to the door, my hand already on the knob. "Riley sounded panicked. Could Virgil have had a nervous breakdown and that's why the doc was calling? Maybe he thinks Virgil's unstable?"

I growled, pissed off beyond belief. I yanked open the door. "No, Riley's just a dick who thought being honest with me about all my personality flaws would help. I asked him a few questions about something personal and he took it as an opening to give me an assessment as to what he thought I needed to work on. Well, there's a reason I tend to keep my mouth shut, but fine, fuck it. If I'm not liked anyways, I'm just going to be me."

"We like you," Stefan argued.

"Right. But you think I'm off. Withdrawn, don't really pay attention or do well with people. Lost in my own world which was why you were trying to get me to be quiet the moment I opened my mouth, right?" I shot back as I set everything up with the projector one of Caleb's people brought in. I glanced at my brother and felt my heart twist in my chest. The look on his face said it all. *Yes.* "Yeah, well, you should be smart enough to not assume you know as much as you think you do."

"What do ya mean by that?" Liam asked quietly, gently. I looked at him and saw nothing but genuine concern in his expression.

"That apparently no one really knows me or gives a damn enough to take the time to see me," I answered before clearing my throat and pulling up what I needed on my tablet. I plugged in the wireless connector to the projector and then the maps, first. "Here are the charted demon attacks from 2000 to 2005. Notice anything?"

"They're pretty even across the board," Caleb hedged. "Except not many in Western Europe."

"Exactly. There were two. Odd for all those countries, right? So look at 2005 to 2010. Same thing. We see an increase, but not in Western Europe. I highly doubt that their warriors are all *that* much better. So I did some more digging." I pulled up two more maps and put them side by side. "These are all the human abductions, missing person cases, and deaths that could be associated with demons in those years."

"There are next to none in Western Europe," Patrick gasped. "Holy shit!"

"Yup. Best way not to draw attention to your area or have people looking into things you don't want eyes on is to have no problems. Now, look at from 2010 until now," I said as I pulled up the map. The East Coast flared up with dots of attacks and kidnappings, deaths, and potential demon-related deaths. "Now what changed in 2010 that could possibly have caused this?"

"Riley and I came up with the bullets," Stefan answered.

"Right, but they didn't know he was there right away. We know that because they tried to attack his old coven last year to get him," I explained. "So what else?"

"You have debatably some of the most powerful founding families in the world all in one region," Caleb answered.

"Yes, but that was always true. What most people don't know and I only found out after some serious digging is that we had two key players turn demon. Torhn, which you knew and you and Micah killed, but he wasn't originally from our coven, so it wasn't attributed to us. He was however in charge of training with our now Councilman Abbott whose *father* did turn demon that year. Then suddenly the attacks increased and we had more demon activity than anywhere else.

"When they found out about Riley being there, up it some more. Explanation, they took the cook from the warrior compound. We find out Cyrus's family is still mostly alive and demons, running the operation according to them. Then we have Barnabas come home, and they try to take him out. Why?"

"He's the last Leopold and it would have thrown the Council into chaos," Stefan answered.

"They could have done that when he was at Oxford. It would have been much easier then without the additional security," I replied, hating that everyone just assumed that was the answer. That was the *easy* answer, but the demons were right on something… We were arrogant. They didn't lose their IQ because they lost their souls. They weren't stupid.

If we didn't start understanding that, all the cool weapons in the world wouldn't save us.

Chapter 3

"He mated," Caleb whispered, his eyes going wide. "If Barnabas died most people would have left his seat to one of their mates, but he didn't."

"Who weren't from founding families, and *that* would have set off some of the Council members. If he died before, Father would have been next in line as the second-oldest founding family on the Council. They wouldn't have wanted that. *That's* what everyone kept missing when they assumed that the demons just wanted to kill the last Leopold. They could have done that years ago.

"It would have put the Mariuses at the head of the Council and with *seven* warrior sons, that would have been a stupid move for the demons. We're just as well respected as the Leopolds, maybe even better known since there are so many of us and we've taken missions all over the world over our years. Victor is debatably the most respected warrior our race has. Then the best doctor our race has mates into our family. Our line taking over the Council wouldn't have helped them."

"But they saw Miles or Digger taking it over as the match that could potentially light the dynamite to make the High Council explode," Stefan recapped.

"Or at least distracted them with their squabbling long enough to do some damage. Then they come for the Kappas. Why would they want them specifically and not just wolves?"

"They were helping our coven deal with their past and become stronger," Patrick answered me.

"Right. But they didn't know about the fae right away, which implies their source wasn't in the loop. Meaning not a founding family or Council member but someone who could have gotten into the Council estate to *accidentally* let the demon Queen Magdalena captured be exposed to the sun, effectively killing him before we could question him."

"That was highly suspect," Stefan agreed. "So you've pretty much ruled out Councilman Abbott even though it was his father that turned demon?" I nodded. I never was a believer of *the sins of the father* and all that shit. Everyone was different. "Who are you thinking then?"

"So say a warrior," I said, generalizing, not ready to get into specifics. "Then the fae come over and we've got another powerful ally, maybe *the* most powerful ally of any coven because the Queen lives in ours. All of a sudden the talk starts that maybe we're building an army, which is ridiculous since we were giving other paranormals refuge, but effective to throw focus off the demon problem.

"It also makes our coven look untrustworthy when we're showing covens how to produce these next-gen demon-fighting weapons. Who would want to use them if they couldn't trust the people they got them from?"

"That's a very good point," Caleb hedged, leaning forward. "I know the Central Europe High Council isn't implementing the procedures we are and making their warriors carry the ammo. I thought it odd but they dodged my questions when I asked about it."

"Then the shit goes down with the margays and their King is attacked. The secret of their blood was highly guarded information that we didn't even know about. You'd have to have lots of pull or friends to know about that. Say like leader of a High Council who has a large margay population in their territory?"

"You think the head of the Western Europe High Council is in league with the demons?" Caleb's eyes looked ready to pop out of his head. I'd get to my proof in a bit, but I wanted to put the idea in their head so I nodded.

"Right. So then we end up having a Kappa who's an Alpha, mated to a powerful founding family. *We* barely learn about all this and the demons take such a risk as to try to take Caven out right away?"

"You think they were targeting Caven and not just trying to attack that night?" Stefan asked, blinking at me in shock.

"Yeah, I highly doubt they just so happen to get in an accident with Darcy's SUV on the way to gathering for an attack," I drawled. "The target was Caven. He's an asset. They needed to take him out before he became as powerful as King Rylan and got the wolves to be an asset. Fletcher wasn't a good or well-trained Alpha. He wouldn't have been a threat to the demons, but Caven? Mated to Gabriel? Oh yeah."

"So you think it had to be one of the warriors that day who bared their necks to Caven?" Patrick asked, getting the point I was making about the inside traitor in our coven.

"I do. The demons knew way too fast for it to be through the normal gossip channels. It was within a few days that the attack happened. The wolf elder explained to them right away why they had done that. If you were the traitor, a wolf who could make a vampire submit like a wolf would have *screamed* power and scared them."

"Holy shit," Liam whispered.

"And of all the lack of attacks in Western Europe, there have been only two in the past few years. The margays, where the goal was to get their blood that can let demons go into the sun temporarily," I explained and then looked at Liam and Lorcan. "And your family. Now why would demons all of a sudden show up at a remote farm in Ireland? There's been *one* demon sighting in Ireland in the past decade. But yet your family gets attacked?"

"Our das hate the head of the Council," Lorcan answered, his eyebrows shooting up to his hairline. "They be the man's biggest rivals. They also be next in line for head of the Council as your da be. They hate Councilman Dubois."

"Exactly. Your dads die and there are several goals accomplished. One, he gets rid of two men who would vote against him and won't fall for his bullshit. Also, they speak out against him. Two, they would side with us. Three, they're *your* family and you're mated to Caleb. How devastated and distracted would the palace have been if they were dead along with Brighid and your brothers?"

"I wouldn't have given a second thought to letting his liaisons in because I would have been attending to other things," Caleb mumbled, shaking his head.

"And if you did, we probably would have," I added. "But it didn't work. So now, the goal is to at least get them out and liaisons in here, in our coven as well, while they're not here to tell you not to because they don't trust the guy. Also, the O'Hagans are stirring up shit that the head of their Council didn't tell everyone that other Councils were giving mandates to pull vampires into covens for protection. He's got witnesses to what can be seen as his screw-up. That's bad for him.

"There's one big piece no one seems to have put together either. Cyrus's dad. The man is in charge of all the demons now basically, from Spain, and yet we really think he'd leave *all* of Western Europe pretty much alone? There has to be a reason for that. Like not shitting where you sleep or drawing attention to themselves by acting like they are perfectly safe there and in control of the demon problem."

"Very impressive," Mareo said. I glanced at him, our eyes met, and I blinked in shock when I saw pride in his. He gave a nod and I noticed Foma doing the same. "Sound logic, impressively backed up facts, detailed research from different angles, and an astounding approach as if you were an outsider as opposed to someone right in the middle of it all."

"Did you just insult Virgil with that last one?" Patrick asked, narrowing his eyes at the fae warrior. "He's one of us."

"No, Pat," I answered, shocked that he immediately came to my defense. I shouldn't have been though. He was one of the few people who always seemed to make sure I was included in things, like the

Christmas present the mates all gave my brothers. "It was a compliment. He was saying that it's easier to see the big picture when you're not a part of what's going on and yet I was able to do that when this all affects me."

"Exactly," Mareo agreed. "No insult was meant. Only the highest praise of a brilliant mind and fantastic strategist."

"Yeah, Virgil's wicked smart," Pat agreed. "He's helped me with homework a bunch of times. I bet he's got as high of an IQ as Riley."

"Seriously?" Stefan asked, glancing between us. I shrugged, rubbing the back of my neck nervously as I set down my tablet. Now that I'd said my piece I kind of wanted to disappear instead of getting attention.

"You had to know how smart he was. That's why he's so quiet," Pat chuckled as he glanced at his mate. Then he frowned and looked at me. "They don't know that, do they?"

"I think you're the only one who's cared enough to pay attention," I answered as I quickly sat back down. I made the mistake of glancing up in between bites of my salad when I reached for my water, Stefan and Caleb still staring at me like I was off my rocker or they'd never seen me before. "Fine. Don't believe me. Whatever."

"No, I do believe you. I think you're right on all of it," Caleb quickly said. "I just don't know what to say, Virgil. I feel like I'm just meeting you or something."

"Yeah, me too and I'm your damn brother," Stefan grumbled. I went to open my mouth but Pat beat me to it.

"And you blame *him* for that? I'm sorry. I think conversations work both ways. He's still your brother. You weren't open about being gay until we met. So Virgil didn't go blabbing he's a genius because he thought you guys might not react well? Geez, proving him right much?"

Stefan stared at his mate a moment and nodded. "You're right. I'm sorry, Virgil. You should have been able to come to me with anything. If you didn't feel comfortable being yourself around me then that wasn't on you. I'll try and keep an open mind and pay better attention."

"Whatever, it's fine," I mumbled, shrugging again. Caleb got up and opened the door, letting them know we were ready for the main course. I hadn't even noticed that he'd sent everyone out during my presentation. Stefan went to speak again and I didn't want to listen to any more of this. He couldn't just say he was sorry and all be forgotten now that I'd proven useful. Tomorrow I'd probably go right back to being ignored. "So what's the plan?"

"If I may?" Mareo asked before anyone could answer. He waited for Caleb to give him a nod before continuing. "I have a call in to our Queen for a personal matter. I feel it best to implore her that I might seek her counsel face-to-face on this matter given this news. She might want to bring along Councilman Marius to see his nephew as long as she's opening a portal."

"That would be okay to say over the phone just in case we're being watched or our phones are tapped," Caleb agreed. "They need to see what you came up with, Virgil."

"Father won't listen to me," I scoffed.

"Yeah, he would," Stefan said gently. "Your brothers might be idiots and blind to what's going on most of the time. Mother and Father aren't."

"If you say so." I shrugged, not willing to take that leap of faith. "Someone else can fill them in."

"No way. You found all this and you need to take the credit," Caleb argued. "I just wonder what else you haven't taken the credit for over the years."

I winced internally, knowing there had been a few times I'd snuck into Riley's lab to help on some formulas when I'd known he'd been stuck. He'd be *pissed* if he knew I'd ever done that. I shrugged again and reached for my glass of blood, chugging the large goblet down. I froze as I went to set it back down, my heart racing.

That wasn't human blood I'd just drank. Why the fuck was Caleb serving werewolf blood? I glanced around, noticing no one else seemed to be acting differently, already having drank some of theirs while I'd been talking. Had I'd imagined it given my conversation with Riley earlier? That had to be it. Caleb wouldn't set us up to turn into horndogs for the night.

Reaching for my water, I quickly drank it down, hoping to snap out of it. It was probably just nerves from putting myself out there for the first time in a long time. I was just about to reach for the pitcher of water when Mareo handed me another goblet.

"Here, you look flushed and thirsty," he said as if it was no big deal, simply having noticed and reached for me.

"Thanks." I took it with a shaky hand, careful not to touch his fingers, and tossed it back. Damn. Same reaction. If it was werewolf blood and not just my mind playing tricks on me, I was screwed. Two of those goblets had to be at least a liter and a half of blood, they were so big.

I'd find out *real* soon if it was shifter blood or just my imagination because the effects would drive me nuts all night if it was.

I listened as we ate, everyone discussing possible ways to get King Rylan here tomorrow and maybe the wolf elder, finally deciding to wait for Queen Magdalena to come and then just go back for them. It took them about five minutes to reach that conclusion and by then I was hard as fucking nails, practically sweating as my body went into hyperactive, lust-filled mode.

"I thought it was very brave and remarkable what you did," Foma said quietly as he leaned in. I shivered as I felt his breath against my neck. Holy hell. I grabbed my napkin and quickly covered my mouth as my fangs popped out. Goddamn it! Why couldn't I control the fucking things around them?

"I agree," Mareo whispered as his hand moved to my thigh. "I find smart men sexy. The way you took control but yet let everyone find their way to your conclusions was impressive. I could listen to you talk for hours."

"Thank you," I practically moaned, my cock leaking at their contact.

"Are you okay?" Foma asked gently as his hand moved to my thigh as well. "Is there *anything* we can do for you?"

"No," I panted. "No. I should go." I cleared my throat and got my fangs under control as my heart sped up even more. I pushed their hands off of me and stood, keeping my napkin over my groin. "Let me know when the Queen is coming or when I'll be needed. I'm going to get some sleep. I'm still tired from the trip."

"Are you sure? We were going to hang out and catch up," Caleb hedged, looking sad for some reason. "I've missed you too, Virgil. We were all friends back before I found out who I was."

"We will tomorrow." I gave him the best smile I could muster. Caleb had been a good friend to me. He had never tried to get me to shut up when I talked. Hell, he'd gone out of his way to talk to me at parties or when he'd hang out at our house. "Just a lot going on that's been wearing me out."

"Just the thought of putting together all that information alone makes me tired for you," he agreed, nodding to the wall where the projection of the maps was up. "I can't even imagine how long that took you."

I smiled politely as I went over and grabbed my tablet. I didn't have the heart to tell him that it hadn't taken me more than a few hundred hours. It had just been something that I'd been curious about at first and I'd started tracking. Then after Caven's attack I really started putting pieces together but really, it hadn't been all that much work for me.

"Maybe Caleb should lock that up somewhere?" Stefan asked as I started to leave the room. "It's got all your evidence on there. We can't risk it going missing suddenly."

"Sure, yeah, that's fine. I have several backups too," I quickly agreed, wanting whatever would get me out of there the fastest. I darted over to Caleb and handed the tablet to him, wishing everyone good night before practically fleeing. I sighed when I was in the hallway but kept moving, several guards and staff around.

It wasn't until I reached the corridor my room was on that I was alone. I practically ripped open the first several buttons of my shirt, hot and flushed in a crazy kind of way. I leaned my forehead against the cool stone wall as I pushed the heel of my hand into my cock, begging it to behave and calm down. I'd never get to sleep with a hard-on like this. I just couldn't seem to get a handle on myself. That *had* to be werewolf blood I drank!

But why just me?

"We could help you with that," a deep voice said behind me. I didn't even have to turn around to see who it was.

"I'm fine," I lied, shaking my head even as I wanted to whimper and beg for them to take me. I went to stand back up to leave when Mareo grabbed my shoulder and spun me around. He pushed me against the wall and kissed me, pushing his larger body against mine. I gasped, shocked at the bold move, and he immediately plunged his tongue into my mouth. Kissing him back, I moaned as two sets of hands moved over my body.

"We see you, Virgil," Foma whispered in my ear as I kept kissing Mareo. Their hands guided me away from the wall and then I was moving backwards towards my room. "Let us show you how special you are like you deserve."

God that sounded so *nice*. To be appreciated for once and not worry. My mind couldn't keep up with my body, the werewolf blood racing through me like a drug. There was this little voice though that was screaming to stop this, that there was something that I needed to remember as to why I couldn't do this.

We got to my room and clothes went flying. I glanced around, wondering how we'd gotten here so fast, panting for air now that

Mareo's lips weren't plastered to mine. I had enough sense left to check that the door was closed before a naked and very gorgeous Foma got on his knees in front of me. Then suddenly the little voice with the warning was dead and I wanted everything they offered. I couldn't say no even if I wanted to with the blood flowing through me.

And I didn't want to.

"Foma has the best mouth," Mareo purred in my ear as his slick fingers moved over my crease. "Suck Virgil off, my love."

"Gladly. I love a big cock in my mouth," Foma moaned before licking the head of it. I gasped as a drop of my pre-cum fell onto his tongue. Holy fuck was that like the most erotic thing I'd ever seen.

"Please, I hurt," I whispered, my body shaking with need. "It was werewolf blood I drank. Don't tease me. It hurts."

"Do you promise to submit to us all night and be ours?" Mareo asked, holding up a hand to stop Foma when he went to swallow me down.

"Yes, I give myself to you tonight," I agreed, having just enough sense to clarify how long I was there.

"Good enough for now," he bitched but waved Foma on. I cried out as he swallowed me down, his light brown eyes staring up at me with lust, groaning at the taste of me. At the same time Mareo pushed a finger in my ass and started stretching me out. "Big cock and tight ass. Yes, you are perfect for us."

I couldn't even say anything. My body was one big nerve ending and globule of need to come. Moments later I was tugging on Foma's hair, freeing his soft curls from the tie, to signal I was coming. He shook his head and kept right on going. I cried out in bliss as I came, my balls almost hurting from the force of it. It seemed to last forever, his mouth never stopping its attention on me.

When I came back down, Mareo was pulling four fingers out of my ass and Foma drew off of me and stood. How had I missed him stretching me out like that? I gasped for air as my senses ran wild, my body craving more and everything from them. Next thing I knew I was on the bed, hands and knees, with Mareo's cock pushing against my hole and Foma's held up to my mouth. I opened for him, getting a smile as my reward as he ran his fingers through my ear-length hair.

The moment Mareo plunged into me, I remembered why I wasn't supposed to give in to them... The fae didn't bite to claim their mates. They just needed to have sex. I felt the bond snap into place and Mareo growled dangerously. "He's our mate. Were you going to tell us ever?"

"Let it go, Mareo. We can talk later. You saw there was a lot going on with him after what happened at dinner. Side with our mate and be what he needs, not another problem," Foma chastised gently.

"You're right. It doesn't matter," Mareo said as he draped himself over my back, pressing his lips to my ear. "It doesn't matter now because you're ours and we're never letting you go, Virgil."

I didn't want to hear talk like that, my lust and hormones making it hard for me to focus even as my brain tried to clear of the fog. I just wanted to fuck. I bucked my hips, letting him know to get on with it. He listened because the next thing I knew he was plowing into me as I deep throated Foma.

I came first, my body needing just a little help and Mareo's massive cock rubbing my prostate being just what did the trick. Hell, I wanted to measure Foma's dick later when I was in my right mind. Maybe in my haze I was seeing more of it than I thought there was, but I was pretty damn sure it was way over a foot long. I couldn't even take half of it into me.

Mareo bellowed out my name as he filled my body with his release. The second he was done, he pulled out of me and flopped down to the bed. Foma pushed me off of him and I rolled onto my back, blinking up at him in shock. He moved between my legs, wrapping them over his hips before plunging into me. Just like before I distantly felt the mating bond snap into place, not being able to focus on it, but knowing that my life would never be the same.

"We're going to love you so good and forever, Virgil," Foma whispered as he leaned over before kissing me stupid. I wrapped my arms around his neck and lifted my hips to meet his. We could worry about whatever else was going on later. Right then I just wanted pleasure. I wanted to let go, deal with my hormones, take the bliss they offered, and give in to my desires with the two sexiest men I'd ever seen.

Chapter 4

Foma

Our mate was so passionate that I was in awe of him. After I took him and we truly mated, I saw firsthand how werewolf blood affected a vampire. Virgil was insatiable. He'd come three times already and here he was, begging, moaning like the perfect horny man of our dreams.

"Please, take me together," he pleaded as he moved to straddle Mareo's hips.

"That's the werewolf blood talking," I hedged, shooting my mate a glance. We were both very big men. We could really hurt Virgil and there were some things that sounded good during the moment that we tended to regret later.

"No, I *love* it," Virgil moaned as he lowered himself onto Mareo's cock, not waiting for help or a green light that more sex was happening. "I had been sleeping with two wolves for months. I'd never been with men before but suddenly I can't get enough of two cocks in me. I think I'm addicted to werewolf blood though and that's why I ended things. I can't believe Caleb served some tonight. I drank more of it than I ever did from Frye or Koi though."

Oh shit. I shared a glance with Mareo and saw that he was concerned as well. Had we basically just given a recovering addict the hit to throw him back into the world of drugs? We were horrible, *horrible* people.

"Whatever our mate needs we will give it to him," Mareo said firmly, snapping me out of my thoughts. "Just tell us if it's too much."

"I will. I promise I will," Virgil whimpered with relief. Mareo pulled him down for a kiss, Virgil's hips moving on their own. I held them still as I added lube to my fingers and started to work his hole even more open so we could both fit. I realized Mareo was working Virgil's cock at the same time to try and take some of the edge off.

On top of everything else, we'd given him a lot of werewolf blood. Great. That would just be the whip cream and cherry on top of my guilt sundae.

"Just like this?" Mareo asked in a husky tone as I slipped in a second finger.

"Harder. Please, I'm almost there. I want to bite you," Virgil begged.

"You can't. Our blood needs to be despelled by the Queen first, sweetheart. Then you can drink from us all you want, okay?"

"Right, yeah. Fae blood would make me crazy," he mumbled. I heard them kissing again and quickly, but carefully stretched out my new mate. I wanted him as much as I did Mareo but I also was nervous. Mareo and I had been together for almost seven hundred years. I'd met him right before I'd turned of age... And the moment I did he'd taken my virginity and we'd realized we'd been mates.

That was a lot for Virgil to walk into. Add to that whatever was going on with his family and friends and we would need to give our mate a lot of love and attention.

When he was ready I pulled out my fingers and pushed my cock into him slowly. Virgil screamed out, his body shaking with need as he moved to take more of me inside of him. "Yes!" I blinked in shock. He was so open, so passionate with us that it was almost the exact opposite as to how his brother seemed to describe him or even what Virgil had said about himself.

So which was the real Virgil?

"Take it slow," Mareo guided as he sat up.

"Don't want to. Want this again," Virgil argued almost manically. He moved his hips as fast as he could, taking more of me into him as some of Mareo's cock slipped out of him. Then he'd impale himself on Mareo's cock until only the head of mine was still inside of him. Hell, he didn't even need our help, it seemed. "Love this feeling. Feel free. The blood is freeing. The cocks are freeing. Confusing when it's over but freeing now. I want. God how I've fought but want this."

"You can always have us now," I assured him as he started to lose rhythm. Mareo saw it too and we took hold of our smaller mate, helping him by moving our bodies to please him. Of course, at six three, most people would say Virgil was tall but since I was seven seven and Mareo was seven six… He was smaller to us.

"So perfect," Mareo moaned as he buried his face in Virgil's neck. "We have searched for you for so long, Virgil. And you're so perfect. I thank the gods for you."

"No one thinks I'm perfect," he gasped in shock. I felt his body shiver at the compliment.

"We do," I agreed, grunting as we took him faster. "You're everything we'd ever hoped for."

That seemed to push the right buttons in our mate because he threw back his head and shouted as he came, his ass clamping down on our cocks. Mareo and I climaxed together, both of us coming deep inside our mate until he was overflowing with our seed.

When we were done, and carefully pulled out of Virgil, we fell to the bed. I was spent, sated and smiling from a wonderful sex marathon. Or at least needing a breather until the next round. I could tell from the way Mareo's chest moved that he was in the same spot.

Not so much for our other mate.

"Which one of you gave me the werewolf blood?" Virgil asked darkly. My head snapped in his direction and I saw some of the lust had cleared enough that his eyes were focused… And pissed.

"You were only here a few days and gave us every sign you knew we were your mates but didn't—" I started to explain as I reached for him. He bared his fangs at me before grabbing the lube.

"Save it. I can't even think past my throbbing cock. You did this and you're going to take care of it even if that means I fuck you both raw all night." The anger in his voice broke my heart. I didn't blame him, now that we knew he had an addiction to werewolf blood and gave him too much. It was just supposed to be a little to take the edge off and open him up.

We didn't mean to screw up this badly.

"Yes, of course, anything our mate needs," I agreed, spreading my legs wide in invitation. His eyes ran over my body until he met my gaze. Then he shook his head. "I can't even look at you." I gave a startled gasp at that and then when he flipped me over. Shit. We really screwed up. He pushed two slicked-up fingers into my ass and I saw the bottle of lube land by Mareo's arm out of the corner of my eye. "Get stretched because you're next. My dick feels like it's going to fall off with need."

I couldn't peek at Mareo. I didn't blame him, which I'm sure he thought I did. I was an adult and I agreed to the plan. I would take responsibility for that. But right then if I saw the sadness or the worry on his face I would crumble. It was hard enough focusing on being with Virgil when I felt like my heart was breaking.

"I've never gotten to top before with a man," Virgil growled as he pushed inside of me minutes later when I was ready. "I like this too. This is good."

"I'm always here for whatever you want or need," I assured him. He didn't say anything, snarling instead as if it had been the wrong thing to say. Then he started a punishing pace. I moaned as my mate sent my body soaring with pleasure. When I could tell he was getting close, I took care of myself, assuming with the way he was acting that it wouldn't be all about me right then.

And rightfully so.

We finished together and moments later he was on Mareo. I watched, completely turned on by the powerful coupling of my mates.

Virgil was so strong. I bet even though he was smaller, he had just as much strength as us and I could tell Mareo loved it as much as I did.

When they were done, I saw a conflicted look cross Virgil's face as he wiped off his cock. He knew we were tired and even as pissed at us as he was, he didn't want to push his mates or take what we weren't willing to give. Our mate had a big heart obviously.

I offered him another blow job for his release, then Mareo did, both of us hoping it showed how much we already cared. Then he took us each once more. Damn, that werewolf blood made him like a machine! There was a nap after that and then several more rounds during which I lost count. Finally a few hours before the sun would be coming up he was spent.

"I will never forgive either of you for what you've done," Virgil mumbled as he collapsed onto the bed, completely exhausted. I felt cold down to my soul at his words. We couldn't even try to explain ourselves because he was out the moment he hit the pillow. I still wrapped my arms around him, Mareo doing the same from the other side of him.

"We'll change his mind and earn his forgiveness," Mareo said in a confident tone I'm sure he wasn't really feeling. There was no way he could after hearing that. Personally, I felt as if my world was crumbling around me.

* * * *

Mareo

I woke when my phone started ringing. I quickly dove for my pants on the floor, answering just in time to catch the Queen. "Good morning, your highness."

"Good morning, Mareo. I apologize for not getting back to you sooner. What is it you needed to speak to me about?"

"It's something of a personal nature but circumstances have changed and it has become very complicated on top of which I need you in person to despell my mate's blood," I answered in a nervous ramble.

"Don't bother. I won't consent to that," Virgil grunted from the bed. I felt my heart break a little more at his words as I swallowed the need to let out a sob.

"Are you okay, Mareo?" Magdalena asked carefully. "Is there something you cannot say to me over the phone?"

"I screwed up with my mate and I might lose him," I admitted, letting Virgil hear my remorse in my voice. "It's very complicated. Michan and Manus O'Hagan are gone, and it involves Desmond Marius, and please, my Queen. I, just, *please*. My friend needs help and that's why I called and now things have gotten out of hand and I need your guidance and wisdom."

There was a pause. "Is it his son you've mated?"

"Don't you dare tell her that," Virgil hissed, rolling over and giving me a death look. But of course, opening his mouth had the opposite effect because the Queen could hear everything probably.

"I'll find Desmond and Elena and we'll be there shortly," Queen Magdalena told me. "We'll fix this, Mareo. Whatever you have done cannot be so bad that he can't forgive you. We will fix this."

"Thank you, my Queen." She disconnected the call and I turned to face a pissed-off Virgil and a freaked-out Foma. "I wasn't going to tell her. I just brought up the despelling of blood because she would *have* to be here for that and it was the best reason to get her here so they could hear everything you came up with on what's been going on."

He narrowed his eyes at me. "Like I could believe a word you said after you drugged your own *mate*." Foma gasped as Virgil leapt out of bed and headed to the bathroom. "Get out of my room and get ready for the company we have coming. I don't ever want to speak to either of you again."

"Virgil, please," I begged as I scrambled to my feet and hugged him from behind. "I'm sorry. It was my idea and it was just supposed to be a little bit to get you to open up. You were so scared around us and we were sure you were our mate and we panicked when we heard you were leaving in a few days and yet you couldn't even be around us. We didn't know about your addiction and we never meant to have those effects."

He shoved me off of him and stared at me in horror. "I don't remember telling you that I thought I was addicted. Now you're going to tell everyone that. You're obviously not trustworthy."

"No, we wouldn't ever tell a soul or betray our mate like that," Foma assured him, moving next to me.

"No, you'd just loosen him up with some werewolf blood so I'd be horny and needy but not a big enough bastard to seek out help from others than my mates when they were here," he snapped. I winced as he got it exactly right. He stormed into the bathroom, slamming the door behind him.

"He'll calm down," I whispered as I moved to pick up my clothes. We needed to get out of there before he came back. Upsetting him any more right then would be the worst thing possible. "He's under a lot of pressure and with whatever is going on with his family he feels alone and now like we betrayed him. We couldn't have known that. He'll see that we're on his side and want him for who he is. He'll come around."

"Except he's not staying here but a few days," Foma reminded me as we quickly dressed before leaving.

"Then we'll have to follow him. Even if that means leaving our jobs and lives here and taking up service to the Queen, we have to show Virgil he's worth whatever sacrifice to us." I paused after we were in our room and pulled Foma into my arms. "I'm sorry, my love. I thought I knew what I was doing. I thought this would work. I thought this would give us our mate."

"I thought so too," he sighed. "It was risky but we couldn't have known all this extra stuff or that we would give him too much. We know the truth about him being our mate and have claimed him. We'll just have to do whatever we need to to show him we're worthy of him now. We can do this."

"We can." I gave him a soft kiss, loving how Foma melted against me when I was tender with him like this... Even after all our years together. "We need to get ready for the Queen and pack a few bags in case we need to leave in haste."

"You shower first then because we never behave when we shower together," he joked, giving me his best attempt at a smile.

"Luckily we heal so fast or I'd still be sore from the fucking our mate gave me," I chuckled.

"He's an animal, that's for sure. Perfect for us in every way. Now we just have to make him see that."

I nodded as I headed to the bathroom. I really hoped we could.

* * * *

Virgil

"Is it true you've mated?" Mother asked the moment she stepped through the portal. It had been five in the morning in Virginia when the Queen had called so we had slept in to past noon which wasn't all that surprising given how late we'd been up the night before.

"That's not why we really called you here," I answered instead of lying to her. Stefan and Caleb stared at me with wide eyes, not knowing what Mareo had said on the phone, just that they were coming and soon.

At least I got breakfast since Caleb had ordered a morning spread for his newly arrived guests because of the time zone difference... Even though it should have been a lunch one with what the clock said in Greece.

"So you lied to me?" Queen Magdalena asked Mareo darkly, power crackling all around her. The man dropped to one knee, whimpering for whatever he expected to come. He shot me a glance that said it all. He would take her wrath to keep the secret that we were mates if I wanted.

And for a second I didn't hate him.

"You, Foma? Are you going to tell me if this man is your mate or not?" the Queen asked. I blinked in shock as my other mate had the same reaction. Showing the respect to his Queen but not willing to betray me. "They're mates."

"We're mates," I said at the same time, not wanting them to get hurt. Then I blinked at the Queen. "Wait—What?"

"I was testing them," she chuckled, gesturing for them to stand. "If you weren't mates then it was a ruse to get us here for reasons that couldn't be stated on the phone and we'd understand that. But they were distressed so I wanted to know what's going on without having to read their minds and see what is private. But they wouldn't deny you and they wouldn't admit to it when you obviously didn't want it known. So they said nothing and were willing to take the punishment."

"I saw that," I agreed, not looking at them. "Look, I don't know what Mareo originally called you for, your highness, but our being mates is not why we wanted you here now."

"It is for us," Foma said gently as he stepped closer to me and my mother who was watching this all like a tennis match. "We very much want Queen Magdalena to despell our blood so you can claim us and take sustenance from us."

"That's *never* going to fucking happen," I snarled at him.

"Virgil!" my parents gasped together but it was my father who went on. "I'm disappointed in you, son. I never thought you would deny your mates."

"Of course it's my fault," I chuckled bitterly. "Unliked, off in his own world, Virgil has to have screwed this up somehow, right?" I saw that both of them pretty much had assumed that. I threw back my head and laughed before focusing on Stefan. "And yet you had *so* much faith that they would see the truth and the real me. Still think they're going to listen for more than two seconds to everything I told you and showed you last night?"

"Virgil, you have to tell them," Stefan implored me. "I don't know what else is going on here but just tell Mother and Father whatever it is so they know the truth. We need to get King Rylan here and start handling everything you discovered. Michan and Manus could be in grave danger. I'm not saying what happened with your mates or finding them isn't important but isn't it something that can be put off until later?"

"I was *trying* to do that," I reminded him.

"Just tell us why you'd deny your mates, son," Father said gently, glancing between us. Then I saw the pitied look he shot my way as if expecting I had a mess of my making to clean up.

"Because they *drugged* me!" I bellowed. "I didn't tell them immediately they were my mates, thrown off by the fact that there were *two* of them and, I don't know, *male*. So at dinner, just hours after meeting me, having guessed that we were mates, they dosed me with werewolf blood."

"You took him against his will?" Queen Magdalena snarled as power crackled around her again.

"Oh no, I was *very* willing," I snickered, pissed off but not wanting to make this any worse than it was. "I was just so out of my mind with lust I forgot that the fae didn't need to bite to claim, that you do it during sex. Of course, they didn't know for sure because I didn't tell them so they didn't claim me against my will. But they gave me just a bit more than the amount of blood to loosen me up that they were shooting for and didn't know that I've been worried I'm addicted to it." I shot them both a dirty look. "Did I miss anything or is that fairly accurate?"

"We just thought—" Foma started to explain sadly but I was too into my rant.

I spun on my parents next. "Thanks for the support and the assumptions your awkward son was to blame for all of this. Now do you want to listen to my answers as to what has been going on or should we just assume I'm dense too and all end up dead? I mean, I could always shut my mouth, keep quiet of my stupid ramblings, and go to my room before I embarrass you any further."

I watched as Father's face paled as the words sunk home.

"Virgil, that was once when you were a boy," he said gently as he stepped closer to me. I shook my head and moved away. "You were telling the head of the East Coast High Council that his horse was lame and he should take better care of his animals and pay attention. I was angry and embarrassed."

"Yeah, you made that *perfectly* clear, Father. Didn't matter that I was right, did it? Wasn't something to be proud of that your *seven-year-old* son figured out a horse was lame but it was embarrassing."

"Yes, you were right, but you still insulted the man by saying he should pay attention," he hedged. "That's why I was embarrassed."

"Well, he should have. A child is blunt and any adult should understand that. He asked me what I thought of the horse. I was honest and you were pissed and embarrassed. But don't worry, you weren't the only one to ever have that reaction. I can name many times when every member of our family has pulled the exact same thing on me."

"That's why you're so quiet and don't tell them how smart you are," Patrick whispered as if figuring out the last piece of the puzzle.

"And why you were so scared to tell us what you'd found last night," Stefan added. "Then quick to say someone else could fill in everyone else."

"Because every time you've opened your mouth to tell them what you know or give them the answers they seek, you end up wounded," Mareo surmised. I met his eyes and did a double take at his reaction.

It wasn't pity or disbelief and didn't hold any signs that maybe I was overreacting or being a baby... He looked sympathetic like he'd been in my shoes and knew exactly how I felt.

"Why is this all coming up now though, Virgil?" Queen Magdalena asked me. I shook my head and she sighed. "Please don't make me read your mind for the answer. I don't like doing that but something more is going on here than a family issue and I'm worried."

"It might be easier if you just see it," I answered as I held out my hand. "And then we should get everyone back home, invite the others over, and get this done in one shot."

"You don't think we should do this here?" Caleb asked quietly.

I shook my head. "I realized while we were waiting that would be a bad idea. You have too many people in the palace who you haven't checked where they originally come from given this new information. We know our house is clean of bugs and listening devices and potentially disloyal ears."

"This is big," Father said curiously, glancing between us.

"Virgil figured it all out and will probably save us all," Caleb admitted. I wouldn't have gone that far or anything, but it was nice that someone did.

"Honeymoon over apparently," Patrick chuckled sadly.

"Sorry, my love. It's just not safe after what Virgil told us," Stefan said quietly as I felt the Queen focus on me. I took a deep breath and didn't hide what had been going on with the wolves I'd slept with, the blood, Riley, and my blowup over it... And that was before Mareo and Foma pulled their shit.

"That was—" She bit her lip and shook her head. "I need a drink for you, my dear. And for the record I've witnessed Riley doing many of the same things he's charged you with so I'd be more than happy to remind him of that."

"Thank you, your highness," I chuckled as I raised her hand to my lips. "But I don't want to fight. He probably was trying to help and thought he was doing the right thing and knew what was really going on. He just didn't. He doesn't know as much as he thinks he does. Maybe I'll thank him one day because apparently it was the straw that broke the camel's back and I'm done giving a shit who I'm embarrassing, who doesn't like what I have to say, or who might get pissed off."

"I think you're long overdue for that attitude and it's understandable how angry you are. Might I make a suggestion though?"

"Of course." She was a good person, wise and kind, and I knew she wouldn't steer me the wrong way.

"You still might want to speak with Ayden. What we see as a child can be quite different than what happened and we only realize that sometimes after age and perspective. I think yours might have been taken away with the amount of people it happened with."

"You saw that too?" I whispered, my cheeks heating up.

"Some." She shrugged. "It was on your mind so it was hard not to. Time to be honest and move past what's happened and focus on what's best for you. Even if that means not conforming with what the rest of your family does."

"We don't care that he's mated to two men," Mother said, hurt in her voice.

"Not what I was talking about," the Queen clarified. My parents shot me a look and I sighed as the Queen gave me a nod.

"I bought one of the houses in the development under a different name. Tyler doesn't even know. I had Ferris help me, saying it was for one of the margays. I don't want to live at the estate or with all of you."

My mother turned away as if I'd just slapped her as my father's eyes filled with sadness. Yeah, that's about how I saw that going.

"Whatever, it's fine. Forget it," I quickly said. "I'm going to go grab my stuff so we can get home and get this over with." I hurried away before anyone could say anything. Maybe I should just leave the coven? After we dealt with the threat of Councilman Dubois and his traitor in our coven maybe I should just start over somewhere else.

Just as I got to my room I realized my mates were running after me. I had just enough time to flick them off before slamming the door in their face. Yeah, moving somewhere and starting all over where no one knew me or could find me sounded pretty damn good actually.

Chapter 5

Several hours later we were all at the Marius estate, gathered in the media room, and I had just finished giving them the same presentation I had last night. And by *them* I mean my entire family and their mates, my mates, who wouldn't stay in Greece even though I told them they weren't welcome. My mother was to thank for that. Along with the Queen, several of her people, Elder Dawson, Barnabas and his mates, King Rylan and his mates, Isaac, Dillon, Darcy, and their mates… Basically *everyone*.

"So what do we do now?" Caven asked me after several minutes of silence, everyone digesting what I said.

"You believe me?" I was shocked, not even able to school my reaction in time and letting everyone see that.

"Yeah, why wouldn't I?" he chuckled. "That was awesome, Virgil. I mean, I couldn't have put that all together ever if you gave me half those answers. When people ask me how it all went down and how this all came to light I'm going to totally be like 'It was my badass, big-brained brother-in-law who figured it all out thank you very much.' I mean, that was just, wow."

"Thanks, Caven." I gave him the first real smile I'd felt in a long time. "I think we should do some recon. I have some potential sites that Councilman Dubois owns off the books and through dummy corporations. They're remote and would be good places for an evil headquarters or nefarious dealings. But we couldn't let all the warriors in on it because we have a traitor."

"I also think I should get closer to this Councilman," Queen Magdalena hedged. "I could read his mind if he doesn't already know that I could. And if he does, that might be a good way to out him as well."

"But would that be wise?" Father asked, glancing at Mother. "Could he do more damage, be more dangerous if he knows we're onto him? He won't have to hide what's really going on then."

"That's a valid point," King Rylan agreed. I put up the map of the locations I'd found in case they wanted it as a reference, excited that I was being taken seriously for once and they actually believed me.

"How did you really figure all this out, Virgil?" Riley asked me quietly. I blinked at him in shock and then growled, pissed he just peed on my parade.

"Oh fuck off, Riley. You're not the only intelligent one in the room."

"That's not what I—" he argued, looking taken aback. I didn't care though. I was still hurt from yesterday.

"You know, for someone so smart it's surprising how dense you can be," I said, smirking when I saw how he bristled. "I know you have interns now, but did you think you had little minions or elves before to help you?"

"What are you talking about?"

I raised an eyebrow at him, waiting for him to fill in the gaps. When I saw he wouldn't I couldn't hold it in anymore now that I knew he'd been judging me. "Funny how you'd find different handwriting on your notes or equations changed when you woke up and went back to it, isn't it?"

"You sabotaged my work!" he gasped and I blew. Whatever piece of me that was still calm was gone at the accusation.

"I didn't sabotage shit!" I bellowed. "I fixed your formulas more times than I can remember. You're a doctor but not the best chemist sometimes. I came up with the perfect ultraviolet compound. Hell, I came up with the equation for the collapsible bullets! Your numbers were off and I didn't want anyone to get hurt when they exploded instead of melted so I *helped you*! Go check your notes and see the different handwriting if you don't believe me."

"Why would you do that? Why would you stick your nose in my work?" he growled, still annoyed. "Who were you to—"

"You singed my father's retinas with a chemical in *our* home, Riley," I practically snarled. "Fine, I get everyone else trusting you since they don't know what it would all mean, especially Micah because he loves you. But I did know what it was. So of *course* I would go see what it really was and make sure Father was okay! I found your notes and realized what you were trying to do. I looked it over and saw how to speed up the process so I changed your formulas."

"And the bullets?" he asked, calm now but still shocked if his rapid blinking was any indication.

"I was curious and couldn't sleep. You and Stefan were talking about it and said you were going to make some the next day and start testing them. I was worried. He knows a lot about guns, but guns involve gun powder which is explosive. He's my brother and Micah almost lost you once and I didn't want him to crumble if you got hurt. So I nosed around and fixed what you had. The casing was too thin. It would have exploded trying to come out of the gun and blown in your faces."

"Why didn't you ever tell us this?" Father inquired quietly. I froze, my chest heaving as I glanced at my father. Realizing I'd been much louder than I thought I was, I slowly turned to face him and understood I'd had *everyone's* attention. Shit.

"Because it didn't matter who did what. It was done and we had a better weapon," I answered honestly. "It was Riley's idea and Stefan was a huge help. I didn't want to make it like Riley couldn't do it on his own after everything he'd been through and needed to do it for his own peace of mind. Plus, he didn't know me. I couldn't get any of you to listen to me most of the time so why would a stranger?"

"Then why tell us the truth now?" Micah asked.

"He pissed me off," I growled, gesturing to his mate. "I come to him for help, finally opening up to someone about something, and he's lecturing me about all my faults. Now he's got the balls to ask me how I really came up with all of this like I'm too stupid to do the research and have figured it out." I narrowed my eyes at Riley. "I'm sorry I bruised your ego and you weren't the one to give us all the answers like always, but don't you dare assume I'm lying or cheated somehow."

"I wasn't, Virgil, I swear. I just thought it was odd that you had all this done and figured it entirely out when everyone else didn't seem to have the first part of this deciphered. I was just trying to figure out your process."

"Must be all that time alone, my OCD tendencies trying to make everything fit into a box," I shouted. "Yes! Okay? I see a problem and I want to make it fit. There were points not adding up in my mind so I sat down and solved the problem. How is that *any* different than what you do all the time? Why am I such an unlikable social reject?"

"Because you don't handle things well," he answered. "You don't know how to be a person and understand that the human condition and life can't fit in a box!" Riley blinked at me in shock like he couldn't believe he just admitted that and I heard several gasps throughout the room. I felt rage swarm through me and I actually pulled back my arm to deck him but in a flash my mates were there holding me back.

"You don't want to do that. His pride is hurt after you just let the cat out that he didn't create all the weapons on his own. Now he's wondering what else you did instead of him and he's lashing out. You're better than that, Virgil. Don't sink to that level," Mareo said gently.

"Come on. Let's take a walk and you can yell at us some more," Foma agreed as he kissed my neck. "You're pissed at us so when he adds to that, what he says seems that much worse. Walk away and you can hash it out with him later after you kick our asses. Don't break things with your brother because you beat on his mate."

That hit home and I glanced at Micah who had moved Riley behind him but looked torn and tortured. I immediately let go and nodded. "Okay. Let's take a walk."

They both sighed and Mareo kissed the other side of my neck. "Thank you, my mate."

"Don't call me that or I really will kick both your asses," I bitched as I pulled away from them. I stormed out of the media room. We got as far as the kitchen and suddenly Ayden was there.

"I'm sorry, Virgil, but I have to," he whispered. He grabbed my hand as he reached for Mareo's hand. Foma got the idea and touched him too. Suddenly we were thrown into a memory.

"Shifter blood to vampires is like strong alcohol to humans," Caleb explained as he rubbed his hand over the back of his neck. *"Maybe tequila? I've heard tequila can make them a little horny too. So let's go with that. It would loosen our tongue, making us honest, and rev up our sex drive. That's my understanding but I've never tried it."*

I felt Mareo's hope that maybe everything wasn't lost. It wasn't the best plan but given I'd shown them signs that I was their mate but completely closed off to their advances and not even willing to talk to them, he was desperate. He glanced at Foma and I saw our mate through his eyes... All the pain Foma had felt at the centuries of not being able to find their other mate.

Then it was like a montage of the memories after they'd been with someone, hoping the attraction they'd felt with that person would lead them to their mate. I saw all the tears they'd cried, all the hope smashed, and even the decision to leave their plane, saying good-bye to everything they'd known.

"I'm scared, Mareo," Foma admitted as he glanced at the portal. *"What if we don't like this world? Maybe our mate isn't born yet and we leave?"*

"The Queen assured us that we can come back," Mareo said gently. "We'll visit every few decades and see if he's been born. I just believe in my heart he's not fae. Our mate will be worth searching for, yeah?"

"Okay, we can do this," Foma whispered. "You're right. Finding our mate will be worth traveling and living in this new world, no matter how scared we might be. He could be searching for us, all alone and not able to find us if we don't cross over."

"We'll find him, my love. No matter how long it takes or what I have to do, I will find him for you. I swear it. I will find the other part of our soul and make us a family."

"You're enough for me, Mareo. You know that," Foma said quietly.

"I know that. I love you so much," Mareo replied. *But I felt his need to find me, and his desire to give Foma the family he'd never really had. He wanted Foma to have everything and was determined nothing would stop him.*

Next it was when they realized I might be their mate and when I had denied them, telling them to leave me alone. I felt their despair and grief that they'd searched hundreds of years for me and I rejected them. Even more than that, they were worried for me. They saw something was going on with me and wanted to help. They thought if I realized I wasn't alone, that they were there for me, it would comfort me.

"I forgive you," I whispered as we came back to the present. "You didn't understand what the blood would really do to me and didn't mean to trick or trap me. You just wanted to help break down the walls I put up."

"Yes," Mareo breathed. "We didn't want to hurt you. We wanted to help, to show you we would do anything for you."

"I believe you." I swallowed loudly and looked down at Ayden. "Thank you. You saved me all that pain and anguish of having to try and deal with what I saw as their betrayal and process this alone."

"You've got enough going on. You didn't need a misunderstanding and good intentions to ruin something that could make you so happy if you let it," he said with a smile. I leaned down and kissed his cheek. "Besides, we're family. Family doesn't ever keep their noses out of each other's business."

"Amen to that," I chuckled. "Can I see you again soon? I need to deal with some other things and what Riley said to me. I want to let go and move on even if it's away from my family. I want to heal and be the man my mates deserve after having searched for me for so long."

"Of course but there's one more thing I want to show just you. I think it will answer some of your questions," he hedged. "We need your mother though too. I have a feeling you don't know the full story but only a part. Elena isn't mean."

"No, she's not," I agreed, not sure what he was talking about. I nodded and realized my mother was there in the kitchen. She came over hesitantly and took Ayden's hand as I did the same. Seconds later we were in a memory from when I was a small boy.

"Desmond, I want to talk to you about Virgil," she said as they sat in Father's study. I hadn't been able to sleep, nightmares about what I'd been reading about demons keeping me up, and I'd gone to find them. They had no idea I was there listening. "I worry he's not normal."

"What do you mean, my love? I know he's oddly blunt and doesn't seem to understand some things that the others have by his age, but maybe he's just a little slow."

"Yes, I know, but at the same time, his studies show the opposite. He learns at a rapid pace. He hasn't been focusing like he was and I realized he was bored. He's accelerated way past where his brothers were at his age."

"So he's smart. That's good news," Father said but then frowned when Mother shook her head. "Just tell me, Elena. Whatever it is we can figure it out."

"It's almost like he learns things backwards. I don't understand it. Maybe I'm not able to teach him. I think he's special, Desmond." It was clear from the way she said the word it wasn't the kind of special that a child would want to hear his parents talk about them but as in special needs. *"I just wish he was normal. I don't—"*

I didn't stay to listen to any more, racing back to my room and crying myself to sleep that night and many nights after. My parents didn't like me. I wasn't like the others and it upset them. I swore that I would try to be the most normal child for them from that moment on so I didn't upset my mother or embarrass my father again. I would figure out a way to be normal.

"Oh, Virgil," my mother sobbed. "You weren't supposed to hear that. You only heard part of it and it's not what I meant. We loved you always. I was upset at my own failings that I didn't think I could give you what you needed."

"I heard what you said, Mother," I whispered. "I didn't even remember that until now." I glanced at Ayden. "I get what you were saying. It explains so much. Why I wanted to fit every mold, not tell anyone ever, and mate a female, have lots of children, and be normal."

"Normal's boring." Ayden shrugged and then gave me a wink. "Now see what your mother felt and what you couldn't understand as a child."

"Desmond, I want to talk to you about Virgil," she said, trying to think of how to phrase what she wanted to say. It wasn't like there were gifted schools back then and especially not for vampires. *"I worry he's not normal."*

"What do you mean, my love? I know he's oddly blunt and doesn't seem to understand some things that the others have by his age, but maybe he's just a little slow."

"Yes, I know, but at the same time, his studies show the opposite. He learns at a rapid pace. He hasn't been focusing like he was and I realized he was bored. He's accelerated way past where his brothers

were at his age." She didn't know how to help me see things in a way I would understand them. She thought *if* she *was smarter she could explain the world and what I needed to know in a way I would understand. God, she was so hard on herself!*

"So he's smart. That's good news," Father said but then frowned when Mother shook her head. "Just tell me, Elena. Whatever it is we can figure it out."

"It's almost like he learns things backwards. I don't understand it. Maybe I'm not able to teach him. I think he's special, Desmond." As much as she loved me for who I was and was proud of me, she worried how my life would be in a harsh world. "I just wish he was normal. I don't know if I can be what he needs. He's gifted. We have a very *gifted* son."

"But with that comes something you're worried about?" Father figured out. Mother nodded and sighed.

"Yes, he doesn't see the world as we do. I fret over this. I'm proud of him. As his mother I love the fact that he sees things differently, is special, and his own person, smart and bright. But also I'm scared that others will pick on him or it will hurt his chances of fitting in. It's a hard world we live in. People fear anything different."

"Like telling Abraham Dragos he wasn't a logical man who didn't appreciate his own people by saying women couldn't be warriors," Father drawled. "Virgil's right and his logic was astounding but I could not believe he just started telling the man that."

"I know it was rude for a child to speak to an adult like that but part of me was just trying not to laugh. Did you see Abraham's face?" Mother giggled, shaking her head. "But yes, like that. I know Virgil still doesn't understand what he did wrong. He just sees we got mad at him for telling us the truth. Do you see how confusing that can be to a small boy?"

"Yes, but we can't just excuse the behavior or he'll make enemies. Abraham was furious. Whether Virgil is eight or not, I thought

Abraham was going to slap him across the room. If I hadn't been there he might have. Virgil could get hurt and I'd never forgive myself. We have to figure out a way to teach him propriety. It's not right and it's not fair, it's just the way of the world. I'm sorry it's going to make him feel like he's done something wrong or it's his fault but it will keep him safe."

"But at what cost?" Mother whispered. "He's special and gifted. I don't want that crushed so he can fit the mold of a warrior and what our society says he should be as a child of a founding family."

"That's for him to decide when he's older," Father said after a few moments. "For now, we protect him. He can be whoever he wants when he's old enough to understand it all but if we don't help him now he could damage his future in ways that can't be undone."

"Right because we ever really understand life," Mother drawled.

"Amen to that," Father snickered. He hugged her close and kissed her cheek.

"You thought I was the good kind of special," I whispered as we came back out of the memory.

"Of course I did," she cried, tears streaming down her cheeks. "You were my special little genius who saw the world in his own way. I assumed I failed you. And then it was just no longer an issue. I thought—I'm not sure what I did exactly. That was when Gabriel got hurt badly on a mission and then suddenly you changed. I supposed it was almost losing your brother that made you see the world differently. I never understood. I am *so* sorry you ever felt that way."

"Me too," I mumbled, pulling away. I got that I didn't take everything the way it was meant but it wasn't just that *one* moment that left me feeling the way I did about my family. There had been comments over the years from my brothers, calling me abnormal or that I was odd, strange, and about a dozen other names. I couldn't just let this all go. "I need some air."

"Please don't leave, Virgil. We're sorry," Father said gently as he pulled my mother into his arms. "I don't know what just happened but I know we love you. We can figure out whatever I'm missing here."

"I'm just—I need—I just want—" I stuttered, never having been able to tell my parents *no* or hurt them.

"We're just taking a walk outside and getting some fresh air," Mareo said quickly before leading me to the terrace doors. "We're not leaving." Foma was right there and the moment we were outside I started shaking with silent sobs. "It's okay, Virgil. Just breathe."

"I don't know how to process this. I want to weep for the boy I was that thought my parents were so ashamed of me," I whispered as I sank to my knees in the grass. "Riley doesn't like me and I wonder which of my brothers think that. Hell, it seems the only people who *do* are the ones who barely know me. Or maybe they do know me. Caven and Patrick like me."

"We like you," Foma assured me as he rubbed my back. "I think you're amazing. You forgave us after seeing what happened. Do you know how rare that is? Most would have dragged it out and still been upset that we wanted to slip a few drinks into you to get you to loosen up."

"What would be the point of that?" I shrugged. "I *was* closed off. I *was* scared. I understood why you did it and after seeing how long you looked for me and how desperately you wanted to find me I feel horrible I made you even have to come up with such a plan."

"As I said, amazing," he whispered as he kissed my cheek. "Tell us what you want, Virgil. Do you want to live in your new house you talked of in Greece? We would live there with you if you wanted."

"Really?" Now I felt shy. I'd been so busy being pissed at them I'd not thought of a future with them.

"We like Caleb, Liam, and Lorcan, but we're not palace people," Mareo admitted with a shrug. "We were closer to there when we heard of the fae coming over so we decided to help our people. My family was lost to me a long time ago and Foma was an orphan from a young age. You might not want to live with your family but I don't think moving away from them right now would be best. This house is still close, yes?"

"Yeah, like ten minutes away," I sighed, leaning into his strong body. "It's all done. I picked out my furniture and everything. I want to see this thing with Dubois through though. I think there's more going on than I know."

"How so?" Foma asked.

I bit my lower lip, wondering if they'd think I was nuts if I admitted what I could barely grasp myself. Then I decided to keep with my newfound honesty. "The amount of demons still bothers me. There's been too many. I mean, hordes of them keep attacking. Where are they all coming from? I'm missing something."

"Then we shall investigate this at your side until you find your answers," Mareo assured me. How long I had waited to hear something like that and feel like I wasn't alone always!

"Then we should get my blood despelled if we're going to be real mates and I'm ever going to claim you," I said quietly.

"Yes!" Foma exclaimed, tackling me to the ground in joy. I laughed as Mareo joined in, both of them kissing me silly. Oh hell, did they know how to set my body on fire. I would seriously have to send Ayden several gifts for his help. He saved my mating and handed me everything I'd ever wanted.

Chapter 6

Foma

"Are you sure?" I asked Virgil again. Once he had decided to despell our blood we had raced inside and found the Queen. Now I was worried we were pushing him too fast with everything else he had going on.

"Yes. I forgive you both. I want this. I want to be happy and screw being normal or what I saw for my life," he assured me again.

"But you wanted a female mate, and children, and that white picket fence." I cupped his cheek, rubbing my thumb over his skin as I stared into those gorgeous kelly-green eyes. "I don't want to lose you but if that's what will make you happy then we have to let you go."

"Don't ever let me go." Virgil mashed his mouth down to mine, kissing me deeply and moving his hips against me until the Queen cleared her throat. I stilled my mate, who was straddling my lap, and sighed as we pulled apart. "We can still have children if we want one day and we'll get a damn fence. You can paint it white while shirtless and I'll be happier than I ever would if you had boobs."

"Good to know," I snickered, shaking my head.

I liked how he was coming out of his shell. I knew it was hard for him but I was also proud of him. It wasn't easy to say *screw everyone and I am who I am* but here he was doing it. I tilted my neck, offering it up to him, and I saw his eyes glaze over. He followed the Queen's instructions, waiting for her to chant the words and make my blood okay for him and then he took a small sip to complete the process.

"You can take more," I offered when he pulled away, worried and a little hurt he stopped so soon.

Virgil smiled at me and then pressed his lips to my ear. "It's a very sacred and erotic act between mates. I take much more and we're going to be on the floor fucking in front of your Queen and my parents. I didn't think that's how you wanted them to get to know you."

"No, that would be awkward," I agreed. He gave me a quick kiss before sliding off my lap. I watched as he did the exact same thing with Mareo and then it was over. Our blood was officially safe for him to drink and he'd never need another to give him sustenance of that kind. Just as we were finishing up, Barnabas, the Queen's grandson and head of the High Council here, came into the kitchen.

"The Council will be assembling in a bit to hear what Virgil has found out. We should leave."

"Wait, you want me to speak to the High Council?" Virgil exclaimed, almost falling off Mareo's lap. "No. Someone else can do it."

"Someone else might be able to repeat what you said but they won't know the answers to any additional questions that might be asked," Barnabas explained with a tight smile. "We need you to do it, Virgil. I'm sorry. Time is of the essence and lives are at stake. I hate to ask this of you but your people need you."

"Fine, okay," Virgil mumbled, his good mood gone just like that.

"We'll be right there with you," Mareo assured him as they stood and we hugged him together. "Then we can have some time to ourselves while they discuss their options. Yes?"

"I'd like that." I smiled as Virgil's cheeks heated up, obviously understanding that we wanted him to claim us. "And then maybe you'd like to see the house?"

"Whatever you'd like, our mate," I agreed, giving him a loud kiss. He snickered and rolled his eyes at my antics. That's what I'd been going for. We quickly collected his tablet and some sandwiches for the drive since our mate *still* hadn't gotten a chance to eat.

Virgil wanted to take his own car so we could come and go as we wanted, but Mareo asked if the wolf Alpha he was related to could join us. We needed him for a personal matter which is why he had put the call in to the Queen.

"Caven, Gabriel, could you guys ride with us?" Virgil called out as his family was getting into several different cars. "I'm sure you can catch a ride back with someone later because we're going to leave right away but I want to talk with you guys."

"Yeah, sure," the man who looked just like our mate agreed. That had to be Gabriel. Mareo told me to drive so that Virgil could eat and he'd hop in the back of the SUV to talk to the Alpha.

"Are you sure this is a good idea?" I asked quietly. "I don't want Virgil to worry we still have feelings for Jordy. He's got so much going on and we need to put our mate first."

"I know, but Jordy's our friend. Whatever is going on in his pack, we can't just leave him there and not help. We promised. Virgil's a good man and will understand."

I nodded. It was the right thing to do. I just didn't want to upset Virgil, especially after he'd just forgiven us. I got in the driver's seat as Mareo got in the one behind me, glancing in the rearview mirror when I heard him groan.

"And of course you heard all that because you're an Alpha wolf," my mate mumbled once we were all in and seat belts on. "We can explain."

"All I heard is you're trying to do right by your friend while taking Virgil's feelings into consideration," Caven said gently as I started up the car. I glanced at Virgil who had turned in his seat and was watching what was going on like a tennis match that confused him. Shit. "Which is good because I adore Virgil and would be really pissed if you still had feelings for another man."

"It's not like that," I blurted out as I glanced at our mate. "As you were involved with someone but ended it before we met, we were too. Except we ended it when we found you. But it wasn't serious. Not on either side. But we like him. He's our friend and he needs our help."

"I'm not mad," Virgil chuckled before biting his sandwich. I pulled out of the parking spot in the massive garage and followed the caravan of vehicles. At least I didn't need directions to where we were going. "You've had sex before me? Oh no, alert the media! I get it. It's all good. I'm not going to shun the wolves I was sleeping with because I found you guys. All that matters now is how we feel about each other and that no one else is on our hearts."

"No, only you and Mareo, I swear," I assured him and sighed in relief.

"Virgil, you were sleeping with members of my pack?" Caven asked with big eyes. "How did I not know this?"

"Because I asked them not to tell since I didn't know how to process what I wanted suddenly and they were good friends and never told. It's not the Alpha's business to know who's sleeping with whom, Caven."

"Right, no, sorry, I know that, it's just, I didn't see that coming," the little Alpha rambled. "Well, I'm glad they were loyal and good to you. Yeah, good, okay."

"So our friend, Jordy, asked us if we could talk to the wolf Alpha in this coven when he found out we'd discovered our mate and he was from here," Mareo hedged. "We didn't know this because we would have helped sooner or given him sanctuary, but he's having problems with his pack. He wants out but his Alpha won't let him leave and none of the packs around him will go against his Alpha."

"Did he tell you why he's in trouble or what was the reason he wanted to leave?" Caven asked after a moment of thought.

"No, he wouldn't tell us. He said wolf business is supposed to stay in the pack but I bet he'd tell you," I answered. "I can tell you that

Jordy's a nice guy. Caleb can attest to that as well. He's sweet, loyal, kind, shy, and just a good person."

"If I didn't know you liked me so much I might start to get jealous now," Virgil mumbled quietly as he stared at his sandwich.

"I have a lot more adjectives that I feel about you, my mate," I said, letting my voice get husky as I took his free hand. "I will gladly list them for you later when you're drinking from me."

"I'll hold you to that." I gave him a wink before focusing back on the road.

"Yeah, I don't know the answer to that either," Mareo said, getting back to Caven's question. "He just said he always seems to be in trouble no matter what he does." There was a pause and I glanced in the mirror to see him staring at Caven funny.

"What do you see? The eyes?" I asked, meeting his gaze when it snapped to mine. "Yeah, I thought that odd too."

"That's what it is!" Mareo exclaimed as he tapped my arm as if showing me he was grateful for the answer. "I couldn't put my finger on it but you're right. He's got Jordy's eyes. I thought it was contacts Jordy wore or something."

"Wait, back up," Caven said firmly. "This wolf has purple eyes like mine?"

"Yeah, is that a big deal? We've never seen a wolf with them before," Mareo said.

"Yeah, it's a really big deal and I'm worried I might know what his pack's doing to him," Caven growled as he pulled out his phone. "Does he have any siblings?"

"I don't know," I answered. Shit. What had we walked into now?

"Get him on the phone and find out," Caven ordered. "Also how fast he wants out of there. I'm calling Elder Dawson and letting him know there's a Kappa who wants out of their pack. He's more than welcome to join mine and tell him we've got Kappas here so he won't be alone or mistreated."

"Right, okay, sure, thanks," Mareo rambled. I glanced at Virgil and he gave me a smile. I wasn't sure what was going on but I knew that wasn't a happy smile. It was more an *I'll fill you in later and it's going to be okay* gesture. Crap.

* * * *

Mareo

"Hey, Jordy, can you talk?" I asked quietly as I turned towards the window of the vehicle.

"Yeah, um, sure, but not freely," he mumbled and then I heard a sniffle. "Someone heard what I asked of you and I got in trouble. I'm not allowed to leave the Alpha house and my Alpha resigned my position for me. Thanks for trying though and it was nice knowing—"

"This isn't over, Jordy," I growled. "The Alpha here in America knows one of your elders. He has purple eyes like you and says there's Kappas in the pack so if you want to come here he can get you out and you'll be treated well here. Alpha Caven wants to know if you have siblings?"

"No, it's just me," he whispered. "Can he really help me?"

"I trust him, Jordy." I leaned over and waited for Caven to pause in his conversation. "No siblings. Alpha found out he was trying to leave the pack and now he's confined to the Alpha house and the bastard resigned from Jordy's job for him."

"Fuck that. Tell Jordy to pack what he can and be ready. We're going to get him help and get him out of there," Caven growled.

"I heard, thank you, Mareo. Thank Foma and thank the Alpha. I just want to be safe," Jordy whispered sadly.

"Why didn't you tell us this was going on?"

"And what would you have done? Come in and tried to rescue me? Pissed off a bunch of wolves and potentially ruined the fae's alliance with the wolves in the area?"

"No, I would have called my Queen and *she* would have done it," I chuckled, smiling fondly. I really did love that woman as did all of her people. "She cares not for the typical politics and games. We are all just people to her and if someone needs help and their own kind are not there for them then it's our responsibility as those who can help *to* help if asked."

"That's nice. I wish more people were like that."

"I get the feeling the coven here is like that," I assured him.

"We are," the few in the car from this coven agreed.

"That's good to know," Jordy giggled. "Thank them for me and I look forward to meeting them."

"Will do." I said good-bye and hung up just as Caven did. He sighed and looked at me with worried eyes.

"The Alpha there never told our council or elders that there was a Kappa born or transferred into the pack. He's been hiding Jordy from everyone. I'm surprised he even let Jordy take the job at Caleb's. Elder Dawson knows an elder in the area who's going to handle it and get Jordy to sanctuary until the Queen can open a portal. She and Elder Dawson agree that they don't want something *happening* in transit if we stick Jordy on a plane."

"Thank you for agreeing to help and doing so this quickly," I replied, letting my sincerity seep into my voice. "Jordy deserves a good life and to be happy. He's been an asset to Caleb and knows how to work the system and all the rules well."

"He might be a good Bevin to your Rylan, Caven," Virgil suggested as he finished off his sandwich. "You were saying that you wanted an assistant to help you integrate the pack and handle the stuff you don't have time for. I know you're looking for Betas and enforcers like Tyler was, but it's a start."

"Yeah, that's actually a great idea," Caven agreed. He leaned forward and gave my mate a big kiss on the lips. "I love that you've started opening your mouth more. Anything else you've got for me?

Can you go visit another part of the world and bring me back some badass wolves to be my Betas?"

"Actually, we might be able to help with that," Foma hedged as I darted a glance to him in the rearview mirror. I nodded, letting him know I was okay with the idea. "You good with the French?"

"I don't have a problem with French people. Don't really know any either though. Why?" Caven raised an eyebrow and glanced between us.

"We spent a while outside Paris about a decade ago," I explained.

Gabriel glanced between us, and seeing the chance to get to know his brother's mates, he took it. "What were you guys doing there? Working?"

"Searching for our mate," Foma answered honestly and smiled at Virgil. "We've been searching for six hundred years."

"Wow. That's romantic," Caven whispered.

"I searched for you almost that long," Gabriel growled.

"Yes, and I was totally worth it. But I get the feeling they traveled all over to search for their mate," Caven replied.

"We did," I admitted. "I met Foma before he was of age and we were mates. From that moment we took just about every available person on our plane to our bed in hopes to find our other mate. When we realized they weren't there, we crossed into your world. Sure, we've gone back and looked—"

"And by *looked* you mean fucked them silly," Virgil chuckled.

"I don't know how you're so cool with that and not a growling, jealous ogre," Gabriel said with a tone of awe. "I still wig if I even hear that Caven was with someone."

"I've been with people." Virgil shrugged and I was proud of my mate's sensibleness. "So have they. Doesn't mean they'd rather be with anyone else but me. I look at it as they've had a *lot* of practice in perfecting all the moves that will bring me centuries of big, fat, dopey smiles."

"I like it. Yes, we will go with that," I agreed, reaching for his hand. He gave me a wink and I turned back to his brother and the Alpha. "We crossed onto this plane and have traveled all over. Every few years we'd go back and bring the Queen some of the rarest and hardest items to find that her procurers could not without great difficulty. That was our specialty. And she would pay us handsomely in gold and we'd go back on our travels to find our mate."

"See, romantic," Caven sighed. "Someday I want to hear all about the world. I can't even imagine what you guys have seen."

"For helping Jordy, I will make sure you even see the pictures we've taken over the years," I chuckled.

"And my sketches," Foma said quietly. I blinked in shock. My mate never let anyone but me see them. He met my gaze in the mirror again. "If Virgil can be brave enough to open himself up and be more honest about who he is, I can start too. These are our in-laws now and Caven's shown to be a good person. He wouldn't laugh or say I'm untalented."

"Of course not," I agreed, smiling at him, now proud of both my mates. "Especially because I've never seen a talent that even rivals yours. Maybe there is one Virgil would like to hang in his new house we'll be living in?"

"Yeah, I'd love that," Virgil agreed. "I think it's sexy that you draw. I'd love to see your work."

"Thank you, my mate. When I get my belongings from Greece you can see some but the rest we have in a storage unit in Germany."

"You're really going to move out, brother?" Gabriel asked quietly. "Have we really been that bad to you?"

"Don't turn that around," Caven growled. "I wanted to not live with all the people and all the pressure and you said you understood. It's not about everyone else always but what he or I needed."

Virgil nodded his head. "That's fairly accurate. I think I just need space at least for a while and to get some things worked out with Ayden. But it's not that you guys have been bad to me. You just don't get me and never really tried to. Admit it, Gabriel, how many times can you even remember, off the top of your head, yelling at me when I was younger that I was a defective little freak and to go away?"

"Gabriel!" Caven growled as Foma followed the caravan into a long drive. This must be the High Council estate.

"I haven't said that in years," Gabriel admitted with a wince. "I was young, not even two hundred years old. And here's this ten-year-old coming out where I'm practicing with all my friends, lecturing me on how to adjust my stance to brace myself for the impact of the strikes I was blocking so they didn't stress my joints and I could react quicker to catch them off-balance."

"I was trying to help."

"It made me look like an idiot to them all," he defended. "I'm sorry I was a jerk but that was a long time ago. It doesn't mean that I didn't love you."

"No, it just told a ten-year-old boy that his older brother, who he loved and worshiped, cared more about what his friends thought of him than that his little brother loved him and wanted to help him stay safe," Virgil said quietly in a broken tone that made my heart hurt. "And I promise you that that's something that doesn't just go away no matter how many years pass."

He was out of the car the second Foma stopped it and I wanted nothing more than to comfort my mate. Foma and I both got out in a hurry and went after him.

"You're a dick, Gabriel," Caven said loud enough for us to hear ten feet away where we were by our mate. I smiled as the little Alpha got out the same side I did and slammed the door. "I know exactly what happened. You were being big, bad, testosterone-filled warrior showing off and looking cool for his friends. That was your kid brother! I can tell you Ayden would *never* have pulled that on me no matter what I said or did.

"That's not what family is supposed to be about. No sex for you! You're an idiot who doesn't think before he speaks and you should know better. I bet that's exactly what all of your brothers have done to Virgil and now Riley has! I don't blame him for wanting to move out. Hell, I want to move out *for* him."

"See, you know you've got three people on your side," I said to my mate, kissing him briefly. He smiled as we watched Caven storm over to us.

"He's an idiot and he doesn't think but I know he would give his soul to keep you safe," Caven said quietly to Virgil so only we'd hear. "You take whatever time you need and I got your back, bro." Then he raised the level of his voice to normal. "And I'd love that kind of help any day you have available. Maybe I'll finally beat King Rylan in sparring with the wooden sticks if I get help taking the force of his blows better so I can turn around and whack him."

"You've already got an elder helping you," King Rylan said as he darted over to us. I realized Caven had known he was close and could hear, saying it then intentionally. "If you've got another ace in the hole that's not fair. You're getting close to my level already. Soon we'll be at swords and there's no way I'm letting you kick my ass then."

"Hey, you've been training since like diapers and I'm new to this," Caven defended. "If I need two people helping me with their mad skills to catch up then it's only fair." He looped his arm with Virgil's and smirked. "Besides, he's *my* brother-in-law. You can't ask him to help you beat me."

"But he's *my* mate's best friend," King Rylan shot back. "Virgil has been to our home many times and is quite close with Ferris. They are like brothers too. I've heard them say it. He would never keep whatever special fighting knowledge he has from me. He's too honorable for that. Besides, we need more instructors now that we're opening the shifters' training center. He could teach us all and then we'd just be on even ground."

"I think that's a wonderful idea," Caven agreed with a smirk. He shot Virgil a wink and strutted off to the front door.

"He's good," Rylan drawled, realizing he just got played. Then he glanced at our mate. "What is it you know that he baited me into wanting to learn?"

"I was like ten," he mumbled. I bumped his shoulder and shook my head.

"Tell him the truth. He asked and no one's judging you here," I pushed gently.

"It's a velocity and impact thing," Virgil sighed. "If you brace yourself the right way for blows when sparring or fighting you're able to distribute the impact better throughout your joints so that no one takes the full force. Which allows you to react faster and catch your opponent off guard. But you guys are already wicked fast so I don't know if that works the same."

"But we're also smaller so balance is that much more important," Rylan said slowly. "I like it. I want to see it soon." He shook his head and rolled his eyes at himself. "After your honeymooning and all that. I know we'll have recon or whatever the High Council decides and you'll want to get to know your mates. But I was serious that we're looking for instructors."

"Really? All the training positions at the warrior compound are filled currently," Virgil hedged, looking excited. He glanced at us with a big smile. "That would keep me local unless there was an emergency. I know we've not gotten that far into discussing what comes next for us, but I assume you wouldn't want me traipsing all over hunting demons."

"No, most certainly not. Unless we were with you," Foma agreed as I nodded.

"Like you couldn't take any of our jobs if you wanted," a man whose name I didn't remember snickered as he walked by. "I've never seen anyone best you in a sparring match in all my years, Virgil. You're the best and undefeated champion and you know it. If the coordinator found out you were mated and wanted a teaching position he'd toss whichever one of us out on our asses to have you take our place."

I glanced at my mate and knew it was probably true with the way he turned twenty different shades of red. Impressive. Smart, sexy, good fighter, sexy, gorgeous, kind, sexy, and all ours.

Chapter 7

Virgil

"What is this about now?" Father asked as he and Mother walked up with Victor, Malachi, Micah, and Riley, most of my other brothers and their mates right behind them.

"Isaac, please," I hissed, not wanting to make this a thing.

"My mate, I do not wish to embarrass you but I would like to know very much what this man is talking about," Mareo said. I glanced at him and saw pride shining in his eyes and a heavy dose of lust. "You wouldn't want to keep something from me when we've been so open with you, would you?"

Oh, he was good. "Fine, but I expect something in return later because you know this will be embarrassing for me."

"Anything and everything you wish, my mate," Mareo promised me in that deep voice that sent a thrill through me. I nodded for Isaac to go ahead as he glanced between us, looking rather confused.

"Virgil's got a bunch of records no one can beat," Isaac hedged. "You guys didn't know that?"

"No, and why didn't we?" Father asked as he glanced at me. I shrugged. "What kind of records?"

"Most consecutive sparring matches won," Isaac answered, scrunching his eyebrows together as if trying to remember them. "Undefeated sparring champ in swords, staffs, gloves, sais, maces, and pretty much anything else we spar or train with. All the climbing drills and obstacle courses."

"You're that fast?" Foma asked me, eyeing me over appreciatively.

"No, not really," I admitted, my face heating up even more. "I just know geometry well enough to get over or around anything the best way. The distance courses I don't ace. The ones with all the stuff in the way I do."

"Who *are* you?" Damian blurted out, his eyes going wide. I felt whatever pride I'd built up at the recognition I'd finally gotten dissolve just like that.

"No one of importance apparently," I mumbled and headed towards the doors.

"Virgil, don't," Mareo said gently as he grabbed my arm. "He's just stunned at the development and learning all of this."

"You know what? Don't side with them," I growled and pulled away. "When we're done here I'll show you the warrior compound. You can see how *hidden* the records and awards I hold are. Isaac fucking knew and I bet it wasn't just because he's an instructor now. Why was he the only one who knew?"

"I knew," Victor said quietly as he glanced around at the rest of my family before walking over towards me. "You know I knew. I've always been supportive and proud of your achievements."

"Yeah, you just never knew what to do with me otherwise," I mumbled, feeling like a little boy again who worshiped his older brother who was like the best warrior ever.

"We never had that much in common but that doesn't mean I didn't love you," he said fondly. "I was old by the time you were born and off on missions but I still made time for you every time I was home and we had fun. It wasn't forced or because I felt I had to. I liked hanging out with my little bro Virgil because you were different. You saw things differently and I thought it was cool."

"Thanks, Victor." I was glad that at least one of them acted like they knew me or liked me. After what Riley said it was like the floor had opened out from underneath me and I was reassessing everything I'd ever known or ever felt about my relationships with people.

"Now go kick some ass and show the Council who Virgil Marius is and why you saw what all the rest of us couldn't." He gave me a wink and I nodded.

"Go ahead, I'll be right in," Mareo said, giving me a quick kiss. "You prepare and check your equipment. I'll find you."

"Okay." I nodded and headed off with Foma, thinking that was weird. Oh well, of a day of total bizarre and new realizations I couldn't deal with every little concern or potential issue. I'd lose what was left of my mind that way.

* * * *

Mareo

I watched as Victor Marius held up his hand to his family, checking until Virgil was out of hearing range before turning on them.

"You will stow your shit and fucking act like adults. Our brother is hurt and hasn't felt he could come to us *all* these years. Do you *really* think that's *his* fault? No. We screwed up. We let one of *us* slip through the cracks. Anyone here not love him?" He waited until everyone shook their head. "Okay, good. That's what I thought. Virgil's quiet. We've all known that always. He's not a bragger. We should have been paying better attention because I bet he knows all about us.

"So not one more word of shock that he's finally opening up or being different than he always has. Not one more guilt trip about him getting space if he wants to move out. He wants to move ten minutes away. You keep fucking pushing or guilting him and he'll move across the damn country or start over somewhere in the human world. He's a middle child and even I know enough about psychology to recognize that part of what's going on is some middle child syndrome.

"But it's *way* beyond that. Gabriel did something that hurt him, I know he wasn't the only one. I caught part of what happened in the kitchen and Virgil thought Mother and Father believed he was an abnormal child in a bad way. There was a lot he heard or misunderstood as a child that led him to think we feel about him the way he does. I get that. But it won't get fixed if we don't handle this better. Savvy?" He narrowed his eyes especially at Riley.

"Yes, I screwed up. I'm sorry. I'm going to apologize," he agreed with a sigh. "I didn't mean he wasn't smart enough to figure all this out. I just wanted to know what sparked the maps and tracing all of this for him. I was trying to use that as a lead-in to apologize for what I said before that hurt his feelings. It went to shit. I suck. I reacted like his mate said and it was my pride that lashed out. I will figure out a way to fix it."

"You also have to keep in mind something else," I said, finally stepping in. I had planned to say a lot but Victor handled most of it beautifully so I hadn't felt the need except for one point. "You all mated first. He felt left out of this family and not accepted. Not normal, even to the ones he loved most. And it seemed even fate agreed by not giving him a mate when you all found yours. Then he finds *them* and we are *two* large fae warriors which you do not have in this family.

"It doesn't take a genius to know he wants to move out before that potentially becomes an issue and he's not normal in your eyes again, whether you say it that way or not. Or whether someone makes an offhanded comment about it while he's dealing with all this. He doesn't want to risk it and I can't say I blame him. Can you? Can you really blame him for wanting space so this situation doesn't implode now that he's mated to two men bigger than him?"

"No, I get it," Damian agreed. "My brothers were great when Cyrus was my mate and even coming to terms with that, he was, um, *bigger*. But they still teased and ribbed me hard about it. That would probably be twice the amount of teasing for Virgil."

"Or you didn't tease him after he saw you get teased and that just showed him that he wasn't loved and invisible," I added, playing devil's advocate.

"Okay, we support his choice to move out," Mrs. Marius said sadly, looking at me with tears in her eyes. "But you promise to protect my boy. The estate gives extra safety to him. I'm sorry he feels we don't love him for who he is and we screwed up but we do. We'll work with Ayden and him to fix this but I want you to understand this is only temporary."

"Or build a house of your own on the estate," Mr. Marius offered. "We'd do that to keep him close and you all safe. Let him know that. Hell, we'll move the house he had built and set it on the estate just as is."

"I will let him know you were willing to go to such great lengths to make him happy, keep him safe, and loved him enough to want him close when I feel he would be receptive to it," I said carefully. They all nodded and we headed inside.

I spent the next hour watching my stunning mate in his prime. He explained everything once again, answering any questions like a pro, and even giving them his best guesses of hideout locations, potential traitors, and directions on what to do next. I held Foma's hand the entire time since I could tell he was as nervous as I was. Our mate needed this to go well and our encouragement.

We were so damn proud of him though it was hard not to be supportive of such genius. When it was over, we fell into step with our mate, ignoring that he was practically vibrating with nerves and need to get out of there.

"Knowing the High Council, they will spend the next few days deliberating on what to do," he said when we were outside.

"Good, then that gives us half the time we'd like to show our mate how impressed we are with him," I said seductively.

"Half?" he gasped as I pushed him up against his SUV. I mashed my mouth down to his, taking what he freely offered and plundering his sweet, sweet mouth as my hands grabbed his firm ass.

"Oh yes. If we got our way we'd spend the next week worshiping your body, you were so sexy and impressive in there, our mate," Foma whispered in his ear. A throat cleared behind us and the two of us growled in disappointment as we let Virgil up. "We're never going to get claimed at this rate."

"No, we're going home now to do it," Virgil promised us. His eyes went wide and I turned to see Damian and his mate, Cyrus, standing there.

"I'm sorry, Virgil," Damian said quietly. "I know who you are. I shouldn't have said that. I was just shocked."

"Go on, amante. Tell him all of it." Cyrus pushed gently, wrapping an arm around his mate. "Virgil is not a man to judge."

Damian sighed and nodded. "I know I'm closest with Vic and I know all of us totally worshiped him as the big bro and kick-ass warrior, but I used to worship you too."

"What? Me? Why?" Virgil gasped as he stared at Damian in shock.

"You made everything look so easy," Damian answered in an exasperated tone, throwing his hands in the air. "You always knew what was what and you were always in control. You never threw a temper tantrum or got jealous or anything. I thought that was so cool and like Father. It was as if you mastered your emotions way before anyone else could ever.

"Look, I get Gabriel was a jerk when you were a kid or something, and I'm not downplaying that but I think it might just be part of being a big brother. He wasn't the only one who called one of his little brothers annoying and threw them out of his room or something. I wanted to be just like you and you used to get so pissed at me for wanting to hang with you."

"Because you were going through my porn, you twit," Virgil chuckled and closed the distance between him and his brother. "I loved hanging out with you and I adored you when you were a twerp. But you were the most curious little bugger ever. And the moment I told you *no* that's what you'd go for. I swear I hid that box in like ten different spots but you'd always find it again."

"That was *porn*?" Damian exclaimed, his eyes practically bugging out of his head. "I thought you wouldn't share your comic books with me! I cried for days because I didn't think I was cool enough in your eyes to get to see your comics."

"No, brother. I would have shared all my comics with you if I'd had any. Why did you think they only had women and no clothes?" I could see my mate trying not to laugh.

"I don't know. I was like six," Damian answered with a snicker. They shared a laugh and another hug. "Love you, okay? I'm glad you're an extra special kick-ass warrior that I didn't realize. That's what I meant by my comment. I want my big brother to teach me all his wicked moves. If I had known, I would have begged you long ago. That's all I was saying. I know who you are, Virg. We all do. Just because we don't know everything or always get it right doesn't mean we don't care."

"Yeah, I'm maybe starting to grasp that," he agreed with a shrug. "We'll see."

"You didn't know I loved to bounce around on fat cock and be bitten constantly, did you?" Damian asked in a cheeky tone with attitude. "Or that my favorite game is—"

"That is enough sharing for today, amante," Cyrus drawled as he covered his mate's mouth with his hand. "He gets the point. Not knowing everything about each other does not mean there is not love or respect there. He gets it. No need to tell him everything that goes on in our rooms."

"No, it's all good, Cyrus," Virgil chuckled as he opened the door to the front seat and the three of us got into his SUV. "You guys didn't know I liked to be double stuffed all night after having drunk werewolf blood." He shut the door so fast he was lucky he didn't close something vital in it. I was sitting in the back and saw Damian's and Cyrus's eyes go so wide they almost fell out of their skulls. "Drive, Foma, drive!"

"Dramatic exit after dropping that bomb?" our mate chuckled as he quickly pulled out of the spot.

"Yeah, I don't know what got into me," Virgil admitted as he turned in his seat, smiling widely. "Damian's always such a smartass and a joker but he's always so happy. I thought why not try it out and see what it's like?"

"And did you like it?"

He bit his lower lip and nodded as he glanced at me, his eyes shining. "Yeah. It was fun to see their reactions and get the last word in. They would *never* have guessed I'd say something like that in a million years."

"It was hot to hear you say it," I growled. "Foma, do you remember the way back? I want to start preparing our mate on the drive."

"I remember. Just don't distract me too badly because I want to see the show," Foma bitched.

"I'm doing this for both of us, my love. The quicker he's stretched, the faster we get to take him together as he said he loves," I reminded him.

"I don't have any werewolf blood," Virgil said quietly. "I've never done it without that."

"You'll be high on us," I growled and practically dragged him into the backseat with me. The moment I had him pinned under me on the bench seat I opened up his pants and shoved my hand down them. "Are you saying the only way you want to feel us is if you have wolf blood?"

"No, no that's not what I'm saying at all," he panted, his eyes wide.

"Then tell me," I demanded as I pulled his dress pants down more so I could get at his tight hole.

"It opens me up. I don't worry. I let go. It's testosterone and Viagra and speed. Endorphins are running wild and there's no pain, only pleasure."

"You're afraid taking both of us will hurt and you won't like it. It will ruin your fantasy," Foma said from the driver's seat, figuring out what I was missing.

"Yes," Virgil admitted.

"Then it's a good thing you're mated to a fae with strong magic who's traveled all over the world," I purred. "I picked up some tricks from a witch who was living in Egypt." I chanted the spell she'd given me centuries ago and my mate gasped, arching his back as he experienced what was equivalent to hours of foreplay and stretching of his hole. He would feel no pain now and be perfectly prepared for Foma and I.

"Thank you for understanding," Virgil breathed against my lips after I moved between his legs to kiss him.

"Anything for my mate." We made out like teenagers, simply learning what the other liked while Foma probably broke every speed limit getting us back to the Marius estate. The moment the SUV stopped in front of the house, I pulled up Virgil's pants, and practically dragged him out of the vehicle with me. Hell, Foma didn't even park in the garage we were so ready to go. That would have taken too long.

Virgil led the way to his suite, holding his pants closed so he didn't give anyone a show. The minute we were alone in his rooms, our clothes started flying and we all fell onto his bed in a pile. He found lube and I quickly poured some on my cock, sitting up and holding it for him.

"We come together as one complete soul, mates forever as you claim me first," I said tenderly as he straddled my lap. Virgil nodded and lowered himself onto my cock. I moaned in bliss.

"I give myself to you freely and for always," he whispered. "To both of you forever."

"Thank you, Virgil. You are truly a gift we will always cherish," Foma whispered. I could tell my mate, who I had loved for so many centuries, was choked up with emotions. I realized Virgil understood it too when he felt one of Foma's tears on his shoulder. "We finally found you. We're complete now. We're a family." Then he gasped and met my gaze. "We were before. I was happy and—"

"I know, my love. I know," I said gently, not feeling insulted or slighted in any way by his words. "I never felt unloved but we were missing a piece to our threesome. Now our hearts are complete."

"Yes, that's what I meant."

"I feel the same," Virgil agreed. "I just didn't know I had two of you waiting for me. Thank you for the love you've already shown me and how quickly you've become exactly what I need."

"It's what being mates means," I assured him.

"No, that's not what it means," he disagreed as he cupped my cheek. "That's the men you are. Both of you. You are selfless, and loving, and kind, and more than I ever dreamed of. I'm so blessed."

"We feel the same," Foma told him as he kissed Virgil's neck. I felt him join me inside our mate, Virgil shaking with need as he gasped in pleasure. "Okay?"

"Yes, perfect. So full and wonderful." Our bodies moved together as one and when it was time, Virgil bit me, drinking from me deeply. I understood what he meant now about it being a private, erotic act that was too special to share… Though part of me wanted to just to show off how beautiful my mates were for all to see what they couldn't have.

Call me prideful.

When we were spent, both Foma and I coming inside Virgil and our vampire mate's seed all over my stomach, we collapsed to the bed. We held each other close and caught our breath before the next round where he claimed Foma.

"I don't want to look a gift horse in the face but there's something I need to know," Virgil said quietly when our hearts calmed back down. He waited until we both nodded and took in a shaky breath. "Are you going to be happy staying here and living in our house? You've traveled for so long and seen so much. I worry staying here in rural Virginia won't be enough for you."

I glanced at Foma and we both burst out laughing. Of course Virgil didn't understand what was going on so when we calmed back down we each gave him a reassuring kiss.

"We hate traveling all the time," Foma explained. "It's horrid. Hotels and rental cars and nothing of your own and living out of a suitcase and blah, blah, blah. Flying sucks and before that it was traveling by boat or horse. Honestly. I'm not sure what's worse with how rude people are in the airline industry."

"In other words, we found a way to make a living as we searched for you," I told Virgil with a big smile. "We don't care where we live. We just want a home again. We want us to all be together, something that's *ours* and not a different bed every night."

"And thank the gods we never have to sleep with another man or woman again," Foma said with a sigh. Virgil blinked in shock at him at that one. "Yes, sex is great and even could be fun at times when Mareo and I shared someone but it was always followed by the letdown afterwards that they weren't our mate. There is *more* than enough chemistry here that our sex life will never get boring and there will be fun had by all for centuries to come."

"You're both such romantics," Virgil whispered and then frowned. "I'm not very romantic. It's always kind of lost on me. I worry I won't be able to romance you the way you want ever."

"Oh, sweetheart," I chuckled, hugging him tightly. "Yes, we're romantics at heart and that's what kept us hopeful we'd find you. But we like to romance. I love romancing Foma. He has trouble accepting it at times and so do I when he does it for me. Will you accept our gestures and show us how you appreciate them?"

"Yes, of course," Virgil agreed. "But—"

"Nope, no *butts*," Foma chuckled, smacking Virgil's. "We like to woo. Then we like to claim who we've wooed as they gratefully show us their appreciation. That's romantic in itself."

"Then I'm just your man." Virgil wiggled his eyebrows at us. "Let me show you what I mean." Virgil rolled him over and lowered himself onto Foma's cock. Then he glanced at me over his shoulder. "Need a written invitation?"

"No, never," I panted. I quickly got into position behind him and pushed into his sweet hole alongside Foma's cock. Dear gods, it was just heaven. I didn't go slow this time, since his body was more than stretched for us. I pounded into him with everything I had, both my mates holding on for the ride as the friction, tension, and movements drove their pleasure to maddening levels.

I watched as Virgil bit Foma, claiming him in the most basic ways as I claimed Virgil again. They came first and I was so enthralled with the sight of it I wasn't prepared for my own orgasm. Screaming out their names, I shot my seed deep inside Virgil, coating Foma's cock with it as well.

"Damn, that was fucking awesome," Virgil mumbled as he collapsed on top of Foma. "We need some individual rounds next too. Maybe after a nap."

"And we need to feed you some more," I said, glancing at the clock. "You've not had enough to eat today."

"Okay, feed me your cock later," he mumbled with a yawn. My jaw fell open in shock. Cheeky mate! I loved it! I saw the lust-filled look Foma was giving Virgil and realized he felt the same. We quickly cleaned up and tucked our mate into bed, wrapping ourselves around him. It was perfect, just as he was.

Chapter 8

Virgil

I ended up being right that it would take the High Council days to deliberate. While they were busy, I knew some of my brothers started investigating potential traitors off the facts I'd collected while I... I enjoyed my mates. In every position, I mean *way* possible.

Ayden did come over several times to sit with me and each of my brothers, working through old memories. Damian had been right. All big brothers can be dicks at times. I just never saw it that way or anyone else doing it to any of my brothers. And after the partial conversation I'd heard between my parents when I young, it just followed me into being an adult.

Funny how that happens. It was almost like we couldn't really understand everything going on when we were young and easily formed opinions and feelings based just on what we perceived.

It wasn't just about the sex with my mates either. I learned *so* much about them. And as crazy as it sounds, I learned a lot about them while having sex too.

Foma was very tender. He was a big softy who loved long kisses, soulful looks, and gentle caresses. He liked to touch and always be touched. If Mareo or I were close to him he was touching us somehow. Not in an awkward or inappropriate, creepy way. Just simple things. While we ate lunch he'd have his hand on one of our thighs. He never rolled to his own side of the bed at night, perfectly happy to be wrapped around us.

And he *loved* oral sex. Oh heavens did he ever. I woke from a few naps and one morning to him sucking me off or eating out my ass. *Lord*, what a talented tongue he had. And he was loyal. He would rather die a thousand deaths than ever betray or hurt Mareo. I could see it every time he looked at our mate.

Mareo had that same loyalty and a very firm sense of honor. He was a warrior through and through. But what I didn't know was that since the fae lived on their plane and there wasn't fighting for them to engage in ever, they trained and were prepared, but they also had other jobs normally.

"So what did you do before you met Foma?" I asked after we showered, dressed, and were about to get breakfast.

"You promise not to laugh?" he mumbled, shy or embarrassed for the first time since I'd met him.

"I promise and I'll do you one better," I purred as I grabbed his ass. "You tell me and I'll give you another fang blow job after breakfast." He moaned and practically chased me out of my rooms. Just to be randy after I claimed them because they had blow jobs that had been promised to them that they'd wanted to collect on… I had bit Mareo's dick when he'd been close. He fucking *loved* it. I mean, went wild and fucked me silly right after he was done coming.

Then Foma had wanted to see what all the fuss was about and we'd had about the same result. Apparently my mates *really* got hot by my getting sustenance from their bodies and they loved the kink factor.

"You already have found our weakness," he growled in my ear as he caught up to me at the top of the stairs. Foma was right there with us, biting back a smile. "Be careful when you play with fire, Virgil. It's not nice to tease your mates or hold your power over our heads."

"I love your fire and passion," I told him honestly. "You can burn me up with it any day you want, my mate. And it's not teasing when I always come through with my promises."

"He's right, Mareo. You have to tell him."

He huffed and gruffed for a few minutes, mumbling under his breath as he pushed open the kitchen door.

"I'm sorry, I didn't catch that," I chuckled.

"What's a cordwainer?" Caven asked, glancing between Mareo and Gabriel. "It sounds dirty. Is that like a cockwaggler?"

"Caven!" Mother gasped in shock.

"Sorry, Elena," he said, not looking sorry in the slightest.

"I *really* have to get used to your impressive hearing abilities," Mareo sighed as he grabbed a plate off the island counter and started loading up with food. "A shoe maker. I used to make shoes. A cordwainer made the fancy shoes and boots. My brother was good at it and became a cobbler. So I made them and he fixed them if need be later. We used to be very close."

"Have you talked to him since the fae crossed over?" I asked, curious since I'd not heard mention of any family of his yet. I knew Foma was an orphan and Mareo's parents were gone, but neither said that they had siblings.

"No, I've not heard of or from Elan and we didn't part on the best of terms last time I saw him," Mareo mumbled. "He thought I was stupid to leave and wouldn't even see me the first time I came back to the plane. After that I stopped trying."

"Mareo, Elan is in this coven," I said gently. "He wasn't here with the Queen the other day but I know him. He was on Caven's security for a while."

"Is he well?" my mate asked quietly, his eyes swimming with emotion. I glanced at Caven, not sure how to answer that. I'd only met the man briefly.

"Elan lived over on this plane for a while," Caven hedged. "He used to procure items for the Queen and his people when the plane started shrinking. I knew he went back for a while and someone else was helping Brio but maybe he changed his mind and thought he should give this world a chance like you did. You should talk to him."

"He said he never wanted to see me again. But thank you for telling me he is well."

"I told you I'd never forgive you," I said carefully, trying to make a point but not rub salt in old wounds. "Things change and people grow up. What can it hurt to say *hi* to him?"

"Please, Mareo?" Foma begged. That surprised me and I blinked at him in shock. "I *hated* that our decision to leave to find our mate because I so desperately wanted the family I never had caused the rift between you and Elan. You were so close. Please give him a chance to apologize or at least mend the fence. You miss him. Don't even try to deny that."

"Okay, yes, I'd like to see him," Mareo sighed after a moment. He leaned in and kissed Foma. "It was never your fault, my love. I wanted to search for our mate as well. Never doubt that." Then he turned to me and gave me one as well. "And thank you for helping me see past my hurt feelings, my love. It is hard to move on when your heart aches from the past."

"I'm learning that and how to—" I started to say and then gasped. I blinked at him.

"Caught what I said there, did you?" He was smiling like the cat that ate the canary. "I thought I'd test it out and see how you felt about it. I didn't want to freak you out with saying it too soon."

"So romantic. I'm telling you. He should give romance lessons," Caven whispered across the table.

"I agree," I told Caven without even looking at him. I only had eyes for Mareo right then. "I love you too. I love you both." I glanced past him and met Foma's gaze. "I love you just as much."

"And I love you, Virgil," he said before practically tackling us together. Mareo peppered our faces with kisses, being the complete goofball when he remembered we weren't alone as we were professing our love for each other. When we sat back up I saw Mother, Marian, a few of my brothers' mates, and even Father with tears in their eyes.

"You're happy," Mother whispered before jumping out of her chair and racing around the table. I thought she was coming to me but she practically dove into Mareo's arms and hugged him tightly. "Thank you. Thank you for making my son so happy." Then she did the same to Foma and I blinked in shock.

"I still get hugs like that," Caven informed me. "She loves to see you guys happy and it's our fault for being your mates apparently." He gave me a wink and went back to his breakfast. Okay then.

"I love you," Mother whispered as she kissed my cheek before hugging me as well. "I'm so happy for you. Whatever you need, Virgil. We're here for you. I'd like to see this house you had built if you want?"

"Soon, yes. I want to show it to my mates first." I was stunned that she was suddenly okay with all of this. I was a little uncomfortable with that.

"Don't overthink it," Caven suggested when Mother sat back down. "You wanted support and now you're getting it. Don't read problems where there aren't any."

"Seriously, are you really only nineteen?" Foma blurted out.

"I get that a lot," Caven snickered. "I promise I still play video games and eat all kinds of shit food when no one's looking."

"And he cusses no matter what the parents in the room say," Mother drawled.

"How come you, Father, and Caven aren't already back at the High Council estate deliberating?" I asked, realizing it was eight in the morning and they'd been gone by that time for days already.

"Because we reached a decision last night about three in the morning," Father answered and then yawned. "We want to send in a team to scout out your locations. It's a starting point at least but while transport is easy with the Queen opening a portal we just don't want to have the team dropped off at the door. We need someone who knows the areas to guide the team."

"Rylan and I can sniff out the areas as we move in from miles away but yeah, landing right on top of the building could end really badly," Caven agreed. I glanced at Gabriel with worry.

"He's Alpha," my brother said, answering the unasked question. "I knew when I claimed him that he was going to be a fighter and in the thick of it all. He's careful, listens, and isn't rash. Do I like it? No. I want him in our suite locked up in bubble wrap, but this is life."

"Does anyone have that map with them?" Mareo asked, glancing at Foma. Father nodded and got to his feet before walking over to where he and Mother must have left their folders and notes when they got home. He pulled it out and handed it to my mate, glancing over his shoulder as Foma did. "We know the providences outside Paris like the backs of our hands."

"We've been to Northern Portugal and Spain many times," Foma added. "Italy, Switzerland, Belgium, England, sure, we know all of these. We could guide in a team no problem. We know how to blend in the regions and even have contacts in case shit hits the fan."

"Okay, then you both are leading the team," Father said with a nod. "We're not including the other vampire warriors other than the ones we know and have trusted with this already. We don't know who the traitor is."

"Rylan said he's coming up with a plan for that besides the Queen or I reading everyone's minds because the warriors are trained to block those types of powers when they focus," Caven added. "Okay so where are we starting?"

"My vote would be Paris. There's several possible locations outside there and while a few will probably be nothing, it would make sense that his main evil lair is close to where he lives. I mean, that's where the Western European High Council is based out of after all."

"That's a six-hour time difference and we wanted to start the recon after full dark their time. So let's say eight just to be on the safe side that most everyone will be home from work already," Victor said quickly. "So we need to be prepped and ready to go by two. Who is all coming?"

"Me, Gabriel, Rylan, Onah, Ferris, Foma, Mareo, and Virgil now," Caven answered.

"Yeah, I'm not letting two of my little brothers and their mates go alone," Victor said with a snicker. "So how does this work to get us back once we find out what we need?" Father and Mother spent the next few minutes, with the help of my mates, explaining the activating stone Queen Magdalena would give us. Basically it was like Dorothy and Kansas. We rubbed it and thought of her and the doorway to her would open.

Wicked cool.

"We're going," Damian said when we finished breakfast. "Cyrus needs this and I'm the best sniper this family has."

"Yes," Gabriel and I agreed as Victor shook his head.

"No," Victor said gently. "Damian, you might have to shoot your fucking in-laws. Could you really do that? And, Cyrus, we might come up against your *family*, man. Don't put yourself in that spot. We got this. Trust us, brother."

"I need to see with my own eyes this time," Cyrus argued. Everyone of course starting yelling as if that would solve *anything*. Yeah, because by now we should know it didn't. I put my fingers in my mouth and whistled loud enough to hurt everyone's ears.

"It's not your call, Victor," I reminded him. "As Councilman, Father named Mareo and Foma leads of the team because they know the area. It's their call." I shot them a sympathetic look and they gave me a curious one back. They knew there was a reason for it but still weren't mad at me for putting them in the middle.

Nice.

"Fill us in then," Mareo said, ignoring the sounds of Victor practically grinding his teeth to the gums. He and Foma listened to both sides of the argument, taking in others' perspectives as well.

When they were done he nodded towards the terrace as he met my gaze. "We're going to discuss it for a moment."

"If you get to decide as team leads, your mate doesn't get a vote then too," Victor bitched.

"No but I've not heard his perspective yet and I've listened to yours," Mareo shot right back. "You have a tough decision and you don't consult your mate for his counsel and to bounce ideas off of?"

Victor glanced to Malachi and sighed. "All the time. Yeah, you're right. I just don't like the situation."

"None of us *like* this, Vic," Damian said gently. "But if one of us went dark side there is not a force on this earth that would stop you from being the one to end it, to save us so we can be with our souls again. Just let them discuss it. Virgil's logical and Mareo and Foma have an outsider's perspective, being new to the family. They'll make the right call."

I appreciated the vote of confidence more than Damian would ever know. Plus, he included my mates in the idea of our family already.

"Why did you get us involved in this?" Mareo asked evenly once we were outside but I could see he was shaking with anger. "We just mate and now you're pitting us against half your family."

"That wasn't what I meant to do," I answered honestly. "I did it for the reasons Damian said. You guys are new to this and you have a different perspective. Victor says no because he loves Damian and respects Cyrus. I say yes because I know Cyrus's code of honor and his love for my brother and that will trump his lingering feelings for his family that are now demons.

"We all could have gone on fighting for hours but the best answer was my mates before my family said things in anger that couldn't be taken back. I promise you that my family won't hold your answer against you after today is over. Even if it goes ass up whatever way you decide, they won't blame you. If they held a grudge I wouldn't have put you in this position."

He nodded as I explained, eyeing me over. Then he glanced at Foma and they shared a look. "Fine, but we each want a fang blow job before we go for the stress this has caused us."

"Deal and done," I chuckled, thinking I got off easy on that one. "Which way are you leaning?"

"Damian is a valuable asset," Mareo answered as Foma nodded. "All your brothers agree he is the best shot and we might need that. Cyrus could be an asset or a liability on numerous counts. Not just could he freeze up if we come into contact with the demons that were his relatives, but someone might recognize him. If they see him they might give us information."

"Or they see him and they sound the alarms because they realize it's him and not his brothers," Foma added.

"That's something I didn't think about," I hedged. "We are planning on staying out of sight though."

"Right but we're coming in from a distance and—" Mareo started to say.

"Carrying weapons," I argued. "It's not like we're walking down the main street here. If we get hooked up, having Cyrus could save our asses because they'll think it's his brother. I say we make sure he's disguised unless we need to play that card."

Foma nodded. "That should work. Yes, then I agree he should come as long as he realizes he is not to engage. He can't go flying off the handle. He stays at the back and covers our rear if shit goes down."

"I think he'd accept that. If he freaks, we're opening a portal anyways and we throw him in it while the cavalry comes." I shrugged since it was the best I had.

"Agreed then." Mareo nodded and we headed back inside. Everyone was watching us and I could tell they were dying to know what we'd said, probably having reached deep into their self-restraint not to have pressed their ears against the glass while we were talking.

"I didn't tell," Caven announced proudly.

"Never thought you would," Mareo replied with a wave. "An Alpha is a position of honor and to have it at such a young age, you must have a very moral code."

"He does," Gabriel agreed.

"We have conditions," Mareo said to Cyrus and Damian. "We want Cyrus to be disguised as much as possible, ball cap, glasses, something. If we're spotted he might be a huge flag and we wouldn't know which way for if we're truly going to be around where his family is. They would recognize him if the resemblance is as Virgil says."

"It is. I didn't think of that," Cyrus agreed. "Except I'm the only warrior of the family so I'm like a larger size of them. I can't pass for one of them if they know my brother or father well. If they've only seen them from a distance then yes."

"Well, that still doesn't change that we want your face hidden then," Foma said, taking in the new information. "And if we see your family you don't engage. We go in, you pull up the rear. Something goes wrong or you can't handle this, we hit the stone and throw you back through the portal while the cavalry comes as my mate put it."

"I agree to your terms. Thank you." Cyrus extended his hand to my mates and they each shook it in turn. Damian did the same and then hugged me before Cyrus did. "Thank you, brother. This means a lot to me."

"You love my brother too much to let *anyone* hurt him or ever risk him," I said firmly. "Even the demons that used to be your family. I don't doubt if the time came you would pull the trigger. Do I want this for you? No, but you know your own mind and what's best for you and Damian better than I do. So I trust you. That's all I told them. Your record as a warrior speaks for itself and Damian's the best shot around so we could use him."

"You're right," Victor agreed quietly. "I'm sorry. I still don't like it but Virgil's right. I *hate* the idea that this is what you might have to do, Cyrus. You're my brother now too and I would save this heartache. I don't want you or Damian anywhere near this."

"We don't want you near it either, Vic," Damian said firmly. "It's just not reality. We're all ass deep in this shit and who do you trust to have your back more than us?"

"No one," he admitted. "Good, so we leave in three hours. Gear up and someone let King Rylan know. Where are we portaling from?"

"The Queen is bringing everyone and their gear here first," Father explained. "Riley has medical equipment here in case anyone gets hurt. The warrior compound would make more sense, but since we don't know who the traitor is…" He trailed off and spread his arms as if to say, *fuck that idea.*

"Okay, so those of us not going, we've got a lot to get set up before it's time," Stefan said loudly, taking charge as the second-oldest brother. "Riley, who do you want to boss around?"

"I'll take Patrick and Malachi," Riley chuckled. "The rest you can boss around for weapons or whatever else you're going to start getting organized." Stefan nodded and then started working with Father and Mother on getting all the extra weapons and supplies we could here right away. Even if we couldn't get to the massive gun hold at the warrior compound, most of the founding families or families with warriors had a selection at their house.

Hell, I'd *seen* the one Isaac had and it would make just about any man hard.

"Virgil, can I have a moment?" Riley asked quietly.

"I don't want to fight, Riley. We have to get ready and I want to spend some time with my mates before we possibly walk into the belly of the beast."

"No, no fighting. Please?" He looked so worried, so earnest that I nodded. Micah started to follow us but Riley waved him off which my mates took as a signal to give us some space as well. Okay then. Once we were in the foyer Riley ran his hands over his face in frustration. "Why is this so hard to say?"

"I don't know," I drawled. "I don't know what you're trying to say. I guess no one likes saying they're sorry."

"That's not the part I'm having a problem with," he chuckled. "I *am* sorry, Virgil. I was an epic-sized douche and came to conclusions when I didn't have all the facts. I suck and I'm sorry. I'm just not sure how to explain why I reacted the way I did. Ayden made me see some things in our session and basically it was fear. We're a lot alike in some ways and it was fear that everyone saw me how you felt your family saw you and I—I don't know.

"I'm not sure it all makes sense in my head yet. I *was* trying to help. I saw you and how you interact with people as me before I found Micah. What I was trying to say is mating changes us for the better. We're always better people after we mate. It wasn't that I was trying to list your faults to pick on you. Fuck, I have the same ones."

"Queen Magdalena pointed that out," I snickered.

"I'm sure she did." He rolled his eyes. "I'm sorry is what I'm really trying to say. I get where you're coming from and I was trying to help you, brother. I'm sorry I botched it to shit and then lashed out when you told me you fixed my mistakes. I sucked again then. And I never said what I should have.

"Thank you. Thank you for saving Stefan and my asses so we didn't get hurt testing the stuff. Thank you for helping us design it all. And thank you for whatever else you've stuck your nose in and fixed for me. I would like to know the list one day."

"When we get back and have some downtime I'll tell you."

"And I'd like to come to you next time I'm stuck with equations or solutions that aren't necessarily medical," he hedged.

"But you have your own think tank now," I teased.

"But it's you I trust more than all of them combined."

I searched his eyes and saw the truth of his words shining at me. "Okay, fight over and I love you too."

"Thank god," he gushed. He hugged me tightly and we joked a little bit more before he headed back into the kitchen.

Moments later my mates came out to find me and I gave them a wink before darting up the stairs. They gave chase and the moment we were back in my suite I dropped to my knees. "I believe the two loves of my life requested blow jobs with fangs." I let them slide out and they both shivered.

It didn't take long until their pants were undone and I was sucking Foma off with everything I had while Mareo was whispering the dirtiest things in my ear while playing with my ass. Then they traded places before each fucking me silly.

That was the most fun I'd ever had preparing for recon and maybe a battle.

Chapter 9

"*Mom*, are we there yet?" Damian whined. "I'm hungry and this is boring and we've not see anything *fun*."

"Seriously, why did we bring you?" Victor bitched and I saw he was trying not to laugh. We were on our way to check out the third possible place out of five, the first two being duds. "Virgil came up with the plan, his mates know the area, Rylan and Caven can smell a bird taking a shit from fifty miles away, and of course their mates wouldn't let them come without them. I'm kick-ass, Cyrus is too, and this is personal for him. Why are you here?"

"Because I have a fabulous ass," Damian answered with a straight face. Then his fangs slid out and he growled. "And I can shoot that bird shitting before it even knows we're close."

"Right. Not sure that makes up for all the wisecracks and comments we have to deal with," Ferris drawled. We kept moving, everyone ribbing each other as Ferris bumped me with his hip so we moved a little off to the side. "You good? I saw I missed your call and then you didn't answer when I tried to get you back. Were you telling me you found your mates?"

"I'm good now," I answered, smiling as I glanced at the gorgeous gods of men that were mine. "I wasn't when I called. I was all muddled up inside and just confused. I felt like a shipwrecked boat and then I found them and I should have been glad but all it did was kind of make me feel like I was drowning."

"I know the feeling. *Believe* me, I know the feeling." It was true. Ferris had been dealing with so much crap when he met his mates and then Rylan lost his parents, became King, and basically Ferris got a son in the form of Rylan's baby brother.

"I know, which was why I called you. Instead I called Riley and it blew up but I'm kind of glad now that it did. I was finally honest about a lot of things and myself for once. It's time to just be me. I'm almost four hundred years old for crying out loud. I'm not going to change into someone else and I don't want to. I am who I am and not letting people see the real me hasn't worked. So time to be me and if they don't like it, they can fuck off."

"Good. I'm proud of you." He bumped my shoulder and I met his gaze. "I always thought who you were was awesome, Virgil. You're a good person, a fierce warrior, and a loyal friend who doesn't do anything halfway. That's something to be proud of, not hide away from the world and those who love you."

"I'm starting to see that. Having mates who love me for god only knows what reason helps."

"Shit," Rylan hissed, sounding more cat than human. "Someone text home base. We've got demons."

"And lots of them," Caven agreed. "At least three dozen. I smell humans." He gasped and looked at Rylan. "You getting that too?"

"Yeah. I'm just not sure what it is."

"Tell us and we won't hold it against you if you're wrong," Victor growled as we picked up the pace. I saw him and Gabriel pulling out their phones as I did. The plan was if we found anything there were three contact points, Queen Magdalena, Tyler, and Father.

"Blood. Lots of blood," Caven replied with a shiver. "I can't even put it into words. But it's different like not fresh on the ground."

"Like bottled up or in big containers?" I guessed, trying to figure out what else it could be.

"Holy shit. Yes," Rylan whispered, his eyes going wide. "I'm scared to think why there are demons, humans, and lots of stored blood in a remote area outside Paris."

"Could they be farming humans instead of just killing them when they get hungry?" I asked no one in particular, more just stating the theory as it popped into my brain. I think part of me wanted someone to say I was being ridiculous… But no one did.

We hurried it even faster after that. This was going to be bad. I felt it down to my bones.

* * * *

Foma

"I'm shifting," Rylan hissed as we got past the gates and perimeter of the estate-turned-factory-looking place. Or maybe it was the other way around. I wasn't really sure. But either way, it was creepy. Damian had been as good with a rifle as his brothers had bragged, taking out guards as he ran, silencer on the gun, so no one would hear the shot. It had been a wise decision to use tranqs though because I had a feeling they wouldn't have gone down quietly dying.

As we went along we severed heads and moved on as they turned to ash. Now that we were against the building, Rylan would be of more use in cat form. His mate, Ferris, took his clothes and stuffed them in his pack as the rest of us started climbing the side of the building. Rylan took several lines in his teeth and darted up the wall as if he was running on flat, even ground. Shifters never ceased to amaze me.

Moments later they were tied off and a few of us each took one, increasing our speed getting on the roof. When we did, Rylan was in margay form and hissing quietly. We went over to him and I felt the need to vomit at what we saw. Virgil had been right. They were keeping humans like cattle… Cattle they were raping and torturing from the glimpse of what we saw.

"Activate the stone," Mareo whispered as I was already pulling it out of my pocket. "Yeah, these fuckers all have to die."

I nodded as I rubbed it with my thumb, thinking of the Queen. There was a glimmer of light, instead of the normal flash, because she was trying to keep the portal quiet but it also meant only one person could come through at a time. Rylan quickly shifted back as people poured out of the portal.

"Can you guys make that jump if we break the glass?" I asked Victor, Virgil, Cyrus, and Gabriel. I didn't know their capabilities and it was a good two stories down to the main floor.

"Yeah, but it's not regular glass. It's bulletproof and light treated so it won't fry the demons," Cyrus answered.

"Leave that to me," Queen Magdalena answered, horror written on her face as she watched what was going on below. "Poor people. What will we do with them? How will we help them?"

"I'm an amplifier," Virgil said. "Dillon's gift is to wipe minds and replace memories. I can amplify any gift or powers. So if we work together, it might take us a few days, but we'll figure out a story and get them back to their lives. For now we bring them back through the portal and get them medical care."

"Right, that's where we come in," Caven told the wolves that had come through. "We can leap right back up. They go down first, start taking out demons, leap down, grab the nearest human, jump right back up, and get back through the portal. That's it."

"Same for us," King Rylan ordered the margays there. "Wolves first as we cover the fae and vampires by shooting the outlying demons if we can. Engage your hypervision." I watched as the margays spread out around the skylight, pulling out weapons and covering all the back corners.

"It's like we know what we're doing," Victor said as his fangs slid out. He unsheathed his sword and flicked it to glow. I thought it was an ingenious invention when Micah had lent me his. Mareo was using Remus's and of course, Virgil had his own, a gift from the mates of the brothers before he'd met us. Which really showed the character of the men mated to this family.

Virgil

"On my count," Mareo whispered, giving everyone the signal to get ready. I braced for it. I was ready to fight to the death for the cause I saw before me. I would prove my mates proud and be the warrior I was trained to be.

* * * *

Virgil

"Don't get dead," Victor growled at us. "That's an order."

"Yes, brother," we snickered. Some things never changed. Centuries of missions with the man and he always said the same thing.

"Same goes for all of you," Queen Magdalena told all her people. "Any of you die and I will find you in the afterlife to kick your sorry butts for years to come."

"Yes, my Queen," they all muttered quietly.

"Three, two, one," Mareo counted down. The Queen flashed power and shot something into the glass, shattering it straight up and out of our way, making sure it didn't harm any of us. Victor, Cyrus, and Mareo tied for first to react, jumping right into the building. I followed a split second after them. As I was landing I saw a demon diving for Damian. I kicked out and nailed it in the head before bringing down my ultraviolet sword.

It sliced through the goddamn demon like butter.

"I love these fucking swords," I yelled.

"Thanks," Damian called out before stabbing another demon.

"Always." I found where Mareo and Foma were and moved towards them, the three of us proceeding as a team to work our way out so more warriors could jump down safely. We sliced through demons, dozens upon dozens of them. All while hearing shots firing from above as the margays took out any approaching ones they could that weren't too close to risk hitting us.

I saw Caven jump down out of the corner of my eye, Tyler and several of the wolves following right after. They grabbed humans and went right back up. When the demons were mostly dead, the margays did the same, grabbing the remaining humans.

The whole battle took less than ten minutes. While the numbers were probably in the demons' favor, they were sorely outmatched in fighting skills and power. I was just about to kill the last one closest to me when I gasped in shock. I hit him with the hilt of my sword instead of taking his head and watched as he went down. I did it again and he was out cold.

"No!" I yelled to Mareo when he went in to finish him off. "No, this one has to live."

"What are you talking about, Virgil?" Victor called out as he jogged over. "They all need to die."

"We need to get samples to Riley," I answered. "I need to identify this one. Who's got the camera and is documenting all of this?"

"Rylan!" Victor called out. "We're ready for you and we need you to start with this demon."

"Why are we keeping one alive?" Rylan asked us as he jumped back down, camera in his hands, and strap around his neck. "What's going on?"

"I know this man," I answered, blinking in shock. "I swear to you that I know this man and he was human. I need pictures to pull his records and Riley will want the same."

"That's not possible. You've got to be mistaken," Victor said nervously.

"I hope I am." I swallowed loudly and looked at him. "But I don't think I am, brother. I know this man." I glanced around and saw who I was looking for. "Damian, come here!" He nodded and jogged across the room with his mate, glancing at the demon at my feet quickly before giving me a confused look. "Look at his face. Really look at his face."

Damian raised an eyebrow at me but did. I saw him start to shake with recognition. "That can't be."

"Who is he?" Victor growled.

"You know the ice cream shop in town?" I answered instead. I waited until he nodded. "The owner's grandson. I've seen him behind the counter."

"When Mother ordered desserts from there for Valentine's Day, she said the woman was a mess because her grandson had up and left, leaving only a note behind to say he was joining the army," Damian said. "It's him. He can't be more than nineteen."

"How can he be demon then?" Gabriel whispered in horror. "We need to get him back to Riley. Can the Queen keep him knocked out or something?"

"Yes I can," she said from behind us.

"Sorry, your highness," he muttered before shaking his head. "I'm just in shock. I didn't realize you were right here."

"As are we all. I will keep him unconscious and get him through the portal. Caven wished me to tell you that all the humans are through as well."

"Good, okay, then I'm needed on that side to help Dillon," I said quietly. I backed away from the demon on the ground, still having trouble facing this new reality.

"You were right," Mareo muttered to me as we each grabbed one of the ropes that had been tied off and dropped down for those of us who couldn't just jump right back up.

"About?" I asked as we started climbing up.

"That there was a piece of the puzzle still missing," Foma answered. We reached the top and walked through the portal. I hated that viselike feeling to my chest when I did that.

"Yeah, but I didn't guess that humans could turn demon," I replied. "I had no clue that's what was going on."

"Wait, *what?*" Father bellowed. Oh shit. I glanced around and realized we'd walked into the ballroom and there were people everywhere who'd just heard what I'd said.

"Shit," I hissed with feeling.

"Pretty much," Caven agreed.

We spent the next ten minutes filling everyone in on what we knew. Damian and Gabriel came through the portal followed by the Queen with the demon and Mother confirmed it was who we thought it was. It was a long night of unanswered questions and trying to process how much our world had just changed.

All while trying to heal and figure out what to do with the mess we'd discovered. Caleb scheduled a secret meeting with the King of the Western European region to discuss what we'd found out and show him our proof. Riley, Cyrus, and Loch, with the help of all the trained medics, were able to save the humans we'd found.

Dillon and I used our gifts to erase the humans' memories and give them plausible explanations for where they'd been and what to tell people once the Queen, Elder Dawson, and Caven had scanned their minds for memories of what had happened. We needed facts about how long they'd been gone, who would be looking for them, and what their lives were like to make the stories work.

After some had new memories, the Queen opened portals and we left where they would be found or could get home on their own without our involvement being discovered.

I felt horrible. I mean, I knew they couldn't find out about our world but it seemed wrong to lie to them and just leave them with a story to tell their families after the trauma they'd been through. Mareo said that my guilt was understandable but really it was a blessing compared to dealing with the memories of what they'd really experienced.

I felt a little bit better when he put it like that. I just hoped he was right. In the end, we saved them from a fate worse than death and I guess there was comfort to be had in that.

But we were still left with more questions than answers we'd found. And I bet I wasn't the only one praying we found them before the demons realized we knew their secret and it meant the death of all of us.

Chapter 10

Foma

After our mate spent tireless hours helping humans get new memories and home to their lives he was exhausted. He slept for a day straight. And who could blame him? While he was out, Mareo and I borrowed one of Victor's cars and met Ferris at the house Virgil had bought.

It was perfect. It was so Virgil and us actually that I knew Mareo saw home in the walls of the house just as I did. And it wasn't just any one thing. It was everything about it, from the layout of the three-bedroom house, to the countertop choices, to the style of the decorating, to the very furniture Virgil had picked.

"It's better than I could ever have dreamed up our home," I whispered.

"He's perfect for us," Mareo agreed. "Three pieces to one whole."

"You guys really love him, don't you?" Ferris asked, smiling widely.

"Yes, we really do," I answered honestly. "Virgil is special in so many ways and I look forward to spending the rest of my life showing him that every day."

"That's good. My best friend deserves that. What can I do to help?"

I smiled at Mareo. We could use Ferris's help actually.

It's truly funny the way a tight-knitted community works sometimes. King Rylan, Ferris's mate, needed some things for the palace that we knew where to get. But it meant getting a portal open.

While the Queen helped us with that, we also found her a few items she needed for some magic she'd been wanting to do and been putting on hold.

"Oh, this is ridiculous," she growled in frustration finally when we came back to the palace. "You're still going to be finding things for me anyways."

"We are?" I asked, glancing at Mareo.

"I would be very disappointed if you were going to stop that role as my warriors," she said carefully. I knew and respected the Queen. She wouldn't order us but she would let us know it was pretty much *yes we would*.

"It's not that we don't want to, your highness," Mareo hedged. "But with us being mated to a warrior here with duties of his own and—"

"That's the point I was getting to," she interrupted, waving off his concern. She chanted under her breath and suddenly there was a stone in her hand. "It's like the activating stone but it's a portal stone of your own. It uses your magic and my own so don't do too many trips in a day or we'll both be exhausted. You're obviously not going to fly all around anymore being mated and a part of this coven and it's of no help to me if I have to come with you."

"Thank you," I breathed, honored by such a gift. "How many is too many trips in a day?"

"A few dozen." She shrugged. Oh, of course to her that was too many. To most it would probably be a few total. Man, she was powerful.

But in the end we had our own way of making a portal. She explained to us how to use it. Either we had to picture the place in our head exactly or we had to picture the exact coordinates of it. Awesome!

After that, everything else we had to do was a breeze. Mareo used the portal stone while I worked on something else for our home. The last being getting our mate out of his bed at the Marius estate and into his bed in our new home. He groaned as I carried him through the portal but didn't wake up right away. He didn't stir as we got him naked either.

He *did* awaken when Mareo used that chant and stretched him out. Virgil cried out our names and started stroking himself in his sleep before his eyes popped open.

"Nice that you even dream about us," I purred.

"Always," he said in a sleepy voice before glancing down at his hand. "Are my mates trying to tell me something?"

"Yes, we want to christen our home," Mareo purred. Virgil sat up and glanced around the room.

"How did I get here? Oh please tell me you didn't carry me here naked while the Queen opened a portal!"

"No," I chuckled and then filled him in. He relaxed then and demanded payment for being kidnapped. "You are *so* abused."

"I am," he agreed, giving me that delicious pout lip. Virgil glanced past me and blinked in shock as he rolled to his knees. "Where did you get that? It's beautiful."

"I made it," I admitted. While Mareo had been gathering our stuff from storage and moving some of Virgil's belongings into the house, I'd been drawing a few projects and finding frames for them. One of them being with Caven's help. He searched mine, Mareo's, and Elena's minds for memories of what the three of us looked like as babies.

"It's amazing, Foma," Virgil whispered as he touched the glass. "It looks more real than a picture." I had sketched a collage of images as if there had been cameras way back then for baby pictures.

"You should see over the headboard," Mareo said proudly. Virgil turned around so fast I was surprised he didn't fall on his ass.

"My god, it's gorgeous," he gasped. He glanced at me with a huge grin. "You are so talented!"

"You like it? I wanted to do something for our home since you had it built and decorated it but I didn't want to intrude."

"Foma, it's wonderful!" Virgil exclaimed and got back on the bed, hugging me close as he straddled my lap. "It's our home. Do as you wish, my love, my talented mate. I adore all of them."

"I'm so glad." I glanced at them, thinking both of the sketches had turned out pretty well. There was one of the three of us, holding each other after we'd obviously been making love though not showing anything inappropriate.

The other was something I caught from an image Caven had showed me from Elena's mind. We had been outside and Virgil was in the middle, Mareo and I had an arm each around his shoulders, and we were both smiling at him with love while Virgil had his head tilted as if trying to see us both at once. It was perfect.

"There's something I need to tell you and I don't want to ruin the mood so I'm just going to say it quickly," Mareo said as he moved my cock to Virgil's prepared hole.

"Okay," our mate moaned.

"Your parents—"

"Please don't start any conversation off during sex with *my parents*," Virgil bitched as his hard-on wilted against me. "Eww."

"Sorry." Mareo chuckled. "Your parents offered to move this house onto the estate if you wanted so we'd be protected with the security there but you'd still have your freedom and the space you need."

"Wow. That's really amazing," he mumbled. I kissed along his neck as I started moving his body. He moaned and his cock filled right back up as Mareo pushed us back to the bed.

"I want to be inside you," Mareo told me.

"You're always welcome there," I moaned, spreading wide for him. He did his magic trick and pushed into me, the three of us joined together, my legs over Mareo's hips as his chest was plastered against Virgil's back. "Oh gods. I want to always be in the middle. Tight hole squeezing my cock while full of cock. Oh gods!"

"Who knew you were so vocal in bed," Virgil purred as he sat up and started riding me. I moaned when Mareo wrapped his arms around Virgil's chest and they both stared down at me, moving together to please me.

"You should see him after several drinks. Two bottles of wine and he's *begging* to be fucked like a slut in front of people," Mareo said in a husky voice, outing my deepest secret. "Foma's a very kinky boy."

"I'm seven seven. No one that tall can be a *boy*," I argued, panting as they moved faster.

"You're *our* boy when we say you are," Virgil growled. My cock twitched inside of him and he gave me a fangy smile. Oh shit. Now he knew I liked being bossed around sometimes too. Nice! "And seven seven or not, soon we're going to double stuff you. And then you and I are going to do it to Mareo. And then we're going to do everything in between."

"Yes, oh yes," I whimpered as they moved faster. "I want everything with you both."

"Right answer," Virgil hissed. I tilted my head, baring my neck to him, and he growled loudly. It wasn't so much that he needed the blood always, though I'm sure he did then because of the trying past few days, but it was more the connection that the bite gave us. Even if he just took a sip I was giving my mate what he needed and damn, I loved the feeling of his fangs in me.

He bit me hard, sending me over the edge. I screamed out his and Mareo's names as I came. Virgil followed me right over, his warm seed covering my body. And then Mareo filled me with his. It was perfect. They fell on top of me as Virgil licked the bite closed. Then Mareo pulled out of me and fell to the side, hugging both of us while Virgil was still lying over me, my cock in his ass.

"I don't feel we should move the house. I like it here, but I would offer another suggestion," I said after my heart stopped racing and I could think again because the blood had returned to my brain.

"Sure, go ahead," Virgil said as he kissed my neck. "Whatever you want, Foma."

"I think we should live here during the week because we'll be busy with work and then it would be nice to just come to our own home and do our own thing," I hedged, glancing at Mareo who nodded. "And then live in your suite at the estate on the weekend. It's like the best of both worlds. No one's feelings get hurt, we get to have some freedom, and the flexibility to change our minds if we want to."

"I think that's a great idea," Mareo agreed. "That way you can keep seeing Ayden with your family on weekends."

"I'm glad you guys are so supportive of that," Virgil said with a happy sigh. "I like the idea too. Especially if I get the instructor job at the shifter training center. I still have to talk to Rylan about that and Father to see how I would even get assigned there. But for now, no one's going out on missions after demons anyways. It's too dangerous with what we've learned. Everything's changed and—"

"Hey, none of that today," I said gently. "We'll figure it all out and the good guys will win. Today is about us and our new house. So we're agreed that we will live at the Marius estate on weekends and here during the week?"

"Yes." Virgil gave me a big smile and a kiss.

"Yes," Mareo chuckled and then growled. "Let's fuck on it. I'm still hard and I love the idea of you taking me together."

"Well, twist my arm why don't you," Virgil purred before attacking our mate. I was right there with him… As I would always be in everything.

THE END

WWW.JOYEEFLYNN.COM
WWW.JOYEEFLYNN.BLOGSPOT.COM
WWW.FACEBOOK.COM/JOYEEFLYNNAUTHOR
WWW.TWITTER.COM/JOYEEFLYNN

ABOUT THE AUTHOR

Joyee dreams of one day living on enough land to have a few horses, and find a couple of cowboys or pool boys of her own. A lover of men, Joyee is all about them in any form in her books; vampire, werewolf, shape-shifter, military…It's all good! She loves to get lost in fantasy that only books can bring. Her wide interest in reading is reflected in her writings, whether short stories, romance, or mystical. Currently Joyee lives with her dog, Marius, named after a vampire from Anne Rice's Interview with the Vampire series.

For all titles by Joyee Flynn, please visit
www.bookstrand.com/joyee-flynn

Siren Publishing, Inc.
www.SirenPublishing.com

Lightning Source UK Ltd.
Milton Keynes UK
UKOW031633120713

213715UK00008B/123/P

Lost

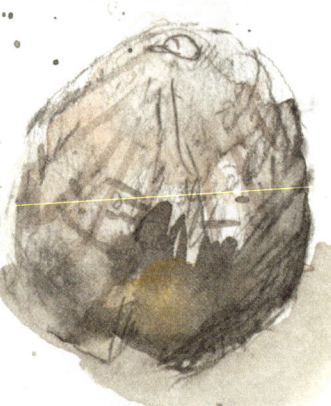

things

28/200

LOST THINGS

Ed Mayhew and Alastair Gordon

Foreword

In the beginning, Al said to Ed, "Let's do a book together."

Or was the origin of this book sooner? The work may have been first conceived on any number of occasions, right back to our first meeting, sharing dinner at a conference, talking about all things arts.

In *Lost Things*, Al composed the pictures; Ed wrote the words. Initially, the paintings came first—with Ed responding in writing. After the first round of compositions, however, it was the poems that prompted the visual element. You can have fun guessing which is which and deciding to what extent it matters.

Some work has source material in the arts. For example, *Lost beauty* was inspired by *Pied Beauty* by Gerard Manley Hopkins. *Innocence ain't all that* pokes irreverent fun at William Blake's *Songs of Innocence*. On the whole, however, this book is based on the stuff we see around us, in a world of lost and found.

We've explored a variety of dichotomies in this book: emptiness and filling, up and down, near and far, understanding and confusion, perception and imagination. One theme that repeats, perhaps inevitably given the collaborative nature of the book, is that elusive reciprocal gift—friendship.

You may have had the experience of rediscovering that old treasured object—perhaps a postcard or photo—that revives a memory, tells a story, puts you back in time to a place made important by those with whom you shared that intimate moment. The musty smell of your find transports you. Somewhere inside, it still holds a hint of sea air. As with an old acquaintance, a facet of your identity sparkles suddenly.

Our aspiration is that you enjoy this book enough to keep returning here. We hope that this book becomes, in turn, one of those old beloved treasures.

Contents

Lost Beauty	1
Nan	3
Filling and emptying	6
Lost property	7
The Elephant's Child	10
Look down	11
Neptune blesses us with rain	14
What's that?	15
Neither/Nor	18
Glitter	19
Object of attention	21
The brick	24
Portrait of the artist	25
Linda's food bar	28
Back	29
Burst	31
Innocence ain't all that	34
Lost property II	35
Divine pea	37
Quadley Bay	39
When we threw them	42
Look up	43
Lost property III	48
Found things	49

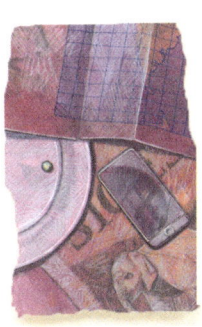

Lost beauty

Glory be to God for lost things —
    For dusk-wrapped sunsets, curled calendars like wood shavings;
      For shed skin, jumble feathers, fashion and fray;
Firm arguments, orbiting grief, plucked strings;
    Landscapes scoped, scraped, scrapped, routed, reborn—replaying
      Industry's never-done demand, "Next please." Said-and-done, filed away.

All things contemporary, erstwhile, spare, strange;
   Whatever is dropped, forgotten (left for dead?)
     Samaritan-restored or trod in soil, all decays;
None more lost than he at hour nine, author of change:
    All praise.

Nan

A souvenir David replica on a pristine mantelpiece,
a knitted, miniature beret on his head.
He looks over at the last Birthday card
that Grandad remembered to give her.
The smell of lamb roast fills every room.
That's my Nan.

Filling and emptying

Our washing basket gasps
as we force in another load.
Pushed down, the lid creaks to a half-close.
A sock sticks out, a lolling, blue tongue.

As I consider this filling and emptying, emptying and filling—
our domestic warfare versus sweat and muck,
marking weekends and weeks,
changing bed sheets, post-holiday resets, and sudden muddy days,

so many emptyings and fillings, spilling into other rooms—
each daily routine marches
before my blinking eyes.

The bed sheets and clothes, filled by us,
and emptied. Waste bins, sinks, appliances, even irons,
pans, plates, bowls,
coats and shoes too, as we empty our houses

and fill the outdoors, where cars, buses, vans, trains,
planes, canoes… are filled and emptied, emptied and filled,
through seasons of nests, buckets, beaches, leaf-strewn paths, frozen drains,
emptied and filled, emptied and filled, filled and emptied.

My breath decants, a somewhere-sigh between weight and wonder.

Like countless stars
burning
to eventual

blackness…

Lost Property

I used to work in lost property,
among the gloves and umbrellas.
Teddy rescues were best:
the anxious kid, fighting back tears and hope;
the heroic reveal!

Once, a child handed in a little brass button at the office.
I thought no one would claim it. But a day later, a treasure hunter came in,
described it with hopelessness, reclaimed it with tears.

The last day I worked there, a lady knocked on the window,
asking if I'd seen a postcard she left on the train.
She'd come all the way from Weymouth to find it.
It was from her Dad, fighting overseas in black and white.
Through creased lips, she told how she lodged it in a fold-out table.
I checked. Nothing.
A second. A third look. No.

She described it so clearly,
I could see it.

The Elephant's Child

I'm holding my son as he cries.
His guts are bloated, his body wretches,
and he's asking, "When will it stop? I just want it to stop."

"I can't. I can't."

I'm shushing him,
telling him stories of times he was sick as a baby,
enacting breathing to show him,
rubbing his stomach.
—"It hurts! Daddy!"—
masking my own helplessness with actions
that may or may not do anything.

Better to try and be wrong.

His breathing's slowing.
I reach for the book shelf—*Just So Stories*—
and read him *The Elephant's Child*.
The melody of the great grey-green greasy Limpopo river soothes him.

As the elephant's nose stretches, the boy wretches—

four hours of gastronomic history spew from him
in a beige, bespotted soup.
Again. Again. And again.
When will it end?
I'm holding him again, settling him with kisses.

"Sh-sh-sh-sh. Sh-sh-sh-sh."

Look down

When you are too tired to look up,
let your eyes examine the earth beneath you—

Look down,
down in the grass,
grass that grows relentless,
relentless in the summer sun;
sun or rain, it does not mind.

Look down,
down at the toys,
toys lost and fallen,
fallen, dropped, discarded;
discarded from pockets, from thought.

Look down,
down away from the sun,
sun reflecting up at you,
at you from hot green earth;
earth of tangles and clods, turning to memory,

memory growing relentless.
Look down.

Neptune blesses us with rain

The clouds above blue Neptune's ice giant
look yellow and red in photographs.

An asteroid crashed into our park last Wednesday—
or perhaps Thursday—a bolt from the blue.

Crows scattered as we crowded the box-shaped crater,
steam rising. Not steam. Ice-cold vapour.

We came across strewn rockets,
arrows jettisoned from Apollo.

"Rained down from the clouds like sweet hail," some said,
like an Elysian dream. But we knew the truth…

Visitors from Neptune's oceans! Explain the flecks on the nose of the rockets?
Simple! Asteroid dust from the flight. Sprinkles? Psh!

Fallen off an ice cream truck, some said; we scoffed.
Whatever they would have us believe—we knew the truth.

What's that?

I once read a book—or a meme—
about how patterns take on shapes and meanings to us—
heart-shaped flowers, owl-eyes on butterfly wings,
Cheshire-cat moons, muddy-bear clouds, and the like.

My daughter's hand bulges with treasure.

It's a "Hundred Acre Wood" day,
oaks intermesh, sway and crackle above us;
we're speaking of Piglet and Pooh,
as we're blustered along.

"Show Daddy?" I ask, and she clutches it tightly to herself.

We picnic on imaginary honey,
sitting on a tall, fallen tree.
When it's time to leave, she's forgotten her treasure.
I scoop it up for her.

My palm reveals what she found, smiling up at me.

Neither/Nor

Drafting a piece on the South Bank, outside rails
that separate the public from the water,
"I've captured a creature—a creation at least."

"Whether it escaped an exotic stall at Borough Market,
or floated here from the North Sea,
drifted up from the deep or down from deeper…" (wild eyes)

Deep creatures, oldest, oddest, closest to earth's core,
appear, to me, the most extra-terrestrial:
neither of this world, nor detachable from it.

"Look again! It's not living; never was! A creation of some
factory in fact. Sprayed with rough paint. Packaging.
The instant discards of a product. Still, I can't be sure."

Unconvinced—it's neither living nor dead—
"Be a dear, if you can, and fill in the last line, please," she said.

Glitter

Tell me why our angels shake glitter
from their wings at every opportunity;

it's futile to clean up after these silver
pipe cleaners and shuttlecocks—
each with a single googly eye.

No use to speculate on
each discarded glittery flake

—like human flecks, their thoughts and wills
move just the same—

but now and then, I simply wonder,
*How did **that** get here?*

Object of attention

New neon running outfit and recently-discovered wrinkles—
a January story.
Rabbit-eyed, she staggers on the tarmac, carrying… it…

Bin bag wrapped—is it a flat boat she's holding?
A comically-oversized skateboard, sans wheels?
Is she a set designer? An artist? Pop-up florist?

Self-conscious, struggling in the wind,
her flighty eyes staccato around me,
ashamed, perhaps, of this curiosity.

What will become of it when I am no longer in view?
Discarded beside the road with despair or disdain,
or in its right home, polished with tiger-eyed pride?

And I—my own December waist bulging from my coat,
chewing a pencil, thumbing the notebook in my pocket—
who was I to her?

The brick

I'm looking at the wall beside our block,
where the smooth level line of the top
breaks uncomfortably,
where one of the bricks has been dislodged.

The brick itself has no particular story.
It has not roamed far, kicked into the corner.
Kicked out by vice, violence or mood?
No, I doubt it was consciously removed.

The wall too, barely notices its absence.
Now it's gone, a mere inconvenience
to the smooth level line of the top, no loss,
new crevice for new moss.

A hooked question mark tugs at my gut, like a crow-beak, curved:
what changes when your absence is observed?

Portrait of the artist

My friend, the artist, working.
He's gathered scraps of memories, tools,
pieces from pockets on spring walks
—that perhaps held a meaning then—
still magic up the scent of heather and the sound of crickets.

He's laying them all out carefully.
A simple composition. Or chance-arranged?
The artist knows—there was some luck about it,
and some aesthetic manoeuvrings—

Man-oeuvre—ha!—he'd like that. Hand-worked.
Art and fiction, arms and fingers.

Oh, there! Look! A detail overlooked.
The translucent sheet where objects rest or slip free. Did you see it?
A frame within a frame. How like him!

He raises his brush, wry pleasure in his illusion
and paints a slight highlight at the top left corner—imperceptible, vital—
pushing his hair back from his eyes.

Linda's Food Bar

My first memory of Linda's Food Bar is a sketch.
I have an inkling of the ink lines—
were they giclée printed?
I remember the large picture in your flat. A real woman in a real place.

Leith. By the docks, I believe.
You noticed her while you were drawing wastelands.
Edinburgh's finest… what? Burgers? Chips? I don't know what you said.

The point was—it was there. There in Leith.

As much a landmark to the locals as Scott's tower or the castle.

The next time I saw it, you had scaled it up, I think.
The same composition. In colour this time. Painted in… oils?
You were still exploring themes of waste lands—me too.
I must have walked near where her food bar used to be.

I'd forgotten Linda,
her food bar,
your pictures,
your lounge in Wimbledon Chase, our early friendship.
But here she is again;
more than a motif.
A memoriam.
A requiem, even.
Even though she may be misremembered,
you won't let her be forgotten;

as much a part of that city as Arthur's Seat or the smell of hops.

Back

"That one's good for lollies." Nope, I shouldn't have said that!
"Quiet, you two! Not today."
"Did you know, sometimes people call corner shops 7-Elevens?"

A surround sound "Why?"

Squeezed in the back between two relentless car seats,
their mummy and mine in the front—
Like two embodied eyes fixed on the way ahead.
They're trying to talk about Christmas,
while I try to distract the littles,
take back my mention of lollies.

"There was a shop that opened from seven—
It's called a 'brand'. It's like Hoover… 7-Eleven."
I struggle for examples.

That's not him, surely?

Cap backwards, backpack, back door, back then
I mocked his weight, laughed when he was late,
and his payback wasn't backchat,
but a glacier of silence that still, now,
eclipses for a moment
the buzzing attention-seeking "Why?"

My friend's fading finger lingers
on the back-doorbell of the rehab centre;
my spine sears as I twist for a second.
Was it me?

"Dad! Dad! You stopped talking."

I flash back to the present crush;
the indicator ticks us homeward.

"What was I saying?"

"Mummy said we could have a lolly from the freezer."

Burst

I'm standing on the exact spot where I threw
everything I could reach at you:
words, images, objects,
blame, pain, shame, rain and rail
in adolescent rage.

It's obvious I should know better
—I shout like a slammed car door—
who cares what the neighbours know?
Loud, screaming, running my red lights,
bees swarming in my throat.

Behind locked patio windows, you're there
—the glass half-mirrors my prowling back to me —
white, with red eyes locked on me,
arms spread wide, goading the temper.
This exact spot.

Once smashed, glass can be reformed;
melt it down, start again. Replacement is easier.
Apologies squeezed out from us eventually,
a sponge oozing crude oil. But something was lost.
We are this forever.

Innocence ain't all that

They fight for first go,
to sing in the show,
to own Mummy's hug,
"I want *my* blue mug!"

To win every snap.

They'll lose this immediacy;
snap out of it, surely?
Self-obsession too simple—
How is it possibly sustainable?

I need *my* self back.

Lost property II

So…
I scribbled the train number
—my manager commanded me to stay, but hey,
I must have been looking for a reason to get out—
and I hurdled the counter.

Three hours later, over the moustachioed manager's
raging cerebral tannoy,
her train came in.

She took my hand—soft, blue veins, high and round rivers.
We had talked little but deeply, and I felt I knew her father
and her struggles.

"It might not be here…" I said,
her eyes holding back tears and hope.

* * *

Ten minutes later, the train preparing to leave Waterloo,
we stepped off with a last backward look.
"You've been very kind," she said,
and I apologised again that I had got her hopes up for nothing.

"Kindness is never nothing," she said,
"You know—today—not having that postcard for the first time
in fifty or more years,
I realised, I remember every word.
You know why—why it's such a treasure?
The handwriting—his patient, painstaking cursive.
He taught himself that. He wanted it to look… historical.
That's my Dad. I remember every word."

She boarded the train back to Weymouth.
I waited and waved.

On a bench by the South Bank, leaning on the back of a full notepad,
I wrote a letter, slowly forming every new character.

Divine pea

Oh divine pea!
I scrape thee into the waste,
Never more to look upon thy face.
Buried and crushed,
Rejected by all.

Thou fell'st, oh pea! And though returned to the plate,
The fluff of the floor made thee obsolete,
Great wondrous pea—once replete
Verdant vine of Eden, plucked,
Packed with companions—
Thou hast survived the tormentuous ice age and the boiling pot
Undevoured, yet now, scraped from the plate of this unseeing world into
The excremental receptacle of the unacceptable.
Oh pea of peas,
Hope still,
Thou rottest to compost to revive us all.

Quadley Bay

The field of rye smiles over us,
Highcliffe Hotel at the foot of the gull-cluttered rock face,
waves above the sea;
glittering, listening waters, nets, buckets, beach balls,
sand ripples.

This place I once called Homer's gut
(round, protrusive and yellow, as opposed to
epic, Greek and, let's say, instinctual);
this bay of shells and shops,
a beach full of froth and souvenirs, bubbles,
sticks, rocks, sticks of bubble gum. Stinks.

My infant hands would scavenge in the sand, like a piper.
A conch as an ear trumpet, listening to the pretend, see.
I liked the tiger shells best.
Striped pebbles too, or quartz-veined, smooth slate skimmers, faces—
I held their cold weights,
the salt smell in grains on my evaporated skin.

Later, the shells of this bay composed a jumble
in a washed-up ice cream tub on our bedroom shelves,
their memories picked away, like creatures their tiger-bodies used to house.
I'd run my teenage finger along their serrated edges, self-heartening.

Many days more than I ever stayed in Quadley Bay,
I remember the smell, shops, sand martens,
the old man with the twisted teeth,
who picked up my sun hat, blown off the windbreak,
laughter creasing his paper eyes at my shy horror,
his teeth growing yellower and more pronounced
as he murmured about mermaids.

When allusions blind, I blink, trick my eyes, my ears, into going there:
riding along the coastal, rhododendron-shaded path,
weighing pebbles and empty shells in small fingers,
turning sand to glass. Your pencil captures three dimensions on a page.

In the sunset, we talk about Quadley Bay, rusing.
As the painter of light plays mental acrobat, tricks
the sight into seeing something that was never here,
in the same weight, by the same measureless phonics,
could the writer of sound craft a phrase to—fool as he is—trick your ear?

When we threw them

When we threw them,
one fell, as expected, down to the grass. Then…

The other rushed in the breeze up
over houses, smokeless chimneys, leaves,
until it rested in a river,
drifted out to sea,
washed onto the shore
of a long-sought country;

where a fisherman, with weathered hands,
unfolded our sodden, tear-smeared note and wondered,
as he dried it in the sun,
What could these symbols mean?

Look up

When you are done looking down,
turn your eyes like the flame of a match.

Look up,
up to the path,
path of earth that stretches away,
away to the alleys, corners, cracks,
cracks like rays of splintering lightning.

Look up,
up to the rooftops,
rooftops gathering moss and cracked gutters,
gutters above you that clog in the autumn spill,
spill sleet in December brightness.

Look up,
up past floating feathers,
up past flocks in flight,
up past clouds and blimps and drones,
up beyond oxygen!

Look up blindly to the halo,
halo that burns us with hope,
hope that grows and never dies,
dies only to rise and rise.

Rise like the flame of a match!
Look up!

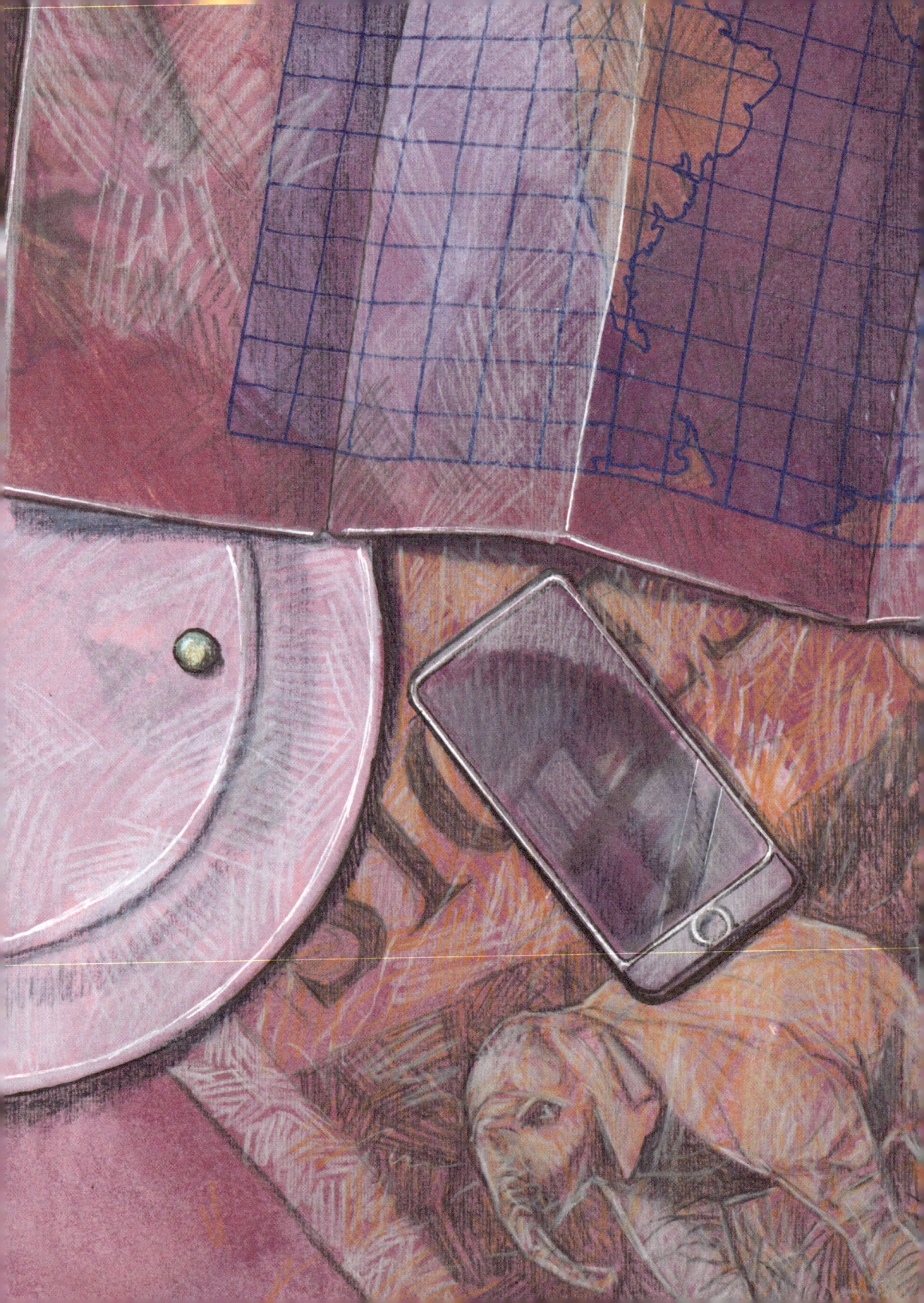

Lost property III

A year later, my phone buzzed.
A photo from an unknown number:
veined, speckled hands—in pied beauty;
a black and white postcard.

Mary.

Found things

You tear back the sheets with a sound like doves;
dust dances like constellations in the beam of the sloping skylight.

In this magnolia attic room, among boxes and dust covers, you rummage.
For no reason you can name, your voice drops to a hush.
"Wow," you whisper, soft as the beige bespotted carpet, "I remember this."

This… wrinkled copy of Just So Stories…
This… scrap of writing in an infant hand.
This… old diary— dare you open it?

Your Hundred Acre Wood memento,
collated, curated, veiled in a muslin bag,
alongside quartz crystals, sea-smoothed glass,
and the sound of Nan's triumphant, "Eureka!"

Over here, a shoe box.
Postcards and pale passport photos;
pressed flowers. A sketch of the South Bank. A letter.

Why do we keep our treasures in shoeboxes?

Down here—look!
A sculpture of perfectly tumbled miscellany.
Why did that glass trinket make you say,
"I'll hold onto that a little longer"?
Why the clay star you made when you were six?
Green glitter still sticks to it.
An odd blue sock encases a harmonica.

You pull a box of files to one side, and underneath,
you uncover out-of-fashion photo albums, pictures scrawled
with clumsy muscles and still-growing fingers,
while you learnt to hold a paintbrush, to evaluate art;
knowing nothing of how wise you would become!

You remember.
You remember.
The sea-echoing shells from Quadley Bay.
The fashion and the fray.
The old book you wrote,
where your friend drew the pictures.

In the twilight, perched on a box, reading your diary
(you gave in to curiosity, and Time snuck out)
sun setting through the skylight,
a mix of moon and sun; day and night;
image and word; seen and heard;
a jumble of fashion and fray;
and shells from Quadley Bay;
a scent of then
found, lost, found again;

Dust and glitter from a handmade star;
kept, treasured, never lost.
After all, this is who you are.

Ed Mayhew and Alastair Gordon – Lost Things

Book design and type setting by Ellie Walker

Copy editing by Miriam Ettrick

Published in 2024 by Morphe Arts, London

Artwork © Alastair Gordon, 2024

Texts © Edward Mayhew, 2024

All rights reserved. No part of this publication may be stored, shared, reproduced or transmitted in any form or by any means without prior permission in writing from the publishers.

A catalogue record for this book is available from the British Library

ISBN: 978-0-9957530-9-9